Mipam
The First Tibetan Novel

ৡৠ৾ ঀ৾ৠৠৄঽ৾ৄৄ৾ৄৠৄৠ৾ৠৄ৾ৠৠৄৠৄ৾ৠ৾ ঀৠ৾ৠৄৠৄৠৄৠৄৠৄ৾ৠ৾ৠ৾ৠৠৄ৾ৠ৾ৠৠ৾ৠ৾
ৠৄৠৄৠৄৠৄৠৄৠৄৠৄৠৄৠৄৠৄৠৄ ৠৄৠৄৠৄৠৄৠৄৠৄৠৄৠৄৠৄৠৄৠৄ ৠৄৠৠ৾

Lama Mipam

Mipam
The First Tibetan Novel

by
Lama Yongden

Illustrated by
Roger Williams

SLG BOOKS
Berkeley/Hong Kong

SLG BOOKS
Berkeley/Hong Kong

This new tradepaper edition published in 2000

First published in 1938 by John Lane, The Bodley Head, London

SLG BOOKS
P.O. Box 9465
Berkeley, CA 94709
Tel: (510) 525-1134
Fax: (510)525-2632
email: mipam@slgbooks.com
Website: www.slgbooks.com

Cover and book design by Yuk Wah Lee
Cover photograph of Chin Rese by Roger Williams
Woodblock prints by Roger Williams
Introduction by Norma Levine
All contributions to this book were made as work for hire

Color separations and printing by
Snow Lion Graphics, Berkeley/Hong Kong

Library of Congress Cataloging-in-Publication Data

Yongden, Albert Arthur.
  [Mipam. English]
  Mipam : the first Tibetan novel / Lama Yongden ;
 illustrated by Roger Williams,-- New tradepaper ed.
    p. cm.
  Originally published: London : John Lane, The Bodley Head, 1938
  Translation of: Mipam
  ISBN 0-943389-33-X
    1. Tibet--Fiction

 PL3748.Y6M55 1999
 895'.43--dc21   99-052397

LIST OF ILLUSTRATIONS

Buddha (thig tshad sketch)

PREFACE TO THE FOURTH EDITION

In the 61 years since Lama Yongden and Percy Lloyd produced the text of *Mipam* "to illustrate (to the West) the ideas and customs of (Yongden's) compatriots," Tibet's identity as a culture and a nation has gone through crisis after crisis. The feudal world glimpsed in *Mipam*, its isolation already breached by the comic dogmas of American missionaries and the rifles of "the Whites," has long been shattered and transformed. Given Yongden's distress at seeing Tibetan culture and spiritual practice "so travestied," it is ironic that the current restoration of shrines and lamaseries would seen in part an effort to cater to Western tourists' in the exotic.

In this context, this book, the first novel ever written by a Tibetan, takes an added importance as an authentic document in the history of Tibet. Fortunately, this aura of importance does not dilute the charm of the story nor blunt the narrator's quiet humor. Perhaps it needs be said that, despite a wealth of mundane detail, this is not a realistic novel nor is it, for all its final focus on the structure and deeper strata of the psyche, a psychological novel. Its style betrays no hint of Proustian or Joycean influences. The characters are clearly types and composites, yet they are drawn with such affection and attention to human detail that they remain thoroughly engaging. It's a refreshing saint who sings well, has a weakness for sweets and drives a hard bargain.

At present, the Tibetan people have regained some small measure of autonomy, having never lost their independent spirit. The future they fashion for themselves amid what Yongden called "the disconcerting play of unknown causes" will, of necessity, include more intrusions, more active roles in the alarums and excursions of the geopolitical drama sweeping the planet. These are a people who took to their hearts the ideal of compassion, not just for clan or species, but for all sentient beings. It is with the hope that their voices will be heard and welcomed in the global discourse, and out of love for the tale itself that we offer this fourth edition of *Mipam*.

The Publishers
Berkeley/Hong Kong 1999
Year of the Female Earth Rabbit

INTRODUCTION

"Portents accompanied his birth". From the compelling opening line of this Tibetan romance we are transported to once- upon-a-time in Tibet, where ragged hermits dedicate their clairvoyant powers freely to others' welfare while black magic sorcerers get paid by arrogant princelings to kill by contract; where wild animals respond like domestic pets to compassion, but true love takes a back seat to the more exalted romance of enlightenment. Hovering behind the scenes like Greek fate there is the force of past life karma directing the action in preparation for the arrival of destiny. This is a thrilling tale of magic and mystery spun into a picaresque novel based on Tibet's most intriguing phenomenon: the conscious reincarnation of lamas.

From the 12th century when the first Karmapa predicted where he would be reborn, Tibet maintained a spiritual hierarchy of wisdom beings in an unbroken lineage from lifetime to lifetime. The *tulku* system developed to recognise, enthrone and educate reincarnated high lamas. To be effective, the system depends on finding the right child. The rebirth is usually accompanied by miraculous signs, and from the start the child shows extraordinary intelligence, fearlessness, and prescience. Even today in Chinese occupied Tibet, miracles occur at the birth of a *tulku*. At the 17th Karmapa's birth in 1985 in East Tibet all the villagers heard celestial music, the unmistakable sound of the conch shell coming from the sky. Similarly, at Mipam's birth, we are told, his mother heard the songs of invisible beings. A leopard appeared near the house contemplating with large attentive eyes the room in which the child was being born. This isn't a fairy tale; we're simply entering the enlightened dimension produced by centuries of Tantric Buddhism in Tibet. The supernatural was natural.

When, through visions and divination, the monks of the former Lama are completely satisfied that they have found the true successor, the child is enthroned in a celebratory ritual. He is then revered as a *tulku*, literally illusory body: the lighter body of those who take rebirth not through the driving force of karmic patterns like ordinary beings, but from the compassionate vow to liberate others from suffering. *Tulkus* receive a strict education in philosophy and meditation, and, if everything goes well, he or she eventually attains the state of wisdom and compassion described as enlightenment.

But what if it doesn't all go according to plan? What would happen if the *tulku* were not recognised, not educated, and left to wander in worldly existence like an ordinary being? And since this book was written, the question could be put in a more treacherous way: what if the child is mistreated, locked up as a political prisoner like the incarnate Panchen Lama, and a pawn recognised in his place? These are both beguiling questions; the former is the basis for this great Tibetan novel.

Mipam is born into a peasant family amidst many auspicious signs, but he is not recognised as a *tulku*. He grows into a greedy, vain, clever little boy, although the signs of an extraordinary power persist - wild animals sit calmly by his side, rays of light appear mysteriously around him, food comes out of a rock to sustain him on his journey. Everywhere he goes he is graced by the protection of an unseen power. He falls deeply in love with the pretty Dolma, daughter of a wealthy Lhasa merchant. In defending her from a violent princeling he incurs the enmity of his opponent's father. He flees to the Chinese borderlands to escape punishment and in a few years amasses enough wealth to win Dolma's hand in marriage. "Shall I succeed?" Mipam asks his clairvoyant hermit guide. The seer's reply - that the future resembles a formation of dust motes assembling and reassembling in response to the choices we make - is lucid, and perhaps the most profoundly memorable reflection in the book.

Mipam does not succeed in his worldly goal. Unseen forces guide him to a more exalted destiny. Dolma frees him from karmic bondage to her. In "the last watch of the night", the veil is torn from his eyes and he becomes the *tulku* that he is, the Lama of Five Wisdoms. The conclusion is so movingly portrayed that one is left with a strangely disconnected feeling of having lived through an extremely vivid reality. It's an archetypal image: in different ways we're all trying to find out who we really are.

In structuring the book as a picaresque novel, the author has an open canvas in which to depict Tibetan life and character: the pretentious astrologer to whom Mipam is first apprenticed, greedy monks and righteous white missionaries, the arrogant prince, the powerful sorcerer from Bhutan, the worldly Bonpo priests. These are captured with lightness and humour and conveyed with unusually penetrating psychological insight, as if a culturally integrated Tibetan were in complete possession of the Western sensibility. This extremely rare hybrid observes, interprets and narrates the story.

Which brings us to the second even more beguiling question. Who indeed is Lama Yongden, and how did he come to write this book? Previously in Tibet, no one had ever written a novel, or for that matter, painted a beautiful woman. Tibet did not develop a secular culture. It was not a country where love between a man and a woman was ever taken seriously. There was no cult of chivalry, no kamasutra, no Mona Lisa. Instead there were cults of the goddess Tara. The greatest respect was given to those who renounced worldly life and travelled the path to enlightenment. Yet *Mipam* is a Tibetan love story, an astonishing event. More than that, it is so deftly executed it could be called a minor masterpiece.

In a brief preface, Lama Yongden presents himself as a Tibetan who coming into contact with the foreigners of the West and their books about Tibetan customs, decided to set the record straight. With the encouragement of his adopted mother, Alexandra David-Neel, with whom he travelled in Tibet, and the literary assistance of Mr. Percy Lloyd of Pembroke College, Oxford, he put the book together. With all due respect to Lama Yongden, it's hard to believe.

In the light of the recent excellent biography of David-Neel by Barbara and Michael Foster (The Secret Lives of Alexandra David-Neel, The Overlook Press, 1998), it's clear that Yongden was a Sikkkimese boy of 14 when he became the servant of memsahib David-Neel. As a matter of interest, while Sikkim and Tibet are neighbours and share a common religion, they are about as similar as England and the US. Eventually Yongden matured into David-Neel's devoted companion and adopted son. But he was always her 'boy', overshadowed by her extraordinary presence, awed by her yogic powers.

In all relationships of this kind, particularly between East and West, the memsahib has the power. The extraordinary David-Neel had it in spades. She had the money: her Penelope-like husband faithfully sponsored her Tibetan odyssey and waited doggedly 15 years for their reunion; she had 3 languages, Tibetan, English and French; she had formidable yogic powers (if her accounts of *tumo* and *phowa* are to be believed); and she had a tremendous writing talent. This first Western Tibetan-Buddhist practitioner was a scholar-translator, an explorer, a yogini and a writer. And she was excellent at all of them. She was also a prototype Western Tibetan Buddhist: self-centred, self-dramatising, strong-willed. An opera singer turned Tantric adept; she was an impossible act to follow. No wonder Albert (her attempt to westernise his name) Yongden met a sad end.

Yongden had been trained as a monk but he had worldly ambitions, so when David-Neel offered him the lure of foreign lands in exchange for unflinching service, he gladly accepted. He played her son when she disguised herself as an old Tibetan nun on pilgrimage and became the first Western woman to see the gilded rooftops of the Potala in the fabled city of Lhasa. She nursed him through fevers and risked her life for him when he injured his leg and could barely walk in a blinding snowstorm. They returned to France and continued their relationship, living together in a large country house in Digne while husband Philip visited on the occasional weekend. Yongden suddenly became a Lama (a title usually reserved only for recognised incarnations or someone who has successfully completed a strict 3 years retreat) and appeared in full Lama regalia to add exotic attraction to the new author's publicity road-show. He sported a beret in Digne, and drank with the locals at the bistro. Though he had an eye for the girls, he never married. David-Neel kept him on a short lead. Uprooted from his culture, Yongden was adrift. He died prematurely at the age of 56 from alcoholism, leaving his adopted mother bereft. David-Neel never wrote another book of significance about the East.

According to David Neel, who kept it quiet, Yongden was actually an incarnate Lama, a *tulku*. If this is true, then Yongden was indeed lost in *samsara*, and it goes a long way to explain the plot of *Mipam*. It was Yongden's story converted to an enlightened conclusion. David-Neel's biographers see her in the character of Mipam: her determination and fearlessness, her meetings with wild animals. The character of Mipam could be an amalgamation of both their psyches. Perhaps Yongden wrote a first draft of the novel, but there is no doubting the hand of David-Neel. The love of magic and mystery, the page turning suspense from chapter to chapter, the keen psychological insights are all her literary hallmark.

All that really matters is that the collaboration was a success. The 'first Tibetan novel,' born from the psyche of a Sikkimese (who may or may not have been a Lama), and one of the most remarkable women of this century is a great read. Enjoy it.

Norma Levine has written two books, Blessing Power of the Buddhas (Element) and A Yearbook of Buddhist Wisdom (Godsfield Press UK, Quest USA). Her articles have appeared in The Times Saturday Review, The Observer Magazine and The Telegraph Magazine. She runs Windhorse Imports, a mail order/wholesale business supplying Tibetan artefacts. email:sales@windhorse.co.uk

THE LAMA YONDGEN

[*The present book is the first to be written by a Tibetan Lama for Western readers.*]

AUTHOR'S NOTE

NEVER was the writer's vocation more unforeseen than in my own case. My life, so it seemed, was destined to be passed, serenely and studiously, in a Tibetan monastery, and had I risen to the rank of a Tibetan writer, my works, in all probability, would have been philosophical treatises, or commentaries on one or other of the numerous doctrines which for centuries past have fed the meditations and the controversies of the learned Lamas of my native land.

That programme was singularly modified by the disconcerting play of unknown causes. Though always deeply attached, in spirit, to my country and the teachings of my Masters—both those belonging to the monasteries in which I have lived, and those at whose feet I have sat, in their hermitages on the roof of the world—I have travelled in many lands, and come into contact with the foreigners of the West.

In this way I came to read, over and above the technical treatises of European Orientalists, books which in the form of novels claimed to describe Tibet and the customs of its inhabitants. In these I found subject for no little surprise. When the hilarity—mingled with some measure of indignation—excited by the extravagant descriptions of certain writers had subsided, I felt that it was undesirable that readers should be led into error by such accounts, since they in their turn might disseminate incorrect notions on the strength of what they had read and believed to be the truth.

On my return to Tibet, I therefore began to collect material which would illustrate the ideas and customs of my compatriots.

I hesitated, in my heart, as to what form my notes should take, when one evening, while camping with my mother by adoption, the explorer Alexandra David-Neel, amid the vast grassy solitudes of Northern Tibet, I happened to speak once more of the distress which I had experienced on seeing the people and things of my native land so travestied. She urged me, then and there, to attempt a faithful description of my people and their ways, in the form of a novel. With her encouragement I collated my notes, and wove them into a romantic drama. While certain persons and episodes were given an air of reality, I took care that my story should be fictitious as a whole, and that no actual characters should be represented.

My book, however, could not have been published in English but for the valuable assistance of Mr. Percy Lloyd of Pembroke College, Oxford. Thanks to his gift of graphic description and his faithful interpretation of the spirit of my book, I am able to offer to those interested in Tibet, in the place of a clumsy narrative from the pen of a foreigner unfamiliar with their language, a piece of competent literary workmanship. I would ask him, here, to accept the expression of my very sincere gratitude, and in this I would like to associate Mrs. Lloyd, for the collaboration which she has so unstintingly afforded him in the course of his work.

LAMA YONGDEN.

Note.—All the names and Tibetan terms appearing in this book have been transcribed phonetically only. The author has made no attempt to follow the Tibetan orthography, which is exceedingly misleading for foreigners. A few examples will suffice: *Cha* (bird) is written *bya; gyalse* (prince) is written *rgyal sras naljorpa* is written *rnalbyor pa*. Despite every care, it has in many cases been impossible to translate the Tibetan sounds exactly into English, for some of these sounds have no English equivalents. The name of Tingley, for example, which in this form has something of its original sound, is really written *Tinglas*.

As far as the Chinese words are concerned, they have been phonetically transcribed in accordance with the pronunciation which obtains in the province of Kansu (North-west China).

Chin Rese

CHAPTER I

PORTENTS accompanied his birth. Before dawn, a supernatural light was diffused beneath the lofty trees of the forest on the verge of which rose the rude dwelling of his parents. There alighted upon its thatched roof a pair of birds with golden crests, although it was not the season for their migration. After a long spell of drought, which had sorely tried the thirsty vegetation and the creatures that depended upon it for their food, quite suddenly, although the sun was shining, the earth was gladdened by an abundant shower of rain. A large leopard appeared close to the house, calm, dignified and unafraid, contemplating with attentive eyes the window of the room in which the child was entering the world, and the mother of the new-born babe declared that she had heard, all about her, the songs of invisible beings.

Puntsog, the village headman, now a father for the third time, having eagerly collated all these events, found in them cause for an illimitable pride, and an intoxicating hope.

He who was making his entry into life surrounded by such portents could not, he told himself, be an ordinary child. In this, his third son, there must assuredly dwell the spirit of some venerable lama, who, in his charity, had returned to earth in order to continue, in the midst of ignorant mankind, his ministry as a compassionate teacher, a guide to the Deliverance from Sorrow.

Why had he, that most saintly of sages, elected that he, Puntsog, and his worthy spouse, should fashion the perishable envelope in which he was once again to become incarnate? Puntsog could not at first understand this; nevertheless, as the days passed by, he discovered in himself virtues and merits which had until then escaped his notice. A month had not

1

elapsed before he had ceased to question the discernment of the sage who had chosen him for father. Indeed, it seemed to him that the choice was amply justified.

Changpal, his wife, received with greater humility the revelation which he made to her of the superior essence of their son, but she did not dream of contradicting him. It was a fact that the most illustrious 'incarnated lamas' (the *tulkus*), and even the Dalai-lama and the Tachi-lama, were generally born of poor families.

The little one who greedily sucked her milk was a *tulku*, then; in that there was no miracle, but only an abounding joy for her, and the pledge of a material prosperity which would overflow from her house to the homes of her relatives, making her blessed and respected by the members of her family and envied by all others.

It was not long before certain of the happy parents' friends and neighbours had openly declared that the infant was indeed a *tulku*, and they even named the lama who had reappeared in his person. To tell the truth, the triumphant father had adroitly helped them to form this opinion.

Now, the lama in question was a very exalted personage, only recently deceased: Mipam *rimpoche* (the 'Precious One'), the seventeenth reincarnation of Mipam the Wonder-worker (*dubthob*) who, some hundreds of years before this date, had led the life of an ascetic on the bare and icy slopes of the Djomo Kangkar (Everest). In the course of his successive reincarnations, the ex-hermit had seen the veneration earned by his austerities, and the miracles attributed to him in his bygone lives, yield ample fruit. His seventeenth successor, lord of the Chös Khor monastery, and of four smaller ones, together with a large estate peopled by tenant-serfs, had lived in opulence, and the eighteenth lama of the line, benefiting by the intelligent administration of the late Mipam's revenues, promised to be even more powerful and wealthy than his predecessor.

When it came to naming the child, his father had unhesitatingly chosen the name of Mipam (the Invincible), in allusion to the origin which he ascribed to him, and to his future greatness.

Two astrologers, being consulted as to the fitness of the *tulku's* choice, both agreed that it was entirely concordant with the horoscope which they had drawn up.

Such was the future they dreamed for their son, these two villagers of Tromo.

This being settled, young Mipam had grown up in the manner of all other little boys. First of all, he had crawled about on all fours; then, straightening himself on his unsteady legs, he had staggered about among the chests and cushions which in all Tibetan houses do duty for seats.

He was not taught to speak. This is not the custom in Tibet. Man, so the Tibetans think, comes to pronounce the words of his mother-tongue as naturally as the animals utter the cries appropriate to the species to which they belong. And experience goes to prove that, without being taught, all Tibetans do talk. Only it is a long time before they do so. When he was three years old, Mipam could still only cry. His stentorian yells, denoting an abnormally robust constitution, were quite explicit and entirely reassuring to his parents, but with the best will in the world it would have been impossible to recognize, in those inarticulate sounds, the melodious syllables of the beautiful Tibetan language.

Mipam had reached his third year when the dignitaries of Chös Khor monastery set about their quest for the new reincarnation of their abbot, Mipam the XVIII. The news spread like wildfire through the land, and Puntsog made ready, against the searchers' arrival, duly to interpret and make the most of the different signs which, in his opinion, identified the personality of his son, thereby proving the legitimacy of his rights to the abbatial seat of Chös Khor.

With a view to paving the way, by assuring himself of the support of the tutelary gods of his ancestors, with those of his wife, and the local deities, and also by creating, by means of appropriate rites, a current of circumstances favourable to his purpose, Puntsog appealed to two lamas of the sect to which he belonged; and in order to leave nothing undone, he also invited a sorcerer, who was deputed to be skilled in securing the good offices of the genii and the demons, or, at least, in preventing them from working mischief. Each of the celebrants was to be attended by several acolytes.

An ox and a pig were killed, and their flesh, prepared in various ways, was to provide the substance of the meal to be served to the lamas and the sorcerer. Another pig and several fowls were to be sacrificed, in the course of the ceremony, by the sorcerer himself.

Changpal sent her two sons to the farmers of the neighbourhood, bidding them collect a number of eggs, wherewith to make the 'Chinese soup', and with her own hands she prepared the beer and the spirits for the lavish libations.

On the day appointed, the sorcerer Bön arrived before daybreak, to begin his office under a tree in front of the house. A little later the two lamas and their attendants, dropping down from the hill-top on which their monastery was perched, appeared on the mountain-side above the village. Preceding them, three novices took it in turns to play the kangling[1] to announce their arrival.

At Puntsog's house, after duly refreshing themselves in the company of the Bön, who had now entered the house, but sat apart from the rest, they all began to read, at the tops of their voices, passages from various Sacred Books, accompanying their reading with the beating of their small drums, the ringing of little bells, and the sonorous utterance of ritual exclamations. As for the Bön, who had returned to his place beneath the tree, he was chanting over his victims, which were laid out on a bed of leaves. The abundant luncheon had given the guests reason

---

[1] Strictly speaking, the kangling is a musical instrument made of a human thigh-bone, used by certain naljorpas; the name, however, is given by extension to a kind of brass cornet.

to hope great things of the dinner that was to follow, and they showed their satisfaction by the vehemence with which they celebrated the rites.

By way of a lucky augury, the superstitious Puntsog had erected a throne in one corner of the room. Symbolizing the future greatness of his son, this throne represented the one that awaited Mipam at Chös Khor. When the ceremonies were over he sat the child upon it, arrayed for the occasion in a robe of yellow silk. At this juncture the *trapas* chanted the final benedictions, calling down prosperity upon the head of the house, his family, and his possessions. Intoning liturgical texts, they made the round of the farm, throwing consecrated grain over people, beasts, and things. A hail of corn fell upon Mipam; his throne was bestrewn with it, and on the floor at his feet the fallen grains formed a circle intersected by rays, roughly resembling the figure of a wheel.[1] Puntsog, ever on the hunt for omens, did not fail to mark the fact, and call the attention of those about him to the augury. All were agreed that it constituted yet another sign which pointed to Mipam as a *tulku* who was to preach the Noble Doctrine.

When all was over, each of the officiants received a fee, in money and in kind, commensurate with his rank. The sorcerer *Bön*, carrying off the best part of the sacrificial victims, retreated to his own quarters, while the *trapas*, well pleased with their outing, and likewise heavily laden with meat and fermented grain, once more climbed, gossiping as they went, the steep paths leading to their lofty monastery.

Left to himself while his parents were dividing among their neighbours the savoury remains of the banquet, Mipam had fallen asleep on his throne.

Despite the signs and omens and the rites duly performed,

[1] In Buddhistic symbolism, the wheel is the emblem of the Doctrine. To 'turn the wheel of the Doctrine' is a classic expression in Buddhist phraseology; it means 'to preach'.

events took an unexpected turn. Guided by certain oracles, the monks entrusted with the quest for their reincarnated lama pursued their researches in other directions. Puntsog had no opportunity of presenting his son to them, or confronting them with the witnesses who were ready to relate the prodigies which had marked the day of his birth.

The authorities of Chös Khor, after examining a dozen claimants, detained three of the boys, who were subjected to the customary triple test.

First, the candidate was required to identify articles which had belonged to the deceased lama; then a clairvoyant had to confirm his identity, and lastly, the rivals drew lots.

In vain did Puntsog multiply his visits and his gifts to personages whom he regarded as influential; Mipam was not included among the candidates, and so he lost all chance of demonstrating the legitimacy of his claim.

While Puntsog was bemoaning himself and weeping over the shipwreck of his hopes, the election took place. The son of a peasant from Yarlung passed the triple test; he unhesitatingly recognized the rosary, the ritual sceptre and the monastic mantle of Mipam the XVII, though they were placed among many others that appeared identical. Three times a clairvoyant lama confirmed his identity, and the divinatory rites and astrological calculations confirmed his verdict. Lastly, in the drawing of lots, which was thrice repeated, his name was three times the first to leave the urn.

The reincarnation of Mipam the Wonder-worker was duly acknowledged. The joyful parents of the successful candidate returned with him to their home, there to await the propitious day when he would make his solemn entry into the monastery.

Two months later, three dignitaries of Chös Khor, accompanied by a numerous following, went to fetch their old lama in his new incarnation.

To the sound of *gyalings*, *ragdungs*[1] and kettle-drums, the procession led off. Arrayed in a robe of cloth of gold, and mounted on a white horse, with two monks walking by his side and supporting him in his saddle, while a third sheltered him under a wide umbrella with a long handle, the child entered the gates of Chös Khor.

Within the boundary walls, surrounded by the low dwellings of the monks, but separated from them by wide courtyards, rose the lama's palace. A lantern, capped with a gilded roof, which was turned up at the corners, and glittered in the sun, rose from the terrace which surmounted the four-storied building.

A wide porch, decorated with frescoes, and approached by a stone stairway, led to the main entrance of the lama's residence. At the foot of the steps the procession drew up.

The oboes swelled their plaintive voices, the long trumpets bellowed more boisterously than ever, and the kettle-drummers, with redoubled energy, made the welkin throb with the rumbling of distant thunder; Mipam, the Wonder-worker, eighteen times incarnate, was 're-entering' his abode.

At the very moment when the young lama, lifted from the saddle by his bodyguards, set his foot upon the first step of his sumptuous residence, the other little Mipam, now reduced to the rank of the rest of the children of his village, was standing, erect and thoughtful, at the edge of the woods close to his house. Slowly he raised his little right hand, holding the five fingers apart, and he who had never yet spoken gravely and distinctly uttered one syllable: *nga* (five)!

A light breeze flitted of a sudden over the forest, and the trees bowed their heads and swung their leafy branches, as though to greet the coming of a victorious hero, or rather, to applaud his setting forth on a glorious adventure. The same

---

[1] *Gyalings*: a kind of oboe. *Ragdungs*: immense Tibetan trumpets. Some of these instruments are several yards in length. When at rest the mouth lies on the ground; when the musicians are marching their long tubes are supported on the shoulders of several men placed at intervals.

mysterious light that had appeared at the time of his birth surrounded the child as with a halo, the beams of which radiated as far as the eye could reach, and Changpal, at work hard by, heard, echoing in the air, the voices of the same invisible choir that had sung while Mipam was coming into the world.

The good woman had not noticed her son's gesture, but she heard the singing, and she saw the extraordinary light. Amazed and troubled, she had intended, on returning to the house, to relate these happenings to her husband; but she found Puntsog prone on his couch, drunk and unconscious. On the morrow, when the impression had faded, her timidity, and perhaps a vague feeling that to reveal such mysteries as this to a profane toper would be sacrilege, withheld her from speaking. She kept silence, but deep in her heart was rooted the conviction that an exalted destiny awaited her child.

Mipam's future, whatever it was to be, whether brilliant or humble, happy or tragic, still remained a secret; but the notorious past of his father Puntsog invested the latter with the melancholy aura of an ill-starred hero.

Puntsog, now apathetic, and a drinker, had once been a chief and a warrior. At the time when the Whites climbed to the assault of the Himalayas, the ruler of Demojong had appealed to the minor chiefs of the adjacent regions to aid him in his resistance. The chief under whom Puntsog had exercised the twofold function of village headman and captain hastily despatched his troops to the assistance of his neighbour.

His 'troops' consisted of a few dozen mountaineers armed with bows and arrows. At their head proudly marched Puntsog their captain, inspired by martial ardour, and never for an instant doubting his power to exterminate the foolhardy invaders. Quickly the men crossed the high pass that divides the Demojong from the Tromo valley, and descended through the forests as far as the torrential Tista. There, in the depths of the jungle, some hundreds of men, working night and day, were manufacturing bamboo arrows.

8

Meanwhile hunters who were skilled in the preparation of arrow-poison coated the points of the arrows and filled the quivers which the combatants carried slung over their shoulders.

Facing them, the civilized Whites, confident of victory with their rifles and their superior numbers, were exasperated by the puerile but obstinate resistance of the mountaineers. Bullets whistled through the brushwood, and one of them found a billet in the body of Puntsog's only son by his first wife.

For three weeks the Tibetans held the invaders in check. But the rifle was victorious. The ruler of Demojong was exiled. A handful of faithful adherents followed his fortunes. Among them was his friend, the Tibetan princeling whose subject Puntsog was, and Puntsog himself, attendant on his chief.

Several years passed. The age of heroism was over; melancholy and dispirited, Puntsog vegetated in the impoverished Court of the *ex-gyalpo* (prince). During his absence his family estates passed into the hands of certain prosaic persons who had divined the issue of the struggle, and had opportunely offered their services, before its termination, to the future victors.

When the ruler of Demojong was authorized to return to his hereditary estates, his friend, the Tromopa chieftain, went back to his own country, and Puntsog, loyal as ever, followed him. But whereas his lord settled down in his little palace and there resumed his usual mode of life, in the case of the ex-captain all was changed: a man of wealth before his epic adventure, he was now almost destitute. The prince condescended, however, to maintain him in his office of village headman, but the gratitude of the masters whom he had defended went no further.

In his dilapidated house, Puntsog had no company but that of two women: his wife, already advanced in years, and the widowed wife of his son.

In accordance with the practice of the country, Puntsog, on his son's marriage, had paid to the parents of Changpal, his

9

daughter-in-law, the price asked by them in compensation for the sums which they had disbursed toward their daughter's upbringing. He had thereby acquired over the girl all the rights of an authentic father, and could in his turn claim the usual gifts from anyone who wished to marry her, but another idea was germinating in his brain.

Twenty-five years had elapsed since the birth of his dead son; his wife had given him no other children, and he could hope to become a father once more only by marrying again. Polygamy, more especially when the lack of descendants is the reason for it, is admitted in Tibet; in that quarter no obstacle existed. But in order to secure a girl of good family he would have to pay a considerable price to her parents, and Puntsog was not prosperous enough to find another such sum as that which he had disbursed when Changpal married his son. The means of dispensing with this expenditure was at hand. Changpal was pretty and even-tempered; it would be difficult to find a more agreeable wife. She was used to living with her mother-in-law and got on well with her. If he should marry her, nothing in his home would be changed; he would run no risk of disturbing its peace by bringing to it a girl with whom his elderly wife could not agree, or who, for her part, would adopt an aggressive attitude towards the older woman.

After full reflection, Puntsog decided to marry his son's widow. Nothing stood in the way: they were in no sense related to each other; 'the bloods were different', and, furthermore, Changpal had not yet borne any children.

What did the young woman think of this decision?—She would probably have preferred a companion less mature than her father-in-law, but her passive character did not permit of resistance on her part, nor did the idea of resistance even enter her mind. The wedding was celebrated quite quietly, and, in the home of the village headman life continued as before; monotonous and active for the two women, and idle enough for himself.

In the course of the years Changpal gave birth to a son who

10

was called Dogyal, and then to little Mipam, whose advent was accompanied by prodigies.

These notwithstanding, Mipam showed no sign of revealing an exceptional personality. He was a taciturn little boy, inclined to be sulky, and also decidedly greedy. There was some excuse for this latter fault, for only a very coarse and meagre pittance fell to his lot in his father's house. Tibetan parents do not believe in spoiling their children.

Every morning the little boy drove his father's cattle into the forest to graze, and all day long he remained there with the little herd. For the first few months his brother Dogyal had accompanied him, but then, since the older boy was able to make himself useful on the land, he was kept busy in the fields. Exceptionally well-grown for his age, Dogyal also went shooting with his uncles and cousins, and sometimes even by himself, returning with a good bag, to Puntsog's great satisfaction. The proficiency of his elder son went far to heal the wound to his self-esteem caused by the reversal of his hopes in respect of Mipam.

But even though the father had renounced the ambitious hopes that had centred on this Mipam of his, who had become so ordinary after such a promising beginning, the child's mother still cherished, at the bottom of her heart, a timid, indefinite hope, a dim faith in the exceptional nature of her silent and gluttonous youngest-born. Of an evening, on returning home from the fields, with aching back, and arms benumbed, and hastily preparing supper for the family by the light of the fire,[1] she would steal a tender glance at Mipam, stretched on the floor with closed eyes, hugging his bowl with his little hands, only half asleep, and ready to wake up as soon as the meal was served.

.   .   .   .   .

[1] Many Tibetan peasants use no lamps or candles. The firelight alone is enough for them. When they want a brighter illumination, they throw on the fire a few very dry twigs or resinous chips, which make a clear flame. These chips of resinous wood are also carried by hand, to serve as tapers, if a light is needed for a moment elsewhere than in the kitchen.

A strange and unforeseen event broke the monotony of family life, and wrought in Mipam an extraordinary transformation of character.

One day the child went to the forest as usual, and the cattle scattered through the underwood in search of forage. In the evening Mipam began to collect them, preparatory to returning to the village. As was their custom, they grouped themselves of their own accord, and set off along the path which they had to follow. Then it was that their young guardian perceived that one of them was missing: the bull, who generally walked at the head of the slower-paced cows. The child's search was fruitless; the handsome bull could not be found. What was he to do? Mipam asked himself in anguish; his father hadn't an easy temper, as bitter experience of cuffs and beatings had taught him. He had no doubt that he would be sent back at once to the forest, to go on looking for the lost animal. There would certainly be no question of supper. . . . Would it not be better, then, in order to save himself a thrashing, and the trouble of making the journey all over again, to begin the search at once?

Night was falling, the impatient cows were lowing discreetly, and some of them were beginning to move off toward the valley. Mipam's mind was made up. Hurriedly he drove his beasts to a path with which they were familiar, and, confident that they would return by themselves to the byre, he once more scaled the sloping mountain-side.

Mipam was quite impervious to fear. This fearlessness of his was due not so much to courage as to a complete unconsciousness of danger. Like other children of Tibet, he had heard terrific tales of demons. He knew that all sorts of beings live hidden in trees, rocks, and springs, ready to play cruel pranks on all who come within their reach. He knew that there were demons who seized little children, and pushed them into the clefts of the rocks, which closed over them again. Sometimes, if the demon was in a hurry, he would leave a little foot or the end of a lock of hair sticking out. From these appalling signs it was known that a victim of the demons was immured in that rock. Mipam knew also that the forest harbours ferocious wild beasts, which issue from their dens at night, and prowl through the thickets in search of prey. He was fully aware of the perils which men and cattle incur when they venture to leave their homes at night. There is safety in the houses of the village, for around them are planted high poles, flying flags on which protective charms are printed. But in spite of everything, Mipam was not afraid.

But he was hungry; Mipam was always hungry. Of the bull not the faintest trace was to be discovered; moreover, the night had grown very dark, with never a ray from the moon. Mipam couldn't see the shape of his hand at the end of his outstretched arm. He stumbled over protruding roots and scratched himself on thorny bushes; and at last he struck his forehead against a jutting rock. The blow dazed him; he sank to the ground, and what with the pain in his forehead and the pangs of his empty stomach, he wept scalding tears. When he had had a good cry he fell asleep, and slipped into another world, where there were no bulls to be sought, and no father Puntsog to be dreaded, and where the gnawings of an exacting stomach were forgotten.

When he awoke it was already daylight; but a strange daylight, more golden than on ordinary days, and the uniform light under the leafy trees seemed to bathe places which would normally have been in the shade. At a distance of a few paces a crouching leopard, motionless, was contemplating him with his large, green, watchful eyes.

'Oh!' said Mipam to himself, when he realized that he was awake, 'can this leopard have devoured my bull?' But the thought that he himself was in danger of being eaten never occurred to him. And because the leopard was very handsome, and he had never seen one alive, and knew that to be so near to a living leopard was a very unusual thing, and also because he was still very tired, Mipam continued to lie where he was, gazing at the animal which was gazing at him.

.   .   .   .   .

Down at Puntsog's, the cows had come home by themselves. Changpal, when she saw that neither their guardian nor the bull had returned, had no difficulty in guessing what had happened. It is a common thing for an animal to lose its way in the forest; Mipam, perhaps, had found the bull late in the evening, too far away to bring it home, and had slept at the nearest farm. The good woman had not worried overmuch, fully expecting to see her son return at daybreak. But the morning wore on, and he did not appear.

Puntsog thereupon ordered Dogyal to go and look for his young brother, and as the ex-captain was above all a practical man, he told his son to take his bow with him, so that he could bag an antelope or a wild goat if he should chance to meet one on his way through the woods.

Dogyal had no great trouble in finding the little herdsman, for the spot where Mipam had passed the night, and where he was still lying, was not far distant from the clearings to which he generally led his charges to graze. The youth did not notice the mysterious light in which that corner of the forest was steeped, but he quite clearly saw the leopard and Mipam, both motionless and quietly gazing at each other. He attributed the boy's immobility to the terror which he must be feeling, and trembling with fear on his account, he shouted out to him, as he hastily strung an arrow to his bow:

'Don't be afraid, Mipam, I'm here!'

Hearing him, Mipam turned his head, and seeing the young hunter bend his bow, with one bound he threw himself in front of the leopard, as he cried:

'Don't shoot!'

Too late! the arrow was sped, the leopard was off in a flash, and it was Mipam who received the poisoned barb in his shoulder.

Horrified, knowing that the wound would be deadly if the poison entered the blood-stream, Dogyal threw away his bow, hurled himself upon his brother, and baring the boy's shoulder, he began vigorously to suck the wound. Dogyal himself was still quite young; he was, indeed, barely fifteen; and half crazed by the uncertainty of not knowing whether he would succeed, by sucking the wound, in preventing the poison from entering the boy's veins, he felt that he had probably killed his younger brother.

In order to obviate all danger to those who consume the meat of animals killed with poisoned arrows, the hunters, as soon as the animal is dead, are in the habit of cutting out a large piece of flesh round the place where the arrow-head has entered. This method alone seemed to Dogyal to be absolutely safe; but what atrocious pain he would cause the child! No matter—anything was better than his death! Dogyal made up his mind.

'I must cut a piece out of your shoulder,' he told his brother. 'If I don't, you'll die. Try not to move!'

He sat down, set Mipam in front of him between his thighs, pressing his knees against him to prevent him from moving, and then, with his knife, he cut out a piece of flesh, which included the wound.

The blood flowed freely, but the child neither cried out nor moved. Dogyal thought he had fainted, but he had not lost consciousness. A singular expression was stamped upon his face; he was staring fixedly before him.

His brother, in great distress, put him, all blood-bespattered as he was, across his back, and proceeded to carry him home. The golden light still lit up the undergrowth, and it accompanied the two children on their homeward way, but Dogyal, as before, did not notice it.

CHAPTER II

AFTER the rough operation which Dogyal had performed upon him, Mipam suffered from fever for a week. Nevertheless, he did not complain, nor did he even open his lips. In vain did his parents try to elicit the reason for the strange impulse which had prompted him to throw himself in front of the leopard, in order to protect it. What had been his intention? What was the motive of such a crazy action? Mipam did not reply: he seemed to be wrapped in a kind of ecstasy, as though contemplating a vision unperceived by those about him.

And then, one morning, Changpal, on awaking, missed her son. They sought him in and around the house, and on the neighbouring farms. He remained undiscoverable. Dogyal explored the parts of the forest that his brother had been wont to frequent; but he was not to be found there.

Puntsog sent for a diviner, but could extract no useful information from him. 'Mipam is living behind a veil,' was all he would say. To what veil did he refer? There seemed to be no sense in his words. A sorcerer *Bön* was called in. Asking for a pig, he slew it as he murmured secret formulae over it. Then, cutting up the carcase, he laid the joints on a bed of leaves and offered them up to his tutelary deity. While these offerings lay at the foot of a tree, the god took possession of the sorcerer, who began first to tremble and then to toss himself about as he chanted unintelligible words. Puntsog, and two of the more intelligent villagers, however, made out that the child had been captured and enslaved by a demon. The god who revealed this fact through the mouth of the sorcerer also informed Puntsog that the demon demanded a cow in ransom for his child. The cow was killed with the same ceremonies as the pig, and just as

16

in the case of the latter, the sorcerer, after a mere pretence of a sacrificial offering, carried off, as part of his fee, the best portions of the animal. Such is the practice of the country.

Despite these sacrifices, the child whom his kidnapper was to return on a duly appointed evening, and leave under a particular tree, did not reappear. When more than a fortnight had elapsed since he had vanished, Puntsog's friends came to the conclusion that Mipam had been devoured by some wild beast, and the headman also began to share this belief. Such a thing does happen in the mountains, and the stupid boy who treated leopards as though they were pet dogs was the very person to become the prey of one of them.

Notwithstanding the supplications of Changpal, who still cherished the hope of seeing her son again, and considered that the celebration of the office for the dead was the very thing to bring him misfortune, Puntsog carried one of the little boy's robes to the adjacent monastery in order that the funeral rites might be performed over it, as representing the dead child's body.

Just when the lama was about to begin the office in his private oratory the little bell that stood before him rang, although he was not conscious of having touched it. A feeling of apprehension seized him. Was it prudent on his part to describe to a child who might still be in this world of ours the paths which intersect in the *Bardo*,[1] and to impress upon him the vision of the disincarnate spirits that wander along them? In so influencing the spirit of a living being might he not run the risk of enticing it prematurely out of its present life? The responsibility which he might incur intimidated the good lama; he signed to the novice who was assisting him to restore to their silken envelope the leaves of the book which he

---

[1] The world where disincarnate spirits wander between the moment of the death and that of rebirth. However, learned Tibetans regard it not as a real place, but as a kind of mirage created by subjective images arising in the consciousness of the deceased.

had already taken out, and wrapped in meditation, left the room.

Mipam, who had narrowly escaped the mist-ridden paths of the world of Shades, was actually wandering on the mountainside. The singular silence which he had maintained since his adventure had masked an intense effort of thought.

His experience in the forest, when he had awakened to find a leopard gazing at him, had endowed him with a curious mental alertness. So the leopard, that was said to be so vicious, could really be friendly! . . . He had seen the big handsome beasts with their spotted coats brought back to the village, still bleeding, hanging by their four paws to a branch carried on the shoulders of two hunters. What harm had they done to the men who had killed them? Perhaps they had done no harm at all! And perhaps, like the leopard, which had seemed as inoffensive as a lamb, the other wild beasts of the forest, and the living creatures that dwelt in the streams, the rocky wilderness, and the black lakes, and the phantoms of the dead, and even that terrible demon who seizes little children and shuts them up in the rocks, his store-rooms—perhaps all might really be friendly. Perhaps it was because the hunters killed them that the beasts of the forests had become unfriendly and baleful! Perhaps it was because men feared and hated them that the spirits and demons had become hostile to them. . . . That fine leopard, which had lain so quietly watching him—had not Dogyal tried to kill it, instead of wishing it well for having behaved like a friend to his little brother?

Oh! how wicked it would have been to let him shoot his poisoned arrow at the beautiful beast that seemed to love him! Mipam's wound was still hurting him, but he did not regret the action that had saved the leopard's life. Distressed because his parents and the village folk did not know what goodness was, he had, to his sorrow, felt himself a stranger among them, and now, although he was so little, he was wandering in quest of his true family, of a land where men do no harm to those

18

who have not harmed them, and do not hastily call those wicked whom they do not know.

As the little fellow, sunk in thought, was sauntering along haphazard, feeding on roots, wild berries, and the *tsampa*[1] with which he had been prudent enough to provide himself for his journey, he saw advancing towards him a long-haired *yoguin* whose pilgrim's staff was tipped with a trident.

'Where are you going, all alone, my young friend?' asked the ascetic, surprised at this meeting.

'I'm going to the land where people love one another,' replied the child, gravely. Then, in his turn putting a question:

'Can you tell me which way I ought to go? It is already a long while since I started, and everything I see looks just like what one can see round my village. The birds and the hares run away when I come near them. The people about here kill them, I expect, as my brother Dogyal and his friends do. These poor animals think I am bad and are afraid of me; if they were stronger they would attack me, perhaps, to prevent my harming them!'

The *yoguin* looked attentively at the odd little wayfarer. He seemed to see the reflection of an inner light shining in the boy's eyes, and to hear, in his childish words, the echo of a doctrine which he had heard on the lips of certain wise hermits.

'Whoever he may be who calls himself your father, you are verily a son of Chenrezigs,'[2] he replied. 'The land you seek is not to be found where you are going. It waits for those of your race to create it. . . . What is your name?'

'Mipam (Invincible),' answered the boy.

'Well named, indeed!' exclaimed the ascetic. 'A glorious name; do you live up to it! But now I am going to give you some barley meal and butter. You must return home. Your

---

[1] *Tsampa*—flour made of barley of which the grain has been roasted before it is ground. It is the principal food of the Tibetans.

[2] *Chenrezigs*. The name of a mythical being who symbolizes infinite goodness and compassion. He occupies, in the Lamaist pantheon, a place infinitely higher than that of the gods.

19

father, the heavenly Chenrezigs, will show you, one day, the way that you must follow.'

Mipam put the flour and the butter in his bag, which was now nearly empty, and as the ascetic strode away, he sat down on a stone.

The pilgrim's words had bitterly disappointed him. Was he to believe him? Were all men, in every place, like those of his village? Did all men really live at enmity with all creatures other than human beings and—as the quarrels which he had witnessed had already taught him—did they also cherish ill-will towards other human beings than themselves? . . . That seemed to him hard to accept.

And why had that holy man told him that he was the son of Chenrezigs? His father, he knew quite well, was called Puntsog, and was simply the village headman, while Chenrezigs, whose picture you saw painted on the temple walls, was a very mighty spirit, with eleven heads and a multitude of arms, to whom you pray that you may be reborn in the Paradise of the Great Bliss, of which he is the sovereign.

The ascetic, who had given him food when for several days he had been on the verge of starvation, was a very good man, but did he really know what he was talking about? Mipam had strong doubts in the matter. It might be that the country he was looking for was a very long way off, so that the holy pilgrim did not know where it was, and in that case he, who was only a little boy, would have great difficulty in reaching it. He was not a fast walker, and besides, it is not easy to find food in the mountains when you do not care to kill birds by throwing stones at them, or to set traps for fish in the streams.

He began to realize the difficulty of his undertaking. He was not going to give in, but he felt the need of kindly advice, and of more reliable information.

Advice and information could be found not far from his village. At the distance of a day's walk there was a hermit who lived in a hut built against an overhanging rock, which sheltered it from the winter snows. Mipam had never seen the

Eleven - Headed Chin Rese

hermit, but had heard people speak of him and his hut. He knew that his father had sent Dogyal from time to time to take food to this holy man. He knew the path leading to the hermitage, though he had never been right to the end of it, and he thought he could reach it over the mountainside without descending to the point from which it started in the valley. He would consult the hermit, therefore, instead of returning to his father. . . . And accordingly the little fellow set off across the mountain.

'You are Puntsog's son, then,' said the *gomchen* to the child, when the latter, presenting himself before the hermit, had explained what he wanted.

Good! thought Mipam, this man sees things clearly; he doesn't take me for Chenrezigs' son! And feeling already at home with him he told the anchorite of his adventure with the leopard, and explained the ideas which this adventure had suggested to him, and all that had followed.

For eighteen years Yönten Gyatso had lived in the hut under the rock, which he had inherited from another hermit, his spiritual master. For hundreds of years, it was said, a *gomchen* had dwelt in that place, disciple succeeding master, in an uninterrupted line, with the object of protecting the inhabitants of the district from the numerous demons who infested it.

While the child was speaking, the hermit recalled the rumours concerning the surprising events which had accompanied his birth. Even if these events were to be regarded as the product of the imagination of Mipam's parents and their friends, there still remained the fact that Mipam's ideas and behaviour were extraordinary. Who had put these ideas into his head? Who was inspiring him? . . . This child of nine must be the incarnation of some holy lama, or even that of a Budhisatva, one of these exalted spiritual beings who at times manifest themselves in our world to work for the enlightenment and welfare of humanity. Since the mysterious but ineluctable chain of causes

and their effects had led the child to him, it was only fitting
that he should welcome him and endeavour to smooth his path.

'Listen,' he said to Mipam; 'the journey that you wished to
undertake is more difficult and longer than you imagined. You
must learn many things before you attempt to make it. If you
wish I will be your instructor, but you must, before everything
else, reassure your family, who will be distressed by your disappearance. You will sleep here, and then, to-morrow morning,
you will take a letter that I shall give you to Passang's farm,
which you know quite well. If you walk quickly you will be
at his house about midday. From there Passang will send you
on horseback to your father, to whom I am also writing, advising
him to bring you back to me in the near future.'

The idea of returning to his father's house did not at all
appeal to Mipam; he had just been savouring the joys of liberty
and a wanderer's life, and they were too sweet to be easily
renounced, but he did not see how he could disobey the hermit.
He would comply with his wishes, but since the hermit was
willing to take him for his pupil, he would stay only a few days
with his father.

The night which he passed in the anchorite's hut was to
remain forever graven in Mipam's memory.

After their meal of roasted grain and buttered tea, Yönten
Gyatso pointed out to his young guest an old piece of carpet,
bidding him spread it out in a corner and lie down and sleep.
Then, paying no further attention to him, he lit a small lamp
and some little sticks of incense, and placed them on a shelf
on which were some books. This was his altar. To which God
or which Sage the spirals of sweet-scented smoke were mount-
ing no one could have said, for on the roughly-hewn shelf there
stood no statue, and the wall was adorned with no picture.

Sitting with crossed legs, his feet resting on his thighs, his
head and bust upright and rigid, the hermit, motionless, was
meditating.

Through the chinks in the mortarless walls and the badly-joined door-boards the air of the forest entered, moist and fragrant. The faint crackling of dry branches and the rustling of leaves betrayed the presence of prowling animals, and from time to time the cry of some night-bird broke the stillness. As the waters of a torrent beat upon an immovable rock, so the waves of life broke all about the silent hut.

Mipam had already passed many a night in the mountains, and his father's house, at the bottom of the valley, was built at the edge of the wood; but having grown up in the closest contact with Nature, and accustomed, as he was, to that particular atmosphere, the things that surrounded him had never arrested his attention. Now everything seemed new to him. He listened and felt with the power of the senses multiplied a hundredfold, or rather, with senses different from those that serve us every day. And what he listened to was not simply the padding of beasts seeking their food through the thickets: what he was aware of was not merely the smell of the wet earth, of the fallen, rotting leaves, the breath of the trees and the fragrance of herbage. A pitiable, passionate choir of voices rose from the encircling shadows, invaded the hut, and crept, suppliant, to the feet of those who dwelt there. It spoke of the pains of sentient beings sacrificed to the wants of others; of cropped leaves, of insects devoured, and of the pain of those who fed on them, eyes on the alert, ears pricked up, hearts quivering with fear, knowing that stronger than they were seeking to devour them in turn. Other harrowing voices bemoaned the horror which some felt for their own acts, when, driven by the imperious tyranny of hunger, they crushed the helpless plants or felt the creatures they were tearing to pieces writhing under their teeth. In horror, in despair, the voices howled or sobbed, timid or clamorous, and what they did not express, what the sad singers were doubtless incapable of discerning in the depths of their dim-lit thoughts, was a consuming thirst after goodness, for the friendship which they found neither around them, nor in themselves.

Still motionless, wrapped in his sombre monastic cloak, the

23

hermit was scarcely visible in the darkness. The little altar-lamp had long gone out; one single stick of incense was still glowing red, on a level with the earthenware stand in which it had been fixed. A tiny point of fire in the darkness, it suddenly gave out two vivid sparks and then died out, and the darkness was complete. Mipam began to weep silently. . . .

At dawn, Yönten Gyatso released his knees from the 'meditation cord' which served him for support and rose to his feet. Had he slept? Had he passed the whole night in contemplation? Mipam was too engrossed in his own thoughts to ask himself the question. He only knew that his host had remained upright and motionless all through the night.

'Go and draw some water for making tea,' the anchorite ordered, and the little boy, taking a bucket, went to fill it at the stream hard by.

When they had breakfasted on buttered tea and barley-meal the hermit addressed himself to Mipam.

'You are pondering over thoughts too weighty for a child of your age,' he said. 'Very few grown men could bear their weight. A noble destiny seems to be in store for you. If I can, I will try to prepare you for it, and to show you the meaning of what you dimly perceive.

'You must understand, you who are so distressed by the malevolence that all creatures manifest toward one another, that at the root of every cruel act there is a false notion of our "I" and of that of others. A wicked man's actions spring from the fear of suffering, or from the desire to increase his enjoyment, without perceiving that in committing these actions he risks, on the contrary, bringing greater suffering upon himself, and instils into his joy the poison of insecurity.

'Some have become wicked because they have lost their way on the journey which you are planning. They thought they had reached a refuge where friendship prevailed; their brotherly trust in friendship has been betrayed, or they have discovered the unworthiness of the heroes whom they once approached with veneration. The bitter grief of their disappointment has turned to hate: and these are they who are most of all to be pitied.

'The ordinary man loves those whom he thinks are good: the wise man extends his warmest sympathy to those whom he sees are wicked, because he has plumbed their misery.

'Doubtless in one of your past lives you have caught a glimpse of these truths, but in your present life you are only a child of nine, and cannot understand them.

'To-day you are to keep in mind these two words only: Pity and loving-kindness. They are the keys to a magic power, and the names of the first stages on the path to the country of your dreams. Hold them in your memory. When you have become my pupil I will teach you more about them.'

Mipam had not understood much of the hermit's beautiful discourse: however, as he had been well brought up, and knew the proper thing to do, he prostrated himself thrice at his feet, saying respectfully:

'I carry your words on my head, *Kushog*.'[1]

The hermit then wrote two letters, one for Passang, the farmer, and the other for Puntsog. In this latter he explained to the headman the circumstances which had brought Mipam to him. He informed him that he had recognized in his son a mind with a very decided bent towards the 'religion' of universal benevolence of the Budhisatvas, and that he would willingly undertake to instruct him.

Yet the wise anchorite never had to take this charge upon himself. He never again set eyes on the little pilgrim who was marked with the seal of the heavenly Chenrezigs, nor did Mipam ever have the chance of hearing from the seer's lips the explanation of his discourse. He would doubtless have to discover it for himself.

Puntsog was sitting out of doors, on a bench against the wall of his house, when Mipam appeared, riding on horseback, and

[1] *Kushog* = Sir.

accompanied by a servant of Passang the farmer. The irascible ex-captain leapt up as he saw him, and with a quick movement seized the heavy stick which he always kept within reach. The child had hardly time to slip from the saddle and set foot on the ground before his father laid hold of him and angrily brandished his cudgel.

'Don't beat him! don't beat him!' cried the servant. 'He comes with a letter from Jowo Gomchen (the lord hermit)! Read it!'

'I have a letter from the *gomchen*,' said the boy in confirmation, struggling to escape correction, but Puntsog had a firm grip of his arm, and the paternal cudgel continued to fall upon the luckless Mipam.

Glaring at the ex-captain with an expression that spoke of fury rather than friendship, the young explorer in quest of the land of universal love began to shout at the top of his voice:

'Let me go! You've no right to hit me! You are not my father, Puntsog! Do you hear—I'm the son of Chenrezigs!'

The stupefaction which overcame Puntsog on hearing this remarkable declaration caused him to unclasp his fingers, and Mipam took advantage of this to make his escape. When he had put a little distance between himself and his father, he turned round, his face red with anger, and began to apostrophize the latter, calling him disrespectfully by his name.

'Heh! Puntsog, you bad man, you dared to beat me, did you! . . . My divine father will punish you. He'll beat you with his thousand arms and curse you with his eleven mouths!'[1]

The old warrior no longer knew where he was. He asked himself if the insolent little fellow who was defying his authority and braving him so boldly, wasn't perhaps a demon, who had animated the body of his son, who had died in the forest, and under that false semblance had come to torment him.

[1] *Chenrezigs*, the personification of goodness and perfect charity, is represented under various forms. One of these gives him a thousand arms and eleven heads.

26

He had not recovered from his stupor when Changpal, hearing the child's cries, arrived on the scene.

The good woman harboured no doubt as to Mipam's identity, and rushing at him, she clasped him tenderly in her arms. The boy submitted to her embrace, but when she wanted to lead him into the house he was once more violently refractory. He would not enter the house of this 'Puntsog' who beat him.

Changpal was bewildered. This was not the first time her husband had corrected Mipam; he did as much to Dogyal, and all fathers do the same. Mipam, who had fled from the house and had caused them so much anxiety, thoroughly deserved to be beaten. She was infinitely happy to see her child again, but she could not blame her husband for having chastised the young vagabond. And how dared Mipam call his father by his name? Where did he learn such insolent audacity? Nevertheless, Changpal's joy in recovering the fugitive was too great to allow her to dwell on such matters, or to be severe with him.

'Come,' said she, 'I'll put you in the *lha khang*[1] and bring you some tea. Your father won't go there to beat you, that I promise you!'

And without awaiting his reply, the sturdy mother deftly lifted her son from the ground and bore him off in her arms. Mipam did not protest, and only murmured in her ear:

'And shall I have some *puram*[2] with the tea?'

'You shall,' Changpal promised.

It was not hard to dissuade Puntsog from following Mipam into the *lha khang*. He could not get his son's strange words out of his mind. Never had any child used language like that. Who on earth would think of calling himself the son of Chenrezigs? It amounted to blasphemy!

---

[1] The room containing the family altar, on which stand one or more images or pictures representing the Buddha, or holy lamas, or saints or symbolic deities of the Lamaist pantheon. Upon this altar, made in the shape of a bookcase, are also laid the sacred books belonging to the family. The literal meaning of *lha khang* is 'House of a god'.

[2] Molasses of sugar-cane, compressed into balls or cakes of different sizes.

'*Om mani padme hum!*' rattled off the captain, to ward off the anger of the 'Lord of the piercing vision,' who, despite his infinite goodness, also assumes, at times, a terrible form: Puntsog had learnt as much from a cousin of his who belonged to a religious order.

Mipam's father was by no means a pious man, and it was not his habit even to recite '*Om mani padme hum!*' His violent temper, over which he had little control, led him, by the law of affinity, to pay homage to a personage whom he considered to be more virile than the Great Compassionate One. In loud tones he hammered out the sonorous syllables of the mantram of Padmasambhava: '*Om gura Padma siddhi hum!*'

The final *hum!*, a mystic exclamation of anger, made the whole house shake when he bellowed it out, and it meant, as a rule, that he was drunk. Alcohol alone evoked in him a display of devotion.

By a natural association of ideas, Puntsog, at the mention of Chenrezigs, thought of his cousin, the astrologer Shesrab. He did not particularly like him, and for this reason had not consulted him as to Mipam's disappearance, but it was generally agreed that Shesrab was a learned man, well versed in the most complicated religious rites, and he enjoyed considerable fame in his native country. This was one reason why Puntsog, who had enough native good sense to doubt his relative's scientific knowledge, and was jealous of his prestige, did not like him, and rarely went to see him.

The circumstances, however, were momentous. The hermit's letter, which he had at last read, perplexed him. Yönten Gyatso advised him to allow Mipam to embrace the religious life, and declared that he had read remarkable signs on the child's forehead. This accorded well with the singular circumstances that had attended his birth. And now the boy was actually asserting that he was the son of the heavenly Chenrezigs!

Puntsog was unaware that the child had got this notion from the pilgrim whom he had met in the forest; the hermit, to whom Mipam had related the incident, had not thought it

Chin Rese Mantra Mandala

necessary to mention this detail in his letter. For Puntsog, therefore, this declaration of Mipam's was most disconcerting. Could it be, despite the opinion of the Chös Khor monks, that Mipam was the authentic avatar of some Holy One, as he himself had believed? If that was so, then all was not lost; he might still hope to end his days in prosperity, as the father of a genuine *tulku!*

This was a serious matter, and in spite of his habitual assurance, and the good opinion he had of his own intelligence, Puntsog felt the need of an adviser. He could see but one available: his cousin the astrologer. He would take more interest than another in Mipam, whose success, by reason of their near relationship, might redound, in honours and profit, upon himself.

Changpal was sent for, and ordered to have in readiness for the following morning some good pieces of dried meat, two dozen eggs, and a sack of malted grain wherewith to make beer. Puntsog was to take all this as a present to his cousin whom he wished to visit.

On the morrow Mipam's father, mounted on his best horse, set out on his journey. In front of him paced a mule bearing the gifts he was to offer to the astrologer.

Shesrab lived less than a day's walk from Puntsog's farm. He was a large, corpulent, cheery person, truculent and cunning, married to two wives, the elder of whom he shared with his elder brother. This latter, a cleric like Shesrab, but peaceful in character, pious and devoid of malice, lived in a modest farmhouse, surrounded by his own fields. Nordzinma, the polyandrous wife, had lived for a long time with her younger and more brilliant husband, the astrologer, who was many years her junior. Later, oblivious of the devotion of his elderly companion, whose assiduous labours had been the means of providing for his subsistence while he pursued his studies of ritual and astrology, Shesrab had not shared his prosperity with her, but had married a widow of means, who was tempted by the honour of being the companion of a famous *tsipa.* Nordzinma, feeling that she was becoming a stranger in Shesrab's house, had ended by rejoining her other husband, and Pema, the second wife, who was rather like Shesrab in character, being equally avaricious and cunning skilfully administered his modest fortune, and cleverly advertised his merits.

'Please condescend to enter, *Aku*[1] Puntsog,' said Pema to her visitor, as she ran to hold his horse's head. 'You have put yourself to great trouble. *Jowo tsipa*[2] will be pleased to see you. . . .'

While Puntsog was climbing up the rough stone steps of a rustic stairway, several young boys—Shesrab's pupils—hastened to unload the presents intended for their master from the back of the mule, which they led away to the stables, together with the visitor's horse.

'*Atsi!* I was not expecting you, *Ajo*,'[3] exclaimed Shesrab, when his cousin entered the room. 'Sit down and make yourself comfortable and drink some tea.'

Hardly were they seated when a small boy of ten came in, carrying shoulder-high, as the rules of politeness require, a large copper tea-pot. He shook it gently, and then poured out some tea into a cup, provided with a saucer that rested on a stand, and a silver lid, which Pema had placed on a low table in front of the thick cushion on which Puntsog was seated.

'Your health is good?' asked Shesrab, addressing his cousin.

'Very good indeed, thank you,' Puntsog replied. 'Your health, also, is good?'

'Excellent. . . .'

The boys entered the adjoining kitchen, carrying Puntsog's luggage. When Puntsog heard them, he rose and joined them. He unpacked the bags, placed the eggs and the meat on the dishes which Pema held out to him, emptied the malted grain into a basket, and signed to the children to take the presents to their master.

Used to the ceremonial, the boys placed the dishes and the

[1] *Aku* = literally, a paternal uncle, but also a term of politeness.
[2] 'The lord astrologer.' [3] Elder brother: a term of courtesy.

30

basket on the floor in front of the couch on which Shesrab was still seated. Puntsog, following them, drew from his breast pocket a small scarf of white tarlatan, and spreading it over his offering, he announced, with feigned modesty:

'I've brought you a few trifles, *tsipa lags.*'[1]

'They are excellent, and you are very kind, elder brother. You have put yourself to a great deal of trouble in bringing all this.'

'No trouble at all,' Puntsog politely demurred.

'Sit down in comfort, and drink some tea,' said Shesrab.

At a sign from Pema, the boys carried the presents back into the kitchen, all but the scarf, which they hung over a corner of the table placed before their master's couch.

Another boy entered once more with the tea-pot, refilled the cups of the two men, and then, walking backwards, left them alone together. They drank their tea in silence. Puntsog was the first to speak.

'I've come, *tsipa lags*, to consult you about a really extra-ordinary affair.'

'I'm all attention,' replied Shesrab.

'It's about Mipam . . . his behaviour is inexplicable. . . .'

And Puntsog related in detail, with many repetitions, all that had happened; how the child had been found seated in front of a leopard, and had been wounded in protecting the animal, and then his singular silence, his flight and his return, furnished with a letter from the holy anchorite Yönten Gyatso, who had offered to take him for his pupil and instruct him in the Precious Doctrine of the Buddhas. Finally, Mipam's astounding renunciation of his father, Puntsog, and his declaration that he was a son of the divine Lord Chenrezigs.

'A la la!'[2] exclaimed the *tsipa*, when his cousin had finished

[1] *Lags*, a syllable without any special signification, but adding a shade of respect or politeness ro the preceding word: *tsipa lags*: honourable or respected astrologer.
[2] A Tibetan exclamation of amazement.

his recital. 'All this is marvellous, unless the whole thing is an illusion produced by some maleficent demon!'

'The people at Chös Khor must have been mistaken,' Puntsog continued. 'Mipam is really and truly a *tulku*, as the signs at his birth denoted!'

'Unless he is a demon incarnate,' the astrologer again objected. 'Such things do happen. Did not the famous wonder-worker, Dugpa Kunlegs, discover one of these baleful beings, in the home of some honest folk, all of whose children born before him had died when quite young? This youngest son alone seemed to grow up in good health. The clairvoyant Dugpa Kunlegs discerned his nature, and foresaw that one day he would kill his parents, if he was not destroyed before he became capable of doing so. He bade the mother throw the child into a lake. She hesitated, but the father, full of faith in the *dubthob*,[1] seized the boy and hurled him into the water, whereupon the child immediately turned himself into a black dog and swam away.'

'Truly, that is appalling,' Puntsog agreed, 'but Mipam isn't a demon, unless he's dead, and one of them entered into his corpse and so brought him to life again. . . . Or else, again, some mischievous sorcerer, on growing old and feeling his end approaching, may have cast off his own body and transferred his spirit into Mipam's, whether he actually killed him or found him already dead. . . . These ideas have occurred to me, but I don't think there's anything in them. Mipam is not dead. All these stories of demons and magicians entering into a dead person's body are ancient history . . . nothing like that happens nowadays. . . . .' And harking back to his pet idea: 'Undoubtedly,' he repeated, 'Mipam is really a *tulku*.'

'But now we must go to work carefully. How are we going to enable him to prove his identity and obtain possession of his abbot's seat? Ought I to send him to the hermit? . . . He has the name of being a powerful magician; don't you think Mipam

---

[1] A sage who works miracles.

32

might perhaps learn from him how to secure the recognition of his rights to the succession as Mipam the Wonder-worker, and sit, at last, on the throne of Chös Khor? . . .'

'Mipam would learn nothing of the sort,' the astrologer broke in abruptly. 'Your head, elder brother, is crammed with crazy notions. The Chös Khor people have chosen their lama. For more than six years he has sat on his throne. The Precious Protector[1] has recognized him as the rightful *tulku*. The question of the succession is settled. You are cherishing crazy ideas, I tell you. Put them out of your mind, and let's think out some rational plan.'

Puntsog gave a sigh of regret, but he had come in search of counsel, and it was therefore proper that he should listen to those who gave it.

Shesrab drew his legs closer together, threw out his massive chest, arranged the folds of his monastic toga upon his shoulders, and with an air of authority addressed his cousin:

'While you were telling me of the strange incidents relating to your son,' he said, 'my clairvoyance showed me the right path for him. You did not ask me to draw his horoscope when he was born; and there you were wrong, but at the time you were so puffed up with the prodigies that you and your wife believed you had seen that you disdained my science. Seeing that we are relatives, I shall repair the harm that was done, but henceforth you must have confidence in me.

'To send Mipam to the hermit would be absurd. We all of us revere him, but what profit is an anchorite to his family? If your son, who seems to be a queer character, were to get it into his head that he was to succeed his master, and occupy, after him, his hut under the rock, you would have to feed him all his life. Is that what you want?'

Without any need of words, Puntsog's face very plainly showed that he was not attracted by this prospect.

'Your son,' Shesrab continued, 'has a leaning toward religion. . . .'

[1] The Dalai Lama.

'I haven't specially noticed it,' replied his cousin, 'but the Lord Yönten Gyatso believes he has.'

'It doesn't matter,' said Shesrab curtly. 'You have an elder son to inherit your property; it will be an honour to you if your younger son wears the monk's habit. That does not exclude the possibility of a lucrative career. What do you say to my making an astrologer of him?'

'An astrologer . . . that's not a bad idea!' Puntsog declared. 'Your position is an enviable one, my honourable cousin.'

'I' owe it to my knowledge,' Shesrab replied with dignity. 'Mipam will have to show great intelligence and assiduity in his studies if he hopes one day to equal me. I'll help him because he is your son. Bring him to me. I will have him received into a monastery by our lama Ringchen Tinglegs; he will then become my pupil and will live with me, and I shall teach him.'

In silence, Puntsog weighed in his mind the advantages and inconveniences of this proposition. To accept it would be to incur a heavy expense. The hermit would doubtless be satisfied if he provided for Mipam's food, and that, in the holy man's hut, might be of a frugal nature. Shesrab was a master of a very different kind. He lived sumptuously, both he and his greedy wife. The parents of his pupils had to supply him with generous contributions of the choicest food . . . and a certain amount of money into the bargain, if they wanted Shesrab to take an interest in their boys, and refrain from employing them in heavy manual work. They had also had to propitiate the lady who presided over the kitchen, and who meted out the portions for the children at meal-times in proportion to the presents which she received from their families: a roll of woollen cloth or silk to make a dress or chemise, or a pendant of coral to attach to a necklace would have to be offered on certain occasions. All this provided matter for serious consideration.

On the other hand, Mipam's peculiar character seemed to presage difficulties for his family. There were grounds for fearing that the boy would evince little aptitude for work in the fields. Young as he was, a tendency towards idle loitering had begun to declare itself, and his gluttony was obvious. He had just shown that he had a violent temper, and he had been audaciously insolent to his father. What would he be when he was capable of using actual violence?

His entry into a religious order would solve the problem. When sufficiently instructed, he would doubtless be able to obtain admission to some important and richly endowed monastery, when his parents would no longer have to support him. If he succeeded in becoming an astrologer, his position would be a hundred times better. In that case he would have every chance of acquiring a handsome competence. As for his father, apart from the honour of having a learned son, he might hope to share in his prosperity. Puntsog evoked a mental picture of a comfortable old age, of rich food washed down with copious draughts of beer and spirits. Such a pleasant prospect was well worth some temporary sacrifices.

Mipam's father woke from his day-dream. He had made up his mind.

'That's agreed, honourable astrologer,' he declared. 'I'll bring Mipam here in the course of a few days. Under your guidance I hope he will rapidly acquire knowledge.'

Shesrab clapped his hand. Hearing him a boy entered with a tea-pot.

'Brandy,' ordered his master with a gesture of dismissal to the child.

A few minutes later Pema appeared, carrying two bowls. On the rim of each, in three different places, a piece of butter was stuck as an ornament. These were signs of good omen, and their number meant that three bowls must be drained in succession.

After placing a bowl before each of the men, Pema left the room, returning at once with an earthenware jar of brandy. Ceremoniously she served her husband, whose clerical rank gave him precedence over his cousin, and then poured the potent spirit into Puntsog's bowl. The two men drained their bowls. The lady of the house refilled them in the same order. They drank once more, and a third bumper followed; then Pema, having filled the bowls a fourth time, took the jar back to the next room. The fourth bowl, and any that might follow it, could be sipped at leisure; the rite was accomplished.

Realizing that the private interview between the two men was ended, the astrologer's wife returned, sitting near them on a cushion. She had some tea brought in for herself, and all three, pleased with the conclusion of the affair, chattered amicably together.

Thus it was decided that Mipam, the juvenile aspirant to universal love, was to become an astrologer.

Lo Khor (Tibetan Astrological Calendar)

CHAPTER III

ON his return home Puntsog informed his wife of the decision he had taken as regards Mipam. This he did in a few terse words admitting of no discussion. Changpal, for her part, felt no inclination to raise any objections. The course her husband had chosen seemed to her a wise one, and though it grieved her to be parted from her son, she was pleased with the prospect of his becoming a cleric, a *chospa*.

A number of careers, some materially profitable, others excellent from a spiritual standpoint, are open to members of the Tibetan clergy. Under the monk's habit every aptitude can be fruitfully developed, and even a total lack of aptitude does not prevent a monk from savouring the sweets of a vegetative existence, from which all effort is banned. That was how Mipam's mother looked at the matter, but she entertained no doubt of her son's intelligence. He was not one to take a back seat: he would become an important-looking astrologer, held in high regard and well paid, like Shesrab, and perhaps even still more highly esteemed, and more richly recompensed than he. Or else a nobler career would attract this singular boy. In her mind's eye Changpal saw him climbing to shadowy heights, vanishing mysteriously in the distance, bathed in a supernatural light like that which had illumined the room in which he was born, like the light in which she had seen him enveloped as with an aureole one morning at the edge of the wood, and like that—but of this she knew nothing—which had filled the clearing where the child and the leopard had gazed like friends into each other's eyes.

And so the worthy mother indulged in protracted daydreams, that were nourished by her extravagant hopes and her infinite tenderness for her youngest born.

.   .   .   .

37

Mipam rode across the mountain accompanied by his father and a servant, the latter leading a mule loaded with provisions for the future scholar and presents for his master. To these Changpal had added a roll of Chinese silk as her offering to Pema, whom she begged to keep a mother's eye on her son.

Mipam's opinion, of course, had not been asked as regards the profession which they had chosen for him. In Tibet the choice of a career for their children rests with the parents. The young boy had welcomed, with seeming indifference, the news that he must leave his father's house to live with and be taught by his uncle.[1] But in reality this feigned indifference masked the elaboration of plans diametrically opposed to those devised by Puntsog. As he ambled along, Mipam was considering his chances of escape. The astrologer's residence was not far distant from the route taken by the convoys of merchants going from Lhasa to India. Many pilgrims also passed that way. Some of these people, who were such great travellers, thought the child, must have visited the happy country where men and animals were all good, and friends with one another. Some, at least, must have approached its frontiers, or would know in what direction it lay. He armed himself with patience. Before he could openly make inquiries he would need to be older, to look, in short, like a genuine pilgrim. But in the meantime he could keep an eye on the passing caravans, and slip into their camps when they halted for the night near his uncle's. He would listen to their conversations round the fire at the evening meal, he would talk to them and question them indirectly. Sooner or later he would learn what route he ought to follow. . . . Then he would slip away, and this time he would never return. As he lulled himself with these dreams the recollection of the days which he had passed in roaming, all alone, over the mountains, rekindled in his memory, lighting in him a flame that seared his heart. Oh! to taste once more that joy of being

[1] Shesrab was the first cousin—the 'brother', as they say in Tibet— of Mipam's father; in accordance with the native fashion of denominating the degrees of relationship he was therefore one of the boy's paternal uncles (aku).

free, of fleeing away from the wicked, of drawing near to those who knew how to love! . . .

For the moment, he rejoiced in the thought of leaving this Puntsog, who claimed to be his father, and dared to beat him. As for questioning his uncle, the learned astrologer, about the country where goodness reigns, the idea did not enter his head. Instinctively he excluded him from the number of those whom he could trust.

Shesrab, although a dream which he had dreamed the night before had disturbed his peace of mind, gave his guests a kindly welcome. In his dream he had seen himself outstretched on the floor before the family altar; Mipam, entering the room, had crossed it, striding disrespectfully over the body of his future master; then he had disappeared, entering the cabinet in which the secret magic rites were performed, the doors of which opened of themselves to admit him, and had then closed behind him. A really bad dream! The least disquieting explanation which the astrologer could find was that Mipam's greatness— of whatever order it might be—was to surpass his own. The prospect did not please him at all. He regretted having promised his cousin that he would take the boy, but he could not go back on his word at the very moment when he had received a liberal contribution on account of the price of his lessons. Pema, who at that moment was putting away the rice, the flour, and the fat pig, killed the night before, which Puntsog had brought, would hardly have allowed them to be returned. The future threatened to be fraught with difficulties, thought the astrologer; he must be on his guard. He had, however, plenty of time to think out some means of warding off the danger, for Mipam was still no more than a child.

For the space of two days, Shesrab, Puntsog and Pema kept high revel together. Mipam joined in the feasting with his fellow disciples in the kitchen. He took stock of them: they were four in number, differing in age and character. Their talk when the mistress of the house was not present, soon informed the newcomer as to the kind of life they led. There was plenty to be done in the astrologer's house, and his pupils, in accordance with the general practice, consecrated by centuries of usage, were also his servants. The lessons were short; the arbitrary Pema quickly roped the scholars into her service. They had to take the cattle to graze, cut wood in the forest, fetch water from the stream, light the fire before daybreak, prepare the morning tea and take it to their master and mistress, who were still abed, and attend to a hundred other jobs.

Mipam pondered what he had heard. How would he be treated once Puntsog had left? He asked himself the question with some curiosity, some anxiety, and a good deal of indifference. What did all this matter?—it would not be for long! Was it not there, close to the house, the road that led far, far away, that would surely take him to the country he sought if he still went on after the merchants had stopped. . . . He would make his escape, of that he was sure.

When Puntsog left his cousin, everything was settled between them as to Mipam's ordination ceremony. The astrologer would consult the head lama of the monastery to which he himself belonged, and the lama's consent to the boy's admission was a foregone conclusion.

Everything happened as he had foreseen.

The monastery of which Mipam was to become a member bore no resemblance to the wealthy monastery of Chos Khor in which his father had hoped to see him seated on the abbatial throne.

Rab-den-tsi, which belonged to the sect of 'Red Hats', who were allowed to marry and to drink fermented liquor, was perched high above Chastong, Mipam's native village, and was the very monastery from which had descended, some years earlier, the *trapas* who had performed at Puntsog's house the rites which were to secure for his son the support of the gods, and bring about his election to the lordship of Chos Khor.

The satisfaction which Puntsog felt on the day of ordination was clouded by that recollection. As for Mipam, he would not have been a child had he not found pleasure in being the centre of a festival, in donning different clothes from those he had worn up to that time, and in receiving gifts from the friends of his family. He knew, too, that his new position as a member of the clergy gave him an importance and conferred upon him privileges which he had not hitherto enjoyed. He would have the right, henceforth, to a place of honour, to a more exalted seat than that of his elder brother, who had remained a simple layman, and the village headman who called himself his father would no longer dare to beat him, seeing that it is a grievous sin to strike one who wears the monk's habit.

The sacred garment in which Mipam was muffled on this auspicious occasion gave the little fellow a somewhat grotesque appearance. Peasants think a good deal about expenditure. To have monastic vestments made to measure for a growing child who could no longer wear them the following year would have seemed to Puntsog an unthinkable absurdity. Nevertheless, the boy must have them if he was to be ordained; moreover, to gratify his family's vanity the novice had to be 'well' dressed. And here the astrologer kindly came to his cousin's aid. For the day of the ceremony he lent Mipam his finest costume: the *shamthabs*, the *todgag* and the *zan*, the three regulation vestments.

That the *tsipa* was a corpulent man, and very tall, while Mipam was a slender little fellow counted for nothing; it is customary for novices to wear, on such occasions, the clothes of their relatives or grown-up friends. The cut of the lamaist costume rather lends itself to this. The *shamthabs*, a piece of stuff of which the two ends are sewn together, forms a skirt, which is drawn tight at the waist by a sash. Over the sash the upper part of the skirt falls in the form of a flounce. By completely doubling the flounce the length of the skirt is reduced by one-half, so that by bundling himself into this doubled skirt a child is able to wear an adult's *shamthabs*. The *todgag*, a sleeveless jacket, the lower part of which is buried

under the *shamthabs*, and is drawn tight by the sash, can also be
adapted to any figure; as for the toga, the *zan*, it is enough to
wrap it several times round the shoulders, and the whole length
can be draped about the child.

Accustomed to makeshifts of this kind, the worthy peasants
saw nothing laughable in them. Bundled up in his uncle's fine
clothes, poor Mipam looked like a moving ball of material,
from the bottom of which emerged a pair of large boots, in
which the little fellow's feet were lost, while at the top a tiny
head wrestled with the collar of the jacket and the thick *zan* that
continually threatened to engulf it.

Between the *trapas*, who were seated in rows in the temple,
which was lit by a number of lamps burning on the altar,
Mipam advanced unsteadily as far as the abbot's throne. His
long hair had been cropped the evening before; the lama had
only to go through the dumb show of cutting it and throwing
it into the air[1] as an offering, as he pronounced the liturgical
words. By his gesture Mipam's separation from the lay world
and his admission into the clergy was consecrated. Drums,
oboes and bells sounded a clamorous greeting, and amidst all
this pandemonium the boy was led first to one of the posts of
honour, at the head of the line of monks, where he was allowed
to sit for a moment, and then to the very end of the line. There,
as the nearest to the door, inasmuch as he was the last admitted
into the Order, he took up his final position on the border of
the quilted carpet, with his legs crossed, and his head erect,
immensely proud, feeling that he was now 'someone.'

A banquet given by Puntsog brought the festival to a close;
and on the morrow Shesrab led Mipam back to his house. His
life as a student was about to begin.

'Come here, Mipam!' called the astrologer.
Mipam quickly drained his bowl of tea, left the piece of

---

[1] In this may be seen a reminder of the tradition according to which
Buddha, after leaving his palace to lead the religious life, threw into the air
the locks which he had severed with his sword.

carpet on which he was sitting in the kitchen, and entered the
room where his uncle was seated on his couch.

The astrologer received his pupil's customary prostration in
silence, and then, speaking in a consequential tone

'You are going to begin to learn. Listen well,'' he said. And
he pronounced loudly and slowly:

'*Di kad. Di kad.* . . . Repeat!'

'*Di kad,*' said Mipam.

'Good! *Dag kis.* . . . Repeat!'

'*Dag kis,*' said the child.

'*Di kad dag kis.* . . . Repeat!'

Mipam remained dumb, and looked oddly at his master.

'Ah! you have already forgotten,' said the latter. 'Listen, I'll
begin again.'

But before he had time to pronounce the first syllable, the
child quickly recited:

'*Di kad dag kis thos pa.*'

'Heavens!' exclaimed Shesrab, surprised and startled. 'I have
not yet taught you as much as that!'

His dream recurred to him; he suspected a supernatural
manifestation.

'. . . *tus chig na*[1] . . .' the boy continued. And there the miracle
stopped.

In the course of the days preceding his first lesson, Mipam,
sitting in the kitchen or before the door of the house, had heard
one of his companions droning out some incomprehensible
words. Endowed with an excellent memory, he had retained
them, and having guessed, from the first words his master had
uttered, what was to follow, he added, of his own accord, the
five extra syllables.

Profoundly perturbed, the astrologer did not guess at this
very simple explanation of the prodigy.

'Go, go,' he ordered. 'Go back to the kitchen. *Ane* (aunt)

[1] Tibetan spelling: *hdi skad bdag gis thos pa dus gchig na*: 'These words have
been, at one time, heard by me.' This is the habitual commencement of the
scriptures which relate the Buddha's discourses to his disciples.

will find you some work. . . . To-morrow you will repeat your lesson.'

Mipam bowed and went out. Pema was at that very moment sending two of the boys to cut wood in the forest. 'Go with them, she told Mipam, 'and bring back a bundle of dry branches.'

The next day Mipam once more sat before his master.

'Recite!' the latter ordered.

'*Di kad dag kis thos pa tus chig na*,' said the lad.

The astrologer was still unaware of the origin of the 'miracle', but he had had time to recover himself.

'That is excellent,' he said to his pupil. 'You are intelligent, so I will give you four fresh words to learn; I give only two to your fellow-pupils. To-morrow you will bring them back to me.[1] Now, listen. . . .'

Mipam interrupted him.

'What is the meaning of what you are making me repeat?' he asked calmly.

The astrologer was confounded. Never, never had any Tibetan child, at any time, thought of putting such a question to his master.

'It . . . it concerns religion,' he replied impatiently. And forgetting that he had not given him any new syllables to learn, he dismissed his disconcerting pupil.

'You can go now,' he said. 'Aunt Pema will find you some work to do.'

But Mipam did not move. He continued to stare at his uncle with an insistence in which Shesrab thought he detected a shade of mockery. At this the astrologer lost his temper.

'You be gone!' he shouted. 'Clear out, or I'll break your bones!' And as the boy made no sign of stirring, he seized the first object that came to hand—a heavy copper bowl used as a slop-basin and hurled it at the head of the impertinent questioner. Mipam dodged out of its way. 'Oohh!' was all he calmly said, as the bowl hit the floor with a thud; then he quietly left the room, without paying his respects.

[1] A literal translation of the Tibetan expression.

Shesrab would gladly have got rid of his embarrassing pupil, but on the first mention of this to his wife she protested. After the generosity displayed by Puntsog in respect of his preliminary presents, a handsome payment might be expected for the lessons given to his son; it would be a great pity to renounce this, and, at the same time, to lose the friendship of a relative, well-to-do and of influence in the district. The skill with which Puntsog had managed to recover, at the expense of persons under his administration, the fortune which he had lost, was highly appreciated by the *tsipa*, and he hesitated to make an enemy of a man capable of employing the same adroitness to his hurt. On his other hand, he could not shake off the impression of his dream about Mipam. If he had reason to fear that the boy might one day supplant him, was it not better to keep him as long as possible under his authority, watching his behaviour, giving the extreme minimum of instruction, and, above all, refraining from teaching him the secret rites of magic? If Mipam were to leave him, he might acquire that knowledge from another master, and employ it to the detriment of the uncle who had turned him out of his house. All things considered, Mipam must remain.

Mipam stayed, then, at the farm, close to the tempting road that led to distant lands. He did not make himself unpleasant in any way. He simply refused—with the stubbornness of a mule—to cut green wood in the forest. 'The branches are the limbs of the trees, he would say. 'To lop them off alive means wounding the trees, and making them suffer.' In the end Pema required him only to look after the cattle, of which he took great care. Another oddity of his was this: in a country where only holy lamas and a few ultra-pious laymen live as vegetarians, Mipam abstained strictly from animal food, for, as he explained, it is cruel to kill beings that, like us, love to live. After a few half-hearted attempts at overcoming his scruples, Shesrab and Pema had not insisted. All said and done, their boarder's frugality constituted an economy for them.

This frugality of Mipam's, however, related only to meat: he was really fond of food, and he greatly missed, in his uncle's house, the sweets with which his good mother had stuffed him, but he said nothing about this. Silent and reserved, he took no pleasure in the games into which his comrades wanted to drag him.

Sitting in the woods and minding the herd, he thought, at times, of the days when he used to take Puntsog's cattle to graze. He recalled his friendly encounter with the leopard, his wound, his flight across the mountain, his meeting with the holy pilgrim who had called him 'son of Chenrezigs' and the tragic and wonderful night passed in the hermit's hut. As the months passed, however, these pictures gradually faded from his memory. He thought less and less about the 'land where all are friends': his desire to escape became less urgent, and was presently forgotten.

On the other hand, his will-power, which was now concentrated on one sole object, grew stronger from day to day: he had a real desire to learn. The methods adopted by Shesrab, and common to all Tibetan masters, were unhappily not such as would lead quickly to knowledge.

While attending to their domestic duties the boys rehearsed the words which their teacher had recited during the brief morning lesson, with a view to repeating them to him on the morrow, when failure would mean a thrashing. So, little by little, the list of the syllables which they murmured grew longer, until it formed the contents of a whole book, after which they began to store yet another in their memory, without ever understanding a single word of what they recited.

They were taught to read in the same way. After some practice in recognizing the forms of the thirty consonants and the signs representing the five vowels, the scholars were gradually initiated into the complications of the double and the triple letters, those which perch on the head of their fellows and those which hook themselves on to their feet. They were taught to distinguish the mute letters at the beginning or the end of words, and the letters that modify the sounds of the consonants which they precede, or the vowels which they

follow. When they had finished studying their letters they
spelt through several hundred pages before they were considered
capable of pronouncing the syllables. Some went no farther,
and never suspected that these syllables could be grouped
together to form words, and that those words had a meaning.

It was then considered that these young blockheads 'knew
how to read,' and they enjoyed, from this fact, a certain consideration among the villagers. The man who could put the
words together as he read a religious book was regarded almost
as a learned scholar.

This is not the case in the towns, where the lettered lamas,
the state officials, and the wealthy traders and their clerks reside,
but the mountaineers of the forests, like the herdsmen of the
grassy solitudes, are deplorably ignorant.[1]

Mipam had to adapt himself to the pedagogic system in vogue
in his country. He never again chanced to question his master
as to the sense of what he was made to learn by heart, or of anything else, yet Shesrab did not succeed in limiting his pupil's
education as strictly as he had planned. The boy was gifted
with a prodigious memory; he remembered, permanently, all
that he heard, both what the astrologer taught him during his
lessons, and the sacred scriptures which he intoned, or the
liturgy of the offices. As soon as he could read he rapidly committed to memory all the books he could lay his hands on in his
uncle's library.

Despite the misgivings which he continued to entertain as
regards the embarrassment which Mipam might one day cause
him, the vanity of the teacher induced Shesrab to exhibit his
remarkable pupil in the villages, when he visited them in order

[1] The above must seem obscure to anyone who does not know how Tibetan
is written. Whereas in the Western languages each word is separate, and
forms a distinct group of letters, in Tibetan each syllable is divided without
any sign indicating those which might be grouped together to form a word.
The grouping of the syllables is left to the sagacity of the reader.

to perform certain religious ceremonies: the offices for the dead, rites to bring prosperity to families and their possessions, exorcisms, or rites propitiating the gods and subjugating demons. On such occasions his nephew did him great credit. By the precocious dignity of his bearing, by his graceful ritual gestures, by the deep bass notes that his youthful throat emitted as he intoned the sacred texts, Mipam proved an admirable acolyte to the vainglorious cleric. As for the study of astrology, Shesrab continued to postpone the first lessons. Privately, he had no intention of ever initiating his disquieting pupil into the science.

Puntsog himself did not manifest any troublesome curiosity in the matter; for the moment he was content with the already flattering success of his son, and he had entire confidence in the master to whom he believed that this success was due. Between two bowls of brandy drained in the company of his friends, he would proudly proclaim: 'Mipam's future is now assured; he can earn his living!'

At the end of every ceremony in which he took part Mipam received, as a matter of fact, a share in the fees paid by the villagers for whose benefit the rites had been performed. These fees were for the most part paid in kind; sometimes, too, in small sums of money. Pema annexed all the provisions for the needs of the household, while Shesrab made his pupils disgorge their share of the money, which he kept for himself.

There was one thing that gave him infinite annoyance. In one respect Mipam was immovable: not only did he refuse to eat meat at the meals offered to the celebrants, but he declined to accept any to take away with him when he left. To refuse a hind quarter of beef or a piece of fat pork was in the *tsipa's* eyes the acme of imbecility. He adroitly arranged for the boy's share to be added to his own, but, often enough the cunning peasants profited by this departure from the normal by adding a portion very much smaller than they would have given to the congenial Mipam himself. This enraged the rapacious astrologer and his no less rapacious housekeeper, but another matter, had they but known of it, would have exasperated them even more.

When an offering in money was expected, Mipam, whose shrewdness was not less remarkable than his memory, contrived to draw the host or hostess aside—and often both of them in turn—and to explain, with cajoling and irresistibly persuasive arguments, that a boy so learned and pious as he ought never to be left without personal resources. He needed paper and ink for copying religious treatises, a task which furthered his instruction and was essentially meritorious. Ani Pema, as his listeners were probably aware, was anything but prodigal, and the meals at the astrologer's were insufficient for a virtuous youth who lived on 'pure' (vegetable) food all the year round. Ought he not, in order that he might have the needful strength to follow his sacred career, to be able to buy, from time to time, from itinerant vendors, a few sweetmeats, which would be good for his health: such as dried fruit, sugar-candy, and treacle cakes? These would not only be helpful to himself, but they formed an indispensable part of the daily offerings presented to the tutelary gods to whom he did homage every morning. Surely his generous donors would not miss the chance of sharing in the merits attendant on the performance of that act of worship. . . . The smooth words rolled off the little rascal's tongue with solemn and persuasive unction: he had a sweet voice and a pleasant expression; they only half believed him, but he amused the farmers, and touched the hearts of their good wives, all of whom would have been happy to have such a nice, clever son. They secretly gave him a few copper coins, or sometimes even a piece of silver. Unknown to Puntsog and Shesrab, the little rascal was saving up his earnings.

Mipam was now over thirteen. Faithful to the reservation dictated by his dread of being supplanted by his pupil, Shesrab had not yet initiated him into any of the mysteries of astrology. And he was never to do so. The destiny of his strange nephew willed otherwise.

The first herald of that destiny appeared, one evening, at Shesrab's door in the very ordinary shape of a merchant from

Lhasa, a friend of Puntsog's, returning, with his daughter, from a visit to one of his brothers-in-law, who lived on the borders of Dugyul (Bhutan). Puntsog had commissioned him to buy him there a length of heavy silk, a speciality of the textile industry of that country. He had intended to present it in person to his cousin Shesrab, but it happened that just at the moment when his friend arrived he was busy collecting taxes, which was part of his duty as headman. He therefore begged his friend to turn aside a little from his path in order to deliver his gift to the astrologer.

The *tsongpa* (trader) Tenzin was a merchant of substance. He owned a good number of mules for the transport of his merchandise, and in addition to his headquarters in Lhasa, he had opened branch-houses for export and import at Dangar, Sining and Peking in China, and Calcutta in India, as well as some shops in certain Tibetan towns. . . . Shesrab, inordinately in love with the good things of this world, and full of consideration for those who possessed them, welcomed his visitor with deferential courtesy.

Mipam knew the merchant, having met him several times in his parents' home; as for his daughter, he had never set eyes on her. It was quite an exceptional thing for her to accompany her father. Only the fact that the little girl's maternal grandmother had expressed a very urgent desire to see the child had decided Tenzin to take her with him when he had to transact some business with his dead wife's brother—a trader like himself— who was living with his parents, the little girl's grandparents.

She came back enchanted with her first journey. To go riding as the only 'woman' with her father and a few servants had put into her head quite a new notion of her own importance: she felt that she was really 'grown up'.

Her name was Dolma; it was a name given to many Tibetan girl children, but that did not prevent her from being very proud of it, and from imagining that Dolma, the goddess, her patron, cherished a particular regard and affection for her. It was perhaps because she had never known a mother's love that

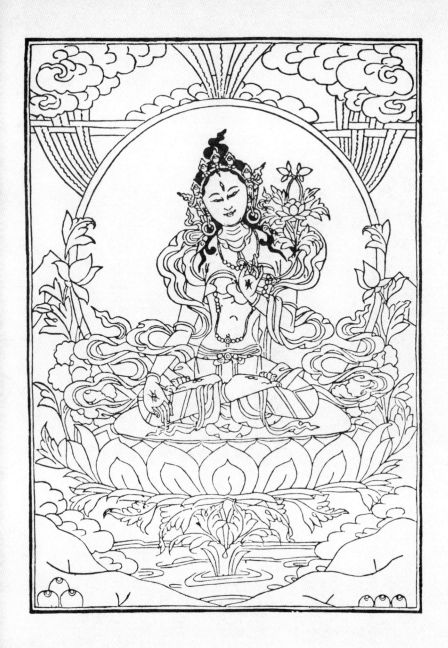

Dolma

the little girl attributed to her divine patron the feelings that she would have inspired in her own mother. That mother had died a few days after Dolma was born. Tenzin had sincerely loved his wife; at first he refused to marry again, but after three years' solitude he ended by living in free union with the widow of a merchant, a capable woman, sober, and of good reputation, who had a head for business. The widow had no children; she possessed, in her own right, a comfortable fortune, and she had also inherited that of her husband. On setting up house together, Tenzin and she had, to their mutual profit, pooled their commercial interests. They felt a mutual esteem for each other, and they lived happily together. Tseringma, Tenzin's second wife, had no children, and she conceived a great affection for her little step-daughter.

As for Tenzin, while he showed himself an excellent father, he regretted, in his heart, that Dolma was not a son, who could have taken his place at the head of the convoys of merchandise when old age debarred him from the fatigue of long and arduous journeys: a son who would have succeeded him when he left this world. Still, he thought, the ill might be remedied. Dolma was quick and intelligent; in her clever step-mother she had a good teacher; she might well become competent to manage the business in Tibet, while her husband could deal with the foreign transactions and take charge of the caravans. All he had to do was to find a son-in-law, who, instead of taking Dolma into his own family, would enter, by adoption, into that of his father-in-law, and would take the place of a son.[1]

He was anxious to give Dolma a husband as kind as he was intelligent. He must belong to a good family, and yet he must find it advantageous to leave it in order to enter that of his wife. In reviewing a list of possible candidates he had thought of Dogyal, Mipam's elder brother, who was nearing his eighteenth year; he was a handsome lad with an open and pleasant

[1] Arrangements of this kind, following an imported Chinese custom, are frequent in Tibet.

face, and an active mind. A sturdy hunter and a tried moun-
taineer, the fatigues of travel ought not to daunt him. With
the pretext of getting him to replace one of his men who was
occupied elsewhere, Tenzin had put Dogyal to the test: the
boy had shown himself adroit, strong, and prompt to understand the requirements of the trade; moreover, his unfailing
good nature had won the merchant's heart. Dolma would
undoubtedly be happy with such a husband.

During his last stay with Puntsog, the merchant had sounded
him on the subject of this marriage project. The village headman hesitated as to whether he should acquiesce; Dogyal was
his eldest son, and it is generally the younger son who is the
subject of such an arrangement, inasmuch as the elder must
continue the father's line. The headman, however, had another
son: Mipam, who promised to bring him great honour as a
learned astrologer. In the sect to which he belonged marriage
was not debarred to members of the clergy. Shesrab was
married; Mipam would marry in his turn, would ensure the
continuance of the family, and would be the sole heir to his
father's property. The proposal, in short, was advantageous to
both brothers. Puntsog gave his consent to it.

Tenzin helped his daughter to dismount before Shesrab's
door, and then ceased to concern himself about her, leaving her
to his hostess. The latter hastened to show little Dolma into
the kitchen, where, with her assistance, she prepared a well-
buttered tea for her visitors. Then, after several times filling
the two men's bowls, she remained with them in Shesrab's
room, examining the piece of silk presented by Puntsog, and
various other trifling presents which the merchant had added
on his own account. He had also, at the request of the kindly
Changpal, burdened himself with a bulky packet of pastry,
fried in butter, which she had made for her greedy Mipam, but
which the no less greedy wife of the astrologer had seized as soon
as she had espied it. Setting half of the pastries aside to eat
herself, she put the other half on a plate, which she placed near

Tenzin, bidding him help himself, and hoping that in his politeness he would not profit too largely by the invitation.

In the adjoining kitchen little Dolma remained alone, seated by the hearth, a bowl of tea and a bag of barley meal set before her on a low table.

The hour was approaching for Shesrab's pupils to return to the house after their labours in field or forest. Their work ended, they liked to linger out of doors, playing or chattering, but Mipam rarely joined them. The atmosphere in which he lived had done something towards lulling to sleep the generous instincts and the rare lucidity which had stamped his childhood with so astonishing an originality. At the present time the modest notoriety which he owed to his exceptional memory pleasantly tickled his childish vanity, and his one thought was to increase it, by learning by heart the contents of an ever-increasing number of books, in order to recite them in a loud voice before the wondering villagers. He had soon convinced himself that the most showy part of his master's learning amounted to that and nothing more, and he doubted, by this time, whether any other learning existed. So, in pursuance of his secret aim of rivalling his uncle, he drove the cattle home as early as he dared, the sooner to take up his books again and memorize their contents as he sat by the fire.

Once more, that evening he returned long before his comrades. The kitchen was almost completely dark in the twilight, and in order to obtain a little light, Mipam prepared to make up the fire.[1] He was approaching the hearth when a branch crackled amidst the reddening ashes; a bluish flame rose from it, fringed with tongues of gold; it lengthened, split in two, united again, and expanded, floating like a veil on the breeze, and through this shifting phantasmagoria Mipam, dumbfounded, perceived

---

[1] The use of lamps is still exceptional in Tibet. The well-to-do use candles imported from abroad; a wick steeped in oil or butter contained in a metal or earthenware lamp often serves at once for a pious offering in front of the sacred pictures and a means of illumination for the room. In many districts the wood blazing on the hearth is the sole source of light.

an unexpected apparition: a little princess was seated on the other side of the room.

From her dress of dark blue cloth issued the wide sleeves of two chemises, worn one over the other, of red and green silk respectively; a long coral necklace hung upon her breast, and a reliquary in beaten gold set with turquoises glittered at her throat. . . . It was in very truth a princess, perhaps even a fairy. What was she doing here?

Mipam timidly advanced a few paces and thus reached the other side of the hearth. The fiery curtain no longer came between him and the strange apparition; all he saw was a small girl with a bowl of tea in her hands.

Shesrab's pupil clearly perceived that this was a real little girl, who had probably come with some visitors whom his teacher was that moment receiving. He did not think she would vanish, as happens in fairy tales, if he approached her; nevertheless, he dared not go nearer.

The little 'fairy' laid her bowl on the table and began to laugh.

'Are you *Aku* Puntsog's son?' she asked. 'I have just come from your home; your mother has sent you a big packet of pastries. . . . I brought it in my saddle-bags,' she added, importantly.

She got up, walked towards Mipam, who still remained motionless, and examined him carefully. The fire was now burning brightly, lighting up the whole kitchen.

'You are very badly dressed,' said Tenzin's daughter, with a little grimace. 'Are you really and truly *Aku* Puntsog's son?'

Mipam drew himself up, offended. You don't mind cows in your best clothes; his gown was dirty, he had torn it in more than one place on the brambles in the wood, but he paid no attention to such trifles: his fellow disciples were no better dressed than he. This was an impertinent little thing, and he was a full head taller than she was. He knew how to answer her:

'I'm the son of Chenrezigs,' he haughtily declared.

The proud little girl was nonplussed. She pondered for a moment; then she said:

54

'*Kyabgon rimpoche* (the Dalai Lama) is Chenrezigs. Is he your father?'

'My father is the Lord Chenrezigs whose images you see in the temples, with a thousand arms and eleven heads,' he replied solemnly.

This was more marvellous still. The little girl was over-whelmed. Mipam was taking his revenge, laughing up his sleeve at the confusion into which he had thrown this impudent critic of his appearance.

'And you, who are you?' he asked.

'I am Dolma,' she solemnly announced.

'That doesn't tell me much,' said the boy. 'There are thousands of Dolmas in Tibet.'

'They are not Dolmas like me!' the girl replied, sharply. She had recovered her assurance.

How pretty little Dolma looked like that, her cheeks flushed with anger! How charming she was, the child princess with her green and red sleeves, as soft and iridescent as a butterfly's wings, and the ornaments that gleamed in the firelight!

She was so pretty that he could not go on feeling angry with her; so fragile that he could not hurt her. Besides, Mipam was not ill-natured.

'So you've brought me some pastries, then, Dolma?' he said, in a conciliatory tone.

'The pastries are for *nemo*[1] Changpal's son,' Dolma prudently replied.

'I am her son,' Mipam declared, 'and I want you to eat some pastries with me. Where are they?'

'I don't know in the least,' the little girl replied. 'I heard my father tell our servant to carry all the bags into the house.'

Hearing that the bags, including the one whose contents interested him, had been brought into the house, Mipam suspected what must have happened. The visitors' luggage was generally stored in a corridor next to the astrologer's private

[1] *Nemo* = mistress of the house. A polite appellation in use among the villagers and other classes of the people.

room. There, probably, Dolma's father had unpacked the presents which he was offering to his host, and this, doubtless, under the eyes of the astrologer's wife, whose curiosity was boundless. In that case the fate of the pastries was sealed. Many previous experiences assured Mipam of this. But to-day the usual thing was not going to happen.

He had shewn resignation as long as he alone was deprived of the dainties which his mother sent him, but he meant Dolma to profit by them. She loved pastries; he had noticed her covetous little smile when he had spoken of them, and her evident satisfaction when he had announced that he wanted her to help him to eat them. He would not disappoint her. She was going to crunch those pastries with her pretty white teeth. He felt that he was strong enough to recover them from the insatiable Aunt Pema, to fight if needs be in order to get them back. Pastries! . . . he would have gone to the ends of the earth for them so that Dolma should be happy and smile upon him. . . .

Mipam was not yet fourteen, but he had all at once become a man. A woman had entered into his life.

'Aunt Pema, I have come to fetch the pastries my mother has sent me: I want to give some to Dolma,' said Mipam, suddenly entering Shesrab's room, and speaking with unaccustomed assurance. His voice was changed: it had become stronger, more serious: the very tone of the words he had pronounced betrayed a firm intention, almost a threat, and the attitude of the boy, boldly confronting his teacher's wife, corroborated the transformation that had just taken place in him.

Dumbfounded, the astrologer and his spouse looked at him in silence, but Mipam had already caught sight of the pastries placed in front of Tenzin. He guessed where the rest of the consignment was: all had happened as he had thought.

'Don't disturb yourself, Aunt Pema,' he said, still in the same decisive tone, 'I will take them myself.' And without more ado he went to a cupboard, opened it, pounced upon the cakes, and put them in a fold of his robe.

The scene amused the merchant. This resolute little fellow,

56

just a little brutal, appealed to him. He saw in him the future brother-in-law of his daughter, a learned ally whose daring would secure him an influential position among the clergy. He would be a credit to his relatives, and his protection might even be profitable to them.

'There are still some more pastries here,' said Tenzin to Mipam, as he pointed with a mischievous smile to the dish in front of him. 'You can have these as well.'

'I am very pleased to offer them to you, honourable trader,' replied Mipam, as he bowed to his uncle's guest.

He spoke, now, with the most exquisite politeness, but he was careful to emphasize the first personal pronoun. '*I* am very pleased to offer them to you.' The pastries were *his*, and *he* was offering them.

Mipam carried the cakes, the infinitesimal cause of future great consequences, to the kitchen, where he enjoyed them with his new-found friend.

Tenzin was to share the *tsipa's* room that night; Pema would give up her place to him, and would sleep in the kitchen. Leaving the two men to drink a last bowl of spirits together before retiring, she spread cushions and blankets by the hearth for her young guest and herself. Mipam and his co-disciples dragged the scraps of carpet and the blankets that served them for beds to the other side of the room, and soon the house was silent, with all its inmates asleep. All save Mipam, who was wide awake and dreaming. His imagination bore him off through the years; he saw the little princess with the features of a tall young girl, and himself with those of a man: a man of consequence . . . he could not imagine himself otherwise. In what his importance consisted, he had no very definite idea. His vision was getting hazy in that respect, but however blurred might be the pictures that rose to his mind, they always pointed to notoriety and wealth. Afterwards, as a desirable and logical consequence, he saw Dolma grown-up, and living with him in a house as fair as his fancy could fashion.

The night slipped by. With his eyes glued to the narrow

window, through the torn paper of which[2] he spied a corner of the sky in which the stars were passing in stately procession, Mipam, motionless, was haunted relentlessly by the same dream. The day dawned, thrusting its pale beams through all the crevices in the badly jointed woodwork: the boys woke up. Yawning they stretched themselves with little grunts, like young animals, broke some dry branches, and lit the fire. Two of them went out, carrying buckets, to fetch water from the stream, and through the door left open behind them the light of day and the fresh, moist air of the forest entered the house together.

The astrologer's wife threw off her blankets, passed a dress over the petticoat and chemise in which she had slept, and murmuring pious formulae the while, she superintended the boiling of the tea, which she wished to be especially good in honour of her guest. In her turn, little Dolma rose, put on her upper dress, readjusted her ornaments, and then, her toilette ended, sat waiting for tea to be served, while she murmured the liturgical invocations to the goddess, Dolma, her patron.

Mipam, with a pensive air, folded his rugs and set to work with his fellow-disciples. He dreamed no longer. The night had enabled him to form a resolve, and when Mipam had decided anything he went straight for his goal.

Their breakfast over, Pema allotted the boys their work; there would be no lessons that day, as Shesrab was detained by his visitor. Nevertheless, the cunning astrologer wanted to impress this friend of his cousin with his solicitude for Mipam, and the special care he gave to teaching him. This, he hoped, would be reported to Puntsog, who would express his gratitude in a tangible form.

'Mipam,' he called. And when the lad was before him:

'Your lesson will be delayed to-day,' he told him; 'I will give it you after *Kushog* Tenzin has gone. Until then, take your books and study; you must not go out.'

[1] In Tibet, as in China, paper is pasted over the windows instead of glass.

58

'Very well,' replied Mipam politely, and returning to the kitchen he informed his master's wife that he had been told to remain in the house.

The other scholars were just setting forth to cut grass and wood in the mountains. Pema commissioned one of them, in Mipam's place, to take the herd to graze, and then went into her husband's room, carrying a large dish of boiled beef, for she was giving the merchant a substantial breakfast before his departure.

Mipam was left alone with Dolma in the kitchen.

'Dolma,' he began confidently, 'I want to speak to you.'

'Speak then,' replied the little girl.

Mipam looked round him. He did not feel at ease in that room, which the mistress of the house might re-enter at any moment. Unconsciously, too, the vulgar setting of the kitchen was repugnant to him; what he had to say could not be said there.

'Come!' he said imperiously, as he roughly gripped Dolma's hand.

'Where to?' she asked.

'Come!' the nervous and masterful boy repeated, as he dragged her out of the house.

Curious to know what this meant, and dominated, unwittingly, by the will of her friend, Dolma allowed herself to be led some distance from the house, under the cover of the big trees.

Then Mipam releasing her hand, looked her in the eyes and said:

'Dolma, I was thinking of you all the night. You will be my wife: I am learned, and I am going to become a rich and important man. Much richer and more important than my teacher Shesrab, or than your father, or Puntsog. We will live in a big, fine house, which I shall have built for you! Say yes!'

The little girl was rather surprised, though not unduly so. She had not, indeed, imagined that Mipam would ask her, that very morning, to marry him, but she was forever expecting, thanks to the interest of her powerful patron, to be the heroine of strange events which would stamp her life as different from that of other maidens.

'Say yes!' Mipam repeated imperiously.

'My father would not allow me to get married,' she answered at last. 'I am only ten.'

'That's true,' replied the boy. 'I, also, am too young to marry you. But in five years I shall be nearly twenty; as for you, you will be fifteen. . . . That is just the time for a girl to be married.'

'That's true,' replied Dolma gravely.

'Well then, you quite understand,' continued Mipam. 'By that time I shall be much more learned than Shesrab, and already as rich, perhaps, as your father. . . .'

'And besides, you are the son of Chenrezigs,' said the little girl, thoughtfully.

Mipam did not expect to be reminded, at that moment, of his relationship to the divine Lord of Infinite Compassion. His heart suddenly contracted. Would that mysterious relationship bring him closer to Dolma, or would it divorce him from her? He did not know, but an agonizing doubt had arisen in his mind, and the picture of the fine house in which he was to live with his beloved seemed to have receded, to have faded almost out of sight.

'Yes, I am the son of Chenrezigs,' he agreed, in a low voice. 'But say yes!'

He no longer commanded; his voice had become almost suppliant, for an unreasoning dread had overcome him.

'Yes,' said Dolma. But she pronounced the word without the accent of dogged resolution, of unshakeable determination, that Mipam would have liked to hear.

With a sudden impulse he took the little girl in his arms and pressed her closely to him. She began to laugh.

'We must go in,' she said. 'My father has to start directly after breakfast, and he will be looking for me.'

60

'And you saw that big dish of boiled meat, and you want your share before leaving,' replied Mipam, to tease her.

'Of course I want my share,' said Dolma, in earnest. 'Come along!'

This time it was she who led the way; Mipam followed her, and the happiness which he had promised himself seemed overcast by a secret sense of uneasiness.

Tenzin was taking leave of his host, and seeing Puntsog's son beside Dolma, who was already in the saddle, he laid his hand on the boy's shoulder.

'Your father has reason to be proud of you, Mipam,' he said kindly. 'Your master has told me how studious you are. Go on learning all you can: you are already well instructed for your age, and one day you will become a great astrologer, a graduate, a doctor, praised and respected by everyone. If ever you want to study at Lhasa, my house is open to you. I am sure you will be a credit to your family and your friends. Continue to work diligently!'

Mipam was overjoyed. No one had ever recognized his merits so eloquently, and at no other moment could praise have been so precious. He glanced surreptitiously at Dolma, who, her eyes sparkling with pleasure, was eagerly listening to her father.

'You are very kind, honourable trader,' he replied. 'I shall do as you say.'

The merchant mounted his horse, his hostess took the bridle, in order to lead it a little way, as a mark of courtesy.

'*Kale jugs den jag*,'[1] cried Dolma to the astrologer, as her horse was about to start; and leaning toward Mipam, who had remained at her side:

'Yes, I say yes!' she murmured, with enthusiastic fervour. 'You will be a great man!'

---

[1] Courteous salutation when bidding good-bye to a guest. Literally it means: 'Sit down quietly.'

CHAPTER IV

THE chieftain among whose subjects the astrologer Shesrab and his cousin Puntsog were numbered had decided that a reading of the whole Kahgyur[1] was to take place at his house. The Kahgyur is the collection of the various Holy Scriptures of Tibet; the reading of it, by monks, at the houses of the faithful, is credited with the effect of attracting prosperity to them, and of securing them and their families against the malignity of the demons who send disease.

All the monks attached to the monasteries situated in the territory under the chieftain's rule were bidden to the palace. The reading of one hundred and eight bulky volumes constituting the Kahgyur, and the performance of various rites, would continue for a month.

Shesrab and his pupils, joining the monks of the Rab-den-tse monastery, to which they belonged, betook themselves, therefore, to the residence of their lord.

There a sorting out was effected; certain monks were admitted to form the choir inside the temple, while others were debarred from that privilege, and were penned in a covered gallery at the entrance to the sanctuary. This classification was based on the comparative erudition of the monks. Those among them who were recognized as lettered were not questioned; they took their place, without any scrutiny, on the low carpet-covered benches reserved for the clergy. But the small fry—young novices or old peasants having nothing about them of the monk save their dress—were confronted with a page of a book. Could they read, or not? If they could, they joined the 'lettered' in the temple; if not, their place was in the gallery where, for a whole month, from morn to eve, they were to repeat 'Om mani padme hum!'

[1] Tibetan spelling: *bkah hgyur*. It means 'Words translated,' the books being translated from the Sanscrit.

The youngsters were not at all sorry to sit in the gallery. There, they enjoyed a certain amount of liberty: their behaviour was not so strictly supervised as in the inside of the temple; they could, on the sly, talk and laugh among themselves. But the elderly monks banished among these turbulent young scamps cruelly felt the humiliation.

There was no need for Mipam to dread being sent outside. When a portly secretary in a fine robe of blue silk brocade put him to the test, he was not content to read the book given to him; he began to drone it out in a deep bass voice, with the inflections of a lama chanting in the choir. Hearing this the secretary lost his habitual assurance. Where did this prodigy spring from? Deeming, nevertheless, that his dignity would suffer should he make inquiries, he silenced the precocious chorister and merely pointed to the temple door with a gesture which meant that Mipam was admitted to sit in the company of the lettered.

The meetings for reading followed one another, day after day, and were both monotonous and noisy. The chieftain's dwelling resounded and trembled as the clamour of several hundred voices started the echoes.

Mipam took part in the buzzing of the choir, regaling himself at meals with the dainties sent by his worthy mother, and thinking of his future wife.

He had been there for more than a fortnight when, strolling round the palace during the midday rest, he espied Dolma playing in the garden with the prince's five children. Was it a habit of hers then, to appear in this sudden and unexpected fashion? Puntsog's son still cherished the image of the little fairy who had appeared to him through a curtain of flames. What was she doing at the palace? Wasn't he mistaken? Was it really she? But the little girl had seen him, and with a joyous cry she ran to meet him.

'Oh, Mipam, you have come with your master to read the Kahgyur,' she said.

'Yes,' answered Mipam, conscious of his importance.

The other children came up.

'Who is he?' one of them asked of Dolma.

The latter reflected for an instant, her pretty face assuming an ultra-serious expression; then, with due solemnity she declared:

'He is the son of Chenrezigs.'

'What?' asked the eldest prince, in surprise, 'are there people, then, called Chenrezigs? I've never heard of one.' And being already a big boy, older than Mipam, he added mockingly: 'Is he the son of the Chenrezigs whose statue is in our temple?'

'Yes, that's just what he is,' replied Dolma, still serious.

Mipam felt embarrassed. As he grew older he had come to understand that Puntsog, the village headman, was actually his father. Yet, on the other hand, his faith in the statement made by the ascetic whom he had met in the forest had been strengthened. He had learnt that certain of these holy men possessed a clairvoyance that allowed them to discern facts hidden from the common herd. The hermit had seemed very sure of what he affirmed. He, Mipam, must therefore be, really and truly, the son of the heavenly Lord Chenrezigs, but he must be so in a special and mysterious way, which he could not clearly understand. These reflections had taught Shesrab's pupil a certain prudence: it was not fitting, he judged, to boast openly of his extraordinary sonship in the presence of the laity and the general run of monks. These ignorant people would not know what he meant, and would simply make game of him. Still, at this present juncture he could not avoid endorsing what Dolma had said.

The prince's son, who had already developed an authoritative manner, asked him sharply:

'Is it true? Are you the son of the Lord Chenrezigs who is in the temple?'

Dolma was looking at Mipam, waiting to hear her words confirmed. He could not deny it.

'I am,' he said.

'How marvellous!' exclaimed the younger of the princes, a child of nine, and he set off as fast as he could go, to the palace,

64

to give his mother the astonishing news that the son of a god was in her garden.

The *gyalmo*[1] burst out laughing when she heard the boy's extraordinary statement, but he, much excited, and anxious to prove his words, seized his mother's hand and dragged her to the window.

Unhappily for him, when she arrived there, the children had passed round to the other side of the house, and as it was the hour for the reading, Mipam had returned to the temple. The lady saw nothing but an empty meadow before her, and began to laugh anew.

'The son of Chenrezigs has gone back to Nub Dowa Chen,'[2] she said.

The little prince did not like to be laughed at.

'You ask Dolma,' he answered; 'she knows him.'

Tenzin, Dolma's father, was the chief accredited merchant of the prince, who, like the majority of wealthy Tibetans, whether laity or clergy, liked to lay out his capital to the best advantage by investing it in commerce. A good business man and lucky into the bargain, Tenzin enjoyed the confidence of his noble sleeping-partner, with whom he was on friendly terms. On her side, the *gyalmo*, his wife, was fond of Dolma, and often had her to stay at the palace, to keep her daughters company.

The imperious little prince did not fail to bring Dolma to his mother to vouch for the veracity of her report, and the latter, when questioned, had to tell the lady all about Mipam. He was, she said, the pupil of the astrologer Shesrab, and very learned; she had heard him more than once declare himself to be the son of Chenrezigs, and she was quite sure that this was the truth.

Her curiosity aroused, the princess sent for the astrologer, and learnt from him that his pupil was the son of his cousin, a

[1] Queen: this title is very freely given to the wives of all the chiefs called *gyalpo*.
[2] The Western Paradise of the Great Beatitude where Chenrezigs dwells.

village headman by the name of Puntsog, who had entrusted him with the boy's instruction. Mipam was then summoned to her presence, and he, though vexed at being questioned, could not avoid repeating his assertion that he was the son of Chenrezigs.

'How do you know that?' asked the lady mockingly.

Mipam, detecting a note of raillery in her voice and in her half-smile, felt affronted. Since they were driving him to it, he knew how to make them take him seriously.

Gravely, thereupon, he related his meeting with the holy *yogin*, embellishing the facts with fantastic details of his own invention. He had seen, for instance, that the pilgrim's feet did not touch the ground, that light proceeded from his eyes, and that while he was speaking he had become, for a moment, gigantically tall. . . . Ah! her ladyship began to become attentive! She no longer thought of mocking! Mipam triumphed inwardly. Unwittingly he had made a good shot; the princess was superstitious, and now felt inclined, if not to believe that Chenrezigs was Mipam's father, at least to think that Mipam was no ordinary boy. Regaling him with buttered tea and parched rice, she sent him away, but continued to think about him. The boy had displayed both politeness and intelligence: his gravity and the important airs he gave himself amused the lady, and at the same time, without her being aware of it, imposed upon her in some degree. She wished to attach him to her own service; he would, to begin with, make an agreeable page, and he could keep her children company; and then, in good time, he might become an excellent steward.

The chieftain's wife was not accustomed to dwell at any length on her projects before carrying them out; her wishes had to be promptly satisfied. A few days after her conversation with Mipam, she again sent for the astrologer.

'Mipam will not be returning to you,' she told him. 'I have sent a message to his father, to inform him that I am keeping the boy in my service.'

In Mipam's country one did not question orders of that kind. It was a practice with the prince to enforce free service, for the space of several years, from the sons of the notables on his estates. If by chance he sent for a peasant's child the parents were overjoyed. It was not altogether a case of a dupe's bargain. A boy in the position of being able to address the chief or his wife privately would become a protector to his family, and even a source of revenue to its members. Petitioners appealing for justice or begging some favour would apply to the relatives of the young protégé, entreating them through him, to forward petitions which, if they passed through the ordinary channels of local procedure, had no chance of reaching the ruler. Such services, naturally, were paid for.

And if it so happened that their son, having reached man's estate, should remain in the palace as steward, secretary, usher, *valet de chambre*, or head cook, although he might not always receive a regular salary, the considerable profits which accrued indirectly from his situation would compensate a hundredfold for the sacrifices made by his parents. For humble folk, more-over, there was the question of self-esteem; their fantastic notions of worldly eminence led them to estimate the position of employee in the personal service of a lord as much higher than that of a private person, or even of a learned monk. Such notions are current in Tibet, and a *zimpon* (first *valet de chambre*) of the Dalai Lama looks down in his turn upon the lords of lesser degree, such as Mipam's new master.

Puntsog was enchanted to learn that the caprice of the *gyalmo* had raised his son to the rank of personal attendant and com-panion of the chief's children. He was convinced that Mipam, clever and learned as he was, would be capable of acquiring, by slow degrees, a position in the palace which would be greatly preferable, for him and his father, to that of astrologer. Besides, there was nothing to prevent his holding several offices at the same time; a functionary might be an astrologer; and moreover, Mipam, by going to live at the chief's palace, was not leaving the religious Order. All he had to do, to remain a member of his monastery, was to spend a fortnight there each year, at the season of the great religious ceremonies.

Just as his parents had omitted to consult him on the matter of making him an astrologer, so they did not trouble to ask their son what he felt about his metamorphosis into a page for the chatelaine. Mipam, however, was not sorry to leave the teacher who had fed him so badly, and had ceased to teach him anything. And then, at the palace he would see Dolma from time to time.

The *gyalmo* lived in a large room that borrowed its light from a loggia overlooking the garden. The dark blue ceiling, traversed by great beams which were painted red, contributed, together with the dark colour of the walls, and the indirect light from the loggia, to make the room rather gloomy, and several massive pillars, narrowing towards the top and crowned with carved capitals, gave it the imposing look of a sanctuary. An altar on which shone perpetually the yellow flame of a large silver lamp, fed with butter, accentuated the religious character of the place. The image of the Guru Padma, flanked by his two fairy-brides, Yeshes Tsogyal and Mandara, was enthroned in the place of honour. Around these three personages were to be seen statuettes of divers deities, several small lamps, which were lit at nightfall, and some silver bowls, intended to contain pure water and the various ritual offerings.

At the further end of the vast room four tiers of thick hard cushions, laid on a platform provided with a high back in red lacquered wood, served as a sort of throne, in front of which was set a table, also in red lacquer, carved and decorated with gilding. Facing this throne, against the opposite wall, two cushions and a few squares of carpet were placed on the floor, to serve as seats for visitors. Some richly decorated cupboards and chests completed the furnishing.

When Mipam was ushered into the princess's room, he had some difficulty in preserving the composure which etiquette demanded. Never had he seen anything so beautiful. As acolyte to the *tsipa*, he had entered the houses of well-to-do people in order to perform religious ceremonies, but the luxury of their dwellings resembled that which now met his gaze as the light of a candle resembles that of the sun.

Guru Padma

Now he was going to live here, and share in the comforts of the lord's family. Gone was the drudgery imposed by the rapacious wife of his uncle the astrologer, gone were the scanty meals which she dispensed with sullen looks. A life of ease was about to dawn for him. Carried away by his childish admiration, Mipam gave no further thought to his old friend, the forest; he forgot even Dolma.

The days, the weeks, the months sped by, tempering by degrees the boy's joyful enthusiasm. His duties were light, the *gyalmo* did not beat him, and he ate abundantly of choice dishes, in addition to the delicacies that he adroitly purloined. Nevertheless, he began to miss the freedom which he had enjoyed in the forest, and he realized now that he no longer had to repeat them he was forgetting the books which he had so laboriously learnt by heart, his knowledge of which had earned him so much credit, and it was not long before the memory of Dolma once more took possession of his thoughts. Before he had entered the service of the princess his little friend had returned to her father's house, and he had not seen her again.

The monotony of the days, one just like another, and of his duties, which led him day after day to perform the same actions, weighed at times upon Mipam. Every morning, when his mistress awaked, he took in her breakfast of barley meal, dried meat, and buttered tea, which the servants brought from the kitchen, and placed in a room which was used as a pantry, next to the *gyalmo*'s chamber. After breakfast the lady proceeded to devotions, made a ritual offering of water to the Yidags,[1] poor wretches tormented with thirst, and prepared the *mandala* of

[1] The Tibetans, together with the Hindus, believe in the existence of certain wretched beings with gigantic bodies, thread-like necks, and mouths the size of a needle's eye. These unhappy beings are born in this form because of certain evil actions committed by them in former lives. Their enormous bodies, running all to belly, demand a great quantity of nourishment, which, with their tiny mouths and their thread-like necks, they are unable to swallow. Out of pity for them, the lamas and the pious laity offer them, every morning, water and food. These, through the effect of the ritual words pronounced by the donor, can be absorbed by the famished *Yidags*. In Sanscrit they are called *pretas*.

offering to the Teacher Padmasambhava, who preached in Tibet about the year A.D. 800.

This *mandala* consisted of a wide silver dish on which various provisions were arranged in the prescribed order. There were to be seen raisins, large lumps of sugar-candy, uncooked rice, various fresh or dried fruits, and pastries. The princess sprinkled them all with spirit, while reciting the consecrated formulae, and Mipam then placed the dish on the altar before the statue of the Guru Padma.

Of this altar he was the sacristan; it was his duty each morning to fill the bowls ranged in a line before the statues with fresh water, and to empty them at sunset. The presence of this water before them at night frightens the images of the gods. By a peculiar optical effect, each bowl of water assumes in their eyes the proportions of an ocean: its surprising appearance so near to them makes them uneasy and robs them of rest. It is not the personalities who are represented by the statues who are afraid, but the effigies themselves. These are supposed to be animated with a sort of life. This 'life' is implanted in them by means of certain rites.

In the place of the bowls, which are inverted after they have been emptied, one or more lamps are lit, over and above the ever-burning lamp which in the home of pious and well-to-do people burns night and day, as was the case in the princess's apartment.

At nightfall, the *mandala* and the other offerings which were laid on the altar during the day were removed. This is the moment when greedy sacristans of Mipam's ilk fish from the bowls what dainties they can, to be hoarded and nibbled between meals.

In the palace the meals were abundant. The prince and his wife breakfasted in comfort, by themselves, as soon as they awoke. About midday dinner was served in the prince's room, when his wife and children usually dined with him. In pursuance of the Tibetan practice, the parents and their children sat at different tables. The chief was installed on a throne of the

kind that stood in his wife's apartment, but of still greater
height and width. The eldest son took his place by the side of
the throne, on a high pile of cushions, and the younger sat near
his brother, but on a lower seat. Facing the throne sat the
mother, at the head of her three daughters, ranged in descending
steps according to their ages. Before each diner was a little
separate table on which the servants placed the dishes and bowls
containing the various courses of the meal.

A supply of food much greater than they were able to absorb
—though they were all good trenchermen—was served to each
member of the family. The meal over, the man who filled the
post of butler emptied into a large receptacle all that remained
in the dishes and bowls. These motley remnants formed the
princely *soslag*, which was divided and sent as a mark of very
special regard to prominent palace officials or visitors of mark.
By a special favour the kind *gyalmo*, who had taken Mipam to her
heart, often handed him, after dinner, her fine silver dish,
which was still more than half full. The boy had then to make
a low bow in token of his thanks, and forthwith to transfer the
contents of the dish to his own. If he happened to be free, he
could eat what had been given him in the pantry; otherwise he
had to hide the succulent leavings, to prevent any domestic
from stealing them while he was on duty.

As he had foreseen, Mipam had an easy time; he grew fat
and continued to hoard. To the little store which he had
amassed behind the astrologer's back he added, almost daily,
the tips pressed upon him by women who sought admission to
the presence of the *gyalmo*. Nevertheless, Mipam was not
happy. His vanity was wounded. He greatly missed the
notoriety which he had enjoyed among the peasants to whom he
went to read the sacred scriptures. He did not cut the figure of
a scholar at the palace; very far from it. The prince's chaplain—
a lama who had studied in the colleges of several large monasteries—ignored him entirely when he came to call on the
princess. One day, thinking to astonish him and compel his

admiration, Mipam, who had seated himself in the passage
before his mistress's door, had begun to recite, in a very loud
voice, an abstruse philosophic treatise which he had formerly
committed to memory. His attempt was not successful: the
lama burst out laughing, and the princess, annoyed by the
impudence of her page, whose declamation drowned what she
was saying, had peremptorily ordered him to hold his tongue.

From that day forward Mipam, who had found it hard to
swallow his mortification, grew less fond of his pretty lady. He
was frankly bored, and wished to leave the palace, but the
question was, how and where should he go? . . .

He often lay awake at night, thinking. He slept in the
prince's room, which was larger even than his wife's. After
serving, in the daytime, as the dining-room and the throne-
room in which the chief gave audience, at night it provided a
resting-place for the whole family.

Each evening the servants brought into the room a quantity
of cushions, with which they constructed a wide, raised bed for
the *gyalpo* and his wife; more provided beds of varying heights for
their five children. The elder son lay on three cushions placed
one upon another; his younger brother on two only. The eldest
girl was allowed two, but these were rather thinner than those
of her young brother; the two youngest sisters had to rest content with one cushion only, and that of the very youngest was
the thinnest of all.

Together with the cushions the servants brought blankets,
some of fine curly wool, in imitation of lamb's fleece, and
coverlets of silk, quilted with wool. Those of the husband and
wife were of Chinese brocade, some red and some blue. All
these bedclothes were luxurious, and fairly dirty. The servants'
greasy hands left their marks on them, and in carrying them
they carelessly dragged them on the floor, which was often
splashed with buttered tea.

Mipam lay on an ordinary carpet, wrapping himself in a
blanket, without undressing; the young princes, tired after
their play, often threw themselves on their mattresses without

72

Amithabha
Opami
the Buddha of endless light

removing their fine silken garments. The *gyalmo*, in her own room with the help of her maids, took off her jewels, her outer dress, and the upper part of her tall coiffure, which was arranged in the Tsang fashion, but the two wooden horns on which this construction rested, which were firmly held in place by the coils of her hair, could be removed only once a month, when the princess had her hair washed and re-dressed by her maids. These two stick-like supports, about fourteen inches in length, projecting on either side at a slight angle, compelled the lady to sleep lying flat and motionless on her back. Accustomed from the years of her girlhood to wearing these horns, they did not seem to incommode her, and her husband trustfully accepted the proximity of his horned consort, who, by a sudden movement, might have blinded him.

In the princely dormitory a lamp burnt perpetually on the altar, where the red Amithabha-Amitayur sat enthroned, the mystic deity of infinite light and life. By the light of this lamp, or on certain nights by the stronger light of the moon, which silvered the paper of the window, Mipam, during his hours of insomnia, contemplated his sleeping employers. At such times a sudden wave of disgust swept over him for these people who lay stretched unconscious on their beds, snoring and stertorously breathing, and a similar disgust for himself overcame him. What was he doing there with these people, in this room, lying at their feet? Was that the life for him? . . . Had he not had visions of fleeing to another place, of a very different order to his present surroundings? Vague recollections of the marvellous ordeal through which he had passed when quite a child, in the hermit's hut in the heart of the forest, rose in his mind, and while the hours dragged on, Mipam, averting his eyes from the sight that sickened him, lay quite still, gazing straight before him.

'Mipam, bring me some *chang!*'

The voice of the drowsy prince startled the boy; he had to rise and fetch the jar that was always ready on a table with the prince's jade bowl, and pour him out a drink. Sometimes it was

the lady who asked for beer or spirits. The heir-presumptive
did his best to keep awake, in order to imitate his parents and
show his importance by having something brought to him to
drink in the middle of the night. Happily for Mipam, the
youth was a heavy sleeper, and was rarely able to gratify his
whim.

The princess was devout in her own fashion. The ordinary
practices of lamaic piety for the use of the laity did not satisfy
her ambitions. She was bent on being initiated into the singular
exercises to which certain *naljorpas* (mystics, yogins) are addicted.
Having heard that a master *naljorpa*, passing on his way from
the country of Kham to Kang Tise,[1] was staying at Nyethang,
she sent a messenger with some presents and a letter begging
him to do her the honour of paying her a lengthy visit.

Invitations of this kind are frequently given. The Tibetan
pilgrims, especially those belonging to the clergy, have their
time at their own disposal. They are often several years on the
road, travelling in easy stages and stopping wherever they please.
Their route is consequently anything but direct; they make
numerous detours, in order either to visit interesting places, or
to stay with hospitable folk who offer them shelter, so that they
may enjoy a more or less prolonged rest, or perform religious
or magical rites for the benefit of their hosts.

Kushog Yeshes Kunzang, the master *naljorpa*, accepted the
invitation on the condition that in lieu of lodgings at the palace
he might have an isolated dwelling in which he could feel quite
at home, and have his suite about him. This latter comprised a
secretary, a steward, two disciples, a cook with his assistants,
and four servants to look after the horses and the luggage, and
act more or less as jacks of all trades. A *yogin* in Tibet is not
necessarily an ascetic who glories in his rejection of 'all the
riches of the world'. Kushog Yeshes Kunzang was wealthy, and

---

[1] A high mountain situated to the west of Tibet: it is a place of pilgrimage
for the Tibetans and the Hindus, the latter calling it Kailasa and placing the
abode of Shiva upon it.

ༀ། ཊི་ལོ་པ་བཛྲ་དྷརྨ།

Yogi Tilopa

prided himself on having reached a degree of detachment from the heights of which he could see himself living in opulence or in indigence with perfect indifference. Whatever truth there may have been in this claim, the fact was that he was travelling like a pilgrim of note. The princess, being duly apprised of this, felt only the greater respect for the master from whom she hoped to obtain instruction of an interesting nature.

As none of the dwellings within a convenient distance of the palace answered to the conditions laid down by the lama, the prince, just as desirous as his wife to have him for a guest, ordered one to be built with all dispatch. Trees were felled, planks cut, and thanks to the efforts of the fifty labourers requisitioned for the purpose, a rustic chalet, with two rooms, soon sprang up on a little plateau on the fringe of the forest, an hour's walk from the chief's mansion. From this latter hangings were brought for the walls, and a quantity of cushions and carpets to serve as seats and beds. A few low tables and another taller one to serve as an altar completed the furnishings. The inner room was to be reserved for the lama; his two disciples would occupy the outer chamber.

A hut also was built a few paces from the chalet, and like the latter, it was divided into two parts. One was to serve the dual purpose of kitchen and dormitory for the servants; the other, separated from the former by a thick partition, was to be occupied in common by the secretary and the steward. Finally, a stable for the horses was provided.

All this work had been completed in the course of a month. After a personal inspection, the *gyalpo* dispatched his secretary to Nyethang, to inform the lama that all was ready for his reception, and that he was expected.

A few days later Kushog Yeshes Kunzang set out for the prince's mansion. On the eve of the day on which he was to reach his improvised residence the prince sent him, to cover the last stage, a magnificent sorrel horse. As a general rule, a change of mount is sent to a visitor of distinction to some point at a short distance only from his host's house, but the *gyalmo* had insisted that her husband should show exceptional respect to the master from whom she was hoping to learn wonderful things.

Kushog Yeshes Kunzang deigned to express his satisfaction with the installation that had been prepared for him. His steward took possession of the provisions of all kinds placed in the cabins for the use of the lama and his suite, and they settled down quietly for a long and comfortable stay.

The third day after his arrival Yeshes Kunzang, duly rested, betook himself to the palace, mounted on the handsome sorrel horse, whose merits he had already appraised during a whole day in the saddle. According to custom, the courtesy mount is returned to its proprietor's stable on the guest's arrival, but on dismounting the lama had so imperiously ordered his servant to tie the horse in the shed where his own horses were kept that the *gyalpo's* men had not dared to lead it away.

'Kushog would doubtless like to enjoy a few rides on the horse,' remarked the princess when this incident was reported. 'See that it is placed at his disposal for the whole of his stay here.'

To give hospitality to a celebrated lama-*naljorpa* flattered the prince's vanity. Few people of importance visited him; he was only a very small kinglet. There are dozens like him in Tibet; the nobility of U and of Tsang looked down upon him or even ignored his existence, and as for the officials of the Dalai Lama, when they chanced to cross his territory in the exercise of their duties they behaved towards him in the manner of authoritative and exacting superiors.

However happy he may have felt in entertaining Kushog Yeshes Kunzang, the *gyalpo* was not at all eager to hear him hold forth on philosophical subjects. A tall, handsome man, and an ardent hunter, he did not by any means flatter himself that he was an intellectual or a mystic. He liked to range the mountains in search of bears or antelopes, to shoot at a target in the garden, and to play dice with his staff; and he felt no repugnance to winning their money. He was a great eater and drinker, and as regards women he was ingenuously sensual, without vice or malice, like the strong and healthy animal that he was.

When he thought he had devoted sufficient time to the lama to satisfy the demands of politeness, the prince bade his chamberlain conduct the guest to his wife. In anticipation of his visit, the *gyalmo* had sent for the chaplain, begging him to lead the conversation into such channels as would induce the master yogin to reveal something of the secret practices which he taught his disciples. Like the majority of his colleagues, Kushog Yeshes Kunzang displayed the greatest reticence in this respect. He evaded all questions. A month slipped by; the lama paid a few more visits to the princess, and the chaplain would frequently go and converse with him in his encampment. These interviews, however, did nothing to further their objective. Nevertheless, the *gyalmo* was more than ever consumed with the desire to devote herself to pious exercises differing from those practised by the ruck of the faithful, and the chaplain, though less intent than she, began, notwithstanding, to think that he might to his advantage complete his book-learning by knowledge of a practical nature which might possibly procure him the power of working miracles.

Ten years previously, a lama of very strange appearance had passed through the district. He was said to be a native of Dugyul (Bhutan), and an expert in magic; and wherever he had stopped, he had left marks of his passage. At the *gyalpo's* palace he had made a mushroom grow on one of the pillars of the temple, and in the presence of witnesses he had twisted into a knot the broad hard blade of a Tibetan sword. The mushroom had gradually dried up, but the knotted sword remained hanging in the temple.

At that time the chaplain was studying in the monastery of Sakya, so that he had not seen the lama work these miracles. The chief was shooting in an adjoining district while these prodigies were being performed at his residence, and his wife had been taking baths at some hot springs in the neighbouring

valley of Phari Dzong. For the very reason that they themselves had not seen them their faith in the miracles and their
reverence for the wonder-worker were all the greater.

And now the chaplain, remembering the Dugpa lama's glory,
had dreams of rivalling him!

It was time for all this shilly-shallying to cease. After discussing the question with the princess, the chaplain went to
the *naljorpa*, and having first pressed upon him a substantial
present, he made his request on behalf of the princess and himself. Both wished to be instructed by the lama and inducted
into the practice of secret methods.

'It is a difficult task,' Yeshes Kunzang declared in a solemn
tone, when he had listened to his brother in religion. 'My very
secret doctrine is profound and subtle to a degree; a superior
mind is needed to understand it. It is hard and brilliant like a
diamond; one must have very strong sight if one is not to be
blinded by its radiance, and a resolute heart to devote oneself
to it. I have, moreover, many doctrines, suitable for different
characters, and adapted to aims of different orders. What is it
you want?—and what does the *gyalmo* desire?'

In common with most of the learned members of the Tibetan
clergy, the chaplain was fairly sceptical as regards the extraordinary knowledge and superlative secrets which the majority
of the *naljorpas* boast of possessing, but for all that he was
impressed. He answered, therefore, that as far as he was concerned he was anxious to acquire breath-control in the practice
known as *lung-gom*, so that his body might become super-
naturally light, and remain seated in the air without support.

As for the princess, he thought that her object was the same.
He had spoken with assurance in explaining his own desires,
but now that he spoke of the lady his tone changed; the sense of
his words was modified by a suspicion of mockery in the inflections of his voice. He had full confidence in his own ability to
achieve his object, and consequently felt that he was deserving
of consideration from one whom he was, after all, honouring
in becoming his pupil. As for the *gyalmo*, she was merely of the

78

laity, without monastic culture, a presumptuous woman who aimed too high and over-estimated her capacities.

The thoughts of his interlocutor were as clear as daylight to the master yogin. He smiled. Was it in approbation, encouragement or mockery? What did his future teacher's inscrutable smile convey? The chaplain was at a loss to understand it, but he did not hesitate to interpret it to his advantage.

'You must first of all, both of you, receive preliminary initiation,' said the lama. 'Then, for the space of three months, you must practise various exercises under my direction. For the whole of that time you will live shut up, seeing neither the light of day, nor any kind of light. Have built, near here, a hut containing two rooms, completely separated from each other and perfectly dark. I will call upon the wife of the chief and teach her how to prepare herself for this retreat; in your case I will give you your instructions here.'

He spoke with authority. Thenceforward, for him, the chaplain and the princess were no longer a colleague and a hostess with whom he conversed with deferential cordiality; they became his disciples, and owed him the triple prostration symbolizing the offering and the absolute submission of mind, voice and body. Yeshes Kunzang, seated cross-legged on a high pile of cushions, had thrown out his powerful chest, and he stared at the startled chaplain with hard, relentless eyes, rather like those given by the painters to the terrible deities whose frescoes decorate the temple walls.

'Now go!' he said, dismissing his visitor.

The latter rose, and knowing what was demanded by the position in which he had placed himself, he prostrated himself three times, and then, with clasped hands and bowed head, begged the *naljorpa* for his blessing. The latter placed his right hand on the head of his disciple, who then retired.

The chaplain was but half content. Kushog Yeshes Kunzang had consented to instruct him, but had taken the high hand with him. When he had respectfully been asked for his blessing, the lama might well have returned courtesy with courtesy, remembering that, after all, he had before him a learned man, who occupied, in the regular clergy, a rank higher than his own. He ought to have acknowledged the humility displayed by his distinguished disciple by touching his head with his own, in token of equality, or at least he should have honoured him with the benediction conferred with both hands. . . . He had merely touched his hair with one hand only! . . . The Dalai Lama himself blesses all the members of the Holy Order, even to the lowest, with one hand. This *yogin* greeted him in the same way:, would he not, on some future occasion, merely stroke his head with his whisk of ribbons,[1] just as he would in the case of a peasant or a woman? . . . But there was no longer any way of backing out of it; he had suffered the humiliation; the only thing now was to profit by it, and learn, as quickly as possible, from the master whom he had chosen, the means by which the supernormal powers attributed to the latter, and to which he owed fame and fortune, were to be acquired.

The princess enthusiastically welcomed the *naljorpa's* reply. At last she was to pass beyond the bounds of her ordinary devotions! The notion of shutting herself up in seclusion (*tshams*)[2] in a room impenetrable to the light, seemed marvellous to her. What would she do in the absolute darkness? That she did not ask herself. Her chaplain had told the lama that she wanted to remain seated in the air without support. It was very proper to credit her with such an intention, but she could hardly believe that she would be capable of accomplishing such a feat. She was not greatly set upon it, in any case; to go into

[1] Mention is here made of the different ways of giving a blessing, according to the degrees of esteem shown to the recipient: with the two hands placed on the head, or one hand only or, thirdly, with the whisk of ribbons, mounted on a handle, which the lama passes lightly over the head of the faithful.

[2] *Tshams* means 'retreat'. There are several kinds of *tshams*. For details on the subject of this practice, see: A. David-Neel, *Among the Mystics and Magicians of Tibet.*

Mahākāla - Gombo Maning

lengthy retreat in the woods and in darkness would satisfy her craving for some sensational religious activity.

That very day she confided her intention to her husband. The prince was mildly surprised. He was anything but devout, but he was not an unbeliever; he felt esteem for those addicted to mystical practices whose meaning is hid from the uninitiated. Without demur he gave his unconditional consent to all that his wife desired.

On the very next day the princess instructed one of the palace stewards to put in hand the construction of a dwelling in accordance with the directions given by Kushog Yeshes Kunzang. Orders were given to the village headmen, to provide compulsory labour, and while their crops were spoiling in the fields they had been forced to abandon, the aggrieved peasants erected the cells in which their devout princess and her ambitious chaplain were about to cultivate the art of levitation.

In addition to the quarters intended for the two *tshams-pas*, as those who go into retreat are called, there was also erected, at a little distance, a hut which served the dual purpose of a kitchen, and, as in the lama's house, a dormitory for the domestics.

On the eve of the day when his new disciples were about to begin their retreat, Yeshes Kunzang shut himself up in the cells which they were going to occupy, and carefully assured himself that there were no crevices through which the light might enter. This scrutiny had already been made more than once by his servants, and every chink and cranny had been stopped. The master *naljorpa* having declared the state of the premises satisfactory, burnt incense and performed the secret rites which would bring into the house currents of favourable influence, and attract the attention of certain deities. The tinkling of his little bell and the roll of his drum could be heard by those outside, but no one might see him officiating.

The entry of the princess and the chaplain into their cells was the occasion for another ceremony. During the night, with the utmost secrecy, assisted by only one of his disciples, the lama traced a symbolical design on a square of white cotton

nailed upon the floor of his room, when various emblematical
objects and offerings were laid upon parts of the design which
represented the abodes of certain deities.

At daybreak the two recluses were admitted into the room,
where they remained alone with their *guru*, who administered
the rites of initiation. Then, escorted by the lama, they made
their way to the habitations prepared for them. Reciting the
appropriate *mantrams* or magical formulae, the master *naljorpa*
led the *gyalmo* up the stairs that gave access to a covered balcony,
on to which opened the cell which she was to occupy, and
ushered her into it. It was a long room, scantily furnished with
a bed consisting of cushions and blankets, and a low table. The
walls were covered with dark cloth. A hatch with double doors
allowed of meals being handed in to the recluse without any
one seeing or being seen by her. In a corner of the room a hole
pierced in the flooring and provided with a lid served for the
necessities of nature, the excretions falling into a pit dug under
the house.

When the princess had entered her cell, her *guru* shut the
door and sealed it with his private seal.

The chaplain was conducted to his quarters in the same way.
Much smaller than the lady's room, his was divided from hers
by a thick partition. The furniture was the same as in the
princess's room, except that the cushions and hangings were of
inferior quality.

Having sealed the chaplain's door also, the *naljorpa* withdrew.

The two recluses were now alone in their dark cells, and what
they did no one but their spiritual master must know.

Mipam, appointed to the service of the chatelaine, knocked
four times a day at the hatch of her room to let her know that
he had brought the tray containing her food. He then waited
until the lady had finished her meal, and had replaced the tray
on the small table between the two doors of the hatch, when
she gave two raps on the inner door. Mipam thereupon took
the tray, handed it to the servant who had brought it from the

kitchen, and then, having carefully closed the outer door, moved away, without withdrawing too far, or else sat down on the balcony, where he also passed the night, lying on a piece of carpet.

This very light task left him plenty of leisure. He loitered about, day-dreaming, and he made the acquaintance of the lama's two disciples. These told him of their country of Kham, and of China, whither they had accompanied their master on a pilgrimage to Omi-shan. Mipam listened to them attentively; his old craving for a wandering life was re-awakened, and seeing that the two young men spent a great part of the day in reading, he felt eager to acquire information.

One day, going in to see his friends, he found them engaged in a heated discussion. Kushog Yeshes Kunzang was out riding with his secretary. As the two young men were alone they did not hesitate to raise their voices.

'You are absolutely wrong,' said one of them to his co-disciple.

'You have not understood a word of what the writer is trying to explain,' the other retorted.

'It is you who have not understood,' replied the first. 'What you are maintaining is the opposite of what he teaches.'

'It is no use discussing the matter,' the second retorted. 'We have only to read what is written; you will see your mistake.'

On which the young cleric got up, fetched a book, opened it, hunted about for some time, turning over the pages for the passage which he wanted, read it aloud triumphantly, and began to comment on it in order to establish the truth of what he had advanced.

Mipam cared little for the subject of their discussion; one fact alone compelled his attention. To these two monks the book said something intelligible, which you could reason about and discuss, just as when someone talks to you. At the astrologer's house the books contained only sounds that you learnt by heart in the order in which they came. This was all the knowledge of which his uncle was so proud, and if his former master knew anything more, he had not taught it to Mipam. A recollection already remote recurred to his mind. Had he not, at his very first lesson, asked Shesrab what the words meant, and had not the latter evaded a reply with such obvious displeasure that his pupil had never dared to question him again?

Fresh horizons loomed before Mipam's eyes. After much reflection, he took one of the young men aside, and told him how his education had fared at his uncle's hands, and how that uncle had evaded his question as to the meaning of what he was made to recite. He finally spoke of his great desire to understand, as the disciple did, the things that were said in books.

'Your case is not unusual,' the monk replied; 'the majority of clerics do not understand what they read. Perhaps your master was one of them, and therefore incapable of teaching you. You must learn the grammar if you want to be a man of letters. I will gladly teach you the elements while my master is staying here, but I must get his permission.'

The *trapa* had no difficulty in obtaining this permission, and Kushog Yeshes Kunzang had Mipam brought before him.

'Ah,' he said, when the boy had greeted him with the accustomed prostrations, 'it is you, is it, who want to learn "what the books say"! You thought that reading meant only producing sounds; many think the same, but it is not so at all. There are, it is true, certain passages written in the language of the gods, and in that of the *dakinis*,[1] and those are to be understood only by very learned initiates, but the greater part of our Sacred Books is quite comprehensible. All the works forming the *Kahgyur* are translations made from very ancient books

[1] The passages he alluded to are those which have not been translated but merely reproduced from the Sanscrit text in Tibetan script. Some of these passages have been corrupted past the possibility of restoration; they are believed by some to be written in the language of the inhabitants of other worlds, and are employed as magic formulae.

written by disciples of Buddha. From these books we know what the Buddha preached, and how he lived, in days gone by, in India. There are also translations of the great religious teachers of India, as well as books written by the sages and learned lamas of our own country, on all kinds of admirable doctrines that neither India nor any other country has ever known, so that Tibet is veritably the Land of Religion, possessing a treasury of teaching vaster in extent than the immeasurable ocean.

'You appear to be intelligent, and your desire to be instructed is laudable; so that when I leave here I will gladly take you with me. You will be able then to learn the grammar, and all that is necessary to understand what the books have to say. In the meantime, profit by the lessons which my disciple will give you.'

Mipam once more prostrated himself to show his gratitude to the lama. Never had he heard a more interesting discourse. How differently he regarded the books now! What had been only dead paper and a sort of monotonous music seemed instinct with spirit and life. He was eager to get into touch with that fascinating world from which the Buddha and the sages still talk to us by the aid of printed signs.

He wished to become learned. To the precious ocean of Tibetan literature he would, perhaps, one day, add a book written by himself.

Mipam was filled with enthusiasm at the thought, and on the following day he took his first lesson in grammar.

CHAPTER V

THE seclusion of the lady and her chaplain was to continue for three months. Around them, the life of the inhabitants of the improvised hamlet flowed gently on; no particular incident marked one day from another. Kushog Yeshes Kunzang rode out on the handsome sorrel horse, accompanied by his secretary. The steward, on the look-out for business, had long conferences with his co-stewards in the chieftain's service. The servants ate and drank for a good part of the day, and slept much of the rest. Mipam studied grammar.

Nevertheless, one night 'something happened'. Mipam was sleeping in his usual place, on the covered balcony in front of the *gyalmo's* room, when a singular noise awoke him. The noise was that of dull blows repeated at rather long intervals. Pom . . pom . . . pom. . . . What could it be? What was happening? No one had been allowed to enter the *gyalmo's* cell. The lama himself had never done so; occasionally he spoke to the two recluses through their hatches—he had exchanged a few words with them the day before—but the doors of the two rooms remained sealed.

Pom . . . pom . . . pom. . . . What on earth was it? Was the lady ill, and was she signalling for help? Was a demon tormenting her? These evil beings delight in tormenting the pious during their meditations. Ought he to call for help, or warn the lama? The boy did not know what course to adopt. Unable to decide, he left the balcony.

Pom . . . pom . . . pom. . . . The same sound was to be heard from the chaplain's cell! There could be no further doubt—the demons were at work. Mipam ran to the hut where the lama and his two disciples were sleeping. At the door, he stopped, not daring to knock. Wouldn't Kushog Yeshes

86

Kunzang be angry if he woke him? He strained his ears in the direction of the *tshams khang* (house for reclusion). There was perfect silence; had the distance muffled that mysterious thudding? He slowly returned to the cells. All was quiet. Perhaps he had better not interfere in things that he did not understand. It was, after all, for the lama to protect his disciples. Mipam regained the balcony and wrapped himself once more in his blanket, but in his perplexity he could not sleep again, and he remained listening until dawn, straining his ears to catch the slightest sound.

It seemed to him that the servant was very late, on that particular morning, in bringing his mistress's breakfast. He was feverishly anxious to hear her take it from the hatch, so that he could be sure that she was still living. He wondered whether he would dare ask her if she was well. The breakfast arrived; Mipam carried it to the princess; he heard her take the tray, and breathed again: she was alive! Later, at the usual signal, he removed the tray, but did not dare to speak to his lady.

But he was curious. His justifiable curiosity was due to his eagerness to learn. He wanted to know what could be the cause, in a *tshams khang* tenanted by devout recluses, of such a noise as he had heard. He could think of only one person who might be able to throw some light on the mystery: namely, the monk who was teaching him grammar.

'Certainly, I know what it means,' replied the young *trapa*, when Mipam questioned him. 'The *gyalmo* and the chaplain are practising *lung-gom.*'

'What's that?'

'It is a method by which all kinds of marvellous results are obtained; you can become extraordinarily agile, and walk for several days on end without eating, drinking, or sleeping; you can make your body so light that it will float in the air, or rest on the tip of a blade of barley without bending it. . . .'

'*Yatsen!* (marvel),' exclaimed Mipam. 'That's miraculous; I've never heard of anything so interesting! Do you think my old master, my uncle the astrologer, can sit on a blade of barley like that?'

'No, decidedly not. None but *gomchens*[1] and famous *naljorpas* are capable of doing so.'

'And what about her ladyship and her chaplain?'

'They probably don't aim at anything so high as that. I know nothing about it. Only Kushog Yeshes Kunzang knows what they are trying to achieve.'

'But this method that goes: *pom, pom,* what is it? Who makes that noise? Since you know, tell me.'

The young cleric hesitated, but Mipam looked at him with such a beseeching expression, and he was such a pleasant lad, that there was no resisting him.

'I'll show you when my master is not here,' he said.

Mipam impatiently waited for the lama to start on his customary ride. As soon as the rider was out of sight he went to find his friend. The monk had warned his fellow-disciple, who had consented to keep watch at the door, to ensure that no one, entering unexpectedly, should interrupt his comrade's demonstration. Seated on a thick, broad cushion, with his legs crossed, his feet resting on the thighs, his hands placed folded, the thumbs uplifted and in contact, Mipam's teacher inhaled deeply and repeatedly, with a peculiar rhythm, and then, suddenly, holding his breath, leapt into the air without shifting his position or using any support. The thud with which he fell back on the cushion resembled, though it was not so loud, the sound that Mipam had heard in the night.

'*Atsi!*' exclaimed the boy, completely taken by surprise.

The monk again breathed deeply, and then, holding his breath, jumped once more into the air.

He repeated this five times. Mipam was dumbfounded.

'Is it possible that her ladyship jumps like that?' he said, in a tone that expressed his incredulity.

The grammarian had relieved his comrade of his sentry-duty,

---

[1] Contemplative hermits.

ༀ ྃ རྡོ་རྗེ་འཆང་ནཱ་རོ།

Gomchen Naropa

and the latter, on entering the room, overheard Mipam's question, and began to laugh.

'That it is permissible to doubt,' he said. 'Before one can do what your teacher has shown you, one must practise for a very long time, sometimes for years.'

'All the same, I heard the sound,' replied Mipam.

'Listen,' said the *trapa*; 'you are an intelligent boy; so your teacher tells me, and you belong to the clergy, as we do; so I'm going to tell you a perfectly true story. What happened took place in my monastery.

'There was a monk who was extremely vain, and was also determined, no matter what the cost, to distinguish himself. So he sought out a master *naljorpa*, with a view to practising *lung-gom* under his guidance. After living beside him and receiving instruction for a time, he returned to the monastery. Assuming a consequential air, he asked for permission to shut himself up in one of the detached huts which are always at the disposal of those monks who wish to go into retreat. This permission he was granted. From outside the hut one could hear the sound of his jumping. Pom . . . pom . . . pom . . . pom. . . . He jumped, it would seem, a surprising number of times, and with quite exceptional vigour.[1] Those who had heard him practising told others of their astonishment. The monks marvelled at his progress, and gathered beside his cell to hear him leap. "He'll end by making a hole in the roof and triumphantly bursting forth into the open," they said. "To judge by the noise he's making, you would think his head must touch the ceiling every time he jumps!" It was so astonishing that one of the heads of the monastery became suspicious.

'This wonder-working recluse was not compelled to live in the dark; it was enough that he should neither be seen nor be able to see the outer world; the little window of his cell was simply covered with paper. Accompanied by a few other

[1] This strange exploit is said to be actually accomplished; it constitutes the final test, by which the *lung-gompas* show their ability. On this subject see: A. David-Neel, *Mystics and Magicians of Tibet.*

monks, the lama stole silently up to the hut, and at the hour when the lamps are lit before the holy images on the altar the invisible recluse began his exercises. Thud followed thud with increasing force and frequency. Suddenly one of the monks, at a sign from his superior, tore the paper from the window. There was the impostor, in the sight of them all, holding a log of wood in his hand, and belabouring a cushion for all he was worth, so as to produce the sound of a body falling from a height.

'He was immediately dragged from his cell and confined in a dungeon, and on the following day he could jump to his heart's content, for they hung him up by his thumbs, and gave him a good beating!'

'Do you think, then, that her ladyship is thumping on her cushions instead of jumping?' asked Mipam.

'I didn't say that, my boy,' replied the cleric, soberly. 'Take my advice; keep your thoughts to yourself, hold your tongue, and speak to no one about what the *gyalmo* does, nor of what you have seen or heard here, or some evil may befall you.' Mipam agreed; he nodded in approval; and he then asked his teacher:

'Can *you* sit on the tip of a blade of barley without bending it?'

'That is far beyond me,' replied the disciple.

'Well,' continued Mipam, after some hesitation, 'can Kushog Yeshes Kunzang do so?'

'He can,' declared the two disciples in unison, in tones of complete conviction.

'Oh!' said Mipam, wondering. 'Have you seen him sitting like that?'

'He doesn't allow us to see him doing such things,' the grammarian replied.

'We are not yet worthy,' said the other monk, solemnly.

'Oh!' said Mipam, again; but with a different intonation; and he asked no more questions.

.   .   .   .   .

Mipam made good progress in grammar, and began to unravel the meaning of what he read; he had watched a *lung-gompa*[1] pupil leaping from his cushion cross legged, and he had learnt a number of interesting things, but he had not seen Dolma again. But already more than two months had elapsed since the princess had gone into retreat; she would soon return to the palace, and then perhaps she would send for the little girl. Mipam lived in hope.

The offer which Kushog Yeshes Kunzang had made him gave him much food for thought, conflicting as it did with his desire to remain near his little friend. The life which he was leading filled him with misgivings. When the lama and his disciples had gone the lessons which he prized so highly would cease; he would once more be in attendance on the little princes, whom he had to amuse by joining in their games and expeditions. But was not this wasting his youth? What would this empty existence lead to? Was it the way to become a man of wealth and consequence, as he had boasted to Dolma? Her father would never give her to a poor and insignificant husband. Must he not leave her in order to make his fortune, and build, on his return, the house which he had promised her? ... To follow Kushog Yeshes Kunzang might lead to the acquirement of wisdom and extraordinary powers. Even if the lama was unable to do so, he, Mipam, would learn how to perch on a blade of barley without bending it. A burning desire to do so possessed him; and he certainly wouldn't hide his accomplishments; he passionately longed for the fame of the wonder-workers, and he at least would be prodigal of miracles. Dolma would regard him with admiration; but her father, the rich merchant, would want money; and even by working miracles, how could he quickly make a fortune?

A prey to painful indecision, Mipam envisaged the two courses which he considered were open to him, all unwitting that the choice was not to lie with him.

One afternoon, on leaving his master, and returning to the

[1]*Lung-gompa*—a man who practises *lung-gom* (breath control).

tshams khang to study his lesson on the covered balcony which served him for a room, he saw Dolma drinking tea, seated on the ground near the entrance to the kitchen. She had been sent to the palace, then, and sooner than he had hoped. Mipam was beside himself with joy.

Dolma laughed her charming laugh: it gave her great pleasure to be welcomed with such glad emotion. She had grown a great deal since the day of her fantastic appearance to Mipam through the flames on the hearth in the astrologer's kitchen. She was now a little woman of thirteen, already versed in business, and a useful help to her capable stepmother.

At the palace, the young princesses found the time hanging heavy on their hands; they were bored in the absence of their mother, and they had begged their father to send for Dolma to keep them company. The *gyalpo* had willingly consented. A messenger was despatched to Lhasa with a letter for Tenzing, who allowed Dolma to travel back with the courier.

The chief's daughters and the rich merchant's child were excellent friends. Dolma was fond, too, of the younger prince, but she did not like his elder brother. He was too masterful; he lorded it over his juniors, and even over his big sister, who was already engaged to be married. They had always to play the games that he chose, and take the walks that he preferred. When he was crossed he became violent. His three sisters were afraid of him, and Dolma avoided him as much as she could.

While conversing with his friend, Mipam did not fail to blow his own trumpet in the matter of the learning which he had acquired. After making her swear to secrecy, he described the exercises in *lung-gom* which he had witnessed, adding that in the near future he would be able to sit on an ear of barley without bending the blade.

'Oh, I *should* like to see you!' cried Dolma, in a transport of admiration.

'You shall see it, I promise, and many even greater wonders!' Mipam assured her.

But while parading the talents which he already possessed, and those which he plumed himself on acquiring at an early date, the vainglorious Mipam had not forgotten the dilemma that had so preoccupied him. If he was to become the magician that he craved to be, he would need a master to direct him. This master he had found: Kushog Yeshes Kunzang would serve his purpose, at least for the preliminary stages of his instruction; but the lama was about to leave the district. Ought he to follow him? What did Dolma think? Mipam consulted her.

'Go to Kang Tise, to the Pal-yul, and then to Kham with Kushog Yeshes Kunzang? Oh, Mipam, what a long way off!' cried Dolma. 'You will be away for years: I shan't see you for ages! Some harm may come to you! Brigands often attack travellers on their way; wicked innkeepers give them poisoned[1] tea to drink; demons lure them over precipices. . . .'

The poor little maiden began to weep. An apprehension which in her eyes was even worse than that of the dangers which would beset her friend had just entered her mind. She could not refrain from expressing it in words:

'Has Kushog Yeshes Kunzang a *yum*?'[2] she asked.

'No, not as far as I know,' replied Mipam. 'His disciples, when they have spoken at his residence in Kham, have never mentioned a *sang yum*.'[2]

'He can't have one then,' said Dolma. 'These great *naljorpas*, who are expert in all kinds of secret practices, have the gods for company. They force the genii to serve them, and

[1] The Tibetans believe that certain people—more especially women—subject to temporary possession by devils, are constrained, when the devil dwells in them, to poison the first person they come across. For this see: A. David-Neel, *Mystics and Magicians of Tibet*.

[2] The wives of lamas, adepts in the esoteric doctrines, to whom marriage is allowed, and on whom, in certain cases, it is actually enjoined, are called *sang yum*—'secret mother'—or, in its abbreviated form, *yum*—'mother'. While ordinary marriages can be dissolved by divorce, theirs is indissoluble. The purpose of this marriage is a mystic one and does not consist in founding a family.

take fairies to wife. When you have become a learned magician, you will no longer think about me.' A prey to infinite sadness, she continued to weep.

'Never, never shall I forget you, Dolma!' Mipam protested. 'If I become a great *naljorpa* you will be my *sang yum*, I promise you. I'll swear to that. But if you wish, I won't go. I'll stay at the *gyalpo's*, or else I'll ask your father to give me a commercial training.'

'Your brother Dogyal is with us already,' said Tenzin's daughter. 'My father is very fond of him, and finds him very quick at business.'

'Yes,' said Mipam, 'I know he's with you. Is he kind to you?'

'Yes, very; but he's so much older than I.'

'Come, now,' replied Mipam, smiling, 'he's twenty, that's not very old.'

'He's not handsome and learned like you, Mipam.'

'He doesn't know so much, certainly,' Mipam conceded, flattered.

'Mipam, couldn't you come and study at Lhasa? You'd find just as good a master there as Kushog Yeshes Kunzang. I remember my father telling you that you could come and stay with us.'

'Yes, that would be a good move, no doubt,' replied Mipam; 'but will the prince allow me to leave his service?'

'But you'd want his permission to follow Kushog Yeshes Kunzang,' Dolma pointed out.

'That's not indispensable. I could leave in the night, or on some pretext or other, either before or after the lama's departure, and join him on the road. He's going to continue his journey. I should soon be far away, where the chief couldn't get me back. At Lhasa, that's different; he's got friends there, and your father is his merchant; if he wanted to, he could have me brought back and beaten.'

'I don't want them to beat you,' protested Dolma, indignant at such a prospect.

Mipam made no answer. He had taken his friend's hand in his, and was dreaming of the happiness of having her for ever thus beside him; but at the same time he saw himself riding across distant lands, gazing on a thousand fresh sights, becoming as learned as his teacher the grammarian, and as his teacher's master, Kushog Yeshes Kunzang. And his heart contracted, for he felt that whatever course he chose, he was bound to suffer, to regret what he had renounced—either Dolma, his little love, or his ambitious dreams.

Dolma roused him from his reverie.

'Mipam,' she said, 'I must go back to the palace. The princesses think I am with the steward's wife or the secretary's daughter, but if I am away too long they'll send someone to look for me. To-morrow, or the next day, as soon as I can escape, I'll come and see you again.'

'Dolma, what a long time we've got to wait before we can marry and be always together!' Mipam whispered as he took her in his arms.

'Two years,' said Dolma: 'in two years' time I shall be fifteen, and you will be more than eighteen; but two years is a long time!'

'Dreadfully long!' echoed Mipam.

The two friends were overwhelmed with sadness. It was not merely the prospect of the long delay that troubled them. An unreasoning dread stole into their minds. What did they fear? They could not have said; they did not realize, as they trembled in each other's arms, that they dreaded the uncertainty of the future, the spectre of separation that rose between them.

Dolma came back neither the next day nor the day after. Mipam was broken-hearted, but he dared not desert his post to go to the palace. Though he had no work to do, he had to remain near the hermitage, ready to answer if the invisible lady should call him and give him an order.

When he absented himself to take his grammar lesson, or to go for a short walk, a servant remained on guard within earshot, to warn Mipam if the recluse should want him, for he alone of all the staff had the right to enter the balcony of the *tshams khang* and address the princess through the hatch of her cell.

For this reason, he could not absent himself for long; moreover, the considerable distance between the hermitage and the palace put such a move out of the question. His presence would be inevitably discovered by the prince's children or the servants, who would inform the *gyalmo* of his escapade. Mipam chafed at the bit and racked his brains to find some means of seeing Dolma again; but a week after their interview she suddenly appeared, breathless with running.

She found the future magician, her intended husband, sitting on the balcony of the hermitage, absorbed in his grammar. Waiting until he lifted his eyes from his book, she signed to him. With two light bounds, like a young leopard, the lad was at her side.

'Go and hide in the coppice down there,' he whispered hurriedly. 'I'll join you in a moment.'

And while she did as he bade her Mipam entered the lama's kitchen. He knew that the servants liked him; he was not afraid of their denouncing him, if they should see him with Dolma.

'I'm going to read in the woods,' he said to one of them. 'Be good enough to listen, in case her ladyship should rap on her hatch to call me; and if she asks for me, come and find me at once.'

The man promised to be on the alert, and Mipam ran to join Dolma.

They sat down side by side and chattered gaily. Dolma brought news from the palace. Life there was dreary. The eldest princess, who was engaged to a *shabpad* (minister), a widower twenty years her senior, was becoming more melancholy every day; the prospect of her coming marriage did not enchant her, despite the high rank which it assured her among the old nobility of Lhasa, and the splendid jewels with which she would be able to deck herself. The chief's second daughter was to be abbess of a monastery at the far end of the province of Kongbu, beyond Giamda, close to the country of the dreaded Popas. On the maternal grandmother's side, the child had some family ties in that region, but the sinister account which the merchants had given of the character of the Popas, whom they described as brigands and cannibals, had terrified her, and the idea of living on the border of their country was nightmare. She often wept, and Dolma was distressed to see her friend unhappy. The third daughter was the only one to display a little gaiety. Her parents had not come to any decision as to her future, or at all events, they hadn't told her of any, and she was still too young to worry about it. The younger of the two princes, recognized as a *tulku* of Lhatsunpa, though there already existed another 'incarnation', was shortly to enter the monastery of Mindoling, to study there.

These details were known to Mipam, but the Tibetans never tire of talking about people of a social condition superior to their own. On this particular day the children had gone down to the river. The elder boy, the one whom Dolma disliked, had insisted on this expedition, which gave him the chance of enjoying a little fishing. The *gyalpo*, seeing no objection to this, had ordered some of the servants to escort the children, to put up a large tent, and provide food for a meal. The whole day was to be spent in the open air.

The stream to which the campers had made their way skirted the spur of the mountain on which had been built the temporary quarters for Kushog Yeshes Kunzang and the two recluses. Dolma had taken advantage of this. While the other girls were hunting for mushrooms, which they wanted to have grilled, she managed to escape. A short climb had brought her to the plateau in which the hermitages had been erected.

The preoccupation about the future which had clouded their happiness at their last meeting did not, for the moment, recur to them: they were genuinely glad to be together, enjoying the present hour frankly and artlessly, like the children they still were.

It is in these carefree moments, when man lives like a flower, all unwitting of the forces whose product he is, that the result of past actions becomes manifested and transform his existence.

The friends were startled by the sound of an angry voice.

'Ah! At last I've found you, Dolma!' someone cried behind them. 'This is why you slip away and leave my sisters to search for you! Why are you here with Mipam?'

The prince's eldest son came up to them, breathless and red with rage.

Some time had passed since Dolma had left the princesses; neither she nor Mipam had realized how long. The girls, returning to their tent with their harvest of mushrooms, had called their companion in vain, and the servants sent to look for her had not found her in the neighbourhood of the camp.

It had then occurred to the eldest boy that Dolma might have conceived the notion of going to get news of the *gyalmo*, of whom she was very fond. Fearing that she might take the liberty of knocking on the *gyalmo's* door, or of speaking to her, a thing strictly forbidden, and displeased with this show of independence, the young prince had hurried up the path leading to the hermitage. It was the same path that Dolma had taken.

What he discovered was worse than he had imagined. Dolma was neither in the kitchen, inquiring for news of the princess from the servants, nor in the neighbourhood of the *tshams khang*. He found her hiding with Mipam among the bushes; they were both so busy chattering that they hadn't heard him come up. So it wasn't out of regard for the health of her protectress that she had so rudely deserted her companions, but simply to meet this peasant's brat!

'Why are you here? . . . I'll jolly well kick you downhill!' he screamed.

Dolma, terrorized, dared not stir, and Mipam knew enough of the customs of his country to be aware that all discussion with the son of a *gyalpo* was useless. Nevertheless, he knew that he would not allow his friend to descend the hill in the company of this young brute.

'Dolma will return in a moment, sir,' he said, as politely as the anger provoked by the *gyalse's* threats to her would permit. 'She's too frightened to come just now; she must go to the kitchen first and drink a bowl of tea.'

'Tea, did you say?' exclaimed the boy, cackling maliciously. 'You be off at once, and make haste, or I'll give you a thrashing!'

Instinctively the girl retreated a step, taking refuge behind her friend.

Mipam did not hesitate for a moment.

'Sir,' said he firmly, 'you will not thrash Dolma, nor will she follow you. I shall let her ladyship know what has occurred.'

'I shan't thrash her, shan't I? You dare talk to me like that? . . . I'll show you, you peasant's brat: I'll thrash her, and you too. . . .'

Rendered furious by a resistance he was not accustomed to encounter, the boy rushed forward, and before Mipam could prevent him he had seized Dolma by the arm and pulled her violently toward him. The girl's feet caught in a root, and she fell to the ground with a cry.

A yell from her aggressor answered hers; with a vigorous blow of his fist, which landed full in the prince's chest, Mipam had sent him rolling down a stony slope. When he rose the blood was flowing from a wound in the head, where he had struck it against a rock.

Although he was two years older than Mipam, and taller, the young prince hesitated to retaliate: his adversary's face bore a terrible expression. There was murder in the air, and he was afraid.

'I'll have you beaten to death!' he snarled, in a voice tremulous with rage and the shock which he had suffered.

He slowly retreated, shifting his hand from his bleeding temple to his face and his aching back, smearing himself with blood, and telling himself that his tragic appearance would increase the severity of the punishment which his father would inflict on Mipam.

.   .   .   .   .

What Mipam had done he had done with the speed of lightning, and now he found himself confronted with an irremediable fact, before he had had the time to give it a thought.

Like many of the feudal princelets of Tibet, the *gyalpo* wielded an autocratic power within the boundaries of his miniature territory. There was not a shadow of doubt that any one who had dared to strike his son would be cruelly tortured; and, should he survive the ordeal, Mipam might expect to be doomed to lifelong slavery in the service of the chief and his descendants.

Dolma was the first fully to realize the gravity of the situation.

'Mipam,' she said, with decision, 'you must fly at once. The *gyalpo* is away shooting; he will not return until the day after to-morrow, in the evening. His secretary and his steward are with him. The others, having no definite orders, will not know what they ought to do. They won't make much of a search for you . . . you'll have time to go far beyond their reach.'

Now that Mipam's wrath had subsided, he recovered his self-possession.

'You are right,' he replied. 'I must start at once. The *gyalse* won't go quickly down that bad path, and by the time he reaches the camp he may not be able to mount his pony to ride home: his back must be hurting him. The servants will carry him, or rig up a stretcher for him. There are only two, you told me; they'll have their hands full. When the *gyalse* reaches the palace it will be already too dark to look for anyone in the woods. I've all the night before me to get a good start. . . . Besides, I shall cut myself a good solid stick, and if any one tries to stop me I'll look after myself all right.''

The boy's eyes became once more hard and determined. Then, suddenly ceasing to think of himself:

'But you, Dolma,' he asked, in an anguished voice, 'what will you do?'

'I? I'm coming with you, Mipam,' the girl replied, seemingly surprised at the question. Wasn't it only natural that she should accompany her friend?

'Where are we going?'

'To Lhasa, to my father. He likes you very much; he won't let anyone hurt you. And then, you know, in Lhasa there are the Dalai Lama and his ministers; there your *gyalpo* is no longer the master. My father is rich; he can give as many presents as are needed for your protection. Come! . . .'

With a firm, quick step she started off, skirting, under the cover of the wood, the huts of Kushog Yeshes Kunzang, the recluses, and their servants. No one must know that Mipam was escaping, nor have any idea of the direction he had taken.

Mipam followed her in silence, thinking of Kushog Yeshes Kunzang and his kindly teacher. Of the matter that had so engrossed his attention there was no longer any question now; he wasn't free to follow them, he would probably never see them again, nor would he ever learn to sit on the tip of an ear of barley without bending the stem. But Dolma was with him: strong and active, she was scaling the steep mountain-side in front of him as though she was his guide. All, then, was well, since his little fairy was leading him. Wherever he might be he would be happy at her side.

The sun had just set; the shadows were gradually invading the forest; Mipam, rousing himself from his reverie, rejoined his friend, and stopped her. He had recovered his assurance, and had formed a plan.

'We are far enough from the hermitages,' he said; 'we shan't come across anyone else. It will soon be dark. We should lose ourselves in the woods; we had better take to the path again and walk without stopping until dawn; then we'll hunt for a hiding-place to rest in during the day, and start off again at nightfall. They are sure to go to look for me at my father's and they'll send a man on horseback along the road to Lhasa,

thinking you'll go back home. We mustn't make for Lhasa
by the direct route; we should only get caught. If you can
manage to keep on walking, we'll look for a side track. I've
got my money; I always carry it on me; we shall be able to
buy what we want to eat.'

'I can walk as well as you can,' the girl replied, proudly, 'and
I know where we'll go. We'll go to Shigatze, to uncle Tsöndup.
You don't know him; he's a merchant, a great friend of my
father's. He's kindness itself; he brings me presents every
time he comes to Lhasa. He has a son, older than your brother,
and two others who are younger; one of them is a novice at
Tashilhumpo monastery. He's got a little girl too. I'm very
fond of them all. Yes, we must go to him.'

Mipam thought well of this idea; he agreed with the plan,
and the two fellow travellers started off again. Before long
they came to a path which led up to a pass giving access to the
arid tablelands which lie between Phari and Kampa. The
track was long and rugged; they did their utmost, yet the first
gleam of dawn was paling the sky when they reached the pass.

Though the track was little frequented, the fugitives thought
it wise to give it a wide berth, so as to avoid any risk of being
seen by a chance traveller. There was a spring a little way
below the pass; they drank of it, and then, on rounding a spur
of the mountain, they came to a little boulder-strewn ravine,
which was not visible from the path. There they lay down to
rest, and in a moment they were both fast asleep.

The year was in its sixth month; warmed by a hot sun,
Mipam and Dolma slept late; when they woke the day was
more than half spent. They were both famished. Although
they would have preferred to wait until evening before resuming their journey, the immediate need of food prevented their
lingering any longer. Moreover, they did not believe that any
search would be made in the direction which they had taken.

On Mipam's advice Dolma removed her jewels, which would
draw attention to her, and concealed them under her dress;
after which they set off again. Twice, as they journeyed on,

Mipam wanted to turn aside and make for a village which he saw in the distance, in order to buy or beg some barley flour, but the prudent Dolma dissuaded him, with the assurance that she could fast a little longer, and that they had better go farther still before they allowed themselves to be seen.

During the night they came to the foot of a little rocky hill, halfway up which there was a cave. Mipam, seeing that his companion was exhausted, decided to halt there. They dragged themselves up until they reached the rocky shelter, and as on the previous evening, the moment they lay down they fell into a sound sleep.

Mipam was the first to wake; the rising sun was flushing the neighbouring heights with a rosy glow, while the valley below them was still bathed in a grey and chilly twilight. The boy remained for an instant motionless, watching the light sweep across the mountains; then, turning his head, he remained dumbfounded. Against the opposite wall of the cave, wrapped in an ample cloak, a lama lay looking at him. Was he dreaming? No, the lama was no shade, but a living man, who was speaking to him.

'Don't be afraid, little one,' he said. 'I am a wayfarer, like yourself.'

Mipam rose, and bowing politely, excused himself:

'Please, forgive me, *Kushog*; it was dark when we came here for shelter, and we didn't see you.'

The sound of voices woke Dolma. She, too, did not at once notice the lama, and raising herself to a sitting posture, she gazed into vacancy.

'Oh! Mipam, I'm so hungry!' she groaned.

'We are sure to find something to eat this morning,' Mipam replied.

Dolma turned in his direction, and saw the lama, who was still lying down, swathed to his eyes in his dark garnet-coloured cloak.

'Why do you let that child go hungry?' asked the lama, turning to Mipam. 'One should assuage the suffering of

103

creatures, not inflict it on them. You ought to know that, you whose hair has been cut.'[1]

This unjust reproach cut Dolma to the quick.

'It's not his fault,' she replied, 'we've no provisions. If you could sell us a little *tsampa*, we will buy it of you.'

'I have no *tsampa*,' said the lama. 'Ask your companion for some.'

'I haven't got any, *Kushog*,' protested Mipam.

'You can have some. He whose heart is filled with love for all existing beings, to him all treasures are open, and he can draw from them to his heart's content in order to relieve their poverty. He speaks the word, and the rivers turn to milk, the stony rocks to butter. . . . Take some meal from that rock!' With a motion of the head, he indicated a projecting rock at the mouth of the cave.

Mipam gazed at the lama uneasily, and Dolma trembled with fear. Still lying down, and wrapped in his cloak, the lama seemed to have grown: standing, he would surely be a giant. His eyes shone like glowing embers.

'You must learn to know yourself,' continued the strange lama. 'Smite the rock!'

Mastered by the imperious tones in which this order was given, Mipam approached the rock, and clenching his fist, he struck it. Miracle of miracles! Instead of meeting the hard surface of the stone, his hand sank as far as his wrist into some soft, unresisting substance. Terrified, he quickly drew it out, and from the hole which it had made a thin stream of fine white *tsampa* began to flow.

'Hold out your cloak to collect the *tsampa*,' the lama ordered once more. Mipam obeyed, and in this way collected a couple of *tés* of meal; and then the miraculous spring ceased to flow. No trace remained of the hole whence it had issued; the rock had again become hard and impenetrable to the touch.

'Go and eat by the side of the first brook you meet,' said the

[1] This means that he belonged to the Religious Order. The laity wear their hair long.

In Dharmsala for Dalai Lama's Kala Chakra,
Roger Williams and his adopted Tibetan Mother.
March, 1970. Iron Dog.

The great Stupa of Bodhi as seen from Williams' work bench.

Williams in front of the Potola Palace, Lhasa, Tibet, 1981.

A NOTE ON THE ILLUSTRATOR

ROGER Williams is an American woodblock artist who works in the traditional Buddhist art style of the Himalayas. The illustrations that appear in this text were cut and printed in the Tibetan Buddhist tradition, using handmade cutting tools, handmade paper as well as handmade ink. The process is very slow but is completely in keeping with the way in which this art-form has been produced for hundreds of years. The prints in this text, for example, took one year to complete.

Mr. Williams lived in Nepal for eight years, where he studied Tibetan Buddhism, Buddhist Iconographics and Tibetan language, as well as woodblock art. A further two years were spent in Kyoto where he studied the Japanese tradition of woodblock art, ukiyo-e.

1936 Fire Mouse	1975 Wood Rabbit
1937 Fire Ox	1976 Fire Dragon
1938 Earth Tiger	1977 Fire Snake
1939 Earth Rabbit	1978 Earth Horse
1940 Iron Dragon	1979 Earth Sheep
1941 Iron Snake	1980 Iron Monkey
1942 Water Horse	1981 Iron Bird
1943 Water Sheep	1982 Water Dog
1944 Wood Monkey	1983 Water Pig
1945 Wood Bird	1984 Wood Mouse
1946 Fire Dog	1985 Wood Ox
1947 Fire Pig	1986 Fire Tiger
1948 Earth Mouse	1987 Fire Rabbit
1949 Earth Ox	1988 Earth Dragon
1950 Iron Tiger	1989 Earth Snake
1951 Iron Rabbit	1990 Iron Horse
1952 Water Dragon	1991 Iron Sheep
1953 Water Snake	1992 Water Monkey
1954 Wood Horse	1993 Water Bird
1955 Wood Sheep	1994 Wood Dog
1956 Fire Monkey	1995 Wood Pig
1957 Fire Bird	1996 Fire Mouse
1958 Earth Dog	1997 Fire Ox
1959 Earth Pig	1998 Earth Tiger
1960 Iron Mouse	1999 Earth Rabbit
1961 Iron Ox	2000 Iron Dragon
1962 Water Tiger	2001 Iron Snake
1963 Water Rabbit	2002 Water Horse
1964 Wood Dragon	2003 Water Sheep
1965 Wood Snake	2004 Wood Monkey
1966 Fire Horse	2005 Wood Bird
1967 Fire Sheep	2006 Fire Dog
1968 Earth Monkey	2007 Fire Pig
1969 Earth Bird	2008 Earth Mouse
1970 Iron Dog	2009 Earth Ox
1971 Iron Pig	2010 Iron Tiger
1972 Water Mouse	2011 Iron Rabbit
1973 Water Ox	2012 Water Dragon
1974 Wood Tiger	2013 Water Snake

Roger Williams

Roger Williams is an American who left San Francisco a few years back on his way to Tibet. The following is from the first letter we received from Mr. Williams early this spring. "My wife and I have been living in Nepal for two years. During this time I have been studying Tibetan Religion and Culture by living with Tibetans and practicing Tibetan Buddhism. Both my wife and I have been initiated into the Kargupa Sect of Tibetan Buddhism. This is the sect, or line of teaching in which Mila-repa was a founder.

"Most of my work has been in the field of Tibetan Buddhist Art. The art of woodblock cutting impressed me upon my arrival in Nepal. I began collecting prints and investigating the art form. As a result of my interest in woodblocks we went to Solu-Khumbu, the area that borders Mt. Everest on the Nepal side. In some of the Buddhist monasteries in Solu-Khumbu, books are still cut by the Monks and a few laymen. We lived for six months with a local buddhist woodblock cutter, Panu was his name. I took teachings from Panu in Tibetan, he spoke no English. He instructed me in the Tibetan style of woodblock cutting. We made my carving tools using wood from a local tree and metal from Swiss mainsprings and Japanese umbrellas. He also taught me ink-making and print making. Together he and I cut the set of 23 blocks which include the 16 arhats and their two supporters; the Gal-Chin-She (Four Great Kings); and the Sakya-Muni. As far as I know another set such as this does not exist. There are many paintings and a few blocks of selected figures from this set available.

"I plan to stay on in Nepal for some time in order to continue my studies which I consider very important. What is left of Tibetan culture will disappear within our lifetime; therefore, it is necessary that what research is to be done on Tibetan Art and Religion must be done now while there are Tibetans who are capable of transferring this knowledge."

lama, and steadily gazing at Mipam with his blazing eyes, he added: 'You are on the right road; go on, you will reach your goal.'

The lad was too overcome by the prodigy whose instrument he had been to make any reply; a lump in his throat prevented him uttering a sound. He tied up his cloak, so forming a kind of pocket for the flour, prostrated himself thrice before the great figure of the lama, and collecting all his courage, drew near to him, and bent double, with folded hands and bowed head, to receive his blessing. Two strong hands emerged from the mantle and rested on his head. Then the lama drew the cloak over his eyes.

In her turn Dolma prostrated herself three times, but the lama did not look at her.

By no means reassured, in spite of the miracle which had been accomplished in their favour, the two friends backed respectfully out of the cave, regained the path, and without exchanging a word, with one accord they set off running.

As soon as they came to a stream they made some balls of meal in the wooden bowl which Mipam had fortunately been carrying in the breast of his tunic when their flight began; but they did not linger, and ate as they walked, being instinctively anxious to put the greatest distance possible between themselves and the uncanny lama of the cave.

'Who could he have been?' Dolma thought aloud, voicing the question which they had been silently asking themselves.

'Most assuredly a saint or a god,' replied Mipam. 'He wasn't there when we reached the cave. Despite the darkness, I should have noticed him. It is thanks to him that we have any food; he was good to us.'

'Mipam, it was you, and not he, who made the meal come out of the rock,' Dolma objected.

'It was I, because he was there, and willed it.'

'It was you, all the same,' the girl insisted.

'Yes . . . I,' said Mipam.

And they went their way in silence, deep in their own thoughts.

Three days later they passed Kuma, a village on the edge of a wide tract of barren, uninhabited land, which was traversed by the road leading to Shigatze. Mipam wanted to buy food there. Though they had eaten of it sparingly, there was only a handful left of the miraculous barley-meal. But Dolma besought him not to approach the villagers, who would certainly ask him where he came from and where he was going, and why. To please her the boy gave in, though he thought it unwise to neglect the opportunity of obtaining fresh supplies.

They had often heard traders speaking of some hot springs which were to be found at the foot of the mountain, some distance from the road. They now set off in search of them, meaning to pass the night beside them, for although it was still summer, the nights are always cold in those high altitudes. The rising steam had guided them to the springs, and they sat down on the warm earth, to eat before they went to sleep. Mipam had taken the precaution of rolling two cakes of moistened meal when they had halted beside a brook during the course of the afternoon; and it was lucky that he had done so, for the sulphurous waters of the springs were far from appetizing.

'These are the last, Dolma,' he announced, as he produced the two round cakes from a corner of his mantle, which he had tied up to form a pocket. 'We shall have nothing to eat to-morrow morning, nor all day long, if we don't come to a village.'

The girl looked at him oddly.

'But . . . you know the way now, Mipam; why should we go hungry?' she said.

'What way?'

'The rock . . . just as the other morning,' she answered shyly. 'Strike it as you did in front of the lama.'

'I had nothing to do with that miracle. What do you

imagine, you silly child? That lama was a saint who took pity on us; it was his power that worked the miracle.'

'Who knows, Mipam, if it was really *he*? Perhaps he simply saw that *you* could do it: that was why he told you to strike the rock. Oh, Mipam, strike this one, too, just where it makes a great hump, like the one at the cave! Strike it, Mipam; meal will come out of it, and water as well if you want it. . . . Strike it, Mipam!'

Dolma was obsessed by the desire to see the prodigy repeated, she longed to feel that it was Mipam, and not the lama, who had performed the miracle. For the last three days she had had only this one thought, and she could contain herself no longer. She wanted to see Mipam perform a miracle!

The boy began by laughing at her too flattering opinion of him; and then, wearied a little by her stubborn insistence, simply to show her that she was wrong, he smote the rock hard with his fist. A few small drops of blood showed like beads on his skin, which he had grazed on the stone, but no stream of *tsampa* or clear water gushed from the rock. Dolma sighed dolefully, greatly disappointed, and Mipam was amazed to feel that although he had not shared his friend's faith in his magic powers, his failure had surprised and depressed him.

Very early next morning they set off again, making for the centre of the valley, in order to rejoin the track. Before they reached it another miracle occurred. On the ground, in front of him, Mipam, who was walking ahead, saw a small leather bag.

He picked it up, and he meant at once to tell Dolma of his find, but she had stopped to adjust the straps that kept up her boots, while he had gone on, and so found himself some distance ahead of her. She had not seen him pick up the bag. It was full of powdered meat.[1] Some traveller had probably lost it on his way to the springs, or coming back from them. Mipam did not fail to form some such theory of how this food had

---

[1] The Tibetans pound up dried meat in a mortar until it is reduced to powder. This powder can be diluted with water and mixed with barley meal. It constitutes a highly concentrated food and keeps indefinitely.

appeared in their path in so timely a fashion. Nevertheless, at the back of his mind another notion was stealthily emerging—the notion of a 'miracle', of gods who had come to their aid, of the goodwill of the enigmatical saint of the cave, which continued to follow them; or else something even more prodigious:

'He whose heart is filled with love for all existing beings, to him all treasures are open, and he can draw from them to his heart's content, in order to relieve their poverty.'

And again, those words that were for ever stamped upon his mind: 'You must learn to know yourself.' Who was he, then? Was he *another* than young Mipam, the son of a village headman, a clerical novice and the servant of a *gyalpo*? Could it be that he was *another* than that Mipam whom he knew so well – *another* whom he knew not at all? This bag that he held in his hand—had he brought it into being by his wish to spare Dolma the torments of hunger, and could he create, in the same way, what was needed to rid all unhappy beings of suffering?

Dolma, walking rapidly, caught him up.

'It was my straps, Mipam; they came undone. It's not that I am tired. Don't think that. I can walk as fast as you like,' she said, anxious to justify her delay.

'Look, Dolma.'

She gazed at the open bag, saw it full of powdered meat, and turned pale with emotion.

'Did you make it spring from a rock, or from the ground?' she inquired, scorning any other explanation.

'I found it, Dolma. A traveller passing this way must have dropped it.'

Dolma shook her head in token of dissent. That she did not believe, and he did not try to convince her of her mistake. He himself was not sure of what he believed.

The journey of the two fugitives was marked by nothing more of any note before they came to Shigatze, where, as they had decided, they betook themselves at once to the merchant Tsöndup, who welcomed them affectionately. After listening to the account which Dolma herself insisted on giving of the reasons which had led to their flight, the good man gravely shook his head:

'Your young friend is a plucky lad,' he said. 'He could not bear to see you ill-treated, but he's put his hand in a hornets' nest. The lord's heir knocked down with a blow of the fist and badly hurt. . . . I can see the scene from here. He deserved the lesson, the young brute, but his parents will think otherwise.'

And, turning to Mipam:

'It's no use bemoaning the past,' he said; 'what's done is done. Don't worry, my boy, no one will come and take you while you are in my house; here you are quite safe. To-morrow Dolma will return to her father. Probably he has already been informed of her disappearance, and he must be feeling anxious, not knowing where she is. By the man who accompanies her I will send a letter to the *tsongpa* (trader) Tenzig; he's an old friend of your father's, and your brother Dogyal lives with him. His advice will be helpful. In the meantime you will remain here. At the house of *aku* Tenzin you might run across some of your lord's servants, and that would complicate matters.'

Very early next morning Dolma, dressed in a pretty robe which had been lent her by Tsöndup's daughter to replace her own travel-stained clothes, and decked out anew in her jewels, bade Mipam good-bye and mounted her pony.

'Till we meet again,' she cried to her friend as she rode away. 'My father will arrange for you to come at once and study at Lhasa.'

But destiny willed otherwise.

A few days later Tsöndup's secretary, who had ridden with Dolma to Lhasa, brought back Tenzin's answer to his friend's letter.

In it he assured Mipam of his warm friendship. He was indebted to him for preventing the son of the chief from mal-treating Dolma, and as Mipam would probably be unable to re-enter his own country for a long time to come, he was going to take charge of his future. He urged the young man not to distress himself on account of the incident, which, regrettable though it was, would lead to his following a more lucrative career than would have been open to him in his own country. In common prudence, however, Mipam had better not be seen at his house in Lhasa until the prince had explicitly declared his intentions.

Tenzin also sent some money to his colleague Tsöndup, requesting him to buy some new clothes for Mipam, so that he might cut a presentable figure in a large town and among wealthy acquaintances.

When he was told the contents of this letter, Mipam experienced a certain disappointment. Still, he understood the attitude of Dolma's father. He did not want openly to defy his noble partner by refusing to deliver up the *gyalse's* aggressor if the prince should send his servants to arrest the boy.

As he said, it would be necessary to wait and see what line the prince would take after the assault upon his heir. But that would soon be known. Besides, the *gyalmo* would be coming out of retreat. She loved Dolma, and she appeared to be fond of Mipam. She knew that her eldest son was a brute: his sisters and his younger brother had often complained of him. She would doubtless try to assuage her husband's anger, and the chaplain and Kushog Yeshes Kunzang would plead for him. The *gyalpo* would probably content himself with forbidding him to resume his service with the princess; he would be banished from the palace, and perhaps from the country; and the better to ingratiate himself with his lord, the abbot of his monastery would expunge his name from the roll of his monks. What did all this amount to? His position at the palace meant nothing to him, nor did his small, unimportant monastery, where he spent only one week in the year. He would have had a happier life at Lhasa. Tenzin had said as much in his letter: the unlucky blow which he had given the *gyalse* would have the result of opening for him a more lucrative career than that of a chief's servant, or a village astrologer. Lucrative—that meant that he would earn more money, and earning money meant obtaining Dolma's hand in marriage. It was only a question of a little patience.

Mipam, heedful of Tenzin's advice, did not repine. A few days later he even felt quite happy. Dolma's father had been generous; the money which he had given his friend's secretary was amply sufficient to pay for two new costumes. One was the complete monastic costume as worn by wealthy clerics: that is, it was freely ornamented with cloth of gold, and covered with a wide mantle of very fine serge.

The other was an ecclesiastical travelling gown in dark garnet-coloured cloth, which revealed a waistcoat of gold brocade, and was fastened at the waist by a sash of the same shade of gold. The better to show his sympathy for Dolma's friend, Tsöndup added to this 'trousseau' two pairs of high boots and a hat, while Dorje, his eldest son, gave him a rosary and a lama's bowl in precious wood.

Mipam was by no means free from vanity. He had been proud of his precocious knowledge, of his ability to serve as acolyte when his uncle Shesrab officiated in the village. He was proud, also, of his ability to recite numbers of texts by heart, and of the deep bass notes which he managed to produce when he intoned them. He was proud of being loved by Dolma, and now he was proud of his fine clothes. Tall, slender, and almost as fair as a Chinaman, his face lit up by his expressive brown eyes, Mipam, though he had no mirror in which to study himself, was quite aware that he was a handsome boy.

Expressing the pious desire to visit the various temples of Tashilhumpo, Mipam donned his clerical clothes, and repaired to the great monastery, moving with measured tread, and draped in his handsome new toga, like a youthful lama of ancient lineage.

Tashilhumpo, one of the most celebrated monasteries of Tibet, the residence of the Penchen Lama—or the Tashi Lama, as foreigners call him—is also the seat of a great monastic university, renowned for the profound erudition of its professors. It lies between its enclosing walls at the foot of a steep mountain, in the immediate neighbourhood of Shigatze.

There is no lack of wealthy *tulkus*[1] among its dignitaries and its students. Mipam, however, attracted a certain amount of attention of which he was quite aware, and which he fully appreciated.

But he also noticed the magnificence of the buildings. On every side victorious emblems and gilded roofs crowned the temples, the assembly rooms, and the tombs of the Grand Lamas. Indoors the accumulation of precious objects was incredible. The place was a treasury of gold, silver and precious stones; in the very floors of some of the chapels enormous turquoises were incrusted.

How mean, compared with such magnificence, appeared the luxury which had so impressed him in the palace of his lord! How naive and foolish had he been to believe in the importance of that petty king; to believe—yes, he had really believed, in common with his fellow villagers, that there existed no power in the world greater than his! What an idiot he had been— what idiots were those among whom he had lived!

Proceeding from deduction to deduction, Mipam arrived at this logical conclusion, this revised opinion of his lord. Since, after all, the *gyalpo* was merely but a petty princeling, it followed that his power must fall very far short of what Mipam had imagined; that he had no occasion to fear the prince, whether at Shigatze or at Lhasa.

Having come to this conclusion, which at once reassured him and flattered his pride, Mipam continued his round of visits to the temples, holding his head higher than ever, draping himself still more elegantly in his fine new mantle, carelessly displaying his waistcoat of cloth of gold, and regarding everything and everybody with an expression of supreme calm and indifference and veiled arrogance in his fine brown eyes. The worthy monks took him for a young Grand Lama of importance on pilgrimage to Tashilhumpo, or recently admitted to one of

[1] Acknowledged saints or reincarnations of great lamas.

the colleges of the monastery, and saluted him deferentially. Mipam returned their greetings with a distant amiability, and when one of the monks approached and besought his blessing, he bestowed it gravely, with one hand only.

Dorje, Tsöndup's eldest son, was rather amused by the airs of importance which Mipam gave himself, but he took a great liking to him, and neglected no opportunity of making himself agreeable. He had shortly to leave for China with a caravan of merchandise, and before his departure he paid a round of visits to various notables of the town, members of the clergy or the nobility, who commissioned him to make purchases for them in China, or entrusted him with the sale of sundry goods: carpets, and pieces of cloth which they had received as gifts, or had accepted from their tenants in lieu of rent. Dorje took Mipam to see several of his wealthy clients, and in the houses of these latter the young man's opinion respecting to the poverty of the 'rich' of his country in general, and of his lord in particular, was more and more strongly confirmed.

Nevertheless, the day was drawing nigh when he would be forced to recognize that however insignificant his feudal lord might be, the latter could find the means to reach his rebellious subject and place his security in peril. Tenzin had still no news of the *gyalpo's* intentions. He dared not institute inquiries about them, even indirectly, fearing, if wind of these reached his ears, to arouse the prince's anger, which might now have abated.

An emissary of the prince had come, immediately after the young folk's escape, to inquire whether Dolma had returned home, and whether Mipam had accompanied her. The merchant had been able, at the moment, to answer both questions in the negative, and since then the *gyalpo* had given no further signs of life.

In point of fact, the *gyalpo* was distraught with troubles of a much more absorbing nature than the necessity of avenging the insult to his heir. A veritable drama was being enacted in his palace.

CHAPTER VI

SINCE the princess and her chaplain had entered their gloomy hermitage, Kushog Yeshes Kunzang had directed them in the performance of the practices which he had prescribed. To that end he communicated with them through the hatches of their cells. Through the inner door he whispered counsel, and listened to the secret confessions of his pupils, respecting their progress or their difficulties.

The period of three months fixed for their retreat would soon be over. Within ten days the two recluses would emerge from their cells. Their eyes long accustomed to pitchy darkness, could not bear the sudden return of daylight; blindness would result. The customary practice is for the master who has directed the retreat to pierce a preliminary hole in the wall of the cell. This the recluse himself enlarges by gradual degrees, and at more or less frequent intervals, according to the sensitiveness of the eyes, accustoming himself by gradual stages to endure the full light of day.

Kushog Yeshes Kunzang began this operation by making a microscopic aperture, with a long needle, in the cement that sealed the joints of the boards of each wall. This his two pupils proceeded to enlarge; then they bored more holes, and by the end of the tenth day their rooms were comparatively light.

At sunrise on the eleventh day the lama went to break the seals on their doors, and bid the two recluses come forth. A number of persons bearing gifts of different kinds were, according to custom, waiting to offer their congratulations.

With all due solemnity, as on the day when he had imprisoned them, making mysterious gestures, and uttering in portentous tones words which he alone understood, Kushog

Yeshes Kunzang set his captives free. First the princess and then the chaplain emerged, moving with uncertain steps after the long period of immobility in their restricted lodging; a little dazed, and tolerably dirty: they hadn't washed for three months.

They were hoisted on to their horses; the prince's musicians beat a roll on their drums, and drew from their hautboys plaintive and stridulous discords; then, still playing their instruments, they set off at the head of a procession, in which the central figures were Kushog Yeshes Kunzang and his two temporary disciples, whom he led back to the palace to enjoy a special banquet.

Valuable gifts, manifestations of gratitude on the part of the lady and the chaplain, awaited the lama. His attendants took possession of them, in order to pack them in their master's luggage, and the *naljorpa* notified the prince of his intention of leaving him two days later, in order to continue his journey to Kang Tise, the sacred mountain.

The *naljorpa's* two attendant disciples took the opportunity of this day spent in the palace to gather fuller information from the chief's servants as to the circumstances which had led to their friend Mipam's flight. The monk who had given him lessons in grammar took advantage of a moment when he could exchange a few words in private with his master, and begged him to intercede in the fugitive's favour. The lama declined to interfere.

'It is useless,' he replied. 'The boy has a path to pursue; obstacles must not be placed in his way. I would willingly have taken him with me, but causes of great cogency are carrying him elsewhere. Let him go where he ought to be.'

The monk had not insisted, but that evening, as he rode in silence behind the sorrel horse which carried the lama back to his chalet in the woods, he meditated on the meaning of that cryptic declaration, and fervently hoped that the 'path' which his sympathetic pupil was pursuing might prove to be a fortunate one.

The next day was taken up with the preparations for

departure, and at dawn on the third day the mules carrying the lama's luggage were loaded up, and he himself came out of his room, dressed for a journey. The chaplain and the *gyalpo's* secretary, with two servants in attendance, had arrived before daybreak to escort the master *naljorpa* for the space of a few hours, as courtesy demanded. A third servant of the *gyalpo's* held the head of the sorrel horse, with its beautiful silver-incrusted saddle. Kushog Yeshes Kunzang motioned to him to bring the animal to the foot of the steps where he was standing ready to mount. The man hesitated. Opening his lips to say something, and closing them without having spoken, he mutely questioned the chaplain and the secretary, who looked away in embarrassment. Meanwhile one of the lama's servants snatched the bridle from the man's hand and led the horse to his master.

The travellers did not follow the steep path by which Mipam and Dolma had fled; they made their way to the main road,[1] which they reached by dropping down from the clearing in which the deserted hermitages stood. After this they rode at leisure, climbing to the high tablelands, leaving behind them the verdant valleys and the crystal-clear torrents. A little before midday the lama gave orders to halt. The beasts were unloaded, the provisions unpacked, the tea-kettle placed on three large stones over a wood fire, and all began to eat. The meal over, the chaplain and the secretary, each with the ceremonial scarf in hand, went up to the lama to take their leave of him, wishing him a good journey and receiving his benediction. Yeshes Kunzang blessed them graciously, passed another scarf round the neck of each, and made his way toward the sorrel horse. The same servant who had held the beast's bridle that morning had grasped it again. Before the lama could reach him, the secretary, respectfully bent double, intervened, another unfolded scarf spread over his two hands.

---

[1] The main road (*lam chen*) is a mere track, not practicable for wheeled traffic, but more frequented by horsemen and muleteers with beasts of burden than the other mountain paths.

'Kushog,' he said, in some embarrassment, 'with your permission we are taking the *gyalpo's* horse back with us.'

'Which horse?' asked the lama. 'You are of course taking back your horses.'

'Kushog, I mean the sorrel horse which the *gyalpo* lent you.'

'Lent!' thundered Kushog Yeshes Kunzang. 'You've taken leave of your senses; the *gyalpo* gave me this horse. Is that, think you, too big a gift in recognition of the honour I did him in being his guest?'

The luckless secretary, charged with so delicate a mission, backed toward the chaplain, seeking his support, but the latter pretended not to understand him.

One of the lama's men cut the discussion short by snatching the horse's bridle, as he had done at their departure, from the prince's groom, and led the animal to the lama, who forthwith mounted and rode away, followed by his little troop, leaving the others petrified.

Their return to the palace was a mournful one; the secretary was only too well aware of the kind of welcome he would get from his lord, and the chaplain, though counting on his office as one of the clergy to mitigate the prince's anger, felt none too comfortable.

Everything happened exactly as they had foreseen. When his secretary announced that he had not brought back the sorrel horse, the chief overwhelmed him with insults; he sent for the chaplain and reproached him with not having profited by his position as Yeshes Kunzang's disciple to make the latter listen to reason; he next inflicted a heavy fine on the three unhappy servants who had accompanied them, and lastly, with various threatening expressions, he bade the secretary set out before dawn next morning to overtake the lama, and recover the sorrel horse.

A few hours later, by the light of a waning moon, the stricken secretary once more left the palace, escorted by two servants. All three had sturdy mounts, and hoped to overtake the lama, who was compelled to travel by short stages, owing to the slow progress of the mules carrying his baggage.

Despite their efforts, they came in sight of the lama's little convoy only after they had passed the frontier of the *gyalpo's* territories. Yeshes Kunzang himself, with his disciples, his secretary, his steward and one servant, had ridden on ahead. It was close upon nightfall when they overtook him, at a spot where he was preparing to camp, near a small farm. The horses of the six travellers were already put up in the stables.

The secretary found it difficult to begin negotiating. The master *naljorpa* inspired him with dread; he believed him capable, if irritated of raising against him certain deities, his special protectors, who would not suffer their faithful servant to be worried or provoked. And failing such deities, or in addition to them, Kushog Yeshes Kunzang could enlist in his service certain invisible but dangerously active demons which he had tamed and enslaved. A great *naljorpa* has considerable magic powers at his disposal, both for helping his friends and for harassing his enemies. With beads of sweat pearling his brow, the secretary came forward, bending lower than ever, presenting, unrolled, a wide silk scarf.

'I see,' said the lama, with condescension; 'you are bringing me your lord's excuses for your imbecility yesterday in asking me to return the horse which he gave me. He has also en-trusted you with a present to accompany his excuses?'

This last remark sounded more like an affirmation than a question.

The secretary felt more and more uncomfortable. Another present indeed! He had to recover the sorrel horse.

'Most honourable, sir,' he began, 'the prince thinks you are labouring under an illusion. His intention was simply to allow you to use the horse while you were his guest; now he wishes you to restore it to him. . . . I have to take it back with me to-morrow morning. . . .'

'Enough of this!' cried the lama, haughtily and finally dis-missing the matter. 'The horse was given to me. I shall not return it. Not that I have any real need of it. I have a score of horses in my stables, in Kham, that are vastly superior to it, and, as you have seen, those I have been travelling with are of no little value; but a lama must not return to a layman the present which the latter has given him. That would imply a lack of charity toward him, for all manner of misfortunes would follow such a restitution. I am afraid that the insistence which your *gyalpo* has shown in wanting to take back the horse he has given me may even now be followed by vexatious consequences for him. As for you, be prudent, and avoid those which might overtake you if you were to persist in furthering his guilty intentions.'

Having delivered this little lecture, the lama entered the farmhouse where he was to sup, and the secretary was left face to face with the peasantry, who had come out to hear the conversation, and were regarding him with hostile looks.

To urge the lama any further to restore the animal was futile, and any attempt to recover it by brute force was utterly impracticable. Over and above the members of the lama's suite, there were on the farmstead a dozen men accustomed to guarding the yaks in the wilds, and skilled in throwing the lasso. If, in the face of all probability, he succeeded in getting the animal out of the walled courtyard and making off with it, the stalwart horsemen who lived on the farm would soon fling their lassos round him, drag him to the ground, and recapture the horse. Furthermore, he had been informed by his colleague, Yeshes Kunzang's secretary, that the *naljorpa* was going on the following day to pay a visit to a Grand Lama, the head of a neighbouring monastery. The farmhouse was on the lama's estate, where he had the right of administering justice, and the lama could have him beaten for attempted theft. There was nothing to be done, absolutely nothing. The poor secretary spent the night in tears beside a little camp-fire which his servants had lit at some distance from the lama's encampment.

And the following day, at sunrise, he saw Kushog Yeshes

Kunzang, surrounded by his suite, ride away and vanish from sight, mounted on the sorrel horse, now lost to the *gyalpo* for ever.

The prince's rage, on receiving his secretary's report, was past all imagining. His roars of fury made such an uproar in the palace that one might have thought there was a tiger imprisoned there.

The secretary was thrown into prison, and informed that, by way of a fine he must forthwith furnish two sorrel horses of equal value to the one he had failed to get back from the lama.

Any further attempts in that direction would have been useless. Kushog Yeshes Kunzang, as he pursued his journey, would be under the protection of the governors of the forts of the Tsang province, who would regard the complaints of a petty *gyalpo* as of very trifling moment. The ex-proprietor of the sorrel horse cherished no illusion on that score. Nevertheless, he did not renounce his hopes of vengeance. When one is unable to achieve one's end openly, there are other means of getting one's way, and the best of these is magic. Now, among his subjects, there was a *Bön* (a follower of the ancient religion of Tibet) who passed for an expert in the magic art; he was the man the *gyalpo* wanted. He had him summoned.

'I want to be avenged,' he said, when the *Bön* stood before him. 'To be avenged on someone who has done me wrong and laughs in my face. It is said that you have demons in your service. Can you send them to injure my enemy?'

Before he was ushered into his lord's room, the sorcerer had already gathered from the gossip of the servants the whole story of the sorrel horse. He feigned, however, not to know who it was against whom the prince wished to employ his services.

'Send demons to attack an enemy! That I can do, my chief,' he replied; 'but just as it is among men—as some are of inferior rank, with only a limited power, while others are important personages, and very influential—so it is among beings of another order. I can command certain of these as their master; there are others whose aid I must implore. And according to the personality of your enemy, the quality of the demons to be launched against him differs. Who is it?'

'Haven't you heard about it?—That lama *naljorpa* who was my guest, and whom I loaded with presents, has stolen my handsome sorrel horse. . . . He must be punished. . . .'

'Oh! Oh!' said the sorcerer, biting his lips and frowning. 'Attack a great *naljorpa* . . . that's a serious matter. Take my advice; give up the idea.'

'I want none of your advice,' replied the prince. 'If you can't be of any use to me, get you gone; I'll apply to someone more capable.'

'You'll find no one more capable than I, my chief,' retorted the sorcerer. 'I only wished to warn you. If you persist in your idea, I must needs implore the help of the most powerful demons. Power must be pitted against power. A *naljorpa*, a master of magic, mustn't be attacked by feeble *mi-ma-yins*.[1] And what chastisement do you desire to inflict on him who has offended you and robbed you of your property? Is it death?'

The *Bön* put this question in sinister tones, and his eyes plumbed the *gyalpo's* heart.

The prince shuddered.

'No,' he exclaimed, 'no, not death!'

'A very serious illness? An accident? . . .'

'An accident . . . yes. . . .'

'A serious one . . . you mean? . . .'

'Serious . . . hmm. . . .'

When it came to furnishing him with precise details, the prince felt ill at ease. Plotting against *naljorpas* is a dangerous game to play. They often know from a distance what plot is afoot against them. It sometimes amused the prince to make fun of what was said on the subject; nevertheless, he was now beginning to feel afraid.

[1] Literally, 'not-men'. Beings inferior to man, and of whom, according to the Tibetans, there exist a great number of various kinds.

'Couldn't the accident concern his property?' he asked the sorcerer. 'His horses, for instance; couldn't they be stolen? Or his baggage could fall into the water on crossing a river. He has stolen a horse of mine; if he were despoiled of all that he has with him, that, I think, would be sufficient punishment.'

'Very well, chief,' was the *Bön's* laconic reply. 'You will give your steward orders to provide me with an ox that I shall need.'

'I will speak to him this very evening.'

'And I'll set to work to-morrow morning.'

The interview at an end, the *Bön* went to the kitchen for some beer. Though he might observe the utmost discretion as regards the conversation he had had with his lord, the fact that the latter had summoned him was sufficiently explicit; the report spread apace in the palace and its precincts that the prince wished to send demons against Kushog Yeshes Kunzang, and all, fearing a catastrophe, trembled with fear.

Two days later the sorcerer took the ox which they had brought him to the foot of a tree. There he offered up the life of the animal to the demon whose help he was imploring; he slew, skinned, and dismembered the sacrifice, and finally, with the help of an acolyte, he carried the flesh and the bloody hide to a shed at some distance from the palace, which had been placed at his disposal. The *Böns*, who profess an ancient religion that existed in Tibet before the conversion of its inhabitants to Buddhism, are not allowed to celebrate their shamanist rites, which include blood sacrifices, near any lamaist temple, and there was a temple in the palace.

In this shed, in absolute secrecy, the sorcerer drew on the hide of the ox the terrible face of the being whom he had evoked. Round this he placed, in a particular order, the various parts of the animal: the head and heart in the centre, the uncoiled intestines framing the whole, and forming what is called the 'wall' of the magic circle. He chanted various incantations before these sinister offerings; then, at nightfall, he retired to the house where he was lodged, for the time being, at the *gyalpo's* orders. During the night the demon was to come and sniff the odour of blood and feed on the subtle substance of the victim. The next morning the sorcerer would know, by the evidence of certain signs, whether the rite had been effective.

The morning dawned, damp and cool, after a night of rain; the sorcerer repaired to the shed. A pool of mud lay in front of the door, and the ground beneath it had been scooped out in several places by the paws of animals. Already perturbed by these suspicious traces of outside intervention, the *Bön* opened the door, and uttered a cry of terror. Of the offerings placed there the evening before, nothing was left but some shapeless remnants. Some dogs, having tunnelled under the door, had entered the shed and regaled themselves on the sacrifice. The large bones, completely stripped of all meat, littered the ground; the hide on which the magic face was traced had been torn to pieces, and partly devoured; on one glutinous fragment, which adhered to the bottom of the wall, the sorcerer could distinguish one of the fantastic eyes of the face which he had drawn, and this horrible eye, besmeared with blood, seemed to hold him with its gaze.

The being whom he had invoked had been vanquished in the fight. Without the shadow of a doubt, Yeshes Kunzang, duly warned by his powers of clairvoyance or his invisible protectors, had punished him. The dogs were but instruments chosen and animated by his will. Had they even been actual dogs belonging to our own world? . . . Now the anger that he, a sorry and foolhardy sorcerer, had aroused in the demon who was to have attacked the lama would assuredly rebound against him who had incited the demon to that deadly conflict. Had he not reason also to fear the anger of the master *naljorpa*, who knew what he had plotted against him?—In these calculations the luckless *Bön* forgot to reckon with a third personage who was more to be dreaded than the demon or the *naljorpa*, seeing that he was nearer.

Immersed in these painful reflections, he did not hear the

123

approach of the *gyalpo*, whom anxiety had robbed of his sleep, and who was eager to make certain, in the early hours of the morning, that the sorcerer had begun to perform the rites. Hearing neither the beat of the drum nor the sound of incantations, and seeing the open door, the prince came forward. If stupefaction had wrested a cry from the *Bön*, it was a veritable howl that the chief emitted when he saw the remains at which the sorcerer was still staring with terrified eyes.

The prince was a big and vigorous man; the sorcerer was old, frail, and feeble. His lord seized him brutally by one arm, threw him to the ground, and overwhelmed him with kicks and curses.

'Ah! you wretched good-for-nothing, so this is your power, is it? Idiot! ignoramus! How did you dare to pretend to my face that you knew all about these rites! . . . Take this, you beast! and that!' And he continued to kick him.

At the clamour he was making, some of the servants ran up, and they too never doubted that the lama *naljorpa* had caused the manœuvres directed against him to miscarry. Their master's brutality to the sorcerer increased their terror the more. Less powerful than Kushog Yeshes Kunzang though he was, the *Bön* nevertheless had many ways of avenging himself on those who injured him. What would happen to the *gyalpo*, and to them, his servants, whom the sorcerer might include in the punishment inflicted on their master? They cried and wept, while the maid-servants prostrated themselves and nothing was heard but cries of 'Have pity, chief! Be merciful, our lord!' But not one of them dared to interfere between the prince and the pitiable sorcerer.

At length the prince, tired of kicking his victim, left the shed. Several of the men thereupon hastened to pick up the *Bön*. Leading him away, they made him sit down, and the women brought him beer and tea.

The man drank in silence, rested awhile, and then got up. He thanked those who had helped him, and rising to his full height, he gazed in the direction of the palace as he uttered these words:

'I see misfortune hastening toward you, chief. You had an adversary; now you have an adversary and an enemy.'

And he went his way before those about him could utter a word; they were dumb with terror.

The chief re-entered his chamber while the news that the *Bön's* offerings had been destroyed, reported by the servants, was spread through the palace. One of her chambermaids told the princess about it, and a small boy in the chaplain's service lost no time in bringing his master the news.

Neither the princess nor the chaplain had yet recovered from the effects of their retreat. With their minds still benumbed by their long inactivity in the darkness, and absorbed in making an inventory of the results of their seclusion, they had paid little attention to what was happening outside their respective apartments. The *gyalmo* was fully satisfied with having been a *tshams-pa*,[1] and she considered that this fact would greatly increase the consideration which she enjoyed—or believed that she enjoyed. The report that she was applying herself to devotions of such a lofty character, might, she believed, come to the ears of those in Lhasa, and at this agreeable fancy she smiled with pleasure.

The chaplain was absorbed in less comforting reflections. He did not see that the arduous retreat to which he had submitted, and the humility which he had been obliged to display before Yeshes Kunzang, had in any way brought him nearer to his intended goal, which was to acquire the power of remaining seated in the air without support, nor, for that matter, of working any other miracle. After the scene which the *gyalpo* had made in respect of the sorrel horse he had kept to his rooms, sulking and chewing the cud of his mortification.

He did not quite understand what his little servant had told him, but apparently the incident was serious, one that concerned the *gyalpo*. He was about to go and make inquiries

[1] Recluse.

when a lad sent by his lady was ushered into his room. The princess requested him to visit her at once.

He found her bathed in tears. She had lost no time in summoning to her presence the people most likely to be well informed, and collecting the information which they had gathered. The upshot of it was that her husband had charged a *Bön* to offer a sacrifice, and that the sacrifice had been spoiled by an adversary. She asked herself, what could be the object of this sacrifice? The chaplain guessed.

'It's about the sorrel horse,' he told her. 'The chief cannot forgive Kushog Yeshes Kunzang for having kept it, and he asked this sorcerer to send a demon against him to punish him.'

'O gods!' exclaimed the wife of the chief, 'we are lost! The idea of pitting that sorcerer against a magician like Kushog Yeshes Kunzang! He knew at once what the *gyalpo* was meditating, and he had the demon conjured up by the *Bön* seized and slain. How are we going to escape his wrath?' And her tears flowed faster than ever.

'The prince,' said the chaplain, 'must at once send a messenger with presents to Kushog Yeshes Kunzang and implore his pardon. You must make him realize that this is the only way to avert some terrible misfortune.'

'I'll go and see him,' the *gyalmo* replied. 'My children will come with me, and you also, Kushog chaplain.'

The latter would dearly have liked to shirk this duty, but he could not. The lady had hastily sent for a box full of scarves and had distributed them to her children, who had come to her room out of curiosity, hoping to learn the fresh details of the drama which was perturbing all the inmates of the palace. She handed a scarf to the chaplain also.

'Let us go!' she said, and they all set off in single file. As the procession advanced along the corridors, officials of the prince's house, for whom the lady had sent, hurried up and fell in; while servants encountered on the way followed behind, eager to learn what their masters were going to say and do.

The whole party arrived at the *gyalpo's* apartment, and while the 'quality' followed the princess, the servants, men and women, remained, all ears, outside the door.

The chief seated in his high seat, was playing dice with one of his cronies. He looked in amazement at his wife and the people with her. All bowed very low. The *gyalmo* presented a scarf to her husband, after which her children, and the other persons who had accompanied her, hung their scarves on the edge of the table which stood before the prince. The lady then signed to the chaplain to come forward.

'Explain everything to the chief,' she said.

The chaplain would gladly have been elsewhere, even in the dark and narrow cell of the hermitage where he had been so uncomfortable. Nevertheless, he began a little speech. To begin with, he diplomatically expressed the regret which they all felt for the failure of the sacrifice ordered by the *gyalpo*. It went against the grain to say this, for in his capacity as a member of the clergy it was his duty to detest and oppose all sorcery and blood sacrifices. He then came to the object of his visit. There was reason to believe that Kushog Yeshes Kunzang was incensed. To incur the peril of his wrath might be disastrous to the prince and his family. Would it not be expedient to do something to placate him?

What was to be done the prince gave him no time to explain. He rose up on his throne, and with a furious exclamation he put a stop to further parleying.

'Get you gone! Get you gone, all of you! You insult me by siding with the man who has robbed and outraged me. Get you gone!'

The lady wept, her daughters moaned, the men appealed in vague tones for pity, and all bowed low; the lay officials hat in hand, the chaplain and the other monks, the sacristans of the temple, by holding out their cloaks in the form of wings or fins.

'You go and ask your father to listen to Kushog chaplain,' said the *gyalmo*, pushing her eldest son forward.

127

The young man shot a vicious glance at her, advanced toward his father, and then turned round and looked the suppliants in the face.

'The chief is right,' he said. 'This lama has offended him, and has robbed him. You are foolish and insolent when you ask your lord to beg his pardon. Dogs ate the meat left in the shed. That's quite natural; there was no need for the lama's intervention. Have you never heard of dogs entering into a room where meat is kept and eating it? It's quite a common occurrence. Kushog Yeshes Kunzang had nothing to do with what happened. The idiot of a Bön ought to have foreseen that the smell of blood would attract the dogs; he ought to have spent the night in the shed, or have got someone else to do so. Don't worry the chief any more!'

The boy was eighteen, and resembled his father in looks, promising to be equally vigorous and handsome. As a rule he was inclined to be taciturn and unconcerned; his resolute attitude now surprised them all and delighted the prince. The lady realized that it would be useless to insist any longer, and withdrew, followed by the others. As the chaplain was about to pass through the door, the gyalpo called him back, and signing to him to take a seat on a cushion set before the throne, he addressed him thus:

'Kushog chaplain, in respect of the attitude which you adopted just now, you were no doubt acting under the orders of her ladyship. We'll say no more about it; of course, it was ridiculous. The lama had nothing to do with the dogs getting into the shed. I was wrong to apply to that ignorant old sorcerer. You know Kushog Zangkar the ngagspa.[1] He lives three days' ride from here, on the borders of the Dugyul.[2] To-morrow you will come to fetch the presents which will be duly prepared for him, and you will take them to him from me, with a request on my part that he will come here with every-

---

[1] Magician.

[2] Dugyul—the indigenous name of the small Himalayan state called Bhutan on the maps, a country distinct from Tibet, having its own king.

thing necessary for performing the rite which kills. I don't want to hear any more from you. Take two servants to look after you on your way.'

And he dismissed the chaplain.

The mission entrusted to the latter was not at all to his liking. He considered that occult ties existed between Kushog Yeshes Kunzang and himself, as is always the case, according to the general belief, between a teacher of mystical science or esoteric knowledge and the pupil who has placed himself, even for a short time, under his spiritual guidance. He, as the *naljorpa's* disciple, owed him the utmost respect, and absolute devotion. The chaplain was aware of the beliefs of the clergy in this connection, and fully shared them. He told himself that he would do better to disappear, and avoid the complicity imposed upon him by his lord. But leaving the country meant giving up his comfortable life in the palace; it meant also abandoning all the property—land, houses and valuables— which he possessed in the *gyalpo's* territory, and becoming, in some distant monastery, an obscure and poverty-stricken monk. The distressed chaplain felt unable to face such disaster.

In the course of the following week he returned with the magician, who was accompanied by one of his disciples and a clerical servant. As soon as they caught sight of him, all the inmates of the palace understood what had brought him.

The chief's resentment was by no means appeased; on the contrary. His eldest son had taken it into his head that Kushog Yeshes Kunzang had covered Mipam's flight by finding him a place of refuge. This was his explanation of the fact that Mipam had not returned to his father, nor had he gone to Tenzin, in Lhasa. The *gyalpo* was now of the same opinion, which made one grievance the more to those which he already cherished. As for the young prince, his desire for vengeance was not satisfied by the punishment inflicted on Mipam's father Puntsog. The hapless headman, all guiltless as he was of his son's fit of anger, had not only been deprived of his office, but his cattle and more than half of his property had been confiscated to the benefit of the prince. More than by the loss of her possessions, the good Changpal was greatly distressed at being still without news of Mipam. What had become of him, her youngest-born, whose childhood had been attended by such prodigies? Was he travelling in the train of the lama-*naljorpa*, as was currently reported? Was he ill or dead? Would she ever know?

In his twofold quality of Mipam's teacher and uncle, the astrologer Shesrab had also been victimized by the *gyalpo's* anger. Though penalized in a much lesser degree than Puntsog, he had been compelled to sell a plot of land, and some of his wife's jewels, in order to meet the fine inflicted on him by the prince. Pema, denuded of her ornaments by her husband, without having had any say in the matter, refused to be consoled for their loss. Therein she found a cause of bitter recrimination, and the existence of the married pair, formerly a peaceful one, was now envenomed by endless bickering. Forgetful of the liberal fees which he had received from Mipam's father, the astrologer never tired of reproaching the latter for having entrusted him with the upbringing of a boy who was destined to cause him such bitter mortification.

As soon as the magician arrived, the *gyalpo* explained what was expected of him. He wished him to celebrate a *dubthab tagpo* in order to bring about the death of an enemy.

Though he affected to consider, with his eldest son, that failure of the *Bön's* sacrifice was merely the work of dogs attracted by the smell of meat, the incident had in reality made a powerful impression on the prince. Actually, in common with his wife and the chaplain, he saw in it the hand of Kushog Yeshes Kunzang. His problem was now, not merely to avenge himself for a wrong which he had suffered, by causing, in his turn, some injury to the person who had wronged him, but also to put himself out of the reach of an enemy who was a past master in magic. Having once been informed of what had been plotted against him, the lama-

naljorpa would not forgive him. So long as Yeshes Kunzang lived, his security and that of his family and property would be perpetually in jeopardy. One thing alone, the lama's death, could give him back his peace of mind. This being the case, the *gyalpo* had decided that a lethal rite should be performed.

The Jowo[1] Zangkar, when the *gyalpo* had laconically expressed his desire, asked various questions relating to Yeshes Kunzang, and learnt all the details of the lama's sojourn on the little plateau among the woods. He asked to be taken there, when he shut himself up for several hours in the chalet which the lama had occupied. On his return to the palace he formulated his requirements. Of these the most important was the construction, on that plateau, of a stone hut of triangular shape. The walls were to be very thick, with deep foundations, and the roof was to consist of large flat stones resting on a few strong beams. When the magician entered the hut to perform the final rite—for which seven days were needed—the door was to be walled up behind him. One small opening would be left, to allow of the passage of the enchanted arrow whose invisible double would strike the prescribed victim full in the heart.

The chief's son—who would be reminded all his life, by an ugly scar, of his fall on the rocky path, the result of a blow from Mipam's fist—wanted the rite to be directed against his aggressor also, so that he too might perish together with the *naljorpa*. When, however, he expressed his desire, the magician looked at him sternly and told him to hold his peace. The chief having summoned him, he had consented to lend him his aid, but he would lend it to the chief alone. The notion of trying to make such a rite answer a twofold purpose was absurd, and offensive to the deities to be invoked.

The Jowo Zangkar, a native of the Dugyul, was not a subject of the *gyalpo*; and he took a high hand with him, having nothing to fear from the prince, but rather exacting his respect. It was clear to the prince that if he wanted the Jowo to perform the

[1] Jowo—lord. A courtesy title given to some lamas, especially to anchorites.

rite, he must avoid provoking him. He apologized for his son, attributing his request to his ignorance of such rites, and the magician withdrew.

Only initiates are acquainted with the rites which are practised in the type of hut which the magician had ordered to be built, but every Tibetan knows what purpose they serve. As soon as they were told what kind of work was expected of them, the labourers who had received *gyalpo's* orders tried to evade the task. To build such a hut was disquieting enough in itself, but after all that had passed the identity of the person against whom the rites would be directed was no secret to any of the inmates of the palace, and the labourers had been informed of the facts as soon as they arrived on the scene. These poor mountain folk trembled with terror at the thought that they would be furnishing, by their exertions, one of the necessary elements of a scheme levelled at the life of a famous lama-*naljorpa*, who, without a shadow of doubt, was the possessor of formidable occult powers. It was to their death that they were being sent. Hoping to be spared a task of so dangerous a nature, they endeavoured to enlist the support of the steward and the chaplain successively. Both shared the belief of those who were imploring their assistance; they sympathized with them, but declared themselves powerless to countermand the *gyalpo's* orders. The *gyalmo* refused to see the workmen, for she realized that she was powerless; neither she nor anyone else could persuade her husband to renounce his vengeance. The young prince, to whom they then appealed, responded with mingled mockery and threats. Their death mattered little to him, he said: they were of no great value, and as he numbered many of their kind among his subjects, his loss would be negligible.

Two of the peasants fled. One of them was recaptured in the forest; he was beaten, and went mad; the other, more fortunate, got away, and was seen no more.

.   .   .   .   .

The hut was completed in ten days. Inside, it was merely a narrow cell, not long enough even to allow the inmate to lie at full length. The celebrants of lethal rites do not actually sleep during the week of their seclusion. They content themselves with drowsing from time to time, while remaining seated with crossed legs.

When the workmen had retired, the magician took up his quarters, together with his disciple and his servant, in the chalet previously occupied by the lama, and all were forbidden to go near the clearing, in the centre of which, close to the chalet, the triangular hut had been constructed.

Before leaving the palace, in which he had hitherto been lodged, the Jowo Zangkar had a final interview with his host. He asked him whether he still persisted in his desire to see the rite performed. To this the *gyalpo* answered in the affirmative, and then questioned the magician as to whether he had no further need of anything. Would he not need some article that had belonged to the lama? Unfortunately he could not provide him with a garment, nor with even a piece of a garment which the latter had worn; Yeshes Kunzang had left nothing behind on his departure.

With an air of contemptuous superiority, the Jowo Zangkar scouted any such suggestion. 'Such accessories are useful to those whose personal powers are feeble,' he said; 'for my part, I have no need of them.'

The chief saw that he was escorted with due honours as far as the top of the path that led to the clearing. There the magician dismissed those who had accompanied him, and shut himself up in the chalet. With his disciple's help he made a quantity of *tormas* (ritual cakes) of varying shapes and sizes. Into some of these Zangkar had to introduce the energy emanating from the magicians of the spiritual line of masters and disciples to which he belonged; into others, the powers of his gods, and of the genii in touch with him. In the central *torma*, triangular in shape, Mahakala, that mysterious being, the destructive force evoked by the magician, would be

incorporated against his will, and would be delivered only after
he had consented to animate the arrow whose invisible flight,
tracing a furrow in the ether, was to strike the specified victim.

All these cakes were placed in the hut by Zangkar's disciple,
on the flat stones which served as an altar.

Finally, the Jowo Zangkar, provided with food and drink,
entered his more than half underground cell, and his disciple,
with the servant's help, walled up its entrance. The disciple
then retired to the chalet, where he had to repeat, without
ceasing, certain protective magic formulae, in order to ward
off the adverse forces which might hamper his master's work,
and to defend him from the anger of Mahakala, who would
not fail to resist the constraint laid upon him, when he was
induced to enter the hut and creep into the *torma* in
which he was to be imprisoned. Whenever the disciple was
obliged to cease his recitation for a moment, in order to eat
and drink, the magician's attendant, who belonged to the
clergy, would take his place. Such protection is indispensable;
for those who practise these rites are exposed to grave and
even mortal dangers if their power of concentration flags, or if
they have not acquired, in the course of their initiation,
sufficient strength to oppose the entities or occult energies
which they attract to themselves.

To curb the impatience which devoured him, and to assuage
the disappointment of being forbidden to approach the spot
where the rite was being performed, the *gyalpo* went off shooting.
He would return, he had decided, on the day when the rite
was completed, and on the following day he would learn from
the Jowo Zangkar if the signs indicating the efficacy of the rite
had appeared. The prince, quite ignorant in the matter, had
not the faintest idea of what these signs might be; he had
heard it said, however, that the head of the slain enemy would
be seen in the midst of the *tormas*, or that blood would flow
from these, announcing his death.

The young prince, who was sulking, declined his father's

ༀ ཉི་འདོན་ཆར་འབེབས་མགོན་དཀར་མཚོན་ལ་དགོ །

GOM KAR, White Mahakala

invitation to go shooting with him. He did not like the chief's attitude toward the magician. He considered that his father ought not to have placed such blind confidence in him. It was necessary, he thought, that some object which had often been in contact with the man they wanted to kill, or some particle of him—a few hairs, or nail-parings—should be used in the celebration of the rite; everyone knew that. Yet the Jowo Zangkar had declared that he could do without them. Was this really because he had faith in his special powers, or else, being afraid to attack them aster-*naljorpa*, did he mean to trick the *gyalpo* by simulating a rite which he knew would be inefficacious?

The young man pondered the matter at length. He greatly resented the abrupt manner in which the magician had rebuffed him when he had asked that the death of his aggressor should be included in the scope of the rite. On the eve of the day on which Zangkar was to bring the rite to a conclusion by shooting an arrow from the opening in the hut, an idea occurred to him.

The act of releasing the arrow was, after all, he considered, the principal and absolutely essential part of the rite. All that the magician might secretly perform in his hut hinged on the arrow; that was the instrument of death. If he could contrive that the arrow should strike and transpierce some object belonging to the lama, the latter would infallibly die: and the same thing applied to Mipam. From that moment his mind was made up. He possessed nothing that had belonged to the lama, save a scarf that Yeshes Kunzang had given him on his departure. The *naljorpa* had held the scarf in his hand for some time before slipping it round the young man's neck. Would that suffice? He was not sure, but he had nothing better, and at all events, it could only reinforce the action of the magician, if he was sincere, and it would render it efficacious, without his knowledge, if he wasn't. In Mipam's case, there was no difficulty. After his flight his blankets and one of his waistcoats had been brought back to the palace.

That waistcoat was just what he wanted. He knew where to find it, wrapped up with the blankets, in a corner of the pantry, adjoining the princess's room, where, when he lived in the palace, Mipam had kept his belongings.

At nightfall the young prince, making a detour through the wood, in order to avoid passing close to the hut and the chalet, bent his steps to the edge of the clearing. He could see, like a point of fire glowing in the dark, the light shining through the little opening in the wall of the hut, in which an altar lamp was burning. That light supplied him with an unfailing pointer, in calculating the direction of the arrow which the magician would shoot from his cell. In a direct line with it he discovered a bush in which he placed, fully outspread among the leaves, the lama's scarf and Mipam's waistcoat. No obstacle lay in the path of the arrow; it must inevitably go through the bush and pierce the fine silken scarf and the waistcoat which it covered. The foliage of the bush, and some high tufts of grass, completely hid them from view.

Having completed these arrangements, the young prince returned to the palace.

Late in the afternoon of the following day he again betook himself, by a roundabout path, to the place where he had stopped the night before. He knew that the arrow would be shot at dusk, and that the Jowo's disciple and servants would immediately demolish the wall that closed the entrance of the hut. While they were thus engaged, he would have plenty of time to see if the arrow had hit the scarf and the waistcoat, to remove them quickly, and return unseen to the palace. It was already growing dark under the trees, and the darkness would facilitate his movements.

The young man, hidden in the thicket, waited for the sun to set. From his hiding-place his eye could sweep the whole extent of the small bare plateau on which stood the sinister triangular hut. This flat piece of ground terminated, at the further end, in a sudden fall of the ground, in perpendicular rocks free of vegetation, and this gap among the trees allowed him to follow the progress of the sun as it dropped toward another chain of mountains, which, at a greater distance, closed the horizon. The moment arrived. The young man crept cautiously out of the undergrowth, and approached the edge of the wood, taking care to keep to one side, out of range of the arrow; then, with his eyes fixed upon the faintly gleaming point which marked the opening through which the missile would leave the hut, he waited. The last ray of sunlight faded; the glowing orb had just been swallowed up in the distance, amidst the crests of the wooded mountains; the *gyalse*, trembling with emotion, moved a step forward in order to obtain a better view. The arrow leapt forth, to encounter a sudden squall, and driven out of its course by the wind, it pierced the young man to the heart. He uttered a cry, and fell dead.

His cry was heard by the disciple and the servant, who were standing one on either side of the hut, ready to rescue their master from his prison as soon as the arrow had been released. They ran in the direction whence the cry had come, and quickly discovered the *gyalse's* body.

Terrified, they returned to the hut, shouting the frightful tidings, and while they hastily demolished the wall which held the Jowo Zangkar prisoner, they repeated their news to him; but no answer came from his lips.

At last the opening became wide enough to allow of their passage. The magician's disciple entered.. Illuminated by the little altar lamp, he saw his master seated with crossed legs, motionless, with dilated eyes: and on his throat were blackish bruises, the marks of a giant hand that had strangled him.

CHAPTER VII

SEATED in his shop, which was crowded with bales of merchandise ready to be carried to China, Tsöndup, with puckered brow, read and re-read a long letter which a messenger of his friend Tenzin had just brought him.

Tenzin informed him that a search was being made for Mipam by an official of Lhasa, a relation of the prince whose son the boy had struck. This functionary's secretary had come to him to seek for news of the fugitive, and having been unable to obtain any reliable information, had announced that his chief would set inquiries on foot in various places where Mipam might possibly be hiding.

At the same time Tenzin told him of the tragic events which had occurred in the *gyalpo's* family in the wake of his attempts to bring about the death of Yeshes Kunzang. He had learnt of these from the secretary, who had come to see him, and the latter, in his turn, had got his information from the *gyalpo's* emissary, who had brought the letter for his Lhasa relative. The man had spent a couple of days in the official's house, waiting for the answer to his master's letter. During that time he had done a good deal of gossiping.

At the palace of Mipam's feudal lord everyone was in a state of profound consternation. The two Dugpas who had come with the Jowo Zangkar, having been warned that the *gyalpo* wanted to have them beaten, had fled by night, by devious tracks, taking their master's body with them. In a bush, opposite the triangular hut, had been found a waistcoat of Mipam's covered over with a scarf. No one could explain its presence in that place, but the prince, beside himself with rage at his son's death, saw in it a sure sign that Mipam had had a hand in the spells which had lured the *gyalse* to a spot where he had no cause to be, and had deflected the murderous arrow in his direction. Cherishing these irrational ideas, the *gyalpo* dreamt of nothing but revenge. He wanted, at all costs, to have the youth whom he called his son's assassin found and tortured to death.

Tenzin felt that it was urgent that Mipam should leave the country.

Tsöndup was of the same opinion. It was unlikely that the chief magistrates of Lhasa or Shigatze would concern themselves with the boy. The *gyalpo* who was hunting him down was of little importance in their eyes, and the tragic issue of the lethal rite, if it ever came to their ears, would hardly incline them to have any dealings with a man who was so manifestly pursued by the anger of the gods, or of some powerful magician.

Nevertheless, a personal friend or relative, such as the official of whom Tenzin spoke, might display greater zeal. It was not very difficult to discover Mipam's retreat. The vain youth, bent on showing off his new clothes, had made himself conspicuous at Tashilhumpo and in the town. He could be seized as he was walking in some isolated spot, or means could be found to lay hold of him in the very house of his hosts, by diverting their attention, and then having him sent under escort to his lord. A trader cannot turn his house into a fortress, nor must he attract to himself the enmity of even the least important of chiefs; that is bad business.

Mipam, then, must be gone, and that without delay.

But Tenzin's letter raised another question. Dolma absolutely insisted upon saying good-bye to Mipam. She realized that his departure was necessary, but she clung to the opinion that it was quite as indispensable to offer a lamp on Chenrezigs' altar, in company with her friend, so that he might be protected from all the perils of his journey. It was because of her, the young girl argued, that Mipam's liberty and even his life were threatened. He had prevented the *gyalse* from beating her, perhaps from killing her. The young prince had had an evil character; she knew him well; in his anger he would have been capable of pushing her over the rocks that bordered the path had Mipam not intervened.

She had insisted that she must be allowed to do what she termed her duty. The greatest misfortunes would assail both her and Mipam, if they did not offer this lamp before the statue of Chenrezigs, in an especially holy temple. Seeing her pale and tremulous, almost fainting with emotion, Tenzin had been unable to resist her. He had promised her that she should see Mipam again. But where were the young folk to meet? He asked counsel of his friend Tsöndup. In any case Mipam must not be seen at his house in Lhasa.

And I am just as reluctant that Dolma should come here, Tsöndup thought to himself. She would distress herself; she would weep, as she did at her father's: that would draw attention to us, and invite questions. Besides, Mipam can't wait for her; the peril is imminent: that infuriated *gyalpo* is clamouring for his death.

Greatly perplexed, Tsöndup sent for his eldest son, Dorje, who excelled in arriving at decisions in difficult circumstances, and of whose liking for Mipam he was assured. When the young man appeared his father gave him Tenzin's letter.

'Mipam must leave to-morrow morning before daybreak,' said Dorje, when he had read the letter. 'He must be well away before it is light.'

'Where is he to go?'

'To China with me; since I'm leaving in three days' time. He will remain there as long as is necessary for this distressing affair to be forgotten.'

The young man reflected for a moment, and once more addressed his father.

'I've got a plan,' he announced. 'Tell me what you think of it.

'With your consent, Mipam will leave with Tingley, who, as usual, is to join my caravan. I can manage to do without him for part of the journey. Tingley is a dependable and prudent person, and he knows the country by heart; he will guide our young friend by unfrequented paths leading from the Giamda highway to the *chang thangs*,[1] and they will rejoin me some little distance to the north of Nagchukha. Starting before me, and travelling more rapidly than I shall, seeing that they won't have pack animals with them, they will have time enough to make a detour and catch me up without causing me delay. In this way you will be rid immediately of Mipam's compromising presence; his safety will be assured, and you will not be seeming to defy those who are looking for the boy, by allowing the neighbours to see that he is travelling with your caravan.'

'Your plan is an excellent one,' replied Tsöndup. 'It has my entire approval, but you forget Dolma. Still, that's of no real importance. I will write to her father that Mipam's departure could not be delayed without grave risk for the boy, and that what she wants is impossible. She will offer, on her own account, a lamp to Chenrezigs, and one to the Jowo[2] as well. As for myself, I will have a lamp lit in each of the temples of Tashilhumpo, and I will offer tea to all the monks in the monastery, so that owing to the merit thus acquired Mipam may have a prosperous journey and good fortune in China. I will write to *aku* Tenzin to that effect; he will tell his daughter and she will be consoled.'

Dorje smiled.

'You are the best of men, my father,' he said; 'your plan is perfect. Mipam sorely needs the protection of the gods, but all that you may do will be powerless to console Dolma, if she

[1] The vast, wild, grassy tablelands of Northern Tibet.

[2] The *Jowo* (the lord) is an ancient statue, venerated in the great temple at Lhasa. It is supposed to represent the historic Buddha at the time when he was still a young prince in the palace of his father, the rajah. This statue is said to have been carved in India, then transported to China, whence the daughter of the Chinese Emperor, Tai Jung, brought it to Tibet at the time of her marriage with King Srongbstan Gampo. It is an object of profound veneration.

MIPAM

has got it into her head that she must bid farewell to her
defender. As a matter of fact, I've provided for this. Mipam
and Dolma will travel separately to Gahlden, which is almost
on the road to Giamda; there they will offer their lamps to
Chenrezigs and will pay homage also to the tomb of Dje
Rimpoche.[1] There is no more hallowed place of pilgrimage in
Tibet. In passing through Lhasa to reach Gahlden, Tingley
and Mipam need not show themselves in the centre of the
town. In the early morning, or toward evening, they will
skirt the city and cross the river at the ferry near Dechen.
Mipam is certainly not watched as yet; it's enough that he
should avoid henceforth any places where they may think of
looking for him.

'Will you write at once to *aku* Tenzin? A man leaving now
will have a full half day before him. He must travel late this
evening, and make good headway; the start he has over Mipam
will leave time for him to see Dolma's father, and for
Tenzin to send her to Gahlden in time to meet Mipam
there.'

'A most excellent plan,' replied Tsöndup. 'Go and tell
Goring that he must leave at once for Lhasa. See that he has
something to eat, and gives a feed of corn to the black horse,
and saddles up while I write the letter. Say nothing to
Mipam; I'll talk to him after we've had our meal.'

The servant left with the letter, and soon afterwards Mipam
appeared, with the merchant's other sons, and all made a hearty
meal.

Dinner over, the young men withdrew to attend to their
several occupations. Mipam, who had none, was about to go
for a walk when Tsöndup detained him.

'Stay here, young man. I've something to say to you.'

'Very good,' replied Mipam.

'You are to leave here to-morrow, well before the day breaks.
Go and pack your things. Dorje will give you some blankets

[1] Honorary title of Tsong Khapa, the founder of the sect of the 'Yellow
Caps'.

142

Tsong Kapa

and one of his warm robes. You mustn't soil your new clothes on the journey.'

'Ah! I'm going to Lhasa! *Aku* Tenzin has sent for me!' cried Mipam, joyfully.

'No,' replied Tsöndup, 'you're going to China. Your *gyalpo* is looking for you to have you killed. Go and join Dorje.'

Once again Mipam's fate had been decided in the space of a few minutes, nor had he had a say in the matter.

Without having consulted him, his father and the astrologer Shesrab had decided to make him an astrologer-monk. Without having consulted him, the *gyalmo* had taken him away from his master and arranged for him to enter her service. And now, whether he liked it or not, he was being sent to China.

Dorje was less laconic in his explanations. Mipam learnt from him the details given in Tenzin's letter respecting the dramatic death of the *gyalse* and the magician from Dugyul, and he was told that in all probability he would see Dolma at Gahlden. This hope put fresh heart into him.

The adventure in itself attracted him. This journey to a distant land, careering on horseback along unfrequented paths, with a hardy companion, and then the stirring life of the caravan as it passed through solitudes haunted by brigands; there was nothing in this to displease him. And lastly China, and the towns where you traded and piled up money. . . . There lay his chance; could he have had a better? One year, two years, and then he would return, mounted on a fine horse, at the head of a convoy of merchandise. This ridiculous affair that was forcing him to fly would be forgotten. After all, he had neither killed nor stolen. He saw himself dismounting at Tenzin's house, and asking him, first of all, for harbourage for his beasts and his goods. And then, the following day, when the merchant could reckon up their value at his leisure, he would say to him, as he presented him with a handsome ceremonial scarf: '*Aku* Tenzin, all this is for you; I can easily

get as much again. In exchange I ask you for Dolma's hand. . . .'
What a fine wedding they would have! . . .

There was a moderate but biting wind blowing, in a clear
sky, studded with stars, when Tingley saddled the two horses
in Tsöndup's courtyard. Under their wooden saddles he carefully arranged the rugs which would lessen their pressure on
the beasts' backs, and would also serve as bedding for their
riders. He then covered the saddles with a square piece of
carpet, and passed over this the straps that fastened the saddle-
bags on either side. The horses were well-bred, swift and
sturdy, the saddles and bridles of good quality, but not
sumptuous enough to attract attention. Mipam wore a heavy
woollen robe of dark red, a little faded from use, but comfortable; Tingley was dressed in much the same way. They
were to pass themselves off as uncle and nephew, travelling
on business.

Tsöndup and Dorje had wished them a good journey the
night before. The merchant had then handed to Tingley the
required sum of money for their expenses on the road. Further
confident of Tenzin's approval, he had in the latter's name
presented Mipam with a hundred and fifty silver sangs[1] to help
him in his early days in China.

Tsöndup having thus made ample provision for the fugitive's
comfort, thought it the better plan to let him leave without
again bidding him good-bye, so as to avoid attracting the
attention of those who might see him leaving the house.

Nothing occurred of any note in the course of Mipam's
journey to Gahlden. Tingley led him through the outskirts
of Lhasa at dusk, and all that he could see of the Holy City
was the golden roofs of the Potala, showing in the last rays of the
setting sun. At the foot of the track which ascends to Gahlden
they slept at the house of some peasants, and in the morning,
leaving their horses in the peasants' charge, they climbed up
to the monastery.

[1] Sang, a Tibetan weight, the equivalent in value, to the Chinese tael.

At the top of the trail, a little to one side, on a small level patch at the foot of a grassy slope, was a tiny tent; Dolma and a maidservant had spent the night there. The man who had been their escort had taken the horses to graze, and would return for them about midday.

'Mipam, I've come to wish you a good journey, and to offer some lamps, so that no harm may befall you,' said Dolma, simply, but her voice was unsteady with emotion.

'I'm so happy to see you again, Dolma,' replied the boy. He was too moved to find words that would express all that he felt.

Hand in hand, they set off for the monastery. Tingley followed them, a few paces behind, carrying a pot of melted butter to feed the lamps. Dolma's maid had prepared it that morning, and had hoped to accompany her young mistress, but Tingley had decided that she had better remain in the tent. He thought it wiser not to leave Mipam, so that he could help him should anything unforeseen occur.

'Whatever happens to you, it is I who have brought it upon you,' said Dolma, dolefully, to her friend. 'If you were to detest me you would be quite justified.'

'I should not be justified,' the boy protested, 'and you know quite well that I couldn't detest you. Don't take things too much to heart; it may be that in the long run all our troubles will turn to our advantage. For my part, I'm quite hopeful.'

'Yes, all will go well with you, Mipam.'

'With you too, Dolma. What is good for me is also good for you, since we ought to share all things in common.'

'I'm very sad, Mipam.'

'I too, Dolma, but I don't mean to lose heart. Listen, in China . . .'

And as they strolled from one temple to another, Mipam confided to his friend the plans which he had formed. He painted for her his triumphant arrival at her father's house, the high price that he would be able to offer to win Tenzin's consent to their marriage, and then the building of the home of their dreams, and long years of happiness.

He had taken from Tingley the pot which the latter was carrying, and from this he poured small quantities of melted butter into the lamps burning on the altars. Dolma and he then devoutly prostrated themselves.

Near a statue of Chenrezigs they came upon a sacristan employed in preparing lamps which he sold to pious pilgrims. Mipam and Dolma gave him some money and asked him to light one hundred and eight small lamps. Pleased with their alms, the monk hastened to set out the lamps in rows on the altar. Mipam and Dolma, after prostrating themselves three times, took each a lighted lamp, which they held out toward the statue, while in their hearts they formulated certain wishes.

Dolma was the first to place her lamp on the altar; Mipam still held his uplifted. Dolma confidently murmured in his ear:

'Chenrezigs surely will hear you; he will fulfil all your desires, since you are his son.'

As he heard his mystic sonship recalled, a sonship which he had long forgotten, Mipam, as though by an unconscious impulse, lifted his lamp still higher, and a prayer ascended from his innermost being:

'May I be thy son in very truth!'

Suddenly the flame of the lamp lengthened, so that the temple, the statue with its countless succouring arms, and the young suppliant were suddenly illumined as by a flash of lightning. Dolma recoiled in fear; the sacristan, after gazing at Mipam with wondering eyes, timidly came forward:

'Chenrezigs has heard your prayer,' he said. 'Never have I seen such a sign. Are you, sir, an incarnated Grand Lama?'

'I am,' replied Mipam, still unreflecting, driven by an impulse of which he was not master.

The monk joined his hands, with the palms touching and the fingers extended, and then, bowing his head, besought the young man's blessing. And Mipam blessed him, as in a trance.

Dolma had tears in her eyes.

'Mipam, Mipam!' she said; 'you will never be a merchant, you will become a lama, a holy wonder-worker greater than Kushog Yeshes Kunzang; but I shall be your *yum* [wife], shall I not?'

'Yes, Dolma,' replied Mipam dreamily.

In silence they came to the venerated tomb of Tsong Khapa. They joined with others of the faithful moving round it in pious procession. An emotion of whose cause he was unaware flowed into Mipam's heart and insinuated itself into his mind, freeing him from all his worries and dissolving the plans which he had made; *another* took possession of him, mind and body.

Near the tomb of the illustrious reformer was a narrow door; beyond this hung a black curtain which hid from view a darkened sanctuary. The two friends entered the door, and Mipam, passing behind the curtain, disappeared into the shadows. Dolma, a little behind him was about to enter in her turn, when an arm, emerging from a monastic cloak, was thrust forth, barring the way, while the voice of an invisible custodian roughly exclaimed:

'Women are not allowed in here!'

Dolma drew back. There was nothing astonishing about this prohibition. Certain temples consecrated to Jigsjed are forbidden to women; that she knew. Mipam, when he found that she did not join him, would return. But Mipam lingered in contemplation of the image of the terrible couple, embracing each other, crowned with skulls, crushing, under their multiple feet, both human beings and animals.

He had seen more than one of these symbolical representations. Not knowing what they meant, they had never arrested his attention, and even at that moment he did not seek to inquire into the significance of the fantastic forms of the 'Father' and the 'Mother' who rose so threateningly before him. Plunged into a sort of trance, he sank into another world, where his faculty of thinking could not follow him,

147

and there remained in him only a confused sensation of finding himself on the edge of a dark precipice, on the point of casting himself over it.

The sacristan, wrapped in his cloak, moved about like some amorphous larva in the darkness, which the light from the lamp burning before the 'Great Terrible One' seemed to accentuate rather than dispel. Mipam's prolonged immobility appearing to him a sign of profound piety, he came forward, holding out a lighted lamp. His intervention partly broke the spell that bound the young man. Mipam took the lamp and raised it, as he had done before the statue of Chenrezigs, but he formulated no petitions.

He then placed the lamp on the altar, left some money beside it, and left the sanctuary, walking unsteadily.

Dolma was waiting for him outside. Her brocade dress flashed with iridescent hues in the sun, and her jewels glittered on her breast; she was indeed a radiant vision, the same darling fairy that he had glimpsed for the first time through the flames on the hearth. Mipam experienced a kind of shock; his heart began to beat violently, and he hurried toward her, his dear beloved, soon to be his wife. Yes, soon. He would exorcise the evil fate which the curious torpor that had seized upon him seemed to foreshadow. His dream would come true. He would make his fortune in China; he would return sitting astride a beautiful horse. The caravan, the numerous bales of merchandise, the smiling *aku* Tenzin, visualized themselves for him in a series of pictures that blotted out the present. . . .

'What, Dolma, are you crying?'

'Why did you leave me all by myself? The sacristan would not let me pass. What were you doing there all that time?'

'All that time? I didn't stay long; the sacristan gave me a lamp, and I offered it. It was the temple of Dorje Jigsjed.'

'Yes, I know that, since women are not allowed to enter. Ah! but Mipam, you are going away; so far, shall I ever see you again? I'm so miserable, Mipam.'

A feeling of painful apprehension clouded the fugitive's mind.

'It is I, Dolma, who have reason to be sad. You have grown into a big girl, the only child of a very wealthy man, a great trader. Many merchants' sons or even young nobles will be dreaming of you, and sending envoys to speak to your father. And what about me, Dolma, supposing fortune were not to favour me in China—if I didn't become rich enough, if your father wouldn't have me for his son-in-law?'

'He will accept you, Mipam,' cried Dolma. And sure of her power over her father, she gravely added, 'I will tell him that I love you.'

The boy shook his head wistfully.

'Mipam,' said Dolma, reassuringly, 'don't be anxious on my account. I told you I would be your wife. I will wait for you. If you are not to be my husband, I will cut off my hair and enter a convent. I swear it. . . .'

She hesitated. An oath ought to have the support of some venerable witness. Whom should she choose? She turned her head toward the monastery. It seemed hostile to her. Chenrezigs had replied to his son's wishes by a prodigy, but he had not looked at her, and she had been turned away from the abode of Jigsjed, when Mipam was lingering there.

She fell back upon herself, on the ancestral faith in the ancient gods of the *Böns* that Buddhism has never been able to uproot from Tibetan soil.

'If I don't marry you, I'll cut off my hair. I'll become a nun,' she repeated once more. *Pho lha! Mo lha!*

Dolma had sworn by the tutelary gods of her father's and her mother's ancestors. It was they, the hoary little defenders of her race, whom she unconsciously invoked to safeguard the humble laywoman's happiness against the vague enemy which she sensed in the vast monastery, seated in triumph on the sun-steeped mountain, the symbol of an ideal that barred her out.

Tingley came up to the young folk.

'Nephew,' he said to Mipam, smilingly alluding to the

fictitious relationship under which they were travelling: 'Nephew, it's time we were off.'

Jerking his head, he pointed to the sun, which had reached the meridian.

It was time to start. Already the maidservant was folding the tent, and Tenzin's servant appeared, leading back the horses, which he had taken to graze.

'Our animals are at a farm at the foot of the mountain,' said Mipam to Dolma. 'Tingley and I are going down on foot.'

'I will come with you,' Dolma replied.

She slipped her hand into her friend's, and they leisurely descended the track in silence. All they could find to say had been said, but the nearer they drew to the valley, the closer they clung together.

Tingley, hurrying on ahead, went to fetch the horses from the farm. The moment for parting had arrived. Mipam pressed Dolma in his arms, looked at her intently, as though to stamp her image for ever on his mind, and then helped her to mount.

'A good journey, good health and good luck, Mipam!' murmured the young girl through her tears. 'Don't forget me.'

'Till we meet again, Dolma; soon, you know; I shall be back soon.'

And whispering into the girl's ear, the boy added, in passionate accents that Dolma had never yet heard:

'I couldn't live without you!'

Tenzin's servant rode off in front. The horses of his young mistress and her maid followed of themselves.

'*Kale pheb*,[1] *kale pheb, Kushog*,' said Tenzin's servants, respectfully.

'*Kale pheb*,' echoed Dolma.

All three trotted off southwards. Standing in the road, Mipam watched them recede into the distance. Dolma's brocaded dress, shimmering in the sun, and her long red sleeves kept her in sight on the dusty track until she was only

[1] The usual polite form of farewell. It means 'go-peacefully'.

an infinitesimal fleck of colour between the blue sky and the yellow earth. Motionless, Mipam continued to visualize what his eyes could no longer see.

'*Kushog!*' said Tingley, sympathetically, forgetful of his temporary role as the young man's uncle.

'*Phai sha sa nes!*'¹ that *gyalpo*! . . . ' Mipam exclaimed wrathfully, stressing the horrible oath.

He sprang violently into the saddle, dug his heels into the horse's belly, and set off northwards at a rapid trot.

'I didn't know, nephew, that you were to be trader Tenzin's son-in-law,' said Tingley, respectfully. 'A father-in-law in a hundred, rich and prosperous, with no other child but that pretty girl; the son-in-law becomes the heir. . . . Oh! . . .' The man clicked his tongue to mark his appreciation. 'In a year's time you will be able to return; your *gyalpo* will have calmed down, if the demons who pursue him haven't carried him off by then. In the meantime there is something to be said for travelling. You'll see, you'll get to like it. I've been to Dartsedo, Peching and Ta Kure² with the traders. I've seen great cities: Lhasa is only a village compared to them. There was every kind of merchandise and there in such quantities . . . things that have never been seen in Tibet. . . . And didn't we eat well there! . . . You'll see, nephew. I don't know where you're going when you get to China, but you won't find it dull, believe me. A man can't stay at home like a woman; he must see something of the world . . . that's life, a good life. . . .'

The honest Tingley was talking partly to cheer up his companion, and also because he took pleasure in recalling his experiences as a traveller, but Mipam was not listening.

Before they came to Medo Kongkar, Tingley left the Giamda

¹ 'Who has eaten his father's flesh' or 'Eater of his father's flesh'. The foulest of Tibetan oaths.
² *Dartsedo* is the Tibetan name of Tachienlu in Szechwan; *Peching* is the Tibetan name for Peking, while *Ta Kure* is the Tibetan name for the capital of Mongolia: Urga, also called Ulan-Bator.

road and made his way across the mountain, following the course of the Kyi chu. The countryside was deserted, and the paths were indistinctly marked. The travellers crossed several passes. Mipam looked with interest at the scenery through which he was riding; it was so different from that of his own country.

During the next few days the travellers took their meals on the banks of the streams. They hunted for scraps of fuel—the dried dung of the yak—and boiled their tea on a primitive tripod of three big stones. At night they slept in the little tent which Tsöndup had given them. This was quite a new kind of life for Mipam, and he was not indifferent to its charms.

One evening Tingley pitched their camp in a tortuous ravine deeply sunk in the side of a mountain.

'Nephew,' said he, 'to-day we won't pitch a tent; we won't make a fire; we'll keep the horses near us, and we'll hobble their fore-feet. The country here isn't safe; the *Jagspas*[1] sometimes cross these mountains and lie in ambush in the path of the caravans. We mustn't show ourselves; the bandits might steal our horses.'

The life of adventure was beginning, fascinating and exciting. That night Mipam slept little. For the first time since he had left Dolma he felt cheerful.

The two horsemen reached a place where the bare earth was hardened by the immemorial trampling of hooves.

'The high road!' Tingley announced.

Mipam surveyed the desert which extended in all directions.

'Is Dorje in front of us, or behind?' he asked. 'How are we to know?'

'That won't be very difficult,' said Tsöndup's servant. 'If he has already passed he can't be very far off, and with the fine weather we've had for the last two days the horses' tracks will still be quite clearly marked.'

[1] Highway robbers, operating in armed bands.

Tingley dismounted, and holding his horse by the bridle, he walked along slowly with his eyes on the ground, examining the surface.

'I see nothing but old hoof-marks,' he said after a while. 'The most recent have been made by a caravan travelling with oxen. Master Dorje is taking mules. It isn't he.'

He continued to walk a little further, carefully scrutinizing the whole width of the track.

'No sign of them,' he concluded; 'your friend hasn't passed yet. We are here before our time. We had better camp at the first convenient place we find and wait for him there.'

'But supposing he has passed?' Mipam objected.

'He hasn't passed,' Tingley quietly insisted. 'And then, if he had, if we didn't overtake him, he would stop and send a man back to look for us.'

'And if he were further off than you think, if he didn't find us, and we were left here all by ourselves?'

Tingley burst out laughing.

'That's very unlikely,' he replied, 'but if things did turn out like that, there would be nothing to fret about. We couldn't take this particular road, because it passes through absolutely deserted country, and we should want a tremendous amount of provisions to get through; but with the food we have we could strike off along another road, further to the east, on which we ought to come across some herdsmen's encampments. We've got money, and we could buy food from them.'

'And where would that road lead us?'

'To Cherku.[1] Many traders, Tibetans and Chinamen, go from there to Dangar, which Kushog Dorje is making for; we could join one or other of their caravans, or we could travel on our own. I've gone that way many a time.'

'But what about Dorje? How uneasy and unhappy he would be not to see us!'

'Uneasy . . . yes, a little, perhaps, but why should he be unhappy? There's no reason for that. Nor is there any real

[1] Often marked on the map under another name: Jakyendo.

reason why he should be uneasy. Our young master has known me since he was quite a little boy. I took him for his first caravan journey when he was nine. He knows very well that I shouldn't let you lose your way.'

'Yes . . . that's true,' agreed Mipam absently.

He felt a little hurt, a little grieved. He had believed in Dorje's friendship. Was it really so shallow as Tingley seemed to think? If he didn't join the caravan, it seemed that his friend would trouble himself very little on his account; less than he would for a bale of merchandise lost, or a mule gone astray. Both of these were dearer to his heart; he would hurry his men off to hunt for them; as for him, poor Mipam, he would leave him to wander in the desert without troubling his head about him. He knew that Mipam was with Tingley; that would reassure him.

Probably this was the sensible way of looking at the matter. Nevertheless, he, Mipam, banished incontinently from his green and fertile valley, dotted with hospitable hamlets, into these savage solitudes, ravaged by boisterous winds, could have wished, in his isolation, to have been encompassed by a more vigilant sympathy. He was alone, quite alone. . . . He suddenly felt cold under his thick gown, but this cold was not due to the bracing air of those high altitudes. Mipam was coming into contact, for the first time, with the indifference of the world about him. This was his first taste of that isolation which is pain before it becomes beatitude.

The two horsemen continued to advance for more than an hour in the direction of a chain of low hills; at their foot they found water, and they decided to remain there until the caravan should pass. At sundown they pitched their tent, tied up their horses near it, and fell asleep, expecting that the trader would arrive on the morrow.

But he came neither the next day, nor the day after.

Despite his natural placidity, Tingley began to find this delay surprising and disquieting. To assuage his impatience, and make their remaining provisions last out, he went in search of some *tumas*, a mealy root with a taste like that of chestnuts. He brought back a fairly large quantity and also found a certain amount of *kyang* [wild ass] dung, and on the site of an old camp, enough yak-dung to serve them as fuel for several days.

On returning to Mipam, who was keeping an eye on the grazing horses, he racked his brains to find some explanation of Dorje's delay, but he himself began to wonder whether he had not failed to detect the marks of his passage. A fresh examination did not yield any more conclusive results. Heavy rain had fallen twice since they had rejoined the main road: it had saturated the ground, and effaced most of the tracks. In his own mind, Tingley had decided to wait for another two days, and then, if Dorje did not appear, to make for the camps of the herdsmen and go on to Cherku.

The young man smiled, and with an absent air approved what his temporary 'uncle' had said to him. He was clearly not listening, but straining to catch the sound of other voices. The charm of the *chang thangs* [the northern grassy solitudes] was beginning to affect him; Mipam had resumed the silent conversations with the invisible presences which had cast a spell over his boyhood in the Himalayan forests.

'Nephew,' said Tingley, with an embarrassed air, on the morning of the fourth day 'we can't stay here any longer; our provisions are almost exhausted; we must set about looking for herdsmen to replenish our supplies. Something unforeseen must have detained Kushog Dorje. He will realize that we couldn't delay any longer. . . . I've had a bad dream, too. Let's saddle up and be off.'

This meant to abandon all hope of rejoining Dorje before arriving in China, but since Dorje had not arrived there was nothing for it but to follow Tingley.

'Yes, let's be off,' agreed Mipam. Tingley went to fetch the horses. Each rider saddled his own, and hung at the back of the saddle a bag containing a supply of fuel. After retracing part of the way which they had already covered, Tingley struck off in a fresh direction. He seemed absolutely sure of his movements, although no trace of a path was visible. Mipam confidently followed him.

On the afternoon of the third day after leaving the high road, they espied some black tents. It was high time. Though they had rationed themselves, they had nothing left but a handful of barley meal and a little tea. The *dokpas* received them kindly, and gave them each a large pot of curd, but would sell them neither flour nor butter. They had not even enough for themselves, they said.

'We shall see to-morrow,' said Tingley to his companion. 'Perhaps I shall find some way of coming to an arrangement with them.'

When the herd had been rounded up again at dusk, the women went to milk the cows, and the milk having been boiled, the travellers were able to drink a few bowls of it. Tingley then helped Mipam to put up their tent and advised him to go to bed at once, as they would have to start very early in the morning. No sooner had Mipam lain down, rolled in his blankets, his head resting on his saddle, than he fell into a deep sleep, and Tingley, who had pretended to be occupied with their luggage, managed to leave the tent without being noticed.

The next morning, when Mipam awoke, his companion was already outside with his blankets and bags, ready to load them on his horse. The young man, a little ashamed of having slept so long, hastened to fold up the small tent; then he put on his boots, fastened his sash, and put on his hat. After the customary polite good wishes to the herdsmen—'A long life, free from illness'—the two men were soon in the saddle and trotting over the turf.

They kept up this pace all the morning. Then, as they were passing a stream, Tingley proposed that they should pull up and have something to eat.

'It will be a short meal,' said Mipam. 'A little barley

moistened with water. We've nothing else left. I envy our horses, that can eat as much grass as they like. A pity we can't graze like them. Do you think we shall soon be able to buy some food?'

Tingley's only reply was an enigmatic smile.

'Let's light a fire,' he said briskly, as he opened his bag of fuel. Mipam was about to ask him what use the fire would be when there was no more tea to boil, but the strange expression on his pseudo-uncle's face was puzzling him, and he said nothing. Had the clever Tingley succeeded in buying a little tea and a handful or two of barley meal from their hosts of yester-eve? He looked with curiosity at the big leathern bag which Tingley was leisurely unlacing. It was neither tea nor flour that came out of it, but a large blood-stained bundle, which Tingley laid on the ground, and when he had unbound the rag in which it was wrapped its contents were revealed as the various portions of a sheep.

'Oh!' cried Mipam, cut to the heart: 'you've killed a sheep!'

'It wasn't I who killed it; one of the *dokpas* saw to that; I only cut it up. The *dokpas* made me pay dearly for it; the cunning rascals knew we had no food left. Anyhow, here's food for several days. And high time too. You ought to be feeling weak, nephew. Come! we're going to grill a nice joint; that will put fresh life into us.'

Mipam was aghast. The feeling of abhorrence which in his childhood had always made him refuse to eat meat was now much less pronounced. At the chief's palace meat was the principal article of diet, and under penalty of an almost perpetual fast one had to eat it except when special dishes were to be prepared. On the eighth, fifteenth and twentieth days of the moon the chaplain abstained from animal food, following the custom of those distinguished lamas who are not entirely vegetarians. He had, besides, a special cook, who drew provisions from the prince's steward. Mipam could not claim any such privilege: the remnants of food which his masters left on their dishes had formed the greater part of his diet.

These remains always contained meat, and Mipam had always been hungry: therefore he ate them. But that cooked meat had come from animals already killed; the idea of having a beast expressly killed for him filled him with horror. This, however, was what had happened.

'Oh! Tingley, how could you!' he began.

His companion interrupted him.

'I know very well that you are of the clergy, and that you ought not to give orders to kill. Do you think I am fool enough not to know that? I took good care to wait until you were asleep before talking to the herdsmen. The beast was killed, cut up and packed before you knew anything about it. Nothing prevents you, now, from eating it. You were not to blame. I know what the custom is, and the right thing to do, you can be sure of that.'

Tingley felt proud of being so well versed in the fine points of lamaic casuistry, and of having under the circumstances, behaved with so much tact.

The meat was grilled over the red ashes, giving forth an appetizing smell. Mipam knew very well how fallacious his companion's arguments were, but his empty stomach was tormenting him. He ate, and as the flesh of the animals grazed on the pastures of the *chang thang* is always of prime quality, he found it good.

Sad at heart, but physically refreshed by this substantial repast, Mipam mounted his horse once more. His enthusiasm as to his journey, and what was to follow in its train, which had been rather damped during the last few days, soon revived, and he felt more optimistic than ever. He no longer regretted that they had not joined Dorje and his caravan; the unforeseen nature of his journey, and his semi-solitude, delighted him. Mipam was not one of those who find comfort in living in a herd.

As he had done a few days earlier, Tingley drew rein on the edge of a broad strip of hardened ground, where the grass,

Mila Respa

thwarted in its growth by the repeated tramping of animals, was cropping up sparsely in isolated patches.

'The high road,' he said. 'Henceforth all will be easy.'

They met with *dokpas* more frequently. Tingley, always with the same tact, the same knowledge of the rules to be observed, continued to provide them with mutton, though Mipam had neither procured nor witnessed the murder of the sheep. He contented himself with eating its flesh, which kept his body vigorous, and his mind sufficiently alert to realize the horror of his conduct and to hold it in detestation.

In the absence of any other form of food, and being loth to interrupt his meditations by leaving his hermitage in search of fresh supplies, Milarespa, the famous ascetic, the spiritual father of the *Kah-gyudpa* sect, subsisted for nearly a year on an exclusive diet of boiled nettles. At the end of that time he perceived, in despair, that not only had he difficulty in standing upright, but that he had become incapable of reflecting and meditating. It happened just then that someone brought him some meat and beer. He enjoyed a few hearty meals, and then, his intellectual faculties reviving, he plunged into profound meditation and attained spiritual illumination.

This story, familiar to Mipam, was to him a great mystery, a disconcerting contradiction. In it he detected a cause of scandal which had furnished an excuse for monks who had no compassion for sentient beings. He could not feel sure that the famous Mila would not have given proof of a higher form of virtue by renouncing his meditations, if he could pursue them only by failing in compassion and setting an unfortunate example. He was not very certain, either, that meditations induced in such a way were anything more than elucubrations of a mind turned in upon itself; detrimental ratiocinations, and an obstacle to the 'profound sight', as his teacher, Yeshes Kunzang's disciple, had termed it.

As for himself, he felt an agreeable glow pass through him after a good meal of grilled mutton. He took to the road

again refreshed and gay, but he continued to pass a severe
judgment on the cowardly consent of his mind to the crime
which procured him that sensual comfort.

The two men halted for a week at Cherku. Tingley had
some acquaintances there among the traders, and he passed the
greater part of his time in long consultations with them, while
Mipam strolled about in the open, or indulged in day-dreams
in the room which they shared. The result of Tingley's
activities was that he and Mipam were to travel with a caravan
going to Dangar, the frontier town to which Dorje was bound.

Mipam welcomed this news without enthusiasm. He had
conceived a taste for the eerie atmosphere of the solitudes; he
instinctively feared that the presence of a number of travelling
companions would shatter the calm and the silence in which
he took such pleasure. He raised no objection, however, so as
not to vex Tingley, whose expression betrayed the keenest
satisfaction. The young man recognized the reason for this on
the day of their departure. His capable companion had taken
advantage of his stay at Cherku to do some business. He was
bringing with the caravan three yaks laden with merchandise.

The slow pace of the big long-haired yaks doubled the duration of the journey. The traders left at dawn and halted a few
hours later to make some tea, after which they kept on
the move until the early hours of the afternoon; they then
encamped until the following day, in order to give their
animals time to graze.

There was no possibility of day-dreaming in the company of
these boors, who became so uproarious every evening, under
the influence of alcohol. Mipam, falling back upon his own
thoughts, endeavoured to forecast the future, to formulate his
plans. What was he going to do at Dangar? What kind of
work, what sort of trade would he take up? Commerce must
be his line. All other careers were now closed to him. And
yet—buying, selling, making money, was that a life worth
living, did it warrant the effort it required? But there was
Dolma. . . . Dolma who could not be obtained without a

great deal of money, merchandise and fine horses. He would have to become a merchant.

A few days before they passed the beautiful lake of Tossu he asked Tingley whether the two traders who were conducting the caravan were living at Dangar. Tingley replied that they both came from Dartsedo, in the Kham country, but that they had branch-offices in several places, and Dangar was one of them.

'All these yaks are theirs, of course?' the young man continued. 'And have you hired those that are carrying your merchandise from them?'

'They bought their yaks, and I bought my three,' replied Tingley.

'What are you going to do with them? Are you going to use them to transport other goods when you return to Shigatze?'

'I shall go back with Kushog Dorje. He will pack his stuff on the mules with which he is travelling now. Yaks are too slow-footed to follow a mule caravan.'

'You've only three beasts; that's not many. These traders will be able to find some use for them, and will buy them from you, of course, if you want to sell them, but I'm afraid, my poor Tingley, they won't give you much for them. They'll profit by the fact that you've got to get rid of them.'

Tingley made no reply, and this was the end of the conversation.

Two days later, quite incidentally, Mipam happened to speak of the yaks to one of the traders' servants.

'We shan't take any yaks back with us, and we shall have very few goods on our return journey,' said the man. 'The traders will take the Nagchuka road, with a batch of fine Sining mules, which they'll sell at Lhasa.'

'Will they be able to get rid of their yaks without losing on them? Is there much demand for pack-animals at this time of year?'

'No, there's very little demand, as this is the season for taking back mules and horses, as my master is going to do, but most of the yaks will be bought by the butchers, who will give a fair price.'

'What! these beasts are going to be slaughtered at the end of their journey?'

'Nearly all of them. If my master loses a trifle on selling them, the loss will be less than the amount he would have paid for hiring the beasts from Cherku to Dangar. So the transport of his goods will have cost him very little. If he has luck, and if there's a good demand for meat, he may even lose nothing. All the merchants rich enough to put down the purchase price of the yaks do the same: it's the most profitable course.'

The man turned to another subject of conversation, but finding that Mipam was distracted and unresponsive, he took his departure.

The unexpected revelation of the fate reserved for the animals on the road before him had staggered the young man.

The surrounding landscape faded from his sight. He saw nothing but the jostling troop of lumbering beasts, with their matted black hair, straining under the weight of their burdens: a sort of sombre river, flowing silently and sluggishly across the emerald grass of the steppe under the wide, luminous sky, so serenely indifferent. He saw the arrival of the poor exhausted yaks, pining for rest, for the bliss which their like enjoy as they chew the cud, lying relaxed in the pastures. He saw the meed which man's ingratitude held in store for them; the knife plunged into their flanks, probing for the heart to pierce, the blood spurting out over the black hair, or the terrible death by suffocation, the mouth and nose constricted by a thong.[1]

Horror of horrors! And these men who, singing and

[1] The animals killed by the Tibetans for the butchers' shops are most often suffocated by this procedure. The Tibetans consider it 'more compassionate'. Besides, they find it preferable that the blood should remain in the meat. In the frontier regions the animal is often killed with a long knife which pierces the heart.

whistling, formed part of this lamentable procession of unconscious victims, did not realize, nor would they ever realize, the
odiousness of what they were doing.

'Uncle Tingley!' Mipam called out suddenly.

Tsöndup's servant, who was riding some distance in front
of his so-called nephew, reined up, glanced over his shoulder,
turned his horse, and rejoined the lad. There had been a
strange note in Mipam's voice; his call had seemed like a cry
of distress.

'What is it? Are you ill?' asked Tingley, uneasy at the sight
of Mipam's abnormal pallor, his terror-stricken eyes, and his
hand trembling on his horse's bridle.

'What are you going to do with your yaks?' asked Mipam
ignoring his question.

'I, *Kushog*. . . . My yaks? . . . Why? . . .'

Mipam interrupted him.

'You're going to sell them to a butcher, to be slaughtered
like the rest. . . . I know now! Answer me!'

'But . . . if I don't find a buyer to give me a good price,
I must. . . . It's the usual thing.'

'Why didn't you tell me that the other day?'

'I didn't want to hurt your feelings; you have certain ideas.
. . . . Good ideas, no doubt, very praiseworthy ideas. You
belong to the clergy, I'm only a layman. . . . But I assure you,
Kushog, that I would have arranged things perfectly; you
wouldn't have noticed anything. Oh! I'm not such a fool as
al! that. I know the proper way to deal with monks. But
who's the idiot that told you about this? Some wretched
fellow who doesn't know what the etiquette is!'

'Be quiet! How much do you want for your yaks? I'll buy
them from you.'

'Buy my yaks? But why? That's not reasonable.'

'I have money, and I'll pay you in advance; this very evening
if you like.'

'Why spend your money? You'll need it. What are you
going to do with yaks?'

'How much?' Mipam asked roughly.

'Well, if you will have it so, I paid thirty silver *sangs* each for them.'

'That means that you want to sell them dearer. You want to make a profit; the butcher would give you more for them.'

'Oh! you are a holy lama, I understand now. Forgive me if I haven't shown you enough respect. But I'm only a layman, just a *mi-nag!*[1]

'Five *sangs* more per yak won't seem to you, perhaps, a sufficient profit. Do you want more? But bear in mind that what I give you will reduce the amount that I can employ to save other beasts.'

'You want to buy others!' exclaimed Tingley. '*Kushog*, there's no sense in it; you can't buy them all.'

'Unhappily not,' replied the young man gravely, 'but one must do as much good as one can.'

Tingley began to feel a kind of shame.

'I don't ask more than the thirty *sangs* I paid,' he said. 'I will trust that through the merits of this good action I may sell the merchandise I've bought to my advantage.'

'Very well,' said Mipam, and he turned his horse's head another way, wishing to be alone.

The caravan continued its slow march to death.

On the evening of the same day, while Tingley was completing the work of unloading his beasts, two yaks which had already been eased of their burdens came and hung about near Tingley; the animals gazing at Mipam as he folded his little tent. In the drowsy eyes of these great hairy creatures the young man thought he could detect a ray of consciousness, a secret appeal from the depths of their darkened minds.

'Tingley, fasten a piece of cord to one of the horns of each of these yaks, find out who their owner is, and buy them for me!'

Tsöndup's man did not dare to protest. He thought his

---

[1] *Mi nag*—'Black man', 'an obscure man', i.e. not enlightened concerning religious matters.

young companion was crazy, but in Tibet every action inspired by compassion arouses, even amongst the coarsest and most materially-minded peasants or traders, an intuitive feeling of respectful admiration. Chenrezigs of the thousand arms, the symbol of Infinite Compassion, was not chosen in vain to be the Supreme Lord and Protector of the lofty Land of the Snows.

Inside his small tent, Mipam threw himself on the grassy ground and sobbed with despair as he thought of his poverty. But it was not because he was too poor to win Dolma that he was so afflicted; what grieved him was the lack of money to save from pain the unhappy brutes that were grazing around him.

CHAPTER VIII

MIPAM pursued his journey, the victim of a melancholy whose cause far surpassed in significance the hapless fate of the yaks which he saw before his eyes. He was haunted by distressing visions of the misery common both to those who inflict suffering and to their victims. He recalled the tragic voices which he had heard, one night long ago, as a little innocent pilgrim, in the hermit's hut in the heart of the forest. He recalled the leopard which he had protected, and his flight from his father's house in quest of the country where all are friends. The product of that marvellous childhood was this tall young man, a future merchant, wending his way to a centre of traffic in the company of predatory traders. He pitied himself, then, for his spiritual fall, and he was filled with speechless anger as he realized the dominant place which material preoccupations held in his mind, and found himself tormented by a growing uneasiness as to his immediate future in China.

Tsöndup had said nothing to him on the subject, and he himself, bewildered by his unexpected departure, and with all his thoughts centred on Dolma, had not thought of asking him for an explanation. Dorje, undoubtedly, meant to give him useful advice, and Tsöndup, in handing him a large sum of money, had relied upon his ability to make a wise use of it, to support himself and lay the foundation of his career. His hundred and fifty silver *sangs* might serve as the initial capital of a commercial enterprise. Many traders who had made considerable fortunes had begun with a smaller sum. He understood that Tsöndup did not wish to employ him, but rather to help him to become independent. Tsöndup probably expected that before long one of the traders returning from

166

China would restore to Tenzin the money which he had taken it upon himself to advance on Tenzin's behalf. To advance, not to give. That was how he must interpret Tsöndup's action; and the repayment of a loan includes interest. It was not only a hundred and fifty *sangs* that he owed Tenzin, but a hundred and fifty *sangs* plus the interest current among merchants. How much was that? He didn't know exactly: at least fifty *sangs* yearly, seventy-five perhaps, or even more. And he possessed only a few silver coins, the balance of his childish treasury, which he had taken with him, tied up in his sash, when he fled from his country. He had spent some part of this during his journey to Shigatze with Dolma, and afterwards Gatahlden, when he had offered lamps in the temples.

He began to laugh ironically, to laugh out of sheer despair, but he did not regret his charitable folly. His distress, on the contrary, increased his love for the creatures which he had saved. He felt a desire to fondle them. He would have experienced a bitter joy in dying of hunger and destitution, abandoned in the wilderness, in the midst of his great yaks, placidly and happily grazing, indifferent to his sufferings, incapable of realizing his sacrifice.

He did not recoil before that end; he was proud to know that he was capable of it; but was it indispensable? At seventeen one has more than one resource, apart from money. He had to win Dolma; he had promised her his love, and a fine house to shelter their happiness; and he owed her these.

And here Mipam, usually so lucidly introspective, hardly realized that he had just been thinking of the conquest of his young mistress in the light of a duty which was incumbent upon him, rather than as the need of his heart and his flesh.

The boy clenched his fists and raised head:

'So be it!' he said aloud. It was the acceptation of the conditions of a battle. What methods he would employ he did not yet know, but he felt that he had it in him to conquer.

On the following days Mipam rode on in silence, elaborating his plans. But the realization of well-ordered plans, conceived and matured in accordance with everyday human wisdom, was to constitute no part of the life of the 'son of Chenrezigs.' Other influences were shaping his life, influences whose springs lay deep in the mystery of the past: what the Tibetan sages call 'the force of old actions.'

Shortly before reaching Dangar, the caravan passed close to a monastery. On seeing this a sudden desire awakened in Mipam. The peaceful aspect of the little monastic dwellings made an imperious appeal to him, and he felt an irresistible temptation to linger beside them. To pass the evening in an inn crammed with rowdy traders who would celebrate their arrival by copious libations of brandy seemed, all at once, too odious, too dreadful to endure. He put his horse to a trot and rejoined Tingley.

'Listen,' he said to Tingley. 'You will continue to follow the caravan. At Dangar, as soon as they have been unloaded, you will take possession of the two yaks that belong to me, which we have marked with a notch on their horns. You will see that they are kept with the three others that I bought from you, and taken to good pasturage. I'm going to stop here. Leave me the tent and the rest of the provisions; you will be able to get food in the town. I am going to rest near the monastery. If, the day after to-morrow, I have not joined you at Dangar, come back here to tell me if Dorje has arrived.'

'Are you ill?' inquired Tingley. 'In that case you would be better off in a room, where they could give you a good dinner, than all by yourself, at night, in the open country.'

'I'm not ill, I am only a little tired, and I don't want a lot of noise around me.'

Tingley had lost the habit of forcing his advice on his obstinate 'nephew'. He did what was asked of him; he promised to look after the yaks, and to return within two days if Mipam did not rejoin him at Dangar; and he rode off after the caravan.

Mipam had quite made up his mind to sleep in his little tent, close to the walls of the monastery; but he felt some anxiety in respect of his horse. Highway robbers do not venture so near the towns; but thieves are plentiful enough, and the horse might be stolen. Why should he not apply to the monastery? Probably one of the monks would allow him to stable his horse. This would give him a pretext for entering the monastery: he was dying to do so. Mipam glanced at his dress. It was in good condition, but dust-stained and faded by exposure to the sun. He had not the appearance of a beggar, but of a traveller come from afar. This was exactly what he *was*, but was it what he ought to *appear*? He decided that it was not. He rode his horse behind a small hillock, to avoid being seen from the monastery, unlaced one of his bags, took out his semi-ecclesiastical costume—that of a travelling lama—put it on, packed his other clothes in the bag, and remounted his horse. Full of assurance, now that he knew he was dressed with becoming elegance, he rode toward the monastery. As he approached its walls two *trapas* (monks), walking in the same direction, greeted him courteously and inquired if he was on his way to the *gompa*, and if he was going to visit one of the monks in their monastery.

'I know no one in your monastery,' Mipam replied; 'I only hope that someone will allow me to put up my horse there for the night, while I sleep in my tent,' and with a motion of the head he indicated the bundle fastened to his crupper. The two *trapas* regarded this well-dressed traveller with marked consideration.

'Most certainly, *Kushog*,' said one of them, 'they will find room for your horse. I'm sure our *gegen*[1] will be happy to render you that service. Would you like to ask him? We will take you to him.'

'You are very kind,' Mipam replied politely. 'I will follow you.'

He dismounted and walked beside the *trapas*, holding his horse's bridle.

[1] Professor.

'Where do you come from, *Kushog*?' asked the elder of the two monks.

'From Shigatze. I came by way of Cherku with a caravan. I have some yaks in it,' he added carelessly.

'Ah, you do some trading,' said the other monk.

'A little,' answered Mipam. 'That is not my principal occupation. I was to have become an astrologer, but I prefer the study of philosophy.'

'Most excellent!' said the monks in unison; their esteem for the traveller was increasing.

Seeing him in the company of two of the inmates of the monastery, and recognizing from his clothes that he was a member of the clergy, the monks whom they encountered in the streets of the *gompa* did not question Mipam.

The professor lived in a little house belonging to the palace of a lama *tulku*, which stood by itself in a courtyard, with a private entrance to the road. Mipam had not long to wait outside. One of the monks who had brought him there returned very shortly, with a companion, and told Mipam that his horse would be stabled and his luggage safely bestowed, and that he was invited to take tea with the professor. Mipam thanked him, took a scarf from one of his bags, and entered the house.

Ushered into the lama's room,[1] he presented him with the scarf, and politely expressing his thanks for the service rendered him, and for his host's invitation, sat down, drank some tea, and ate a little barley meal.

As his two pupils had already done, the professor asked Mipam where he came from, and what was the object of his journey, and many other questions which compelled the boy to draw upon his imagination rather than reveal what he did not choose to tell. Now, once he began to embroider, Mipam was given to representing himself as what he wished to be rather than as what he actually was. And so, without deliberate

[1] The title of lama is given by courtesy to all learned and distinguished monks, even if they have no authentic right to it.

intention, he conveyed to his host the impression that he had before him a young monk of good family and fairly well-to-do. One detail helped to confirm the professor in this opinion. Mipam, on being asked whether he had any acquaintances in Dangar, replied that he was joining his friend Dorje there, the son of the trader Tsöndup of Shigatze, and that he would also be calling on the agent of the trader Tenzin of Lhasa, who was a great friend of his father's. On hearing these names the professor exclaimed that both men were well known to him.

Several lamas belonging to the monastery, and among others the incarnated lama (*tulku*) who owned the house in which he was lodged, had business relations with the agents of these two merchants. From that moment Mipam ceased to be a stranger, and inspired them with complete confidence. They could not think of letting him camp in the open; he must sleep in the monastery, and as the permission of the head of the monastery was necessary before they could put up a guest for the night, the professor gave a scarf to one of his pupils, which he was to present to the dignitary with a request for the necessary authorization.

This was granted, and after partaking of a generous supper Mipam was ushered by one of the *trapas* in attendance upon the professor into a smaller courtyard, which gave access to two apartments, one on either side. The young man's blankets and bags had already been carried into one of these rooms and placed on the platform which served as a bed. A small lamp was burning on a bracket.

'*Kale jugs den jag*,' (sit in peace), said the *trapa*, as he withdrew.

Left alone, Mipam looked around him, inspecting his quarters. The inventory of his lodging did not take him long for the room was empty. Longer than it was wide, at each end there was a platform. The door was in the middle of the outer wall, and on either side of it was a large bay window, filled with an ornamental trellis, covered with translucent paper.

171

Mipam spread his blankets on the platform, and divesting himself of all but his trousers, he went to bed; but the thoughts that kept surging into his mind prevented him from sleeping. He was no longer thinking merely of his future in China, but of the very near future, which, when the sun rose again, would be the present, and which he would have to face. By entering the monastery, by accepting its hospitality, he had foolishly created additional difficulties for himself. On the following day he would have, as was usual, to show his gratitude to his host by making him a small present, and he would also have to pay for the corn and hay supplied to his horse. But he had come to the end of his money. The few coins he had left would not be sufficient to cover this expense. What was he going to do? How could he possibly extricate himself from his awkward predicament? He could find no solution to the problem.

His lamp went out, and he lay, with his eyes open, in the dark. Then, after a few moments, he perceived several slits in the paper stretched over the bay window which he was facing. He had not noticed them as long as his room was lighted from within, but now the dim radiance of a clear night filtered through each of these little openings. One of them framed a star, and lower down, in another, danced a twinkling yellow light that seemed to come from a distant lamp.

He was not, then, alone in this part of the buildings, as he had believed. There was some one living on the other side of the narrow courtyard. This proximity, of which he had been unaware, was at once a comfort and an annoyance. He felt vexed at having revolved the material difficulties of his position in his mind, just as though he had expressed them aloud within the hearing of indiscreet ears; on the other hand, the little light seemed friendly to him. Its intermittent flashes were like sympathetic appeals. 'Come! Come!' it said, gradually hypnotizing the young man, and drawing him with a gentle influence, persistent and irresistible.

'I must have air,' thought Mipam drowsily. He rose,

donned his old dress, and went out. Leaning against the door-post, he inhaled deep draughts of the fresh night air. Why did his neighbour so stir his curiosity? he asked himself in astonishment.

Facing him, the twinkling radiance of light continued its 'magnetic appeal, casting its light in waves on the paper that closed the bay windows of a little building identical with that in which he was lodged.

Mipam succumbed to the attraction. At close quarters, he thought, he would doubtless discover some little rent which would allow him to obtain a glimpse of the interior. Crossing the courtyard on tiptoe, he approached one of the windows. He examined the impenetrable paper screen, resolving to make an opening in it with his finger-nail, so that he might behold this bewitching light, that seemed to draw his heart from his breast. Thereupon a quiet voice, gentle yet authoritative, pronounced a single word:

'Enter!'

Mipam was not startled or astonished. He was in a peculiar state of consciousness, somewhat resembling that experienced in a dream, when one accepts without surprise the most fantastic happenings. Besides, he was vaguely expecting 'something.' That 'something' had occurred. 'Enter,' he had been told. He entered.

The room in which he found himself was large, and was evidently built between two courtyards, for opposite the door by which he had entered was another exit, and on either side of this door was a bay-window. But instead of being carefully screened with untorn paper, like that which had defied Mipam's curiosity, the bays and the door facing him had a dilapidated air. The paper which was pasted across them hung down, torn, in scores of places, exposing to view wide expanses of sky and dark masses which appeared to be buildings.

On one of the *kangs*, near one of these shabby windows, an old monk was seated, wrapped in a tattered monastic mantle.

Behind him, fastened to the wall, hung a large painting representing Jampai-yang, the mystic Lord of Science, patron of the 'Lettered,' and at the foot of the platform was an earthenware brazier, the top of which was broken. The room was devoid of furniture, and the corner in which the old man was seated was dimly lit.

Since he had been bidden to enter, Mipam naturally expected to find someone in the room, but he had expected, more than anything, to see the lamp which had, in the first instance, attracted his attention, and afterwards had so strangely forced itself upon his notice; the lamp which was the very cause of his presence there. But no lamp was visible; yet, for all that, there was light. Somewhat mystified, the young man bowed and endeavoured to make some apology, though he had no clear idea as to what he ought to apologize for; but at the sound of his stammering phrases, as he was advancing toward the old monk, the latter interrupted him.

'Sit down!'

He waved his nocturnal visitor back, ordering him with a gesture to remain near the door by which he had entered.

Mipam sat down on the floor.

The old man scrutinized him without speaking, and Mipam, not knowing what to say, was silent.

'Why is your mind tossing like the waters of the Tso Nyönpo on a stormy day?' said the monk at last. 'The waves which it raised in the ether struck upon me even here. What matters it that, to-morrow, you must confess to the professor that you have nothing to offer him in return for his hospitality? That will cause him no suffering. He is rich. It's you who will suffer, in feeling yourself humiliated by that avowal. Why did you boast, why did you change your dress, desiring to appear a man of importance, and why did it give you pleasure to realize that you were succeeding in your design? The moment of pleasure has passed; the moment that follows is painful. Who but yourself has troubled the serenity of your mind, by filling it with joy and grief? Where do you come from?'

Jampai-Yang

Mipam opened his lips to reply that he had come from Shigatze, but a wizened hand, half emerging from the ragged mantle of his interlocutor, with a calmly imperious gesture, bade him keep silence. The strange old man looked at him fixedly for some time, and then his gaze appeared to return to some object within himself; like the Buddhas, painted on the walls of the temples, he 'looked inwards.'

Mipam dared hardly to breathe.

'You saved five yaks from death; that is what deprived you of your money, and you wept because you were not able to save a greater number. Chenrezigs likewise despaired because he could not free all beings from sorrow.'

The name of Chenrezigs seemed to have, on the seer, the effect of a stone which a traveller has not seen in his path, and against which he stumbles, and thereupon suddenly perceives the surroundings of the obstacle which has forced itself upon his attention.

'Chenrezigs,' he murmured. 'Someone called you "Chenrezigs' son." I see him in the forest. You are quite little. And . . . what is that scar that you have near your shoulder? . . . . A leopard friend . . . he was looking at you. . . . Go, my son, go and sleep. All is vain but kindness.'

Much impressed, if somewhat startled by the old man's clairvoyance, Mipam prostrated himself three times, as men prostrate themselves before the Grand Lamas, and left without uttering a single word.

The courtyard, which he had to cross again, seemed darker than when he had left his room. He turned toward the seer's lodging: the lamp which had so mysteriously attracted him was no longer shining.

Fatigue overcoming the various preoccupations to which he was a prey and the emotions which he had just experienced, Mipam ended by falling asleep, but his sleep was not of long duration: he woke at dawn. The question of his departure at once presented itself to him, but it did not cause him the same acute anxiety. As if he had found it in his sleep, the solution of the difficulty flashed upon him. He must wait at the monastery for Tingley to come and fetch him, as he had asked him to do. Tingley would have money, and would lend him the sum which he required in order to take an honourable leave of his host. The fine monastic vestments which Tsöndup had had made for him at Shigatze were sufficient security; he would give them to Tingley to sell. With the product of the sale Tingley would repay himself, and would return him the balance. Nothing could be simpler.

The plan was perfect, but the first step depended on the professor rather than on himself. With what pretext could he remain until the following day as his guest? He was thinking this over when the door opened, and the monk who had brought him to his room the night before entered with a young novice, who was carrying a pot of tea, a bag of barley meal, and a brazier filled with red-hot cinders to keep the tea-pot hot.

'You are doubtless tired, *Kushog*,' said the monk, seemingly somewhat astonished to find Mipam in bed. 'You have had a long journey.'

Mipam had a sudden intuition: a way of remaining in the monastery had occurred to him.

'I had fever in the night,' he replied, 'and I feel dizzy. On our way here we encamped in some marshy places, for the sake of finding good pasture for the animals. I don't think that has done me any good. Thank you for the tea. I don't need any meal. I have some in my bag, and some dried meat as well. I shall soon be better, and able to leave.'

'There's no hurry, *Kushog*. Stop in bed and keep warm.'

He noticed the case containing his guest's bowl,[1] opened it, took out the bowl, filled it with tea, and handing it to Mipam, withdrew.

'How is my stratagem going to work?' Mipam asked himself. 'I shall have to say I'm worse, presently, so as not to leave

[1] The Tibetans usually carry a private bowl out of which they permit no one else to drink.

when I said I should.' However, he was given no time to worry about the matter. The monk who had brought him the tea re-appeared.

'*Kushog*, the professor has sent me to tell you that you must not leave to-day if you are feverish; you must rest and eat well. If you like, we will send some one to Dangar to let your friends know that you won't arrive to-day.'

'Oh! a thousand thanks!' cried Mipam. 'The professor is very kind. A day's rest will certainly do me a great deal of good. I felt very tired last night, and had a headache; that was why I wanted to sleep quietly in my tent instead of passing the evening with my fellow traders, who were going to celebrate their arrival. To-morrow I shall be perfectly well. One of the trader Tsöndup's servants has been travelling with me; not seeing me arrive to-day, he will come to look for me, and not finding my tent pitched, he will certainly ask for news of me at the monastery, Please convey my best thanks to the professor.'

Once more alone, Mipam cheerfully dressed himself. He poured himself out some tea, made a ball of meal moistened with tea, took some dried meat from his bag, and began to eat with a good appetite.

The ideas which are held by the Tibetans regarding the diet suitable for invalids differ completely from those of the Chinese; for whereas these latter advocate a drastic dietary, and even complete fasting, their western neighbours have great confidence in the good effects of intensive overfeeding. Mipam could therefore eat to his heart's content without fearing to arouse suspicions as to the genuineness of his indisposition.

About midday the monk came to ask him if he felt better, and whether he would like to dine with the professor, or would prefer to have something to eat in his room. Mipam declared that he was much better, and would have great pleasure in accepting his host's kind invitation. As he left his room he glanced at the little house on the other side of the courtyard.

It seemed untenanted. And so it had appeared to him all the morning, when he had examined it through the slits in the paper pasted over his windows, without being able to surprise the slightest movement, the least sound that might betray the presence of an inmate.

'Who lives there?' he asked the monk.

'No one,' replied the latter. 'The two rooms looking on to the courtyard are used to lodge visitors who come to see the lama, his steward, or the professor.'

'No one?' repeated Mipam, in perplexity. Had he then dreamt the extraordinary interview of the night before?

His perplexity showed itself on his face when he entered the professor's room. The professor thought he saw in Mipam's face the marks of the fever of which he had complained.

'Ah! yes,' he said, as he looked at the young man, 'one can see that you are unwell. No doubt the effects of fatigue, and also of camping in the marshes. But that won't last. Above all, eat well; there is no better remedy for fever.'

Mipam did justice to the meal: ill or well, joyous or sad, he was always hungry. Emotions of any kind had no effect whatever on his perennial appetite.

After the meal, a monk wearing a handsome monastic costume, with a waistcoat of cloth of silver, came to see the professor. Mipam was informed that the visitor was the *nierpa* (steward) of the lama *tulku*, the owner of the building, and that he answered to the name of Paljor. The steward had learnt that a friend of Tenzin the trader was with the professor and, as he knew the merchant, he was curious to see his young friend.

Mipam repeated that his elder brother lived with Tenzin, that the merchant was an old friend of his father's, and that, he, for his own part, was intending to trade in China. The conversation then turned on commercial matters, of which Mipam knew nothing, and precisely because he was ignorant of the traditional methods of the traders, he expounded others of his own invention, to the astonishment of his hearers. As

178

he was naturally eloquent, and spoke with assurance, they, without clearly understanding his explanations, admired him and recognized in him the making of an enterprising merchant who might look forward to a most successful career.

'Will you be kind enough to come round to my rooms for a moment, *Kushog*?' the steward asked him, as he rose to return to his own quarters.

'With pleasure,' replied Mipam.

'I have,' the steward observed, when they were seated in his comfortable room, 'a certain quantity of goods that have been given to my lama and to certain dignitaries of the monastery, which they, knowing my business abilities, have entrusted to me. I was thinking of handing them to a Ziling merchant to sell, but from what you have just explained to us I believe you to be cleverer than he. You will probably get a better price for the stuff. Would you like to see it?'

'Thank you, I should,' Mipam assented, in tones expressing the prudent reserve of the experienced salesman.

The steward thereupon took him into a very large room which was piled high with quantities of miscellaneous goods, comprising articles of food, textile fabrics, and carpets.

'What is there here that you could find a sale for?' asked Paljor, who evidently took Mipam for an experienced trader.

Mipam had not the least notion, but if he lacked commercial experience he had plenty of assurance.

'I cannot take a great deal,' he replied, 'as I propose to take Chinese goods with me on my next round.'

The two men employed the rest of the afternoon in making up the consignment which Mipam was to take with him. They discussed the prices, which Mipam invariably considered twice as high as they should have been, and finally it was arranged that in two days' time the young man should bring his yaks and take delivery of the bales.

Everything being arranged, Paljor invited his new representative to eat with him, to seal their agreement; then, the meal over, Mipam retired triumphantly to his room. He was no longer the pauper of the evening before; he had in his possession the first elements of a fortune which he felt that he was competent to build up.

'Dolma,' he murmured, 'if you could see me, you would be proud of me!'

But Dolma was far away, and close at hand was a mystery which forced itself upon Mipam's consideration: namely, the room opposite his own, which he had entered the night before, and where an old monk had reminded him of incidents in his life that not a soul in this monastery could know of. The room was untenanted, he was told. Well, then, he had dreamt it all: had dreamt of the singular appeal of the lamp, of crossing the courtyard with the desire to look into the room in which the light was shining, of the sudden invitation to enter: all this he had dreamt. It was strange, but possible; certain dreams leave an impression as real as that produced by actual facts. And yet. . . .

Through the slits in the paper of his windows, he continued to peer at the little building which confronted him. He waited for its windows to light up, but they remained in darkness.

Thereupon he went out, crossed the court, and stopped at the same spot as on the evening before, hoping to hear the same command to enter; but not a sound! He ventured to push the door; it opened. Darkness reigned within, which the feeble light from the courtyard did little to dispel. Facing him, the two bays and the door, with the torn paper, that led into the open on the other side of the building, should have shown in paler patches against the surrounding darkness, yet he saw nothing before him but the blurred outline of a wall. The room seemed shrunken, the platforms at each end seemed to have become shorter. He moved forward toward the door which he had seen the night before, and collided with a wall. This was not an illusion, due to the darkness, but a real wall, extending from one end of the room to the other, and with no opening in it.

Mipam went out, wishing to make sure whether, against all likelihood, he had entered another building. There was no other building there. The narrow courtyard was enclosed, on one side, by the room which he was occupying, and on the other by the mysterious chamber which he had entered the evening before, and to which he had just returned. How could it differ from the room which he had seen? The probabilities pointed to the fact that it was, in reality, as he saw it now, exactly like that which existed on the other side of the courtyard. Yet he wasn't demented; he recalled, in all its details, his interview with the old monk, and the spot where it had taken place. Then . . . then it really was a question of a dream.

Well and good, he had dreamt, and dreams of that kind are sent by friendly deities. His dream had recalled to him the thoughts that had filled his childhood, and his marvellous journey through the forest in quest of the land where all are friends.

Why had he listened to the *yogin* pilgrim he had met in the forest? Why had he returned to his father? Who knows where he would have arrived in this world, or some other, if he had continued his journey! Now, he was a trader; he *had* to become a trader, a wealthy trader. . . .

The next day, toward the middle of the morning, a monk led Tingley to Mipam's room.

'I've just been told that you've had fever, *Kushog*; I'm very sorry to hear it,' said Tsöndup's servant as soon as he entered.

Mipam smiled:

'I'm quite well, Tingley, don't worry. Has Dorje arrived?'

'He has been at Dangar since the day before yesterday.'

'Have you found out why we didn't meet him on the Nagchuka road?'

'He was obliged to delay his departure from Shigatze, he told me; I think it was on your account. He'll tell you all about it.'

'Tingley, we're going to drink some tea—the steward is

going to give us some—and after that I shall leave at once with you for Dangar. I must hire a large room there, and to-morrow we'll come back here with my yaks to fetch my merchandise. I've become a trader, Tingley.'

Tingley was inclined to think that the fever was making his fellow-traveller wander in his mind.

'All right, all right,' he said in the conciliatory tone one uses with the sick.

Mipam read his thoughts, and burst out laughing.

'I'm quite well, I assure you,' he said. 'Come and see the steward and the goods he's entrusting me with. But first you must lend me some money. I must make a present to the professor who has put me up, and to the monks who have been of service to me, and have taken care of my horse. I've hardly anything left. I'll give you, as security, the monastic costume that *aku* Tsöndup had made for me; it's quite new and of good quality; you shall sell it and pay yourself back out of what you get for it. I'll take the surplus.'

'I'll lend you the money you need, *Kushog*; I don't want any security, and you can pay me back when you like,' replied Tingley, quite hurt at realizing that Mipam, since their transaction with the yaks, thought him interested and distrustful.

He drew some silver ingots from a bag which he carried strung round his shoulders under his outer garments, and handed them to Mipam.

'We'll weigh them in the steward's room, if you haven't your scales,' said Mipam. 'Let's go to him.'

It chanced that Paljor had met Tingley, the year before, at Tsöndup's office, and remembered him. Thanks to this circumstance, Tingley's appearance as the young man's companion confirmed what he had said as to his friendly relations with the rich merchant, Tingley's employer, and the steward congratulated himself on his notion of entrusting Mipam with the sale of his goods.

Dangar is a very small fortified outpost, at the further end of the Chinese province of Kansu, on the threshold of the great solitudes of northern Tibet. A certain number of whole-sale Tibetan merchants own houses there, where they lodge during their stay in the town, and which they use also to warehouse their stocks.

Despite the fact that there is at all times a considerable floating population of Tibetans in Dangar, the town has retained a Chinese appearance. Mipam scanned with interest the shops bordering the narrow street into which he plunged, after passing through the arched gateway cut in the small enclosing wall. What a motley collection of articles was exposed for sale, skilfully displayed to tempt the passerby! The Tibetan merchants are ignorant of the art of display, and, except in the open markets, the goods remain hidden indoors. Mipam had not seen the Lhasa market, and that of Shigatze seemed to him much less interesting than this line of shops, wide open to the street, exposing all their contents, and so presenting a lavish display.

From his saddle, Mipam scrutinized also the features of the shopkeepers seated behind their counters, and of the people whom he met. These Chinese looked to him very different beings from his fellow-countrymen. Slight and erect in their tight-fitting robes, very pale and serious, giving one the impression that they were pondering some clever move, they seemed to him enigmatic and disturbing; they would surely be redoubtable adversaries in business, and it was with them that he was about to measure himself as a merchant. Mipam began to suspect that the exercise of his profession, in China, would not be all plain sailing.

The welcome that Dorje gave him caused him a certain amount of disappointment. He was expecting a cordial interest, and inquiries as to his health, and his journey, and also, if not some excuse, at least some explanation of his friend's failure to meet him at Nagchukha; but Dorje's first words were:

'Why didn't you come here with Tingley? What were you doing at the monastery?'

'Eh,' answered Mipam with a smile, 'I'm of the clergy, Dorje. A monastery is the very place for me.'

Dorje did not appear to appreciate the joke.

'Have you come to China to play the holy lama?' he retorted, in unfriendly tones. 'And what's all this story about some yaks you bought with the money my father gave you; what do these fancy notions mean?'

Mipam felt no further inclination to jest: the tone in which Dorje was speaking to him jarred on him.

'The story of the yaks is my own affair,' he answered coldly. 'As soon as I can, I shall repay uncle Tenzin the hundred and fifty silver *sangs* which your father lent me in his name. Is that all you've got to say to me, Dorje?'

Tsöndup's son was not ill-natured; Mipam's strange behaviour had annoyed him, but he bore him no ill-will.

'Sit down; we'll have something to eat, and talk at the same time. You are a young mad-cap, that's all. To-morrow I'll fix things up for you.'

'I've already fixed them up, Dorje,' Mipam answered, quietly. 'But tell me why I didn't find you on the Nagchukha road? Tingley and I waited four days for you to pass.'

'Something annoying happened,' replied Dorje, whose face again wore a vexed expression.

'On the day after your departure a client and sleeping partner of my father's, one of those on whom you called with me, sent for him. Your *gyalpo's* cousin, who is on good terms with him, had written to him, begging him to make inquiries about you. As your brother is living with uncle Tenzin, it might be supposed that you would be found at the house of a friend of Tenzin's or a friend of his friends. Now, my father's client had seen you; it wasn't necessary, therefore, to send his people to inquire about you; he knew where you were. He had liked you, and he didn't wish you any harm; nor did he wish to cause any annoyance to my father, but he hadn't the slightest desire, for our sake, to embroil himself with a government official.

'Being unable to deny that you had stayed with him, my father informed his client that you had left. Left—where for? —He pretended he didn't know, as you yourself, when you started, had no settled plans. You might possibly be going to Kham. The thing was plausible; with Ghalden as your objective, you would take the Kham road. But the *kudag* wasn't deceived by that subterfuge: he realized, instantly, that you were going to travel with me, and he told my father so. My father denied it, but then he considered that it had been unwise to lie to a person of high social rank, who had long been a sleeping partner of his.

'You see how it was: the *kudag* would have told his friend in Lhasa that you had left Shigatze, and that he didn't know your whereabouts. Now, later on, the Lhasa man might chance to realize from the fact that you had joined my caravan, that we had arranged your flight. In that case he would have reason to suspect that his friend had known of our stratagem and had given it his support. He would have been vexed; he would have reproached him with his apparent duplicity; while the *kudag*, in his turn, would have accused my father of deceiving him, and of making him seem a liar, who was protecting a boy escaping from correction by his lord. In his anger he might have broken off business relations with my father, and have even withdrawn the capital which he has invested with us . . . You see how it was. . . .

'So, to make it quite clear that there was no connection between your departure and my own, I waited ten days before starting. I knew quite well that you couldn't wait so long for me. What you would do, what route you would take, I didn't know, but you were with Tingley, and were supplied with money; there was, therefore, no cause to worry on your account. And here you are safe and sound, after all, as I had expected.'

Mipam had listened to this lengthy explanation without saying a word.

'I understand,' he said, after a pause, when Dorje had finished.

185

On the one side, commercial interests at stake, and the fear of alienating an influential partner: on the other, a fugitive persecuted by a grotesque despot who wanted his blood. The choice was soon made. The boy had been given money and a guide; this was generous treatment; He had become a nuisance; he was got rid of, and abandoned in the desert. 'There was no cause to worry about him,' Dorje had thought.

'I understand,' repeated Mipam.

He was silent for a few moments longer; then he spoke very quickly and coldly.

'Commerce is very interesting,' he said. 'I think I shall succeed in it. I've already begun. You won't have to concern yourself about me. This will put your father quite at ease as regards his partner and the officials in Lhasa or elsewhere. From to-morrow I shall set up as a merchant. I have already a certain amount of merchandise. I didn't waste my time at the monastery, as you suppose. Now I must be going. I've got to rent a room to stow my bales in.'

'Where did you get these goods, and what are they?'

'You shall see: I'll show you them the day after to-morrow.'

'Then you won't stay here? I can find room for you in the house.'

No, thanks, I had better be alone; I shall learn my way about all the sooner.'

'As you like. Come and eat with me whenever you like.'

'I shall be very pleased to, you may be sure.'

The two young men parted amicably enough, but Mipam's naturally affectionate heart was wounded by what he considered desertion on the part of his friend. When one loves, is one so calculating, so reasonable?

Tingley was waiting for Mipam and took him to see two inns at which the merchants were accustomed to lodge. In one of these the young man found what he was looking for: a room large enough for his needs, furnished with two plat-forms (*kangs*), of which one would serve for a bed, while on the other he could put some of his stock. Tingley was to find the man who was looking after the yaks and collect them, and take them on the following day to the monastery.

When he had left, Mipam tied his horse up in the stable, saw that he was given hay and corn, and carried his saddle into the room where he had already put his luggage.

He was glad to find himself alone, and to make his own arrangements. He was no longer the little boy dependent upon others, always obliged to obey. Henceforward he would do as he pleased: he had suddenly become a man, a merchant who had to earn money to live, to repay what he owed, and save money too, if he was to extend his business and become wealthy. This would mean hard work, and a struggle, but the prospect of a fight delighted him. Dolma would be proud of him.

The room in which he now found himself, with its walls of sun-baked earth, blackened by smoke, was not in the least like the *gyalmo's*, but when he thought of the latter he was amused by the admiration which it had once inspired. And what had it really been?—a cage for a slave! He had escaped, and he was fortunate.

Mipam got the innkeeper to explain where he could find the Tibetan commercial agent, on whom he proceeded to call. Without the least timidity he confronted the portly merchant, whom he found enthroned, full of his importance, on a corner of the *kang*.

The young man introduced himself as a tyro in commerce, already provided with a certain amount of merchandise, and desirous of information as regards the Chinese merchants of Sining with whom he might trade.

Though his great height and his resolute air made him appear at least two or three years older than he was, the agent thought Mipam very young to start in business as a principal. In the ordinary way the trade is learnt in the employ of a merchant, unless one happens to be the son or relative of one. But Mipam was elegantly dressed, and spoke with assurance, and this meant that he had money. The agent felt disposed to treat him with consideration. He invited him to take tea with him, and gave him all the information he required. Then, as other merchants came in, beer was served also, and the men began to talk business. Mipam, quick to note all that was likely to be useful to him, did not miss a word of what was said. He referred quite casually, in the course of conversation, to his friendly relations with Tenzin of Lhasa and Tsöndup of Shigatze, His family must be wealthy, thought the merchants; and wealth in Tibet confers the right to great esteem.

One of the merchants asked Mipam what his father's profession was.

'He's an officer, a captain,' replied the young man remembering that this title was sometimes conferred on Puntsog, in memory of the battles in which he had led his archer 'heroes.'

A captain . . . that was a nobleman, or little short of it. Mipam was giving himself a nimbus of aristocracy.

'Why did he wish to be a trader?'

'I want to become very rich.'

'And why was he so anxious to be rich?'

'To secure the wealthy girl I love,' answered Mipam, laughing.

All echoed his laughter, imagining that this son of a good family had cast his eye upon the daughter of a minister or of some other great noble of Lhasa or Tsang, and no one suspected that the girl in question was the daughter of their colleague Tenzin.

On the morrow Mipam, having duly secured a footing among the merchant folk of Dangar, returned to the neighbouring monastery.

CHAPTER IX

MIPAM, in the company of his partner, the steward Paljor, was superintending the lading of his merchandise in a spacious courtyard on one side of which some stables were built.

'Could you have imagined, *Kushog*, when you entered this *garba*[1] four days ago, that you would begin your career as a trader here?' the steward jestingly remarked.

'I didn't exactly foresee that,' answered Mipam. 'All I knew was, that I *had* to stop here. Your monastery called me when I passed near it with the caravan. But I'm not at all certain that its appeal concerned my profession of merchant. Perhaps it was a question of something loftier than commerce.'

Mipam was thinking of the singular 'dream' which he had experienced, and was seized with the desire to revisit, in broad daylight, the room which he had entered at night.

'Some gods or *bodhisatvas* must haunt your monastery, *Kushog* steward,' he observed to his partner. 'I felt them brush past me when I slept here. I am of the clergy, and though I am taking up commerce, I know that all things that are of the world have but little value. "As pictures seen in a dream, so much we regard them," it is said.'

'That's very true, *Kushog*. You understand religion. One day when you have made your fortune, you will have a fine house built in a monastery, where you will live in peace, reading our Sacred Books.'

'I am a *sha mar* [a monk of the Red Cap sect]. I shall marry and live with my wife and my family, but I shall certainly

---

[1] *Garba* is the name given by the Tibetans of this region to the almost princely residences belonging to the lamas *tulkus*, in the enclosure of a monastery.

189

have a dwelling in one of our monasteries, so that I can go into retreat there from time to time.'

'Excellent, *Kushog*! There are *sha mar* who are very learned in the religious doctrines, and who are possessed of great spiritual powers. Some of them are famous hereabouts.'

'It was there, was it not, that I lodged?'

With a gesture Mipam pointed in the direction to which his back was turned.

'Yes, just behind the wall against which that little old building is leaning.'

'Is there not a narrow courtyard, where two rooms face each other?' Mipam particularized.

'There is. One stands against that wall, which divides it from the one that faces in this direction; the other is on the opposite side, as you say. It's the quarter reserved for our visitors.'

As he was speaking, the steward also pointed to the small building and the wall to which he had referred. The young man turned round, mechanically following with his eyes his companion's gesture.

On the threshold of the dilapidated lodging which he was now facing stood an old man draped in a ragged mantle. Mipam instantaneously recognized him: it was the seer who had spoken to him in the night. Then he had not dreamt the interview!

'Who is that monk?' he breathlessly asked his partner.

'A poor lunatic whom our lama lodges and feeds out of charity,' replied the steward in an undertone. 'We don't know who he is, nor whence he comes. He speaks but very rarely, and then to say things devoid of sense. He never leaves his room, and never has a light burning there. That's one of his manias: he says he can illuminate everything with his mind. Poor man! I wonder what can have brought him outside. . . . Oh, but look, he has already gone back to his room.'

Here Mipam, seeing that Tingley and his mate had almost finished lading the yaks went out to them.

'I shall be busy here for some time yet,' he said to Tingley.

'Since you have brought a man, you can both of you return to Dangar without me. Wait for me at my inn, and we'll sup together.'

'Very well, *Kushog*.'

Mipam returned to the steward.

'I should like to talk to that old monk,' he said to him.

'Why? Of what interest can he be to you?'

'Won't you allow me to do so?'

'By all means, if you wish, *Kushog*. I only warn you that if he answers you he'll talk sheer nonsense. But he's quite harmless, not at all excitable. You've nothing to fear from him. He has never annoyed us. Would you like me to go with you?'

'No, thank you, I would rather see him by myself.'

'As you wish.'

The steward left the courtyard, vaguely uneasy. This sudden fancy of his new partner seemed to him very strange. Why did he want to talk to that old madman? Could it be that he himself was a trifle deranged in his mind?—In that case, hadn't he been imprudent to entrust him with his merchandise? But perhaps it had nothing to do with that. Who knows if the young man hadn't conceived some notion about the identity of the poor old lunatic, and wanted to verify it by conversing with him? That was possible, and the thought reassured him as to the fate of the capital which was leaving him on Mipam's yaks to brave the hazards of commerce.

Mipam pushed open the tottering door of the wretched lodging on the threshold of which he had just espied the old monk, and entered. He found himself once more in the setting he had seen in his dream. At the windows the paper hung down in tatters, and through the slits were to be distinguished the roofing of the stable, answering to the dark outlines of the buildings he had seen in the night. A painting, portraying Jampai-yang, the patron of the 'Lettered,' was hanging on the wall, and the brazier with its broken top was standing at the foot of the *kang*. Seated on this latter, and swathed in his ragged mantle, the old man silently regarded him. Save in two particulars, the scene reproduced his vision. The room he was now looking at was smaller than that which he had surveyed three nights ago, and on the side opposite the entrance it was bounded by a blank wall. Otherwise he recognized in it the same peculiarities which he had noticed in his nocturnal investigations of the night before last, which had induced him to attribute his interview with the old *trapa* to a dream. He had then collided with a wall in his attempt to reach the further exit. And now, in broad daylight, he found that the door which he had entered twice, in the course of two successive nights, was not accessible from the old monk's lodging. What on earth was the meaning of this phantasmagoria?

'Why let yourself be troubled by things of no importance?' said the old man slowly.

'*Kushog*,' answered Mipam, 'I know you; it was you who called me the first night I spent in this monastery. I know your room too, but . . . but I did not enter from this side, and yet I saw you; I saw your room as clearly as I see you, and as I see it now. But then, there were two doors, facing each other; one could pass from the courtyard on which my room opened to that from which I have just come, and yet now there is a wall between the two—a solid wall, with no passage through it. *Kushog*, explain this to me, I entreat you. I can understand nothing at all; it will drive me mad.'

'Mad, it's I who am mad. Paljor has told you so. What do you want with a madman?'

'Sir, I know you are not mad. You are a holy wonder-worker. Do explain.'

'Explain what? He who is capable of understanding has no need of explanations, and whatever explanations may be given him, he who is not apt of understanding will understand nothing at all. You have already forgotten how one day you drove your arm into a rock more solid than this wall and drew meal from it. Meal from a rock! Ha, ha, ha! How impossible!

Only a madman could imagine the like. You are just as mad
as I am to have thought that you held meal in your hand.
But you ate it, and it nourished you. That's enough.'

'How do you know all that, *Kushog*? The other night you
reminded me of things I did when I was a mere child. . . .'

'Beings bear their past written upon and in them, and one
needs but to know how to read it.'

'How is it stamped upon them, and by what signs? And
how can one read within them?'

'How can one see through a wall, my son?'

Mipam started:

'See through a wall, do you say! . . . Is that it? . . . I saw
you through this wall when I was in the other room. . . .
But that's impossible. One can't see through a wall.'

'All that we see, we see *through* something. It may be
through a fog or through the divagations of our minds. Why
not through a wall, provided we haven't the preconceived idea
of the existence of an impenetrable barrier? Is the contact of
the eye necessary for pictures to appear to us? Do you not
see forms when your eyes are shut? Don't you see them in
your dreams? But what you don't see, my son, is *yourself* and
that, alone, is of any consequence.'

'*Kushog*, since you can see written on me the events of my
past life, you know also what I am engaged in. Tell me, shall
I succeed?'

'The future! You want to know the future; you think it is
written on you as the past is written. It is actually in this past
that the germ of the future resides; the *rgyu* [the principal
cause] is there, but not the multiple *rkyen* [secondary causes]
which are to fashion the germ, to fortify or enfeeble it; which
from the minute seed are to make the mighty tree, or else to
destroy the young growth as it breaks through the ground,
reaching towards the light. The future exists, but solely in
the causes which can engender it, as the tree exists in the seed.
The potential combinations of those causes are infinite in
number; they comprise the meeting between the forces

193

generated in our world and those emanating from other worlds. How can he, who belongs to any particular world, he whose conceptions are limited to the things of that world, how can such a one foresee the irruption of extraneous forces whose nature and activities are different from all he is capable of knowing?

'Do you know what form the future has to the eye? It resembles the dance of the dust-motes in the air along the roads on days of drought. There they lie and rest upon the road, ready to respond to the stimulus which stirs them to action. The wind blows—and there they are, those particles of dust, rising and travelling and dancing, meeting, colliding, fore-gathering, forming indefinite patterns that fall apart before one has time to realize to what they bear a resemblance. They are abortive sketches of what might have been and will never be because some sudden shock has broken up their formation in the making.

'The pictures of the future one may envisage are merely probabilities and never certitudes.'

The ideas expressed by the old man were too complicated for Mipam's understanding. The young man's simple belief, derived from those current in his environment, was that a learned astrologer, and, better still, a holy wonder-worker, could predict, with absolute certainty, the fate of an individual and his enterprises. He timidly returned to his query.

'Reverend sir . . . my business?'

'Your business . . . it appears that it ought to prosper. You are competent to make a success of it. . . . It will prosper. . . . Are you satisfied now?'

'Yes, surely, *Kushog*; but one question more. . . . Be kind to me, *Kushog*. Please be good enough to tell me. . . .'

He paused, embarrassed.

'It is the girl of whom you are thinking, isn't it? It's of her. For a long, long time your paths have crossed for good or ill. Many a time, in the course of your past lives, have you travelled together. You separated, only to meet anew. And here she is

194

once more upon your path. But fellow wayfarers do not always keep together. One tarries, plunges into a side path, lingers in some wayside inn, or, wearied, sits down at the foot of a tree, while the other presses on and passes him. . . .

'Go, go your way, young merchant. A wall is before you whose stones are fancies; mists of imagination hedge you in. Ha, Ha! . . . I'm mad, my boy. Mad as the traders who think they can see through walls; mad as the muddle-headed stewards who dub insensate what they cannot understand. Ha, ha!'

Mipam felt ill at ease; the old man's uncanny laugh disturbed him. He prostrated himself in farewell, and left the room. He did not doubt the old monk's possession of supernatural powers: of that he had given proof in divining his past, but he had not explained the miracle by which he, Mipam, had seen from one room into another through a wall, and had conversed with someone on the other side of that wall.

He had also declined to prophesy anything precise as to the success of his business ventures and his marriage with Dolma. All that he had said was incomprehensible. Was he to believe Paljor, who had warned him that he would hear but the wanderings of a madman? Mipam, with a humility born of wisdom, was inclined rather to think that his lack of intelligence prevented his understanding the gist of the strange monk's words. He felt, however, no keen desire to do so. No sooner had he left the courtyard to rejoin his partner than all his thoughts were once more centred on his trading and on Dolma. The wall that hid and barred him from himself rose up more solid than ever; the mist grew denser.

What man calls chance is ability more than anything else. The clairvoyance, the sureness of logical deduction inborn in Mipam, together with his untiring energy, won him rapid success. He applied to his business qualities that he might have employed in loftier pursuits, continuing to ignore his essential personality, resting content with making his way among the blind beings instead of cutting loose from them.

Eighteen months after his debut he forwarded two hundred and fifty silver *sangs* to Tenzin, in repayment, plus interest, of the hundred and fifty which the latter had lent him on his departure from Tibet, and by the same messenger he sent to Dolma and her stepmother two rolls of fine Chinese silk.

Mipam had been anxious to retain a domicile in Dangar: he liked that little town on the borders of the great Tibetan solitudes. Between two of his business journeys he rode as far as the shores of the Koko Nor (the immense Blue Lake) and spent several days there sleeping in a small tent, almost forgetting that he was a merchant, and extending a willing welcome to his boyish memories, which at other times dared not seek admittance to a mind so wholly immersed in commercial projects. Lying at full length in the tall grass or upon the mauve and pink pebbles, spangled with silver, he smilingly called up the vision of the little Mipam of long ago. With tenderness he listened to the faint and remote accents of the youthful mystic voicing his aspirations and his childish dreams. Then, as the holiday which he had allowed himself came to a close, he bade farewell to the frail, beloved phantom, that faded without protest, gentle and melancholy, and he who returned to Dangar was the keen, hard-working, avaricious merchant, already held in high esteem by his fellow traders, who were surprised to find such skill and tenacity in a boy still in his 'teens.

As soon as his resources permitted, Mipam left his room at the inn. He continued to dislike crowds and noise, and was not insensible to a certain comfort. Further, he considered that the fact of possessing a place of residence would give him a standing by which his business would profit.

A small house being offered for sale, Mipam had been able to purchase it by instalments. It was not yet the 'beautiful home' promised to Dolma, but a young wife could live in it without being too unhappy. The house, built in the Chinese fashion, comprised a shop having a frontage on the road. By the side of the shop a door gave access to an open passage, leading to a courtyard, at the end of which rose a modest building consisting of a room on the ground floor and one above it. A wooden balcony ran the whole length of this latter. The sides of the courtyard were occupied by a stable and a kitchen, near which there was a well.

Mipam let the shop to a Chinaman. The ground-floor room at the end of the courtyard served as a storeroom; Mipam also received there the people with whom he did business. The first-floor room constituted his private quarters, to which only his friends were admitted. These were few in number; Mipam kept very much to himself. During his visits to Dangar he devoted to study the time left over from his commercial occupations. The head cashier at Tenzin's office taught him bookkeeping, and how to write business letters in Tibetan, and a Chinaman instructed him in reading and writing the elementary characters of his language, such as were needed in commercial correspondence.

Mipam was still fond of dress. He considered, not without reason, that his success was due to the handsome costume which he had worn on visiting the monastery of Dangar. Had it not, by influencing the professor and the steward in his favour, facilitated his first steps, which might have been arduous and painful? When he thought of his exceptional luck, Mipam included, among his benefactors, the five yaks which he had saved. The merits of his act of charity were bearing pleasant fruit. He insisted that their keepers should take good care of these great animals, each of which wore, in one of its pierced ears, a tassel of red wool, indicating that it was 'life-given'—destined to die a natural death.

In Mipam there was no tendency toward asceticism. In his new position he was just as greedy as he had always been. The meals in his house were lavish in quantity; that was one of the reasons why Tashi, the first servant he had engaged, and later, Kalzang, the supplementary servant, gave him such zealous service. What other master would have fed them so well? They had never met one; and for a Tibetan of their class to eat well is the height of happiness. Though he doled out alcohol in moderate doses to his two men, Mipam himself drank none, nor did he gamble; two things which afforded great surprise to his colleagues, who were, for the most part, far from sober, and hopeless gamblers.

Some business transactions with a Tibetan chief in the neighbourhood of Payenrong led, indirectly, to Mipam's making the acquaintance of some white foreigners who resided in Dangar. He had heard it said that some *Philings* (foreigners, and more especially the English) were living in the town and preaching their religion there, but as he was nearly always away travelling, and as during his short periods at home his occupation kept him indoors, he had never had occasion to meet them.

These foreigners were Protestant missionaries: an Englishman, a Mr. Peary, a man of fifty, his wife, who was of Dutch extraction, and a young Australian, their assistant. In addition to a room for Church services, the Mission included a dispensary and a boys' school for boarders and day pupils. The son of the chief of Payenrong, a boy of eighteen, named Tobden, was a boarder. Neither his father nor he had the remotest intention of becoming a Christian, but the chief thought it would be useful for his son to be taught in the Western method, and also to learn Chinese in the ordinary way. Such an education, he thought, would procure for Tobden a lucrative post in the Chinese administration controlling the Tibetan province of Amdo.[1] Now, the Mission school gave its teaching free. To be admitted as a boarder it was sufficient for the pupil to contribute an adequate quota in kind to the common dietary. The chief had been enchanted with these advantageous conditions, and, on their side, the worthy missionaries considered that the presence of the sons of good families among their pupils would give the Mission a standing among the natives, and would help them to effect conversions; in which the good people were under a delusion.

[1] Amdo is a large territory situated on the north-east of Tibet, and partly included in the Chinese province of Kansu.

'Go and see Tobden, from time to time, when you are in Dangar,' the chief had said to Mipam. 'I shall be glad for him to have your company. Young as you are, you are already a man of good position, and successful in business; you will be a good example for him.'

And so it happened that one day Mipam visited the Mission.

A young Tibetan of eighteen summers, even though he be a boarder, cannot imagine that anyone should be allowed to interfere with his movements. He is willing to admit that he ought to be regular in his attendance at lessons, inasmuch as the object of his stay in the institution is to acquire learning. But he is already up in arms against the notion that he should be obliged to take his meals at strictly fixed hours. Why can he not have his portion kept back for him in the kitchen? Who would be inconvenienced by that? As for the thought of being shut up within the walls of a courtyard or a garden during the leisure hours of the day, this would offend all his ideas of good sense, if he could conceive that anyone could be capable of devising such a regulation.

Mr. Peary was perfectly well aware of this aspect of the senior pupils' mentality; much to his regret, he had to consent to their passing through the gate of the Mission, to wander round the little town, facing all the different temptations which—lacking Grace—these poor pagans, he thought, were unable to resist. Nevertheless, in a lodge adjoining the entrance-gate a Chinese porter, and a Christian to boot, exercised a general control over all who entered the Mission. This porter stopped Mipam.

'What do you want?'

'I've come to see the Chief of Payenrong's son; Tobden is the name.'

'What is the motive of your visit?'

'Motive? . . . why, to see him. His father asked me to call and see him.'

'Who are you?'

'Am I by any chance at the Potala, in the palace of the Dalai

199

Lama, and are you his chamberlain, or his master of ceremonies?' Mipam asked ironically.

The old Chinese, offended by this raillery, replied in portentous tones, which he thought imposing:

'You are at the Mission, at the house of the Reverend Peary.'

'That I know. I'm not asking to be taken to him,' answered
Mipam, not at all impressed. 'I merely want to see a Tibetan
boy called Tobden. Hurry up, my good man. I've no time
to waste; go and look for Tobden or tell me where I can find
him.'

The porter wavered.

'Very well, my friend,' concluded Mipam. 'Stay here, I
shan't be long discovering Tobden. If he's as big as his father,
it won't be easy to hide him.'

'I'll go and call him,' cried the Chinese, stopping the
impatient visitor, who had already passed the lodge. 'You
wait here.'

He departed, leaving the young man to wait in a small
room whose walls were plastered with pictures and inscriptions,
reproducing, in Chinese and Tibetan, texts from the Bible,
quite incomprehensible to one unversed in all the doctrines
to which they referred. Mipam ran his eye over them absently,
to be pulled up by a picture portraying a procession of people
amusing themselves in various ways, drinking, playing dice,
and careering on horseback in the company of women. All
were trooping joyously under a large porch, on the farther side
of which they were seized by devils of various hues, and
hurled into a sea of flames. Another procession, less numerous,
was composed of men and women of conceited bearing, advancing with melancholy looks toward a narrow door, behind
which they found a very steep stairway, leading to the summit
of a mountain.

Mipam had seen at the doors of village temples frescoes
representing analogous scenes, but in these the faithful advancing toward Paradise had not a sorrowful air, and instead of
swarming up an arduous stairway they sauntered gleefully along

a gorgeous rainbow. Badly versed though he was in the doctrines of this religion, Mipam knew that these pictures were the work of ignoramuses addressing other ignoramuses.

'That picture interests you, my young friend?'

Someone who had just come up asked him this question in Tibetan, but with the oddest of accents.

Mipam turned round. A stranger was standing behind him. A stout man, with a pleasant, pink, chubby face framed in straw-coloured hair; while his eyes. . . . Mipam was petrified with astonishment—he had pale blue eyes, like those of the huge dogs that guard the herdsmen's tents in the wilderness.

'That picture interests you?' the stranger repeated amiably, with an engaging smile.

'No!' replied Mipam still staring at the extraordinary eyes of his interlocutor

He realized that the man of abnormal physique who was addressing him must be the master of the house. By an effort of the will, wishing to appear polite and well-bred, he turned his eyes from the object that so fascinated him, and courteously explained what had brought him there.

'I'm in business relations with Tobden's father,' he said. 'He asked me to go and see his son, and to do what I could to amuse him during my visit to Dangar. I've come to ask him to eat with me.'

'In business relations?—You are a merchant, then; with what merchant are you employed?'

'I manage my own concern,' Mipam answered, in the tone in which he might have proclaimed his title of Emperor of the world.

'Oh, you'll excuse me! You are very young to be a master. Are you married?'

'No.'

'What part of the country do you come from?'

'From a great distance from here, to the south of Lhasa.'

'Indeed! . . . I don't think Tobden is free yet; the lesson in Chinese is probably not finished yet. In the meanwhile, come and take a cup of tea with me. I will have Tobden told that a friend of his father is here.'

'You are very kind.'

'This way, follow me.'

In the dining-room into which Mipam was ushered Mrs. Peary and Mr. Simon were about to take tea. On the table were a small milk-jug, a small sugar basin, and a small plate with some small slices of bread and butter. Everything seemed to Mipam abnormally small. Mrs. Peary herself was not tall, but her breadth made up for her height. Her hair, drawn smoothly back in the Chinese manner, made her appear as if she had been wearing a kind of yellow skull-cap, and her eyes looked even more colourless than her husband's.

Mr. Simon was young, tall, and slight; his head was covered with almost black hair, and his brown eyes gave him an expression that Mipam recognized, with relief, as honest and normal. When he was invited to sit down he instinctively drew his chair toward that one of these human beings with whom he felt a vague racial relationship. The Pearys must for certain belong to the category of the *mi ma yins*.[1]

Mrs. Peary handed a cup of tea to Mipam, and offered, first of all, to help him to milk, which he energetically refused, and then to sugar, which he gladly accepted.

'Our guest is already the head of a business house,' said Mr. Peary, addressing his wife and Mr. Simon. 'He trades with the chief of Payenrong, the father of our pupil Tobden. He has come to see the boy. I found him waiting in the porter's lodge. He was very interested in the picture portraying the contrary fate of the sinners on their way to hell and that of the faithful who have accepted *Kunchog's* pardon, and walk sustained by His grace.'

'Your picture is ugly,' replied Mipam, 'and that stairway

[1] Literally, the 'not-men', one of the six classes of beings tabulated by the Tibetans. It comprises genii, spirits, demons, etc., some friendly, others hostile to humans, or alternately one or the other, according as one is pleasing or displeasing to them.

overgrown with thorns is displeasing. Our painters represent that sort of thing much better. I could supply you, for a modest price, with a very pretty picture. In it the people wending their way to Paradise would wear a happy look, and would be taking an enjoyable stroll on a wide rainbow, preceded by a well-dressed lama. In Tibet also scenes of that sort are to be seen painted at the temple doors, but only in the villages, and even there they don't figure inside the temples themselves.'

'Why?' asked Mr. Simon, who liked to learn.

'Because they represent the beliefs of the ignorant. Those to whom the Doctrine is familiar know that hells and paradises exist only in our minds, and they free themselves from them by effacing them from their thoughts.'

Mipam repeated the fine sentence which he had heard from his teacher, the disciple of Kushog Yeshes Kunzang. He would have been at some pains to explain its meaning, but he felt that a saying borrowed from a learned lama like Yeshes Kunzang must have a very profound meaning. Mysterious as it remained to him, it had a persuasive ring that attracted Mipam. He had heard, also, the mystical verses of Milarespa chanted:

> *Sems rang nas chyung*
> *Sems nang la thim.*
> *It arises from the mind*
> *And in the mind it sinks.'*

Involuntarily he hummed the melody. Mr. Simon seemed interested. Mrs. Peary appeared to be trying hard to hold herself in hand.

'Those are false ideas,' she declared at last. 'Heaven and Hell are terrible realities. Those who deny their existence will one day be convinced of it to their undoing. *Kunchog* gave His only begotten Son to be slain that our sins might be forgiven and that we might enter into Paradise for all eternity. They who decline His gift, in this world, will burn eternally in the next.'

'Oh!' exclaimed Mipam, 'that is wicked, absolutely wicked! It is cruel to give anyone to be killed. For my part, I saved five yaks from death, so preventing their being sold to the butcher, and I was distressed that I hadn't enough money to buy a greater number of them, and save them as well. And then, you are mistaken. One cannot remain for ever in a hell or a paradise, because there, as here, one must die some day, and, being dead, one is born again in the place to which the fruits of one's actions lead one. But what are you saying about *Kunchog*? *Kunchog* has no son. *Kunchog* is not a person; it's a name that designates, in one, the Buddha, his Doctrine, and the religious Order. That is why we say *Kunchog Sum*.'[1]

'*Kunchog* is not that,' Mrs. Peary corrected him. 'He created the heavens and the earth and all that therein is. His Son came down to earth to save sinners. . . .'

'You're wrong, you're wrong, *Cham Kushog*,' protested Mipam. 'You're not Tibetan, and I know better than you what the words of my language mean.'

'We must give him some tracts for him to read and understand. Arthur, give him the Gospel of St. John too.'

'I will,' replied Mr. Peary.

Then, to the great stupefaction of Mipam, the good lady began to intone a strange hymn with Tibetan words, to music which had absolutely nothing Tibetan about it.

'Join in, join in!'

The singer, pausing for a moment, issued an imperious

[1] *Kunchog* signifies 'rare, excellent'. It is as Mipam puts it, the usual appellation for the trilogy: the Buddha, his Doctrine, and the Order of monks, his disciples: whence the expression *Kunchog Sum*, the 'three rare-excellents'. The Tibetans believe in the existence of *gods*. These form one of the six kinds of beings they acknowledge, but the gods, *lha*, have not the eminent and unique dignity of the 'rare-excellents'. The Protestant Missionaries settled on the frontiers of Tibet have selected this term *Kunchog* to translate the foreign word God, hence the continual misunderstanding between them and those whom they address. The Catholic Missionaries translate the word God by *Nam gi dagpo*, the Master (or the Owner) of the Heavens.

command, in English, to her husband and Mr. Simon, to mingle their voices with hers.

Thus urged by her, they obeyed: Mr. Peary willingly, his assistant with a visible lack of enthusiasm. He would have preferred to go on talking with Mipam.

The chorus was in full blast when Tobden appeared in the doorway. With a masterful gesture Mrs. Peary forbade him to advance, but Mipam, insensible to the charms of the vocal music with which they were regaling him, and not initiated into the polite customs of the West, rose and went toward the boy.

'You are Tobden,' he said. 'One couldn't make a mistake; you are exactly like your father. I am Mipam, a merchant of Tromo. Your father asked me to come and see you. I am taking you to eat with me this evening.'

Peary and Simon stopped singing, but Mrs. Peary imperturbably finished the hymn.

Mipam saluted all three politely, expressed his thanks for the kind reception they had given him, and left the dining-room with Tobden. Together they crossed the courtyard, making for the exit, when Mr. Simon rejoined them.

'Mr. Peary asked me to give you these tracts. . . . Will you wait for a moment?' he said to Mipam.

He entered a little building and came out again almost at once, holding in his hand a tiny book and some printed sheets.

'This will enlighten you on our holy religion,' he said, handing them to Mipam.

'Thank you,' said the latter.

'You must come and see us again. I should like to have a chat with you.'

'Thank you,' repeated Mipam. 'You are very good.'

The two young men passed through the big gateway into the road. Tobden burst out laughing.

'They're extraordinary, aren't they, *Kushog*?'

'Very curious indeed,' declared Mipam. 'I had never yet seen any foreigners. What funny eyes they've got! Yet they seem to see clearly, just as we do. It's not an illness that has washed the colour from their eyes. They are white by nature, like those of the herdsmen's dogs; you'd say that cheese was oozing out of their heads. It's horrible!'

'Not beautiful, certainly,' Tobden agreed.

'And why did they suddenly start singing?'

'That's their way of praying to their *Po-lha*.[1] They make us sing too, every day, in class.'

'Can you sing like them?'

'I can.'

'It's not beautiful, like our *gurmas*.'

'Quite the reverse.'

The young men began to talk of other things, and presently arrived at Mipam's house.

'Here we are,' said Mipam. 'The house and shop belong to me.'

'Upon my word,' Tobden exclaimed, in admiration, 'you are rich, *Kushog!*'

'No, not yet, but I'm young, and shall be rich in time,' said Mipam, as he showed Tobden into his private room.

He went up to the window which opened on to the balcony and clapped his hands. Two vigorous '*lags*' answered him from the kitchen, and a moment later one of his servants entered the room. Mipam ordered him to get a course or two from the adjoining Chinese restaurant, to supplement the soup and the boiled meat which were to be cooked at home.

After the moral shock which the revelation of the fate reserved for the yaks from Cherku had given him, Mipam had turned vegetarian again, though less rigidly than when he was a boy. His relations with his colleagues and his clients compelled him to invite them to dinner; but except in the case of a few lamas or very pious laymen, a meatless dinner is an inconceivable thing to a Tibetan. What could they find to eat? The culinary art is little developed in their country, and the small number of dishes which they know how to prepare all contain meat, and indeed are frequently composed of meat

[1] The god of their paternal ancestors.

alone. Mipam, therefore, resigned himself to giving meat to his guests, and as after once tasting it he had become fond of it, he succumbed sometimes to the temptation and partook of it with them.

He could not make an exception of Tobden. He was treated to boiled mutton and *mogmogs*, that delicious hash of savoury meat, enclosed in a ball of dough and then steamed.

The son of the chief of Payenrong was a nice boy, cheery, care-free, and good-natured, generous on occasion, but rather dissipated. He liked strong drink, and the agreeable burning sensation as it slips down to the stomach; he liked the excitement of gambling, and above all, he liked women. He was indignant with his father for having put him to school with the missionaries. He appreciated their teaching, and being aware that it might help to secure him a lucrative position, he worked well, but he felt that he might just as well have attended the classes as a day-boarder, if his father had rented a room for him in the town—a course which would not have interfered with his personal freedom.

Mipam, easy-going and independent, seemed to him just the person to make an effective accomplice in the stratagem which he was elaborating in order to escape the supervision of the Peary household.

'You mustn't call me *Kushog*; I'm not so much older than you, and we are of equal rank; you must call me Mipam,' the young merchant said to his guest. The familiarity which this permission authorized encouraged Tobden to confide in Mipam. Having drunk several bowls of spirit after dinner, in which his host did not join him, Tobden approached the subject nearest to his heart.

'Haven't you any womenfolk with you?'

'I am not married.'

'I'm not speaking of a wife. I mean a mistress, like other traders have?'

Mipam was chaste without effort, from indifference, but he was not prudish. He burst out laughing.

'When I leave on a journey, I take my servants with me, and so the woman would remain by herself with the merchandise. Eh! that means a temptation which few can resist. She would have, no doubt, some other friend who would replace me when I was away, and my rolls of fine cloth might well be transformed into clothes for my deputy. No, Tobden, solid bolts on solid doors and no women inside, that's what a merchant's shop wants when he is away.'

'You are doubtless right. But I suppose you send for women when you are here? I, you see, have always got to put the Peary off the scent. You cannot imagine how inquisitive and sly he is. He has the elder pupils spied on by villainous old Chinamen, who profess to be of his religion just to wheedle money out of him. He spies on them himself too. Do what you will, he always manages to know where you go. . . . Look here, my friend, could I bring some women to your place? The Peary would be less suspicious; I'll tell him that you are inviting me to dinner, and if any of his Chinamen get to know that women have dined with us, I'll tell him they came for you.'

'Not a bad scheme, but it won't suit me. I don't want women here. They're never satisfied with the present they are given, and always try to collar something extra.'

'You've got a nice opinion of women.'

'A very prudent thing to have.'

'How do you manage, then? Do you go to them? . . .'

'They don't tempt me. I find them ugly and stupid.'

'There are some pretty ones among them, I assure you. I can introduce you to some beauties.'

'You'd have your trouble for nothing, old man. I bear in my heart an image so pretty that all the girls you could show me would appear, in comparison, just hideous baboons.'

'Oh! oh! Where does she live, this beauty of yours?'

'In Tibet. She'll be my wife when I've enough money to persuade her father to give her to me.'

'Oh, that's serious, a wealthy girl and of good family . . . but that shouldn't prevent your having a good time, since you are here all alone. But you're economizing, aren't you? Your future father-in-law is exacting. All fathers are. I have an elder sister, and I can assure you her husband didn't get her for nothing.'

There was a turn in the conversation, and after that, as it was getting late, Tobden took leave of his host, for he had to be back at the Mission before nightfall.

The months slipped by. Owing to Tobden's presence in the Mission, the young merchant continued to keep in touch with the Pearys, and Mr. Simon sometimes came to call on him.

To the attempts they made to convince him of the erroneous and absurd nature of the Lamaic beliefs, Mipam replied by pointing out the contradictions existing between certain of their own theories and the actual facts. When they spoke to him of the love of God for His creatures, he reminded them of the universal distress of all sentient beings, a prey to sickness, old age, and death. He drew a picture of the tragedies of Nature, the feebler serving as food for the stronger: the insect devoured by the bird, the roebuck by the leopard; he referred to the anguish of the tree rooted to the soil, that feels the parasite clinging to it, growing and choking it, or the mosses and lichens weaving around its motionless boughs a winding-sheet to strangle it. If we had not lived other lives, before our present life, where then would be the justice, the divine goodness, when some are born blind, infirm, or stupid? Who is it that finds amusement in creating them so?

The Pearys, from lack of arguments, found this hard to answer; they were so incrusted in their beliefs that they refused to examine them critically. Mipam's retorts slid off their minds like rain from the burnished leaves of the holly, and the obstinate repetition of their affirmations, which never answered his objections, increased the young man's aversion for their pitiless religion.

Mipam found Mr. Simon easier to understand. He felt

sympathetically drawn toward him. An incident of which he was a witness still further increased this instinctive liking.

One day, when he was returning from a visit to the herds-men, having brought back a load of butter, he went to offer two pieces to Mrs. Peary, in acknowledgment of the tea which she had offered him whenever he had gone to fetch Tobden. He found the Pearys and Mr. Simon in a parlour where they received the natives whom they did not wish to admit into their dining-room. The visitors consisted of three Chinese, a middle-aged couple and the husband's aged father. Mrs. Peary was exhorting them with authority and some irritation.

'That's a pagan superstition,' she said. 'If you wish to be baptized, and have your sins washed away, you must give it up. You must burn the tablets of your ancestors and the images of the false gods which you have in your homes, and after that you will dine here with the Elders of our Church, some Chinese who have been redeemed by the blood of Christ, and who will enter into Heaven.'

The husband listened with bent head, the wife wept, and the wrinkled face of the old man grew rigid: he appeared to be waging a battle with himself.

'That's settled, then,' Mrs. Peary continued. 'To-morrow two of the Elders will repair to your house to be present at the burning of the idols, and the day after to-morrow you will dine at the Mission and eat meat with us.'

She made a movement as if to rise and dismiss the Chinese, when, unexpectedly, the old man interposed:

'No,' said he.

'What? No?—Do you refuse to destroy the objects of your idolatry, or to reject a ridiculous superstition? If your obstinacy is such as to make you repel the salvation that is offered you, your children will accept it and will do just what I have said.'

'No,' replied the old man straightening his bent back. 'In this country, the father is the master. In my house, they shall not burn the tablets in which dwell the spirits of my ancestors, nor the statues of the gods whom they have venerated. That would be committing murder. Any of my family who encourage the butchers by eating meat will be driven out of my house. A son whose heart is so void of pity for the sufferings of the poor animals would be capable of killing his father and mother if it profited him to do so.'

'It isn't necessary to eat meat to be a Christian,' Mr. Simon remarked in a conciliatory tone.

'Not necessary if one does without it for reasons of health or because one doesn't like it,' retorted Mrs. Peary. 'But with these people it is a superstition, the superstition of not killing animals, and that is contrary to the order established by the Lord.'

'One can't affirm that with absolute certainty,' Mr. Simon made bold to reply, mildly: 'It is written: "I have given you every herb bearing seed, which is upon the face of all the earth, and every tree in which is the fruit of a tree yielding seed; to you it shall be for meat."[1] There is no question of butcher's meat.'

The untimely erudition displayed by the Australian angered the arbitrary Mrs. Peary; she turned furiously upon him and overwhelmed him with a flood of words in English.

The old Chinaman and his son gazed at them in silence; the woman continued to weep, and Mipam, his packet of butter in his hand, realizing that the moment for presenting his gift was ill-chosen, was thinking of politely withdrawing. He made a sign to Mr. Peary, who, having vainly endeavoured to stem the vehement eloquence of his spouse, had sunk, inertly, into his arm-chair; he showed him the packet, and laid it down in the embrasure of the window, pointing to Mrs. Peary, to indicate that what he was leaving was intended for her. Then, raising his hat, he made for the door.

His movement put fresh life into the assembled company, hypnotized by Mrs. Peary; Mr. Simon spoke some words in English, rose, nodded kindly to the tender-hearted old pagan,

[1] Genesis i. 29.

211

and left the room. Following his example, the Chinese got up; first the father and then his obedient children.

'You have forgotten what you have been taught for a whole year—the gospel of Grace, the gift of Life Eternal, the Heaven that baptism was to open to you!' cried Mrs. Peary.

'I shall follow my fathers; I shall go where they have gone,' the old man placidly replied.

'But you!' insisted the lady missionary, addressing the two who had not spoken.

'The duty of the son is to obey his father,' answered the man. The woman still kept silence, but she grasped the robe of her husband, her master and her guide.

In the courtyard Mipam paused as Mr. Simon followed him, on his way back to his private quarters.

'That Chinaman was right,' Mipam said to him. 'To cause the death of innocent beasts, to eat them, is cruel: it is a devilish act. Why force those to do so who, happily, have always abstained from being a party to such a thing? That is undoubtedly wicked.'

'It is,' murmured Mr. Simon.

'Since you agree, say so to these Chinese. Here they come.'

The trio were slowly making their way toward the gate.

The son of the obstinate pagan went up to the Australian and shyly asked him:

'That material, sir, which you gave me to make you a suit, ought I to return it to you?'

'Why?' asked Mr. Simon in astonishment.

'If we are not baptized, if we don't come to church any longer, do you want me to make up the suit all the same?'

'Yes, of course, my friend. And you shall make me others as well, when I need some,' warmly protested the young missionary. 'You're a good tailor and an honest man; why should I withdraw my custom from you?'

The Chinaman looked gratefully at his client, and his wife who had ceased weeping, gave him a childish smile.

'Tell them that you too don't approve of eating meat, and that his father was right to feel pity for animals,' Mipam suggested, speaking in Tibetan to Mr. Simon.

The latter shrugged his shoulders sadly.

'One of these days, my friend,' he said. Then he passed under the arch that gave on to the little garden at the bottom of which was his lodging, and disappeared.

'I'll tell you what he does not want to tell you,' Mipam declared to the Chinese.

He took the old man by the arm.

'You gave a good answer to the lady with the white eyes, old father. Animals suffer as we do; to kill them is wrong; you do well not to allow meat to be eaten in your house. Our holy lamas don't eat meat, and when we sinners do so, we know that we make ourselves into beasts of prey, and that the Buddhas turn away from us.'

'Good, good, I see you understand,' replied the old man. 'Well, that's ended.'

But what was ended, he did not explain.

The father passed through the Mission porch; the son followed him, and the wife followed the husband.

The vision of Mr. Simon sorrowfully returning to his own rooms haunted Mipam for the rest of the day. He pictured the missionary a prey to a painful conflict of thought and a target for the resentment of the Pearys. Beyond all dispute, Mipam told himself, Simon had a good heart, but he dared not follow the generous impulses which came to him. Why? Was he afraid of the Pearys? Could they harm him? The young man knew nothing as to this, but passing from deduction to deduction, his inventive mind came at last to the conclusion that Mr. Simon—for the moment at all events—was unhappy and lonely. From that to wishing to assure him of his sympathy and to help him, if it lay in his power, was but one step for the compassionate Mipam. He returned to the Mission at dusk, and this time, without asking for

Tobden, he passed straight into the Australian's garden and entered his lodgings.

In the small room that served him for a study, Mr. Simon was seated in an arm-chair, close to the table. He was evidently doing nothing, for he had not lit his lamp, and the room was already too dark for reading or writing.

'What, you here?' he said, greatly surprised at the trader's visit.

'Am I disturbing you?'

'No. I hope you are not in any trouble?'

'No, nothing of that sort. . . .'

They looked at each other in silence. Mipam, who had found his impulse quite natural when he left his house, now felt embarrassed. Could he say to this foreigner: 'You are unhappy; I've come to offer you my services?' Perhaps, after all, Mr. Simon was not unhappy: he might think his visitor impertinent for having supposed that he was, and for having allowed himself the liberty of telling him so.

'Why have you come?' the Australian asked kindly.

His voice was friendly, with a sad, weary note in it. Mipam wavered no longer.

'Since I left you after your . . . dispute with Mrs. Peary, about those Chinese, I have done nothing but think of you. I thought that you might be feeling sad, and I came. . . .'

'That's kind of you, very kind,' answered the Australian, greatly touched. 'I am delighted with your visit, more than delighted. Do sit down.'

They once more fell on silence.

'You don't get on with the Pearys, do you?' said Mipam. 'With Mrs. Peary less than with her husband. Your religion isn't like hers. Mrs. Peary is not compassionate and you are. . . .'

'You can't understand,' said Simon gently.

'Yes, I can. I've read the story of Yeshu Massika[1] in the

[1] Jesus Christ, as he is called in the Protestant Missions on the Tibetan frontiers. In the Catholic Missions they simply use the word Jesu.

book you gave me. In it is related how Yeshu went, one evening, into a garden, at a time when he was dreadfully sorrowful: the people he had held to be his friends were forsaking him. It is plain that he and they didn't think alike, as is the case with you and the Pearys. When that happens, each goes his own way, without bothering about him whom he leaves. His father, too, had abandoned him, so I read in the Book.

'Yeshu was undoubtedly a good man, though he sometimes made statements that were quite erroneous. He said—I read that in the Book—that his God, whom he called his father, fed the birds. That's not true. The birds, like other wild creatures, have great trouble to find their food, and when winter comes, with the frost and the snow, many of them die of hunger. The God of Yeshu, moreover, let him be killed without protecting him. That wasn't good of him.'

Mr. Simon could not forbear smiling. The picturesque logic of Mipam's comments on the Gospel gave him an insight into the inner feelings of native hearers of his Sunday sermons.

Artlessly the energetic Tibetan proposed what seemed to him a reasonable solution.

'If the Pearys behave disagreeably, don't remain with them, but take up your quarters somewhere else, and if you have lost your faith in the religion of Yeshu, leave it, but don't allow it to distress you.'

The young missionary closed his eyes for an instant, seemingly absorbed in the contemplation of a picture which he saw within himself.

'Friend,' he said in a low voice, 'you came to see me because you thought I was unhappy and lonely; ought I to desert Him Whom all abandoned? . . . '

'I understand,' said Mipam after a pause.

Raising his hat, he bowed and left the room. Mr. Simon, his elbows on the table, dropped his head between his hands; perhaps he wept, but no one was there to see.

CHAPTER X

MIPAM continued to maintain friendly relations with Paljor the steward, his first partner, to whom he owed the facile and fortunate opening of his commercial career. Paljor having lauded the young man's ability to the administrators of the monastery estates, these latter had accepted him as an accredited merchant, and had frequently entrusted him with the sale of the goods presented by the faithful or delivered by the tenants of their Grand Lama and Lord Abbot.

Mipam, therefore, from time to time, went to spend a day or two at the monastery. He eagerly embraced these opportunities of revisiting the mysterious monk, the inmate of the house in which prodigies were performed. He found him always seated on the platform, in the same place, wrapped in his ragged mantle. In vain had Mipam begged that he might be allowed to offer him some new clothes and make his wretched room more comfortable; the old man had always obstinately refused to accept anything whatever.

'A fool, a real fool,' the monks would say, their commiseration mingled with a touch of contempt when informed of his refusal. And everyone, extremely puzzled, asked themselves what reason could induce a young, intelligent trader to pass so much time with that old imbecile. What did they say to one another during those interviews? Had they been present, their conviction as to the incurable madness of the poor monk would probably have been extended to include his young visitor.

Mipam often remained seated for an hour at the foot of the platform without eliciting a single word from the seer, who did not appear to be aware of his presence. Mipam spoke to him, but he did not seem to hear, and the young man had to leave him without having been vouchsafed a word or a look. At other times, on the contrary, the old man gave him the counsel or the teaching which he needed, before he had preferred any request in the matter. But whether he spoke or whether he remained silent, an atmosphere of peace flowed from him. Mipam felt that the old man was guiding his thoughts, was shedding light on the obscure problems that had defied his investigations, and lifting veils behind which he glimpsed the confused images of a life very different from that which he was leading. At such times he would objectively contemplate Mipam the trader as a stranger, quite separate from himself; but the Mipam who remained, watching his double recede into the distance—this Mipam he could only dimly distinguish. Profoundly troubled, he suddenly tore himself away from the fascination of these nebulous visions; silently prostrating himself, he left the still impassive old monk.

Over and above the question of profit, his relations with foreigners gave Mipam the pleasure of contemplating, from close at hand, the sayings and doings of people moved by an entirely different mentality from that of the Tibetans. Inquisitive and thoughtful by nature, he never wearied of these observations, which he found diverting or distressing, according to circumstances. For that matter, he often misunderstood the sentiments by which the 'whites' whose words and acts he was considering were actuated, and his incomprehension of the conceptions current in the West evoked in him sudden explosions of raillery or horror, the comical side of which he himself could not perceive, nor could the persons who occasioned them. 'That stupid pagan!' said the latter with disdainful pity; 'These wicked idiots!' thought Mipam.

East and West considered each other without sympathy.

One morning when Mipam was breakfasting in his inn at Gomi—a small town in Amdo, on the banks of the Yellow River—a Chinaman presented himself at the half-open door.

'I should like to speak to you,' said he.

'Come in; sit down and drink some tea.'

And Mipam called to his servant, to bring a bowl and pour out some tea for his visitor.

'And now, what is it you want of me?' asked the trader after the Chinaman had drunk his tea.

'I want to become a *Tien du tan*—a Catholic.'

'That doesn't concern me, my friend,' replied Mipam, greatly surprised. 'I'm not a *Shinfu*, a priest; I'm a lama, and have nothing to do with the religion of Yeshu. You must apply to the priest of the Roman Catholic Mission.'

'I know, I know, but you're acquainted with this priest. You go to see him. Quite recently you sold him some butter and some peas for his horses. You might speak to him for me.'

'Speak to him yourself. I can't interfere in this, as I am not of the religion of Yeshu.'

'I've already spoken to him.'

'Well? . . .'

'He's quite willing for me to go to his church when he worships Heaven by singing and gesticulating, but he doesn't want to pour water over my head.'

'Is that absolutely necessary?'

'Indispensable. The priest won't protect me if he hasn't wetted my hair. It's a symbol among those of his religion.'

'Ah, you're in need of protection. You're afraid of the magistrate? What have you done? Stolen? . . . eh?'

'No, no,' protested the Chinaman. 'I have stolen nothing. It's about an inheritance . . . a plot of land. My brother claims that it ought to come to him. . . .'

'And of course you claim that it's yours,' interrupted the trader, laughing, 'and you think the priest could persuade the mandarin to decide in your favour.'

'That's exactly what it is; you've guessed it. But he'll do so only if I'm really of his religion, if my hair has been wetted. I'm certain of that; those who go to his church and are well informed have assured me of this.'

'I see,' said Mipam, 'but why won't he pour water on your head? He has probably realized that you don't believe in his religion, that you are only trying to find a way of getting the plot of ground. They are artful, these priests.'

'Not so artful as all that; besides, they want to get plenty of people into their church.'.

'Then why does he refuse you?'

'Because I'm quite by myself. He wants to pour water on several persons at the same time.'

'Why not go and ask some of your friends to have their hair wetted, so as to do you a good turn?'

'It can't be done; they must be people belonging to my family. And sometimes, in the country, the priest insists on more than that: he wants to wet the heads of all the peasants of the same village on the same day. He says that one single convert among all those of a different persuasion cannot observe the customs of his religion. You see, it's like this: the village headman becomes *Tien du tan* (Christian), and then he says to the others, to the members of his family and those under his authority: "You must become *tien du tans*; it will pay. I've seen to that." And the priest gives out that a hundred or two hundred men and women have adopted the religion of Yeshu.'

'But you are not a village headman; what is your job?'

'I'm a miller. The priest would be satisfied to have my family.'

'And your father is not willing?'

'My father is dead. The matter concerns my wives.'

'How many?'

'The "great one," from whom I have a son, the first "little one," who has given me two sons and a daughter, and the second "little one," who is almost a child.'

The smile which accompanied the mention of the second 'little one' enlightened Mipam sufficiently as to the Chinaman's feelings for her. She was the favourite.

'Follow me carefully. The priest wants me to keep only

the "great one" and the children,' resumed the miller, 'and insists on my sending away the others. The first "little one" has lived with me now for fifteen years, and has given me two sons. The second "little one" I bought when she was still a child. She was brought up in my home before she became my wife; her parents and her grand-parents are dead. Where will she go if I send her away, who will give her to eat? And then, there are certain signs that she's with child. . . . But the priest won't listen to reason: the "great one" only must remain in the house, the others must be driven out, or I get no water on the head.'

'It's abominable! altogether abominable!' cried Mipam passionately. 'To throw out of your house women who have trusted you and are the mothers of your children! Only a demon is capable of such cruelty!'

'The "great one" won't hear a word of it; she has a great love for the two "little ones"; the youngest is like a daughter to her; she was brought up by her. And then, there's my old mother too, who is strongly opposed to my acting against the family laws which have come down to us from our ancestors.'

'She's right, quite right,' Mipam strenuously insisted. 'Go back home and give up once and for all this idea of adopting such a cruel religion!'

'There's the land . . . ' the Chinaman reminded him calmly.

Mipam, in the indignation evoked by the suggested abandonment of the two poor 'little wives,' had forgotten all about the motive which had induced the miller to consider the adoption of Christianity.

'Ah yes, the plot of land,' he murmured, as he thought the matter over. Suddenly an idea occurred to him:

'All that can be arranged,' he announced to the Chinaman. 'The *tien du tan*[1] (Christians), are not the only ones who are competent to plead your cause before the magistrate. There are also the *fu ien tan*[2] Christians. They have a home

---

[1] The followers of the 'Religion of the Law'—i.e., the Protestants.
[2] The followers of the 'Religion of Heaven'—i.e., the Roman Catholics.

near Gomi, that I know; I have recently sold them some wool. Go and see them; they will probably be less wicked. This I can tell you! I know a Chinaman at Dangar who belongs to them, and who has kept his two wives. Since they have allowed him two, they will just as readily accept three. What harm is there in having several wives, if it so pleases one, and one is good to them? Go and see the *fu ien tans.*'

'I can't,' answered the poor Chinaman, dejectedly. 'My brother, the one who is quarrelling with me over the land, has just been received among them!'

The comedy was food for laughter, but the trader, already aware of the way in which Chinese intrigues are carried on among the lower orders, saw only the practical side of the matter.

'There ought to be some other means of influencing the judge,' he said after a moment's reflection. 'For instance, if you could prove to him, without the shadow of a doubt, that you are right, that the ground belongs to you. . . . One doesn't know; sometimes when the right is really on one's side, the magistrate may happen to acknowledge it. Have you papers and witnesses that you can produce?'

'I've got witnesses and papers as well, but my brother has had some false deeds made out and has already handed them to the judge.'

'It's you who say they are false.'

'They are, I promise you. Why should I lie to you? It isn't you who are going to give sentence.'

'Do you know Tsung, the big merchant?'

'Everyone knows him, he's a man of consequence.'

'Go and see him from me; I'll give you my card. Tsung is a friend of mine. He is wise and influential; you can get good advice and protection from him.'

The Chinaman thanked him, took the card Mipam had given him, and departed.

The business that had brought him to Gomi being completed, Mipam left the neighbourhood, and forgot the petitioner with the three wives. After his departure, however, the Chinaman's cause triumphed, and it gave rise to some unexpected incidents.

Tsung, the rich merchant, did not like foreigners; he was fond of Mipam, and the man whom the latter had recommended to him was in danger, should the protection of his own people fail him, of breaking with the traditional customs of China. Here was a reason why a virtuous disciple of Confucius should constitute himself his defender. Tsung, however, would champion only a just cause. He examined the papers shown him, questioned the witnesses presented to him, and not only convinced himself that the miller had an irrefutable right to the land in dispute, but also obtained proof that the title-deeds handed to the magistrate by the brother were fabricated.

He thereupon sent for the petitioner and persuaded him to resort to the last resource which, in these provinces, Chinese justice puts at the disposal of those who regard themselves as the victims of injustice. This is the 'cry,' the appeal made to the magistrate, by beating the drum hung at the entrance of his residence. To this 'cry' the magistrate must respond immediately, by seating himself in his tribunal and hearing the crier's' plea. Woe betide the 'crier' if he has ventured to employ this extreme measure when his cause is not entirely just; for justice, offended by his imposture, will take vengeance upon him by inflicting a pitiless beating.

Emboldened by the encouragement and the presence of Tsung, the miller passed through the portico of the magistrate's dwelling, fell on his knees before the drum, and grasping the mallet hanging by its side, struck it several times, and then bawled out, as he had been taught, his appeal to justice.

The poor man actually 'cried.' The fear which he felt had almost made him forget the cause which had led him to accomplish his audacious act, now irremediably consummated. The deep, lugubrious tones of the big drum and the sound of his own voice had terrified him, and his 'cries' were, more than anything else, cries of terror. What was going to happen to him? . . .

An official, correctly attired in black silk, with a solemn bearing, appeared in the doorway and signed to the miller to come forward. The miller rose and advanced unsteadily, followed by Tsung, who exhorted him to have confidence,

A few minutes later he fell on his knees and made *kowtow* before the magistrate, who, seeing that the plaintiff was accompanied by Tsung, somewhat relaxed the severity of his expression. The merchant had a good reputation, and was said to be very wealthy: his protection had weight behind it.

The miller put forward his claim, produced his written proofs, and named his witnesses, and Tsung deduced that he was convinced of the petitioner's veracity, failing which he would never have consented to champion him. The miller's right to the title appeared well established. The magistrate decided that he must come before him again, together with his brother and the witnesses for both parties.

A week later, all these people met together at the court. The falsity of the documents presented by the miller's brother was proved beyond any possible doubt, and the plaintiff was declared the legal owner of the land which he had claimed. This part of the case was settled, but there remained the injury done to the magistrate by the man who had dared to deceive him by presenting false title-deeds. This, in China, constitutes a much more serious offence than the intention to defraud a brother of property belonging to him.

'Let this man be taken at once to prison,' ordered the mandarin. 'I shall decide later as to the punishment to be given him.'

He had hardly finished speaking when one of the prisoner's friends, who had come to hear the verdict, hurried from the court and ran to inform the Protestant missionary of the fate of one of his flock.

The missionary was an Irishman from Ulster, still young, tall and thin, with light red hair and grey eyes, ardent, zealous, and subject to sudden fits of passion, the prevailing motive of which was not malice, but an unshakable faith in his superiority as a white man and a Christian over the yellow pagans, even were they as distinguished for learning as was the magistrate who had just condemned the forger.

When he learnt the verdict, the Reverend O'Kelly bounded from his arm-chair, rushed to his room, seized some pyjamas and a blanket, and carrying them over his arm, dashed from his house, leaving the Chinaman who had brought him the news gasping.

There was a fair distance between the Mission and the *yemen*. O'Kelly's athletic legs made short work of it. The magistrate was still seated in his tribunal, engaged in hearing other cases, when the fiery Irishman burst in upon him.

Pushing the astounded claimants aside, Mr. O'Kelly planted himself before the magistrate, trembling with indignation.

'You have had Su-chin thrown into prison!' he shouted in hurricane tones. 'Put me in prison too!'

Flinging wide his arms, to emphasize his heroic challenge, Mr. O'Kelly exposed to view the striped rainbow-hued pyjamas which he had brought for his night in durance vile.

Calm and collected, the magistrate raised his small black eyes to the tall son of Erin.

'I haven't the right to lock you up,' he gently replied, 'and I assure you I regret my inability to do so.'

Signing to one of his assistants to collect the petitioners and defendants in the case which had been interrupted, he resumed his interrogatory.

Mipam learnt of this dramatic ending of the miller's trial only when he had occasion to return to Gomi, where it was told him by an eye-witness.

Seated in his cheerful room at Dangar, and feeling sad for no apparent reason, Mipam was gazing through the open window at the sun, which was setting over the battlemented walls of the town. In his mind's eye he saw, beyond those ramparts, the unpeopled wastes of the grassy solitudes, furrowed by the tracks leading southwards to Lhasa. Soon it would be time for him to set off across the wilderness to gather the reward of his labours. If his fortune did not yet equal that of his childish dreams when he fled from Tibet, it was nevertheless enough to allow him to present himself to Dolma's father. He had become an acceptable son-in-law, and a keen merchant like Tenzin could not fail to foresee, after the success that had already crowned his youthful efforts, that further successes would follow in its train. He had better not wait any longer. Nearly four years had now elapsed since he and his young friend had parted, by the roadside, after their pilgrimage to Gahlden. To him, whose mind had been immersed in commercial schemes, who had been bent on one aim alone, the acquisition of wealth, the years had seemed to pass quickly, but to her, who could only wait passively, they had no doubt seemed long. Yes, it was time to bestir himself.

Tashi, his head clerk, who had gradually made himself conversant with Mipam's affairs, could make his usual rounds in his absence, while his faithful partner, Paljor, who was extremely shrewd, would willingly consent to advise him. Besides, he would not be away for long. It would perhaps be unwise to journey from Lhasa to the valley of Tromo, where his parents lived. The prince might have him seized and wreak upon him his long delayed vengeance, but he hoped that Changpal and Puntsog would come to Lhasa for his marriage. The festivities over, he would take Dolma away, and if she did not like Dangar they would live at Sining, a large city not far away.

His mind was made up; on the very next day he would begin his preparations, and as a beginning would go and bid Mr. Simon farewell. He had not seen him since the evening he had left him in his darkened room, evoking the memory of that Yeshu whom, the Book said, his friends had deserted, and whom he, Mr. Simon, was unwilling to abandon, even if he could not believe that all he taught was true.

225

A saintly man, this Mr. Simon, thought Mipam. Had he had a knowledge of the exalted doctrines which our wise contemplative hermits teach, he would doubtless have come very near spiritual illumination; he might even, perchance, have attained that Deliverance which is like the awakening that puts to flight a haunting dream. But for him the path to it was beset by obstacles. As the result of acts committed in former lives, he was born in a country where the doctrine of the Buddhas is unknown. Yet by coming to China he had drawn very near to it, Mipam reflected. And before leaving, he must have a talk with the steward Paljor. He would go to the monastery, and he would crave the blessing of the old monk, whom, in his innermost heart, he regarded as his *guru*, his spiritual director . . . and why should he not take Mr. Simon to the old man who read men's minds? He would know the fitting thing to say to him, he would know how to teach him, to make him see, that he might recognize the right path, and be delivered from the sadness which weighed upon him. That was what was needed. He, Mipam, was only a stupid merchant, he could be of no use to Mr. Simon, but the holy wonder-worker could. The very next day he would consider how best he could arrange that interview.

Mipam was absorbed in his charitable intentions when his servant entered the room.

'Master, a man has come from Tobden, who is at the foreigner's school. He asks you to lend him a pair of boots and some garters. It's Tobden who needs them.'

'Some boots for Tobden? . . . What does he want with them?'

'I don't know, *Kushog*.'

'Send the man up.'

'Very well.'

A few minutes later a Tibetan was shown in to Mipam. His smiling air went to prove that the business that brought him had nothing tragic about it.

'*Kushog*, it's Tobden who has sent me; he wants you to lend him a pair of boots.'

'You are poking fun at me; what does this pleasantry mean? Tobden has got plenty of boots.'

'Certainly, *Kushog*, there are some in his room at the school, but he isn't there. It's so that he can come to see you that he's asking for boots. His have been taken.'

'His boots have been stolen. . . . But where?'

The Tibetan's smile grew broader.

'He's with a woman, *Kushog*.'

'Well, well, and she's stolen his boots. . . . That's very odd! I believe, comrade, that you are telling me a story to get the boots for yourself, without paying.'

'No, no,' protested the Tibetan. 'I'm an honest man. I'm employed in the salt department; I can buy myself boots when I need them. The woman hasn't stolen Tobden's boots; it's the foreigner who has taken them.'

'What are you talking about?—If Tobden was in a woman's room, the foreigner certainly wasn't with him.'

'He was. Not for the same reason as Tobden, of course. He came to find him and take him away. Oh! you should have heard what he said to him! What he said to his little friend! Both of them would fall in the fire and frizzle for ever. . . . He yelled! . . . yelled! . . . and Nordzinma, who is afraid of nothing, laughed! Tobden was furious. People ran up and down and joined in the laugh when they heard what it was all about. He's got no shame, that foreigner! What was he doing there? . . . When he saw that he was being made game of, and that Tobden wasn't listening, he collared his boots with the garters inside them. Ah, and his sash too; I was forgetting that: Tobden wants you to lend him a sash as well!'

'That's fantastic,' exclaimed Mipam. 'But how do you know all this?'

'I was there, *Kushog*, with a neighbour of Tobden's little friend. We were drinking beer with the door open. We saw the foreigner enter the courtyard; with him was a Chinaman who was pointing to Nordzinma's room. He didn't stay long:

he was evidently afraid of Tobden; these Chinese are not brave like us. My little friend understood in a twinkling. "He has come to take the chief of Payenrong's son by surprise," she said to me. "I'm going to try and get him in here; if I can keep him here for a moment, you go and tell the young man, so that he can get away." She went out, put herself in front of the foreigner, smiled, jabbered, invited him to come and see her, and asked him if he'd come to distribute little story-books or pretty pictures. She would like some pictures, and she looked at him so fetchingly. . . . Oh! ho! she's pretty, my little friend! I spied on them through a hole in the window-paper; if I'd been in the foreigner's boots, I couldn't have resisted her; but he, all he did was to insult her, and then I went out to give him tit for tat. But he didn't hear a word; he was like a madman. He hurled himself against the door of the room where Tobden was, and with kicks and blows of his fist he broke it open. Then, as I told you, he began to threaten them with fire and demons. I went to see what was happening, and my little friend with me.'

'What's all this?' she said to him. 'They're doing no harm to anyone. If your parents hadn't done the same thing, you wouldn't have been born!'

'It was then that everyone roared with laughter, and the foreigner seized the boots and the sash and made off with them. I don't think he really knew what he was doing, he was so angry. I saw the Chinaman who had brought him waiting for him in the street. I ran up to him and thrashed him in a way he'll remember, to teach him to spy on honest Tibetans. Then I returned to my little friend. The chief's son stood spirits all round to all who were there. Several of the men wanted to lend him their boots so that he could go back to the school, but Tobden, who is very proud, doubtless found them too worn, and asked me to come and borrow some from you. He does not want to return to their school. He wants to come here.'

'Very good,' said Mipam, much amused at the adventure.

Then, addressing his servant, who had remained in the room through curiosity, he said:

'Get a pair of new boots, some garters, and a red sash from the store, and take them to *Kushog* Tobden.'

'Very well,' replied the man.

'That's it,' said Tobden's envoy; 'you can't lend him yours because they're clerical boots, and your sash is yellow.[1] I hadn't thought of that. You are perhaps a *gelong*[2]?' he added—for this would explain why Mipam did not care to go in person to rescue his friend from the house of the harlot.

'You've guessed it,' lied Mipam, who divined what he was thinking.

An hour later, Tobden, hilarious and just a little drunk, entered Mipam's room, profuse with his protestations of gratitude, and at supper he retold the story of his adventure.

'Mr. Peary will turn you out of his school,' Mipam concluded.

'He wouldn't turn me out because I'm the son of a chief, and he likes to have distinguished pupils, but I don't want to return to him. I'm a man, Mipam; I shall soon be twenty; I can't let myself be treated like a child.'

'I know that,' Mipam said to soothe him. 'But there are your studies. Your father sets great store by them. What will he have to say?'

'I already know Chinese pretty well, and our own language quite well, and I believe I could manage to obtain a post as second interpreter in the magistrate's *yemen*. I shan't get much pay, but in that billet one can count on the presents offered by the petitioners whose requests one translates. And then people come to ask your advice, or they beg you to present their

[1] The boots of the clergy, which are simpler than those of the laity, have red tops, and are not ornamented with applique work in green cloth, or embroidery in vivid colours, like those of the laity. The yellow sash is a distinctive badge for monks.

[2] *Gelong*, a monk having received the major ordination and bound to celibacy, even in the sect of the 'Red Caps', who sanction marriage in the case of monks who have received only the minor ordination.

petitions to the mandarin. To belong to the household of an official is always a profitable thing. I shall be able to pay for my lodging, and for masters to pursue my studies. My father will willingly continue to supply me with food; that won't ruin him. I'll ask him, too, to send one of our boys to me as a servant. . . . Mipam, I shall be like you, living in my own place, with a servant to bring me my meals at any hour I like. I'll invite you to eat with me. . . . How pleasant that will be! I'm sick of their school and the clock that calls us to eat even if we aren't hungry, and orders us to bed even if we aren't sleepy. No, Mipam, I shan't return to the foreigner, and you are going to be a good friend, and come with me to my father, to explain everything to him, so that he doesn't get angry, and gives me money to make a home for myself.'

'He'll tell you to go back to him at Payenrong.'

'No, I shall get the post of second interpreter; I know I can get it. It's only a question of offering·a present to the mandarin's secretary. I know him. My father will be satisfied and proud of my success. Old Peary will choke with vexation. Mipam, you'll give me the present for the secretary, won't you? I'll repay you later.'

The young rascal had the gift of the gab. Mipam had to laugh; there was nothing in his character to incline him to severity.

'I'll give you the present,' he promised, 'but I can't undertake to go to Payenrong. I've decided to leave very shortly for Lhasa, and I have to make my preparations.'

'To go and see my father won't take you long; a week at the most. And then, perhaps he will ask you to do some business for him in Lhasa. You really can't leave without having seen him.'

The artful Tobden had hit the mark; the magic word 'business' had an irresistible effect upon the trader.

'You're too clever for me, comrade,' he said, clapping his friend on the shoulder. 'I'll go with you to Payenrong.'

Yielding yet again to the entreaties of the young libertine, who did not want to see Mr. Peary any more, Mipam called next day at the Mission, to inform its irascible director that Tobden refused to return to the school. At the same time he was able to recover the boy's clothes and books.

The young merchant did not at all enjoy the commission with which his madcap friend had entrusted him, and the idea of having to listen to the long declamations of Peary and his wife as to the immorality of their pupil distressed him. On the way to the Mission he decided to see Mr. Simon about the matter. Simon would surely agree to repeat to Mr. Peary the little that Mipam had to say. He had in any case intended to speak to the Australian with a view to taking him to the monastery where he could make the acquaintance of the seer. The circumstances offered him a natural pretext for his visit; he could broach the question of a meeting between the missionary and the old monk without appearing to have come expressly for the purpose.

Mr. Simon was writing in his room when Mipam entered.

'Welcome, friend,' he said. 'I haven't seen you for ages. Have you been away on your travels? Is business still going well?'

'Better and better, thank you. I've been absent from Dangar. I've come to trouble you. You probably know what happened yesterday between Tobden and Mr. Peary.'

'Yes, I do.'

'Tobden is rather dissipated in his way of living, but I can't understand why Mr. Peary interferes in things that don't concern him. I'm bound to tell you that his behaviour, in the matter of that woman, is regarded very unfavourably by everyone in the town. He ought not to have gone to her rooms. And why did he go off with Tobden's boots? What on earth did he mean by that? It's the act of a madman!

'To come to the point, Tobden doesn't want to return here. I shall accompany him to Payenrong in a few days' time. His father will be informed of all that has passed, and will decide as he thinks best. Tobden is a man: he can't be watched and ordered about like a little boy.'

'Mr. Peary's intentions were good. I dare say his manner of showing them was extreme. I can understand that Tobden doesn't want to return to the school. It's a pity; he was a good pupil.'

'I believe he'll be able to continue his studies. He has a billet in view that will allow him to do so.'

'Ah, all the better. He's intelligent. . . . He wanted to become some sort of official.'

'I will ask you to see that Tobden's things, which are in his room, are given to my servant, who is waiting in the courtyard.'

'You had better go and see Mr. Peary about that.'

'I would rather avoid him. He would overwhelm me with recriminations concerning my friend; it would serve no useful purpose.'

Mr. Simon smiled.

'I'll do what is needful,' he said.

He sent for a Chinese usher and ordered him to have the trader's servant taken to Tobden's room, where he could help him to pack the young man's clothes and books.

'Are you thinking of making a long stay at Payenrong?' asked Mr. Simon of Mipam, when the removal of Tobden's effects had been arranged.

'No, just the necessary time for concluding the business that takes me there. I shall try, first of all, to help Tobden to obtain the post of second interpreter at the *yemen*, which is vacant. If he gets it he will arrive at his father's house like a conqueror, and will receive nothing but compliments. I don't know why he is so anxious for me to accompany him. He doesn't need anyone to stand up for him with his father. He'll get a good welcome. But I'm leaving for Lhasa.'

'A long journey. I know that you Tibetans don't consider it too much to take the trail for three months on end. You are great travellers.'

'It will take me much less time than that. I shall use all

possible despatch. I'm not travelling on business, and I shall have no beasts of burden with me.'

'Ah! . . . .'

'Mr. Simon, when I return I shall be married. I shall bring my pretty wife to call on you.'

'Who is she?'

'The daughter of the trader Tenzin, who has a branch office here.'

'A big merchant, Tenzin, according to all accounts. I wish you the best of luck. But I shan't have the pleasure of seeing you on your return. I, too, am going away.'

'Where are you going? For how long?'

'I'm going to the coast, to Shanghai, first. Before coming here I had begun my medical studies: I am going to resume them in order to become a doctor.'

'It's a fine thing to be a doctor. Why didn't you go on with your studies?'

Mr. Simon was seemingly gazing through the window at the shrubs in the garden, but what he really saw was himself, as he had been several years earlier, when he had suddenly dropped his studies to become a simple missionary, thinking that the saving of souls was of greater value than looking after bodies.

'I had no doubt taken too much upon myself,' he said, pensively. 'I am only a blind man myself, and I thought I could enlighten others. I hope now to succeed in the humbler duty of relieving their physical sufferings.'

'That means that you no longer believe in Mr. Peary's religion, and that you don't want to preach it any longer,' concluded Mipam, with the simple and ruthless sagacity peculiar to him. 'But because you are good, you have pity on the sick and wish to heal them. How much time do you require to complete your studies?'

'About three years, I think.'

'In three years, then, you will come back here?'

'Here or elsewhere. . . . I can't tell where they will send me.'

233

'Send you? You won't be able to go where you like?'

'Probably not, my friend. I belong to a Missionary Society, and I shall be sent where a doctor is wanted.'

'Doctors are wanted everywhere. I wish you were coming back here. Why do you want to remain in Mr. Peary's Society, if you no longer believe in his religion?'

'It's not Mr. Peary's religion, trader, it is the religion of Yeshu.'

'And you don't want to leave Yeshu, you told me so; but Yeshu is not Mr. Peary and his friends. Moreover, since you no longer believe what Yeshu said. . . . I know you don't believe any longer.'

Obstinate and convinced, Mipam returned to his idea; his unbending mind could not conceive of a sentimental compromise.

'Faith, trader, is perhaps, after all, a small thing, an illusion born of a presumptuous opinion of our ability to discover the truth. We think, we imagine we have grasped something which is real and certain, and we say we believe. Who are we, poor beings with narrow, feeble minds, to dare speak of certitude? On what should we base it? Can we conceive what God is, what His designs are, why living creatures swarm into the world, to suffer and then to disappear? What rash and blind temerity on our part to think ourselves capable of doing so! Who knows what Yeshu believed in His innermost mind; who knows what He thought at Gethsemane and upon the Cross? How can I, I a puny pigmy, explore the heights to which He soared, He, the all-Pure, the all-Holy, the all-Great?

'What I know is that He loved men, that He tried to teach them to love one another. Faith is a small thing, my friend; love is of greater price. It matters little what I may believe about the cause of the sufferings of those around me. They suffer, that is a fact; in endeavouring to suppress a part of their ills, I follow the dictates of my heart . . . more than that I do not know.'

Mipam felt at once touched and troubled. He admired the

spirit of charity that animated Mr. Simon, and he realized, at the same time, that the humility into which the missionary was sinking, as into a quicksand, barred him from the path to the mountain-peaks which the Masters of his country point out to their disciples. Doubtless neither Mr. Simon, generous and saintly though he was, nor he, who, having disowned his childhood's dreams, was only a commonplace merchant, could hope to attain, in their present life, those far-off summits, but they could set forth toward them. Other lives, many other lives, would follow this; dying in one, they would be born again in another; and just as one climbs, one after another, the steps of a staircase, so they could rise toward the light. But Mr. Simon was not ready to answer the call of those who teach the severance from every tie. His loving heart remained attached to his master Yeshu, though he detected errors in his doctrine, and he, Mipam, who had set foot on the journey toward the land of universal friendship, had abandoned his marvellous journey for the love of a·woman. Attachment! whatever its object may be, sublime or childish, attachment is the source of sorrow!

Ought he to mention the seer of the monastery to Mr. Simon? . . . Perhaps.

'Before you leave Dangar, Mr. Simon,' said Mipam. 'I should like you to go and see an old lama who lives in the monastery. A sage without needs, without desires, who can read the thoughts of others. You do not know what our religion is. You have only come across ignorant monks, just as absorbed in amassing money as we traders are. It would be as well for you to know what our Masters teach, so that you will not carry back with you, to your own country, false ideas about us.'

'My country? I don't think I shall ever return to it. I shall remain in China. There is no lack of doctors in my country: I shall be more useful here. And then . . . I understand what is in your mind; it's kind of you, and I'm touched by it; I'm grateful to you for it, but it's all to no purpose. I don't seek to be instructed, to understand, to attain anything. I have but one feeling: pity, and I want no other guide.'

Mipam realized that all insistence would be in vain.

'One day, in a forest,' he said with emotion, 'when I was a little child, a holy ascetic told me that I was the son of Chenrezigs, the Great Compassionate One. It is you who are his son, Mr. Simon.'

'All who have pity on the unhappy are the sons of the same Father, trader,' answered the Australian, holding out his hand to Mipam in the Western fashion.

Mipam was never to see Mr. Simon again.

Tobden obtained the post which he coveted, and the journey of the two friends was a merry one. The chief was agreeably surprised to learn of his son's unexpected nomination to an official post, and Tobden did not fail to remind his father that Mipam had contributed to his success by his valuable present to the mandarin's secretary.

The chief expressed his lively gratitude, and generously repaid what his son's friend had spent, by presenting him with two handsome Sining mules. He then suggested that Mipam should accompany him to Lhabrang, as he had been informed of the arrival there of some horses which the trader might care to buy. Mipam could not decline to look into a matter which promised to be profitable. Two or three good horses, together with the fine mules which had just been given him, would form an excellent present to offer to Dolma's father, and so dispose him in his favour.

Mipam therefore proceeded to Lhabrang, where, together with two horses, he bought various goods, which he secured at a price that left an ample margin for profit. He knew that he could sell part of his stock at Lanchow; he therefore hired some mules, organized a convoy, and set off thither. In this large town many Chinese and foreign articles are offered for sale, which the rich lamas of distant monasteries buy, without haggling, at three times their value. So able a merchant as

Mipam owed it to himself to profit by such an opportunity. He made some purchases, organized a fresh convoy, set off for Lanchow, sold his goods, bought more, and again resold them. He was lucky, and made further expeditions which duly brought in grist to the mill, and it was three months before he got back to Dangar. The season was too far advanced to cross the northern solitudes. At that period of the year the herdsmen withdraw with their cattle into the sunny recesses of the mountains, where they are sheltered from the wind. Not a tent is to be seen beside the tracks; it is impossible for travellers to obtain fresh supplies on the way. The pastures, covered with snow, afford no grazing for their beasts, and their owners can no longer find the dried dung which serves as fuel. Mipam had to postpone his journey until the following spring.

CHAPTER XI

THE postal service is an innovation of relatively recent
date in Tibet. It extends practically only to the two
roads joining Lhasa on the one hand to China, via Chiamdo,
and on the other, to India, via the Himalayas. Between Dangar
and Central Tibet no regular postal service exists. The Tibetans
are not accustomed to receiving news from their own people
while they are away on a journey, and they rarely think of keeping them in touch with what is going on in their absence.

Since his arrival in Dangar, Mipam had seen Dorje, the son of
Tsöndup of Shigatze, on one occasion, and the Tibetan trade-
agent had twice handed him letters from Tenzin and Dogyal,
which had been brought by caravan traders. In one of these
Tenzin thanked Mipam for the repayment, with ample interest,
of the hundred and fifty silver *sangs* which Tsöndup had given
him, in his name, on his departure from Shigatze. Dolma's
father was pleasantly surprised on receiving this remittance,
which he was not expecting, as his intention had been to make
a present of the money to his young friend. However, as this
repayment was evidence of Mipam's prosperity, he rejoiced
at it, and wished him further success. Of Dolma there was
no mention in either of his two letters, except that she was in
good health. From Dogyal's letter Mipam learnt that Tenzin,
keeping only the interest on the money, had sent the hundred
and fifty *sangs* to their father Puntsog. He congratulated his
younger brother on the rapidity which had marked his rise
as an independent merchant. There was perhaps a shade of
envy in his congratulations; he, the elder, was only an assistant,
whereas Mipam enjoyed the delights of independence.

Somewhat laconic, though affectionate, these letters did not
warn Mipam of the precarious position to which the prince

had reduced Puntsog, with a view to revenging himself upon him for the supposed crime of his fugitive son. Tenzin and Dogyal agreed that it was best not to trouble Mipam at a time when he must give all his attention to the conduct of his business, if he wished to continue the success which had hitherto attended him. Without the knowledge of the chief, whom he thought quite capable of taking offence at his intervention, and confiscating his remittances, Dogyal sent money and provisions to his parents, so that they did not lack the necessaries of life.

The second time he received news from Lhasa, Mipam found in a parcel containing various presents from Tenzin a note which Dolma had slipped into it. 'Aren't you soon coming back?' the young girl wrote.

It never occurred to Mipam that he might live in Lhasa. There he would have no position, whereas in China his status was becoming more and more assured. But now that he had decided to see Tenzin in the spring, and to ask for Dolma in marriage, he employed the winter months in embellishing his house. He had already enlarged it by the construction of an extra room. This he furnished comfortably, so that Dolma, should she decide to live in Dangar, would have a private room to which she could retire when he was receiving his fellow-merchants.

The New Year coming round once more, Mipam entertained his friends in his house, and went round to them to make merry. These rejoicings continue during the whole of the first month of the year in the homes of well-to-do Tibetans; Mipam was enjoying his full share of them when one day, at the close of a banquet, the most startling news that he could possibly have imagined shattered his peace of mind.

He was dining with the trade-agent, and amongst the latter's numerous guests were three pilgrims, pious middle-class people from Lhasa, who had made a pilgrimage to some of the holy places to be found in China. They had gone to Omi-shan, the mountain on the summit of which the shadow of the Buddha may be seen rising in mid-air; then to

Riwotsenga, the mountain dedicated to Jampai-yang, the
tutelary deity of the 'Lettered;' thence they had repaired to
Sining, and there they were awaiting the departure of the first
spring caravans, with a view to returning to Lhasa with one of
them. Some friends of the agent, who knew one of the pilgrims,
had brought them to his house.

The travellers had just learnt from a fellow guest that Mipam
was on friendly relations with Tenzin, the trader, and that the
latter was an old friend of his father.

'I'm also a friend of Tenzin's,' one of them observed to
Mipam. 'So you are the younger brother of Dogyal, who is
going to marry Dolma. We shall certainly attend the wedding.
Won't you be coming to Lhasa about that time? Tenzin,
before I left, told me that the date fixed for the wedding would
be an auspicious day in the third or fourth month. He consulted a learned astrologer in the matter. The astrologer had
not concluded his calculations when I left Lhasa. Have you
heard from Tenzin recently? Do you know exactly when the
marriage is to be?'

Mipam saw everything reeling around him; he felt the house
sinking under his feet, and bearing him down with it to a
bottomless abyss. His interlocutor's voice, and the voices of
the other guests, sounded to him, of a sudden, like the roar of
a torrent that was rolling him over and over in its course, and
bearing him out of the world. He gripped the cushions on
which he was sitting with both hands, and making an effort, he
was able to answer:

'I know nothing about the date. I haven't had news of my
brother for a long time.'

Already well primed with beer and spirits, Mipam's informant
had hardly noticed the young man's distress, and not realizing
that the trader had taken no alcohol, he put it down to the
first stages of drunkenness. All the agent's guests were already
more or less intoxicated, which was in itself a compliment to
the liberality of their host. This fact enabled Mipam to leave
the room without attracting much attention.

He returned in haste to his house, with a plan already made. The next day, or the day following, at the latest, he would start for Lhasa. The first month of the year had hardly begun; the marriage was to take place at some time in the third month at the earliest. If he hurried, there would be time for him to intervene.

The evening was too advanced for him to think of going to the monastery. Even if he rode hard, he would arrive there after the gates were closed: he·must wait until to-morrow. Mipam had counted on entrusting his partner Paljor with the supervision of his affairs. Tashi, the senior member of his staff, would stay in Dangar and engage an assistant to work the indispensable rounds with him. Kalzang, his junior, would accompany him to Lhasa, and at the monastery he would doubtless find two or three monks accustomed to crossing the solitudes, who would be glad to make the journey. He would take the two fine mules which the chief of Payenrong had given him, as well as the two horses purchased at Lhabrang, in addition to the mounts for himself and his men. Thus provided with remounts, he could negotiate long stages, and at a good pace. Moreover, to-morrow would be the sixth day of the moon; for more than a fortnight it would light their way; they could travel at night, which would keep the animals on the move and prevent their suffering from the frost.

He would push on as fast as he could. Who knew to what extreme measures Dolma, without news of him, might have recourse? He saw her, in his mind's eye, with her hair cut short, and clothed in a nun's dress. How bitterly he reproached himself for not informing Tenzin of his intentions! He had wanted to wait until he was richer, always richer, so that he could astonish the great merchant by the presents which he would offer him in return for Dolma's hand. His pride and his lack of enterprise had betrayed him. Tenzin would no doubt have contented himself with the success which he had already achieved, foreseeing a wealthy future for him. His marriage with the friend of his childhood was so firmly rooted in his mind that he had deemed it a thing inexorably fated, and the idea that Dolma could marry any other but himself had never occurred to him. Not for one moment had he imagined that his brother Dogyal, living with Tenzin, and now his right-hand man, could have been chosen by him for his son-in-law. He understood it now, however. It was but a logical sequence to Dogyal's adoption by Tenzin. This marriage may well have been concerted a long while ago between Dolma's father and his own. It was with a view to this that Puntsog had agreed to be separated from his eldest born, of whom he was so proud. At the very moment when he espied his little friend through the flames on the hearth in the house of the astrologer, she was, perhaps, already intended for Dogyal. How was it that he had never thought of this in the course of the intervening years?

Oh! if only he could have foreseen this, he would have . . . What would he have done? . . . That he could not decide, but he accused himself of having left undone what he ought to have done, and he tossed about on the cushions of his bed, stifling his cries of rage in the long sleeves of his robe. Dolma! Dolma! She must be cursing him for his silence, his inaction, his imbecility. . . . Dolma! Dolma! He had left her alone, like a cast-off chattel, his little one, his dearly beloved, Dolma! . . .

Well before sunrise, Mipam was trotting along the road to the monastery. When he arrived there the stars were still shining in the paling sky; on the roof-terrace of the assembly hall the novices, blowing into their conch-shells, were summoning the monks to their morning congregation. The outer boundary gates had just been opened; through the narrow alleys, which were thronged with monks proceeding to the assembly hall, Mipam made his way to his friend's quarters. The steward, like many of the monastic officials, was dispensed from attending the morning office, save on the days of the great religious festivals. Mipam knew that he would find him at home.

'What brings you here at this hour?' cried Paljor, surprised to see the young man enter his room. 'Did you arrive last night—did you sleep here?'

Then, despite the darkness in which the room was still plunged, he noticed his friend's distressed appearance.

'What is it?' he asked, with solicitude. 'Has anything serious happened? Are you ill?'

'Nothing wrong so far as business is concerned. I'm not ill. . . . I must start for Lhasa to-morrow.'

'To-morrow! At this time of year! But why?'

Mipam hesitated. Should he confide the true object of his journey to the steward? He must give him some plausible reason. His partner must not suspect him of any reprehensible action. It would be better, doubtless, to tell him the truth.

'You will keep my secret, keep it strictly, won't you?' he asked.

'*Yum chenmo!*[1] replied the *nierpa*, with a solemn oath.

'The father of the girl I want to marry is about to give her to another.'

'Oh!' exclaimed Paljor, sighing with relief. He attached small importance to such a contingency, for he had dreaded some business catastrophe. 'You had perhaps aimed a trifle too high. You never told me which was the family in question. The girl's father is doubtless a rich *kudag*?'

'It's Tenzin, the merchant.'

'But in that case there is every chance that he would prefer you to another; you have told me that Tenzin is a friend of your father's.'

'That is so.'

'And you are a merchant, as Tenzin is; a prosperous merchant, an excellent man of business. Who is the son-in-law of whom he is thinking?'

'My elder brother Dogyal, whom he has adopted. He has been living with him for several years and has assisted him in his business.'

---

[1] An oath on the Sacred Book, the Prajna Paramita, to which the Tibetans apply the deferential epithet of 'Great Mother'.

'He'll give him another of his daughters. Has he only one?'

'One only, and no son. I've been a fool, to think only of my trade, of amassing enough property to ask for her hand; and I was so sure of succeeding! It was all settled in my mind. Alas, I have delayed too long! Well, I leave to-morrow. I've come to ask you to supervise my affairs while I'm away. The older of the two boys, Tashi, will remain at Dangar; he knows my ways and my clients.'

'You can count upon me. Have no anxiety.'

'I have none.'

'I wish you good luck in your venture, but don't take the matter too much to heart, my young friend. There are plenty of nice girls, and many a father would be glad to have you for a son-in-law.'

'It's Tenzin's daughter whom I want.'

'He'll probably give her to you. You have a convincing way of putting things. It's not easy to resist you. . . . Your journey will be a hard one. How many men are you taking?'

'Kalzang is the only man I have available; and that's my difficulty. I thought I might find two or three monks here, seasoned travellers, who would like to go to Lhasa.'

'All monks like going to Lhasa, but what you want are stout fellows whom you can trust. I'll give you one of my own men, and I know two in the adjoining mansion who will be delighted to make the journey. Their lama is, for the moment, in Mongolia; my colleague, the steward who manages his house, will grant them leave. So there you are, everything is settled. Now to breakfast.'

The meal over, Mipam paid a visit to the old seer. He wished to ask his help, to beg that he would exert his super-normal powers to influence Dolma's father, from a distance, and constrain him to give him his daughter. But when he found himself face to face with the old man he dared not put his wish into words: in the atmosphere that surrounded him all such desire evaporated. Perturbed and full of anguish as he was, after a moment in the wonder-worker's presence

Mipam felt a wave of quietude pervading him, that irresistibly submerged his preoccupations, his revolt, his grief, and his will to fight for what he wanted; even the vision of Dolma grew fainter and seemed on the point of fading away altogether. Behind his closed eyelids he saw this impalpable tide reach his little fairy, who was dressed as in the days of their first meeting; he saw it reach the green and red double sleeves that floated about her dark robe like the wings of a startled butterfly; the tide rose, reached her shoulders, was about to touch the throat at which the gold reliquary was suspended. . . . This was more than Mipam could bear. He leapt to his feet, and bowing respectfully with folded hands, he craved the old man's blessing. He knew that it was useless to tell him anything. The seer had read his thoughts and had answered them, and Mipam refused to accept his answer.

Placing his two hands on the young man's head, the seer broke the silence:

'The last watch of the night,' he said.

And with the utterance of these cryptic words, he relapsed into contemplation, and seemed thenceforth oblivious of Mipam's presence, and of his departure.

In the bluish light of the moon, shining brightly in her first quarter, a group of horsemen were trotting across the snow-clad steppe. Around them, bounding the vast tableland, the dark masses of mountain ranges with rounded summits could be dimly distinguished; a wolf howled somewhere in the wilderness, and from the lake which they were skirting there came a loud booming sound as though great trumpets were blown beneath its ice-bound surface.

In the heavens the crescent moon grew red as it sank toward a mountain-top: and the head horseman scrutinized the white plain in search of a camping-ground. The road had been gradually approaching the mountains; a gap between two spurs seemed to indicate that it turned in that direction; in the opposite slope, which faced southwards, they might find some ravine free from snow. Without a word the leader, followed by his companions, put his horse to the gallop; once they had rounded the outlying spur of the mountain the hard, wiry grass was visible, and at some little distance they saw the gleam of an ice-free river, flowing across another plateau.

'Halt! Unload the animals, and walk them about. Don't let them cool down too quickly!'

The men mutely obeyed. One of them went to fetch water from the river, drew a little dried cow-dung from a sack which was included in the baggage, and lit a small fire. Fuel was scarce, and had to be used sparingly. The tent was pitched and the tea boiled, and the travellers ate barley meal and dried meat with their buttered tea. Horses and mules were given a ration of peas, and then, being well covered with rugs lined with sheepskin, they were left free to crop what they could of the frozen grass. One of the travellers, wrapped in his fur-lined robe, rolled himself up in a thick blanket and lay down in the open, his rifle by his side, keeping an eye on the horses, and rising from time to time to bring back to the camp those that had strayed too far. The leader and the three men slept in the tent, lying on the ground, completely clothed, their feet encased in their felt boots, their heads hidden under blankets drawn tightly round them, with a saddle for pillow.

Mipam was on his way to Lhasa.

Despite his urgent reasons for haste he was obliged to halt for a few days at Cherku. Horses and mules had been hard worked and insufficiently fed on the way; they had to be rested and fed. The men, too, were tired, though they had tried to hide their fatigue from the trader. Without knowing exactly what had induced him to undertake a forced journey in this inclement season, they had learnt from Paljor that his motive was a serious one, and the latter had urged them to serve the trader to the best of their ability; to spare him, as far as they could, the worries inseparable from such a journey, and not to trouble him with their questions or their chatter. All four were honest fellows, and did their best to do as they had

246

been told. But they found it very difficult to ride in silence. Tibetans are wont to cheer their long stages with humorous anecdotes, songs, and bucolic pleasantries. But Mipam, the merchant whom they knew and esteemed, was strangely altered: his face, generally smiling, wore an expression which they had never seen upon it, and there was a strange glitter in his eyes, which seemed always to stare at some invisible object. He hardly ate, and when those who slept beside him woke in the night they often saw him seated with open eyes, absorbed in his eternal contemplation. How had the jolly merchant been so transformed? What alien personality had entered into him? He seemed to have grown taller, and his voice, on the rare occasions when he spoke, had now a tone of command which none dared to resist. The liking which his companions had felt for him at Dangar was replaced by an astonished respect, not unmingled with fear. Who was this new Mipam? they asked themselves.

One evening, when they came to a sheltered camping-ground, a bear, alarmed by their presence, fled from a cave which the darkness had hidden from them. It halted at some little distance, within sight of the den from which it had been dislodged, and when Mipam called it—wonder of wonders!—the animal slowly returned to its lair, and passed the night asleep a few paces from their tent.

'It would have been wretched wandering about without shelter,' the young man remarked.

Such things were related of hermits who were wonder-workers; but Mipam was only a trader. Whence did he derive this power?

The fine weather continued to favour the travellers. The snow, which lay very thick on the summit of the passes, made their passage difficult, but it was pleasant to ride through the sunny valleys, and the temperature grew gradually milder. The riders reached the main track from Chamdo to Lhasa; though they were still far from the end of their journey, the most arduous part of it was over.

247

At last, one afternoon, the five horsemen saw the glitter of the Potala's gilded roofs, and Mipam recalled the evening when he had left them behind him in the darkness on leaving Tibet for China, where he parted from his dear Dolma after a brief farewell at Gahlden. She had loved him then as dearly as he loved her; he remembered how, without a moment's hesitation, she had accompanied him across the mountains when he had fled his country after striking the brute who had maltreated her. Every single incident of their short journey, and the happiness which they had experienced, re-awoke in his memory.

Now he was returning to take her and carry her away . . . his Dolma! He felt capable of contending for her with Dogyal, and with Tenzin. He was no longer the little boy who could only run away; he had become a man who could fight.

It was not the noisy, crowded caravan of young Mipam's day-dreams that halted before Tenzin's gate, but a company of five silent horsemen, whose features told of the fatigue endured on the way.

While the men were unsaddling the horses and leading them to the stables, Mipam was conducted to that part of the house where Tenzin, who was immediately informed of his arrival, was awaiting him.

'I could not have imagined that you could come from Dangar at this season,' said the astonished merchant, as he took the scarf which the young man offered him; 'but I am glad to see you. You are greatly changed, you were only a little boy when I saw you for the first time in your village. You have travelled a long way since then. From all I can hear, you're a trader of mark over yonder and a wealthy man.'

Hearing the horses stamping in the courtyard, he opened the window and stepped on to the balcony. For a few moments he inspected the animals critically.

'Are these mules yours?' he asked, at once picking out the two big black ones.

248

'Yes, and the horses, too.'

'Fine beasts. They represent quite a bit of money. And who are these men?'

'My servants.'

Tenzin nodded.

'I was not misinformed,' he said. 'You are a wealthy man.'

'Wealthy, no, uncle Tenzin, just comfortably off. Riches will come later: I'm young, and my business is prospering.'

'They'll come right enough; you can count on that, my boy, you're on the high road to them. My wife has gone out with Dolma; you'll see them presently. Dogyal has just left for Calcutta; he won't be back for six weeks or two months. But you'll still be here then.'

A maid brought them tea, barley meal, butter, dried meat and biscuits. Mipam ate and drank a little as he waited for one of his men to come and tell him that the toilet of the horses and mules which he wanted to present to Tenzin was completed. His men, assisted by Tenzin's servants, had worked quickly. The animals, curry-combed, their manes and tails plaited and decorated with red and green ribands, and with long scarves hanging from their necks, had been led into the middle of the courtyard. One of the men came up to the room in which Mipam was conversing with his host, and signed to him from the doorway.

'Will you come on to the balcony for a moment, uncle Tenzin?' said Mipam.

'Very good,' politely replied the merchant, rising.

The young man, thereupon, drew a scarf from his breast pocket, unfolded it, and offered it to Tenzin, pointing to the two mules and the two horses which his servants were holding by the bridle:

'Uncle Tenzin,' said he, 'I ask you to accept these four beasts. It is only a poor present, but show your kindness by accepting them.'

'These four beasts! They're splendid. A gift worthy to be

offered to the Dalai Lama himself! I'm going down to look at them!'

In an instant Tenzin was in the courtyard, inspecting the animals. Without being abnormally rapacious, he was always delighted with any addition to his possessions. He imagined the satisfaction which he would derive from exhibiting the four handsome animals to his friends, and informing them that they were a gift. In Tibet the importance of the presents which a man receives is a mark of his social rank and power, and a source of pride.

Tenzin had welcomed his young friend with affection; he now treated him with a kind of deferential gratitude that seemed to augur well.

While the merchant, having ordered one of his men to mount the horses and mules in rotation, was watching them as they trotted round the large courtyard, his wife and daughter returned.

'Wife! Daughter!' he cried. 'Mipam is here! Come and see the lovely beasts he has given me!'

The young man greeted his host's wife, and while she, as curious and interested as her husband, drew near to examine the animals, he grasped Dolma by the arm, and whispered in her ear:

'Dolma, I've come to fetch you.'

'Yes, Mipam,' answered the young girl.

Her answer lacked the frank enthusiasm for which he was looking, and he noted that Dolma's eyes had lost their old expressions of daring and determination. Her voice and glance betrayed a sort of lassitude and constraint.

'You still love me, Dolma?' asked Mipam, painfully surprised.

'Oh, yes, Mipam.'

This time the words were spoken with an unmistakable accent of sincerity, but the abounding joy that Mipam had hoped to hear in them was wanting. He dropped his friend's arm and gazed at her attentively. The little girl whose picture he had cherished in his heart was hardly recognizable in this grown-up Dolma, who was fully developed, and a woman in all her ways. She was richly clothed, as in days gone by, and her dress was like that which she was wearing when Mipam had seen her for the first time: a robe of dark blue cloth, from which emerged the silk sleeves of two blouses, worn one over the other—one green, one red. Dolma was undeniably pretty, but time seemed to have woven around her a tenuous veil as the pale mosses wreathe the trees of the Himalayan forests. The years had softened the bold brilliance of her eyes, had fettered her movements, and had, perhaps, attempered her heart and mind as well, stifling in them the impulsive independence which had set her so apart from other young girls of her age. Dolma, his own Dolma, appeared as through a veil, which must be torn aside before he would see her real self. A physical pain gripped at Mipam's heart, like that which he had felt when, on his way to China, he had learnt that the yaks of the caravan were to be slaughtered at the journey's end; like that which he vaguely recalled having felt, in his childhood, during the night that he had passed in the depths of the forest, in the hermit's hut, when the sorrow of existing beings was borne in upon him.

Dolma, too, was watching him, and doubtless perceived something unusual in his face.

'Mipam,' she said, 'you have become a great merchant like my father, but you have the face of a holy hermit.'

The young man trembled; for Dolma's remark matched his own thoughts.

'I became a merchant for your sake, Dolma; you know that I love you above all things. It was so that I might marry you. Was it not a promise that we made to each other?'

'It was, Mipam.'

'To-morrow I shall ask your father for you. I have a home in China ready to receive you, and if you don't like it I will buy another.'

'Yes, Mipam,' answered Dolma. And this time happiness seemed to lend strength to her voice.

When they had re-entered the house, Mipam presented Dolma and Tseringma, his hostess, with the gifts which he had brought for them: a roll of Chinese brocade and a very fine turquoise for each. Tseringma showed her delight, and drawing a happy augury from the pleasure which she evinced, the young man hoped to find an ally in her, to support the request which he was about to make to her husband.

Next morning, after breakfasting with his host, Mipam approached the subject which had led to his journey.

'Yesterday, uncle Tenzin, you were surprised at my arrival in Lhasa, and I didn't wish to tell you just then why I had come. If you are not engaged for the moment, would you care to have a talk?

'By all means, Mipam; what is it you wish to tell me?'

'Uncle Tenzin, I think I might assume that you would be neither sorry nor ashamed to have me for a son-in-law.'

Tensin did not answer. He was reflecting.

'I was not expecting that you would make such a request,' he said, after a moment's silence. 'Was it for this that you came to Lhasa?'

'For this alone.'

'Dolma is to marry your brother on his return from India. It's a settled thing.'

Mipam thought it better not to seem already aware of the fact.

'Uncle Tenzin, neither you nor Dogyal can possibly know what I am about to tell you, and Dolma has evidently not dared to mention it. A long time ago, when you went to Dugyul with your daughter, you passed a night, on your way back, at the house of my teacher, the astrologer. Do you remember? You had just come from my parents' house, and my mother had entrusted Dolma with some pastries for me.'

'I remember it quite well. Your uncle's wife had put the cakes in her cupboard. You went to look for them there, and

how boldly you asserted your right to them! She was quite
taken aback and your uncle dared not say a word. They looked
so abashed, I wanted to roar with laughter. What a young
rascal! You were promising well . . . and you haven't belied
that promise. . . .'

Mipam interrupted him.

'Well, uncle Tenzin, the very next day, before your departure, I asked Dolma to become my wife, and she gave me her
promise.'

'Ha, ha! Better and better! What a boy! How old were
you then?'

'Thirteen.'

'And Dolma was ten. And these children decided they would
be married! Ha, ha!'

'We were certainly very young, but that promise to become
husband and wife we repeated again at Gahlden, three years
later, when I left for China. And if I've worked with so much
ardour, if I've already made for myself such a good position
for a young trader. . . .'

'A very good one, Mipam; you may be proud of it. I could
never have imagined such success in a boy of your age.'

'Well, uncle Tenzin, if I strove to succeed it was because I
was thinking of Dolma, because I wanted to be able to ask
you for her hand. You are wealthy; I knew that your son-in-
law should at the least appear capable of becoming a wealthy
man. Uncle Tenzin, what must I offer you to become Dolma's
husband?—Dogyal is, I am sure, less well off than I am, and
long before you thought of making him your son-in-law, Dolma
and I had decided on our marriage.'

'Dogyal has nothing but what I give him, Mipam; he's in
my employ, and not a merchant on his own account as you
are; but you're mistaken if you think that your childish project
preceded mine. When you saw Dolma for the first time, I had
already agreed with your father that if your brother Dogyal
showed a disposition for business and behaved himself well, he
should marry Dolma and become my son and heir. Your elder

brother is honest and a good worker; he is capable of making an
efficient manager of a business firm that is already well established. I don't think, Mipam, that he could have done what
you have done. People from here who have been to Dangar
have spoken to me of you, and have told me what is said there
of your extraordinary ability. They admire you. But the
husband of my only daughter must be my heir, and he must
first work under me. I am not yet old enough to renounce the
personal management of my business. A subordinate position
is not the thing for you. You are used to being your own
master; there must be only one master in a house, and here it
is I who am the master. . . . And again, I promised your
father to be responsible in this way for Dogyal's future; this is
not the moment, now that he is impoverished once more, to
break my promise.'

'What is that you say? My father is poor?'

'Quite so, Mipam. I didn't wish to let you know it, thinking
it better to spare you useless worries at a time when you had
need of all your wits to make your way in a foreign country.
At such a distance you could not have been of any use to your
parents. I have provided for that; they have never lacked the
necessaries of life.'

'But how did it happen?'

'You were the cause of it, my poor Mipam. Not being able
to get hold of you, the *gyalpo* revenged himself on your family.
Keep away from his territory, whatever you do. Time has not
appeased his anger; if he can lay hands on you, he will have
you tortured, you can count on that.'

'Uncle Tenzin, I should like, all the same, to go and see my
mother. My dear mother, always so good to the naughty little
boy that I was! Do you really think, if I went there by a
roundabout route, and only spent a day with her, that I
couldn't go to our village? I would take a good horse, and
come back another way. The prince thinks I'm a long
way off. . . .'

'It's no good, Mipam, you will never see your mother again.'

'What?' cried the young man.

'She has been dead nearly a year.'

Mipam did not utter a cry; not a word came from his lips; but his eyes closed, and the blood left his face, which assumed a deathlike pallor. Tenzin thought that he was fainting, and rushed to support him, but at his touch Mipam re-opened his eyes, rose to his feet with an effort, indicated with a motion of the hand that his host was not to distress himself, and left the room.

'Never would I have imagined that this hardy lad was so sensitive!' thought Tenzin, more disturbed by Mipam's silence than he would have been by tears and a loud demonstration of sorrow.

'Cham! Cham!' he cried, calling his wife. 'Come here and have some beer sent up.'

The trader felt the need of company, and a bowl of strong drink to restore him after his emotion.

'That proves that he's got a good heart, and that he loved his mother,' said Tseringma, when her husband had described the effect produced on Mipam by the sad tidings which he had given him.

'Obviously, obviously,' replied Tenzin. 'But Mipam has been queer since his childhood. Do you remember what his brother told us about him? When he was still only a child, he threw himself before a leopard in order to save its life, and was struck by the arrow meant for the animal; and then he ran away from home. Tsöndup's son, too, had a queer story about some yaks which Mipam bought: how he spent all he possessed in order to prevent their being sold to a butcher.

'His success as a merchant, too, is extraordinary. Whoever heard of a boy of seventeen undertaking such business transactions quite on his own, and amassing a fortune in the space of four years! It's wonderful, but a little disquieting. One would say that Mipam is a man of a different kind from ourselves. . . . Guess why he's come here, in winter, over the frozen steppes? . . . It was to ask me to give him Dolma in marriage. It appears that when the child was only ten she promised to be his wife. He says she renewed that promise to him at Gahlden,

when she went there to bid him farewell and offer a lamp with
him to Chenrezigs. Do you remember how she insisted on
seeing Mipam again before he started? . . . Has Dolma ever
spoken to you of this plan of marriage?'

'Never, but girls keep many things to themselves.'

'Women, too, no doubt,' chaffed the merchant, looking at
his wife. 'In any case, Dolma is to marry Dogyal on his return
from India; that's all settled.'

'Dogyal will be a better son-in-law for you,' declared
Tseringma. 'He's a devoted assistant, and is not given to
fancies like Mipam. With Mipam you never can tell what's
going to happen: he might get tired of a merchant's life, and if
some fresh crotchet took hold of him, he might leave home to
go who knows where, to look for who knows what, as he did
when a child. He's violent, and respects nothing when he is
in anger. He struck his lord's son. I don't like that. The
young prince was vicious, that's certain, but he wouldn't have
killed Dolma; and she was wrong, after all, to desert the princesses in order to look for Mipam. He might behave again
in such a way as to get us into trouble. It was on his account
that your business relations with the *gyalpo* were broken off.'

'That's of no importance: the prince could no longer be
useful to me. He's almost ruined. He has got no money left
to invest. He's pursued by a curse. Doubtless the curse of
that lama-*naljorpa* of Kham, who went off with his horse, and
whom he tried to kill by magic. Those lamas of Kham are
powerful magicians. Who knows if there actually isn't some
sort of bond between him and Mipam? Dogyal told us that his
brother was staying with this lama when the *gyalmo* went into
retreat in a hermitage.'

'Yes, that may be so,' said Tseringma. 'And who knows if,
after all, he didn't have something to do with the *gyalse's*
uncanny death?'

She reflected for a moment, and then continued:

'Master, you can't break your promise to Dogyal and his
father. He must marry Dolma. You'll find no better son-in-
law, none more submissive, more respectful.'

256

'That's what I said to Mipam; there must be only one master in a house, and I intend to remain master here. There is no place in my house for an undisciplined mind like his.'

'Wait. Don't reject Mipam in too much of a hurry. He's rich and generous. He might, while keeping up his business in China, become your partner, and an excellent one at that. Why let the property which he's amassing go to another family? Why should not Dolma marry both brothers? It's the custom. Dogyal would remain in Lhasa; Mipam would come here from time to time, and would not stay long enough to cause you annoyance. I regard him as you do: he's odd, disturbing; it may be that he's in secret communication with some god or demon in his service, or with a magician who exerts his power on his behalf. Be careful not to irritate him. Better have him with us than against us.'

'What you say is very true, Tseringma; your advice is always sound. Yes, here's the solution. Dogyal, the elder, shall marry Dolma as arranged. In the marriage settlement we'll insert the name of Mipam as second husband, and all will be satisfied. My mother was the wife of three brothers; it's the recognized thing, and in this way the family property will not be dispersed. Dolma will be rich and happy, and if Mipam, by any chance, takes it into his head to leave her, she will still have the steady-going Dogyal left.'

Congratulating themselves on having so cleverly arranged matters, the husband and wife drank together and planned the preparations for the wedding festivities.

Mipam, who had left Tenzin's house without realizing what he was doing, wandered aimlessly through the town. One single thought filled his mind: his mother was dead, he would never see her again . . . never, never. She had loved him more than her first-born. Until now he had hardly appreciated this, but he saw, in a flash, that she had expected something more from him than the satisfaction which a good son may give his mother. 'The gods sang in my room at the moment when you were born, and "signs" appeared around our house,' she had told him long ago. He was too young, then, to heed her words, but their meaning came home to him now.

From the son born in the midst of prodigies, Changpal had hoped for a prodigy; she had hoped in vain. He was not a wonder-working saint, and having left his father's house so early, he had not even had the opportunity of proving himself a good son. Now that he had returned, capable of understanding, and capable, perhaps, by the force of his affection of working the long-expected miracle, his mother was no longer here.

He recalled the religious songs of the poet-ascetic Milarespa, which the begging pilgrims sing for alms at the villagers' doors,

> *'When I had a mother I was not by her side,*
> *And when I returned to her, my mother had died.'*

The impermanence, the unreality of the things of this world, of which the seer of Dangar had sometimes spoken, rose insistently before his mind. What was all this display that surrounded him, these houses, these people that he met in the streets the great temple of the Jowo[1] and the massive palace of the Dalai Lama enthroned upon the hill?—All these were but unsubstantial pictures, which would fade away as the image of his mother had done. Oh! to see her again, to clasp her in his arms! . . . . But before him lay nothing but emptiness. And they had perhaps met thousands of times in the course of their successive lives, coming to birth and meeting once more, dying and separating, without ever arriving at a true mutual understanding and love.

Then his thoughts turned to Dolma, to her distant, passive demeanour, and suddenly there once more rose before him the vision which had driven him from the old seer's room on his departure from Dangar: the intangible wave, advancing slowly, irresistibly submerging all that surrounded him, and reaching Dolma, still impassive, almost inert.

As at Dangar, a rebellious reaction banished the hallucination. Lhasa, and the things of the world to which Lhasa belonged,

[1] A celebrated statue of Buddha which is worshipped in the great temple of Lhasa.

resumed their semblance of reality, and Mipam once more began to think as men do think in this world. In the place of the sorrow which his mother's death had caused him he wanted to put his love for Dolma. A being who loved him had been taken from him; he stretched out his arms to grasp another by whom he wished to be loved. Oh! the misery of the man whose headlong course carries him from one love to another, never allowing him to attain to love!

He walked on and on. He was calmer now, but he preferred to be alone rather than return to his host and become the object of conventional commiseration, and presently he found himself before the monastery of Sera. A number of monks were returning thither after spending the day in town. For them the monastery was only an inn from which they escaped as often as they could, on business or pleasure bent, to buy and sell and gossip. . . . One might just as well become a merchant, openly, as he had, as lead that kind of life. Nevertheless, the great monastery seemed to shine with a beauty of its own. Its array of small white houses, screened from the outer world by the high boundary wall, might have been so many sanctuaries for thoughts very different from those that swarmed outside its walls, so many refuges in which noble minds might have created good influences which they could have sent forth into space from all the gilded *gyaltsans*[1] with which the roofs of the temples and palaces of this monastic city were bristling. Of what significance were these emblems of victory if they did not mark the victory of that gift of gifts, the refulgent truth, the conquest over false and evil thoughts, the triumph of good?

'To those who have the thoughts of an ape, I will give the pure ray of the purest light; the Knowledge that delivers from sorrow. . . .'[2]

[1] *Gyaltsan* means 'sign of victory'. They are for the most part gilded ornaments of pointed or cylindrical form narrowing toward the top. They are placed on the roofs of temples or the Grand Lama's palaces.

[2] The Buddha is made to utter these words by the author of the *Gyacher rolpa* (a romance on the life of the Buddha, translated into Tibetan from the original Sanscrit poem called *Lalita vistara*).

Now, where had he heard these words? He could not remember.

Yes, when he had married Dolma, and she was living with him at Dangar, he would buy a monk's house in the monastery in which his friend Paljor the steward resided, and he would go and stay there from time to time. How good are solitude and silence! Side by side with the world in which live merchants and their like, there exists another world, and it was this that attracted him.

It was late when Mipam returned to Tenzin's house; a servant was waiting up for him, as his employers had already retired to their rooms.

'It isn't prudent to be out of doors after nightfall, *Kushog*,' the man remarked to Mipam. 'There are robbers prowling around who beat and rifle belated passers-by. The mistress has had some supper taken to your room, and I will bring you up some tea.'

'Thank you,' said Mipam.

When he rose the next morning Mipam determined to resume the conversation with Tenzin which he himself had so abruptly interrupted under the shock of the emotion evoked by the news of his mother's death. He must convince Dolma's father and win his consent to the marriage. Tenzin could still adopt Dogyal if he chose; this would ensure that he would not be deprived of his services, and Dogyal would be no worse off, seeing that he would inherit from his adoptive father. For himself, Dolma was all he asked for. He would gladly undertake to renounce all rights of succession to his father-in-law's property, and he felt confident that he could make a fortune which would prevent his wife from regretting such a step.

In this way matters could be easily arranged, but Dolma must help him, must show the decision and strength of will of which she gave proof as a little girl. He must see her alone and talk to her. She desired their marriage as much as he did: they had only to work together to secure Tenzin's consent.

Mipam had no difficulty in obtaining the desired interview

with his beloved. He had decided to go and offer lamps to the Jowo, in memory of his mother; he told Tenzin's wife of his intention, and asked her to allow Dolma to accompany him, as she had known the deceased. Tseringma now regarded Mipam as her stepdaughter's future husband, and an admirable future son-in-law; she gave him her best smile, praised his pious purpose, and then, after ordering a piece of butter to be melted in a bronze pot which was wrapped in a thick piece of felt, she was about to order a servant to carry it after the young people.

'I'll carry it myself,' said Mipam.

'No, I'll carry it,' said Dolma, politely.

'Do as you like,' said Tseringma, realizing that they wanted to be by themselves.

The young people then set off.

'Dolma, do you remember the day we went to offer lamps at Gahlden?'

'Yes, I remember it quite well, Mipam.'

'I was very sad at parting from you, Dolma.'

'So was I, Mipam.'

'You knew that I would come back and fetch you.'

'I knew you would come back.'

'Well, here I am, Dolma. We must be married very quickly and then we'll go to China. Do you remember our tramp across the mountains, when we went to Shigatze?'

'We had a lovely time, Mipam, such a lovely time! . . . never have I been so happy.'

'We shall have a still better time, now. We shan't have to hide, we shan't be afraid of being pursued and beaten; we shall have horses, servants and any amount of provisions. We had none when we ran away and you were hungry. . . . Do you remember that?'

'You brought meal out of the rock, and the gods threw a bag of powdered meat in your path. . . . Mipam, do you still get meal out of the rocks, and do the gods still feed you when you're travelling?'

Mipam felt embarrassed. He had attributed this second miracle to a perfectly natural cause—a traveller had dropped a bag; and as for the first, he regarded it as a demonstration of power on the part of the holy man who had slept in the cavern.

'I've always had enough to eat; there was no occasion for miracles.'

The young girl held her peace, she appeared to regret this absence of the marvellous in her friend's life.

'I let your mother know about it, Mipam.'

'What did you let her know?'

'The wife of one of my father's clerks comes from Dugyul, and she went to see her parents. Before she left, I described how you had plunged your arm into a rock, and how we ate the meal that flowed from it after you had withdrawn your arm. I told her, also, how the bag of powdered meat was given to you by the gods, and I made her promise to repeat all this to Mistress Changpal. She did so. I know that, because your father sent me a letter with some biscuits which your mother baked for me. In the letter he said that your mother was very happy to hear it, but not at all surprised; that she well knew that you were a god incarnate, since the gods had sung in her room when you were born. And the woman and her husband who went to your parents' house to take them some presents from my father told me, also, that your mother was overjoyed, and that your father said once more: "They may deny it as much as they like, Mipam is certainly an incarnated lama." '

In Mipam's heart there welled up a song of thanksgiving. His mother had hoped to see him perform miracles, and she had heard such miracles ascribed to him. By them her favourite son had discharged his debt of gratitude and had brightened the last years of her sad life, the life of a mother bereft of her children. What a consolation for him!

The two young people paid their devotions before the statue of the Jowo. Mipam gave an offering to the sacristan, which was repaid with obsequious obeisances, and then, together with

Dolma, he climbed up to the roof-terrace of the building. There, finding the solitude which he desired, he approached the subject of their marriage.

'I was talking last evening with your father, Dolma. He did not welcome my request as I expected. He wants you to marry Dogyal. That you know, no doubt?'

'I do, Mipam.'

'How came your marriage to be decided on?—You ought to have spoken, you ought to have told your father of the arrangement between us; you should not have let him give his promise to Dogyal.'

'My father told me that he had promised your father a long time ago that Dogyal should be my husband. That was settled when he took your brother into his house, before we met.'

'I reproach you with nothing, Dolma, yet if I hadn't come back, you would have become, before long, Dogyal's wife instead of mine. Is that what you desire?'

'You misunderstood my father. Mistress Tseringma explained to me, yesterday evening, that he wants both of you to be my husbands.'

'No!' cried Mipam.

'Yes, I assure you he does. My stepmother told me so.'

'And you accept that, Dolma, you wish to be Dogyal's wife as well as mine?'

'It's the custom, Mipam. Grandmother, my father's mother, who now lives in a convent, was the wife of my three grandfathers. I could say nothing; father is the master.'

'Do you love Dogyal?'

'He's kind, and works hard, but he's only a merchant.'

'I, too, am only a merchant.'

'You are a merchant because you've had to earn money to live, and you wanted to earn money for me as well, but you are really anything but a merchant. The holy man in the cave saw that, and I, Mipam, know it too. I have thought of you so much, and have seen you in my dreams; sometimes you appeared all encircled with light, like the Buddhas.'

'But you want, all the same, to marry Dogyal.'

'It isn't I who want it, it's my father. And then, since you'll be my husband, too. . . .'

'No!' cried Mipam, interrupting her, 'it's Dogyal or I; make your choice.'

'You, of course, Mipam.'

'That's really true?'

'Why don't you believe me?'

'I want to believe you, Dolma. Since things are so, you must speak to your father. You were courageous before; why have you altered? Do you remember?—You told me that if you couldn't be my wife, you would cut off your hair and become a nun. Tell him that. Make him understand that it isn't the practice in China for a wife to have several husbands, that I don't intend to agree to such a thing, and that you don't either. You mustn't wait any longer; you'd better talk to him to-day. I'll speak to him as well. Between the pair of us, we'll persuade him.'

Dolma made no answer; she was weeping softly.

'Please, Dolma, don't cry; all will come right, I'm sure of it.'

'No, Mipam, my father won't change his views. He loves Dogyal, and wants to keep him with him to look after his interests. Father is ageing; he's still in very good health, but he's afraid, in a few years' time, of not being able to take such an active part in his affairs. I know he thinks a great deal about it; he says, at times, that he feels old age creeping on, and it greatly distresses him. He's so attached to his business, and he doesn't want anybody else to be at the head of it, while he has to remain sitting at home, drinking beer and reciting prayers. He would wish still to be the master, even if he had to give the necessary orders from his room, and that, he knows, he can do with Dogyal, who is obedient, patient, and very respectful.'

'Let him keep Dogyal, then! For my part, I'm going to carry you off.'

'Oh! Mipam!'

The young girl continued to weep in silence.

Mipam felt his heart sink. He found no help in her: she had lost the will to fight.

'Listen,' he answered. 'You must exert your will, our happiness is at stake. I shall do my best to convince your father, and you, for your part. . . .'

He paused, reflecting. Dolma's inertia did not give him the smallest hope that she would be able to confront Tenzin and conquer his obduracy if he, Mipam, could not manage to do so. It would be better, then, that Tenzin should believe her resigned and submissive. He would not, in that case, think of watching her. And for his part, he had made up his mind. If the merchant would not consent that Dolma should be his wife alone, he would escape with her to China.

Ought he to acquaint her with his design? He feared lest she should take alarm, and lest something in her behaviour should put her perspicacious stepmother on her guard. Yet he wanted to make sure that she would be ready if an elopement were necessary.

'You don't seem very courageous, Dolma, nor very determined to defend our happiness,' he said dejectedly. 'Don't speak to your father, then; I'll be responsible for that; and I am sure I can make him change his mind. If I fail to do so, you must slip away quietly and accompany me to China. That is really what you wish? You know, you swore to become my wife; you cannot go back on that. Promise me once more, by the Jowo!'

'By the Jowo!' Dolma repeated, trembling.

'And now we will offer another lamp together to seal our promise.'

They went down from the terrace and made their way to the altar, which was resplendent with light.

'You offer the lamp, Dolma,' said Mipam. 'It's to confirm your promise. As far as I'm concerned, there's no need to bind myself by an oath. My heart clamours for you, and I dare dispute you with the Jowo himself.'

* * * *

The further discussions which Mipam had with Tenzin left him no hope of bringing the merchant round to his standpoint. From the very first he was persuaded of that, but he judged that it would be more adroit on his part to let Tenzin think that he still had hopes of convincing him, and that he would continue to adduce arguments in support of his wishes. The object of this stratagem was to occupy the obstinate merchant's attention. Tenzin, for his part, believed that Mipam would end by coming over to his way of regarding the matter, and would agree to share Dolma with his elder brother, and, as his second son-in-law, would become a profitable acquisition.

Mipam, on the contrary, was making preparations for Dolma's escape. He had every confidence in Kalzang, the man he had brought with him. Like Tashi, his head clerk, whom he had left at Dangar, Kalzang was a half-breed, born of a Tibetan mother and a Chinese father. He had no trouble in understanding the reasons which actuated his employer.

'These Lhasa Tibetans are real savages,'[1] he declared. 'Only savages could think of giving several husbands to the same wife. It's putting things upside down. It's logical, on the other hand, for a man to have several wives.'

'I agree with your first statement, but I'm doubtful about the second,' Mipam answered, laughing. 'After all, certain women may take as much pleasure in having several husbands as the husbands take in having several wives. These are things without importance. Every man is free to order his life as he likes, always providing that no one suffers thereby. For my part, I mean to be Dolma's only husband, and to have no other wife. Since her father persists in wishing to give me my brother as partner, I have decided to take Dolma away to China without his permission. It remains to be seen how this can be managed.'

The two men held a long private conference in the country, far from prying ears, and weighed up the situation under all its aspects.

[1] Polyandry does not exist in Eastern Tibet.

266

To carry Dolma away by night was impossible: her step-mother slept, most of the time, in the same room with her; the big gate of the courtyard, the only means of access to Tenzin's residence, was closed every evening at nightfall, and near the gate several of the servants were lodged. On the other hand, Mipam could hardly carry the girl off in broad daylight. Were she to be seen by any of her acquaintances leaving Lhasa on horseback in his company, these latter, finding something suspicious in the fact, would not fail to talk about it in town. Tenzin would soon learn of it, and would have no difficulty in tracing the fugitives.

After carefully considering several plans, Mipam decided on the following. He would feign to return to China, and would allow several days to elapse, so that Tenzin might believe him to be well on the way home, and then he would double back to the outskirts of Lhasa, and wait for Dolma on the date agreed upon. He decided also to put Tenzin off the scent by telling him that he was going to Tsetang to buy some serge, and that from Tsetang he would join the Chiamdo road, without passing through Lhasa, making his return journey through the Ga country, which can be easily reached by secondary trails. Dolma's father would escort him as far as the banks of the Kyi river; after the present which he had received from Mipam, Tenzin could do no less. He, Mipam, would then cross the river, and ostensibly take the road to Tsetang, but instead of going thither he would cross the mountains to the north of Samye, which would take him back into the neighbourhood of Dechen, close to Lhasa. He would recross the river at some other point than that to which Tenzin had accompanied him, and would wait for the appointed day, in some outlying spot to the south of the city. In the meantime he would procure a horse for Dolma to ride, and some mules to carry the provisions. With the advent of spring there would no longer be any hardship in travelling; he would leave Lhasa by a road that started from behind the monastery of Depung, and led to the great lake of Tengri Nor. It would never occur to Tenzin to

search in that direction; he would be much more likely to inquire
for him at Tsetang, so losing several days, which the fugitives
would utilize in reaching the northern solitudes.

It remained to decide how Dolma was to leave her father's
house. It would have to be during the evening, so that the
darkness would prevent an immediate search, and enable
the travellers to put a substantial distance between them and
Lhasa. Dolma, in her present state of fright and want of energy,
would not go alone, after dark, from Lhasa to Depung; she
probably would not dare cross the city boundaries. Some
one must accompany her from the door of her house, someone with whom she could leave the house without attracting
attention.

Kalzang solved the problem. 'Some woman,' he said, 'must
undertake to wait for her near Tenzin's house. She must
provide herself with a little *todja*.[1] At the corner of an alley,
in the shadow of a doorway, in any secluded spot, Dolma will
hastily smear her face, which will make it difficult for anyone
to recognize her in the dusk. In this woman's company she
will leave the city in the direction of the Dechen road, the
one that leads to Chiamdo, which you say you want to take.
I shall be waiting near the road with a horse for Dolma; we
will pretend to be going toward Dechen, and then, as soon
as the woman is out of sight, we will skirt round Lhasa and
come to rejoin you close to Depung.'

'The plan is not a bad one,' declared Mipam, 'but where is
the woman?'

Kalzang knew a woman who would readily agree to play that
part if promised a sufficient reward. She was the sister of a
woman who kept a small restaurant at which he had often
eaten, since his arrival in Lhasa. She seemed fairly greedy for
gain, and not overburdened with scruples. He would say that he
was acting on behalf of the son of a noble family, who was in
love with Dolma. Her fear lest the young man should punish

[1] A sort of brownish resin which Tibetan women smear on the face to
protect the skin from wind and sun.

her for any indiscretion would effectually prevent her from gossiping.

'You will give her twenty silver coins, and promise her another hundred when she joins you with Dolma,' said Mipam in conclusion. 'I'm going to announce my departure to Tenzin; you must see at once about buying the animals we need.'

The conference was at an end. Mipam went back to his host.

'I'm about to leave you, uncle Tenzin,' he said, after the evening meal. 'I propose, since I'm not far from Tsetang, to go and buy some serge there. I shall be able to dispose of it in the Amdo monasteries. I have nothing more to say in the matter which brought me here, but a day will come when you will regret having refused to give your daughter to such a son-in-law as myself.'

The young man seemed deeply to regret his failure. Without being unduly cast down. His attitude, a perfectly natural one, was that of a man who is resolved to make the best of a painful situation. Tenzin was completely deceived.

'I haven't refused to have you for a son-in-law, my boy,' he answered. 'Quite the reverse. Your brother and you will marry Dolma, according to our country's custom, which is a wise one. In this way the property will not be dispersed and the family will be wealthy. In their turn, Dolma's sons will share one wife; my grand-daughters will be asked in marriage by wealthy merchants, who will pay a good round sum to their parents, and all will live in comfort.'

'There's a certain amount of truth in what you say, Uncle Tenzin. It was probably in China that I conceived this repugnance to share my wife with another, but I can't get over it.'

So ended the discussion between Mipam and the merchant, and the young man appeared to be completely engrossed in his commercial schemes. Two evenings before his departure, Kalzang engaged the attention of Tenzin and his wife by inspecting with them the saddles which his master wanted to buy. Mipam, for his part, led Dolma to the stables, to show her the mules and the horse which he had lately acquired.

'Your father is obdurate, Dolma,' he told her. 'I've done my best to convince him; I'd have given him the price he wanted; but the thought of marrying you to both of us is fixed in his mind; he won't renounce it. You will leave with me: I've arranged everything. Look at this handsome horse; it's for you. It has a wonderful amble, always quite uniform; you'll never get tired. I'm going to make a sham departure, and in a week's time I'll be back to fetch you. I've arranged my plans so that your father won't think of looking for you on the road that we shall take. Be careful to remember the date in which we start; it will be the eighth of the month, a propitious day. I shall not be able to show myself here, as your father will think I'm already far away. A woman will come and fetch you, and will take you to the place where Kalzang will be waiting for you with the horse. I shall be quite close at hand, but it's better that the woman shouldn't see me. Your stepmother goes to the temple of the Jowo, and makes the rounds while telling her beads, on the eighth and fifteenth days of the month; and I heard her say that on the eighth of this month she will remain there for twenty-four hours,[1] fasting and reciting prayers with some of her friends. That will be an exceptional opportunity for us. You must find some pretext to avoid accompanying her. Pretend to stumble as you go down the stairs, and hurt your ankle; you can declare that you would not be able to go the rounds and make the prostrations. At dusk you will be at the little window that lights the saddle-room and looks on to the road. The woman will come there and will say: "Jowo knows" to which you will answer "Dolma knows." Then, making sure that there's no one in the courtyard, you'll slip out and follow the woman. Even if one of the servants were to see you leaving the house with a woman he wouldn't pay much attention, but it's better

[1] An exercise in common use in Tibet.

that you shouldn't be seen. That's settled, then, isn't it, Dolma; you have quite understood what you've got to do? Repeat it to me.'

Dolma, trembling and with tears in her eyes, repeated in a low voice what her friend had told her, and Mipam once more felt depressed as he noted the lack of enthusiasm and moral courage with which she faced an adventure which would have delighted her four years previously.

'Dolma, aren't you glad to be leaving with me, to be with me for ever?'

'Indeed, I am, Mipam. It would be lovely to be with you always.'

Her words had an unmistakable accent of sincerity. They expressed the girl's whole-hearted longing to pass her life by Mipam's side, yet her declaration was tinged with a shade of regret. As she made it she seemed to be already mourning a cherished dream.

'Dolma,' replied Mipam, 'you are a little upset by the idea of this flight of ours; you had dreamt of a gay wedding, with crowds of guests, and banquets, but what does all that matter to us? You will be happy, because we shall love each other. I'm not taking you to poverty; you will want for nothing; and life in China is pleasant. And then, didn't you promise to be my wife? You promised it more than once, and even before the Jowo.'

'I did, Mipam.'

At this moment the voices of Tenzin and Kalzang could be heard as they left the stores; Kalzang was speaking very loudly to warn his master. Mipam clasped Dolma passionately in his arms:

'My wife—for me, for me alone. . . . Dolma?'

'Yes, Mipam,' replied the young girl, trying to stem her tears.

Two days later, Mipam left Lhasa with his men and his mules and horses. As he had foreseen, his host accompanied him as far as the banks of the River Kyi, and Tenzin saw him ride off along the road to Tsetang.

Tenzin had not been altogether pleased with Mipam's visit; the obstinate boy would have nothing to do with the scheme suggested by Tseringma. Hitherto the merchant had felt that he had found in Dogyal the son-in-law whom he desired. Mipam had troubled his peace of mind. Dogyal would always remain a desirable son-in-law, but Mipam, it was clear, had a more brilliant commercial career before him, and Dolma—one couldn't close one's eyes to the fact—loved him. . . .

Returning home with a certain misgiving, Tenzin found his daughter lying on her bed, bathed in tears. Mipam, it was only too evident, had brought trouble to his peaceful hearth; but the merchant was not the man to give way to vain lamentations; he was accustomed to get his own way.

'Don't cry, little one,' he said to his daughter; 'Mipam is the younger; his presence at the wedding, and his consent, are not necessary to make him your husband. It will suffice for the elder son to marry you; I will have Mipam's name entered after that of Dogyal in the marriage contract. When he comes to Lhasa again he will have changed his mind, and will be very glad to learn that you are his wife also.

'Your father has only your happiness at heart. Mipam is a clever lad, but at times cranky; one never knows, with a mind like his, what he may decide to do. If he were to desert you, when he was your only husband, that would be most unfortunate for you, while in marrying a steady husband like Dogyal you can rely on a good companion who will make your life comfortable.'

His little homily ended, Tenzin left the room, in love with his own wisdom, and repeating, with a knowing smile:

'I will have his name entered in the marriage contract.'

CHAPTER XII

IN the narrow rectangle of a window beside the gate of
the great courtyard was framed a pale face with distorted
features. Not far away a woman was loitering beside a shop,
watching the entrance to the Tenzin residence. The sun had
set, and in the darkening sky the moon was shining in her first
quarter. It was the eighth day of the month by the Tibetan
calendar: a day devoted to works of charity and pious exercises
by the majority of the faithful, and to a more prolonged meditation by the spiritual *élite*. The minds of all turned toward the
Buddha and his Doctrine, from which each one borrowed what
he could discern and digest. Mystical thoughts, puerile or
lofty, filled the atmosphere of the great Lamaic city; occult
forces were at work. . . . Bathed, quite unconsciously, in that
singular atmosphere, two children were striving to defend
their love.

The woman, to justify her prolonged station before the shop,
bought a pair of straps, paid for them, and moved away,
brushing against the walls. Presently she approached the window
at which she was expected, saw behind the grating the pallid
face, the eyes dilated with fear, and murmured:

'Jowo knows!'

'Dolma knows!' replied a trembling voice.

'Hurry! I'll wait opposite the gate.'

She moved on a little way, then stopped, making a pretence
of replacing the old straps of her boots by those which she had
just purchased. The courtyard was empty, as was the balcony
overlooking it; and the windows opening on to it were closed.
No more favourable conditions could have been desired. There
was Dolma. When she reached the gateway, the woman held

273

out her hand and drew her forward; with one step the girl was outside.

'Quick,' said the woman; 'no one has seen you!'

But Dolma resisted the pressure of the hands that sought to drag her away; her body, shaken with a nervous tremor, came to a standstill; her features contracted, and a gleam of madness shone in the depths of her dilated pupils.

'Don't stay there; come!' the woman repeated.

Dolma did not seem to understand; confused sounds buzzed in her ears, and the ground seemed to rock under her feet.

'Come, come along; you'll feel better in a moment; we'll stop a little further on to let you rest.'

It was now the woman's turn to tremble, but from impatience and fear lest someone might come up.

'I cannot,' stammered Dolma.

Mipam ought to have been there, to lift her up and bear her away in his arms. In his intention of remaining at a safe distance had he erred from excess of prudence, had his plan been too cleverly conceived? But a man cannot carry a girl in his arms, in the heart of Lhasa, without attracting the attention of the crowd. Is she hurt? is she ill? where are they taking her? who is she? . . . How many questions would be asked! No, Mipam could not have done such a thing, but the woman was going to risk it. If she only could carry her just to the corner of that alley close at hand, the girl, once out of sight, would have time to recover her wits. At all costs she must drag her away from the gate. She stooped down a little, embracing the girl.

'Put an arm round my neck; I'm going to carry you,' she said.

But the movement which Dolma made was not what she expected; at the woman's touch the girl suddenly recoiled, so that she found herself once more within the walls. A servant appeared in the courtyard, coming to close the great gate. Seeing his master's daughter, and a woman stooping in front of her, a strap in her hand, he misunderstood the stranger's intention and took her for a hawker.

'It's no good insisting,' he said with a laugh. 'Semo Dolma wears only silk garters, and those her father sells.'

Then, slowly, he closed the heavy wooden halves of the gate. Dolma fell back, and they fell to with a deep, imperious, mournful clangour.

At some distance from the road, hidden behind a knoll, Mipam was seated. He had driven a picket into the ground, and had tethered his horse; and now he was waiting. Night had fallen, feebly lit by the crescent moon; there was no traffic on the road, and no light was shining in the windows of the monastery houses of Depung—the largest monastery in Tibet— whose imposing bulk could be descried outspread at the foot of the mountain. Nearer Mipam, encircled with trees, the residence of the State Oracle loomed mysteriously in the darkness. Mipam waited. Soon his dear one would be there; he would take her away, would keep her beside him all his life . . . all this life, and all the lives to follow. He would keep her for ever, in this world and in others. But was this really the first time he was waiting thus to carry her away and make her his companion? . . . A feeling more tenuous than a memory mounted to his brain, coming from unplumbed depths. He was imbued with the feeling that to-day's adventure had happened to him before. Dolma . . . had he already loved her, had he already wrestled with those who wanted to take her from him? Oh! the mystery of our past lives that are moulding our present one!

A bell rang out; the muffled sounds of a drum beaten in cadence spread over the plain: the Oracle's disciples were saying a nocturnal office.

As the time went by, Mipam's impatience subsided rather than increased. His thoughts, turned toward the past, strove to divine what Dolma could have been before her birth as Tenzin's daughter, what had been the manner of this previous meeting, and what had been the fate of their love; for that love, he was persuaded, did not date only from the day when the 'little fairy' had appeared to him in his uncle's kitchen; it dated back, far back, from the illimitable past. Mipam was dreaming, wide awake.

That 'illimitable past' seemed to him a dim remoteness in which nothing could be distinguished but the vision, dwarfed by distance, of a Mipam and a Dolma holding each other by the hand.

He started, without apparent cause, and returned to a consciousness of the present realities. Dolma ought to have been there a long while ago, but no sound announced, in the oppressive silence, the approach of the riders. The emptiness of the plain outstretched in front of the monasteries produced a strange effect upon his mind. It was to him an image of the emptiness in which his own life was passing, despite the success of his enterprises, despite the friends he had made, despite his dear mother's love, despite Dolma's. He called to mind that a learned monk of the Lhabrang monastery had one day quoted to him a passage from a book held in great veneration by the Buddhists of India.

'I am nowhere anything to anyone,
And nowhere is there anyone who can be anything to me.'[1]

'Dolma!' he cried; but his cry was unspoken, and did not break the silence.

Dolma . . . why did she not come? . . . Mipam shivered. Was she faithless to her promise, did she refuse to leave with him? . . . But no, the muffled sound of horses' hooves hammering the ground reached his ears and drew near. Dolma was coming. He leapt up and hurried to the road. The shadow of a horseman emerged from the darkness, coming in his direction. An instant later Kalzang dismounted before him. He was alone.

'And Dolma?' asked Mipam feverishly.

'She has not come,' replied Kalzang with embarrassment.

'The woman on whom you counted has broken her word?'

[1] Visuddhi-Magga, chapter xxi.

'No, not that. She saw the trader's daughter and spoke to her. Semo Dolma even came outside the courtyard for a moment, and then didn't want to go any further; she went in again; someone came to shut the gates and the woman had to go. But she's ready to try again; she wanted me to bring her to you so that she could explain what happened, and also tell you how she means to manage next time. She hung on to my horse . . . she is in despair at losing the reward on which she was reckoning; so I decided to bring her. Hear what she has to say. Your features will hardly be recognized in the darkness; even if, by any chance, this woman has seen you at uncle Tenzin's or elsewhere, she won't know you again. Just pull your hat over your eyes. She will think you are the young nobleman of whom I spoke.'

'What end will it serve?' replied Mipam wearily. 'Well, let her come; I should like to know what happened.'

Kalzang left him, to return a few moments later, leading the luckless emissary, and the horse which was originally meant for Dolma, on which the woman had been riding.

Bowing low repeatedly as soon as she saw Mipam, she endeavoured at once to justify her failure, but the young man checked her threatened flood of words.

'Nothing but a strictly accurate account of what happened. And don't try to lie; I've the means of knowing the truth and of punishing you if you don't tell it me.'

In the imperious accents with which these words were uttered, the Tibetan woman thought that she recognized a nobleman, made a fresh obeisance, and gave a faithful account of her interview with Dolma. Then, seeing that Mipam remained silent, she offered, timidly this time, to make another attempt.

'Go and wait for me a little farther on, with my servant,' he ordered her.

The woman went off without venturing to answer. It was high time. Mipam could no longer contain his grief. He sat down again where he had already waited so long;

and he was still too prostrated to form a resolution of any kind.

So the dream which he had cherished since his childhood, the dream toward which for many years all his thoughts had converged, for whose realization he had laboured with such diligence and energy?—that dream had come to nothing, through Dolma's fault. It was not that she had turned away from him, that some other love had replaced the love she had felt for him. No, of that he was certain. His beloved loved him now as she had always done, and was suffering at this very moment as he himself was suffering; but as she grew up she had been cramped by her upbringing, by the customs and ideas of those about her; she had ceased to be herself, to become one of the crowd, a sheep wandering, head down, with the rest of the flock. Dolma no longer knew how to will ; she could do no more than lament the happiness which she dared not approach.

Poor, poor Dolma! To be pitied even more than he! Poor, poor beings, who, by the million, stretch out their arms toward the object of their desires, and, when it comes within their reach, draw back, not daring to grasp it!

Following the habitual bent of his mind, Mipam enlarged the circumference of his vision. Apart from his individual sufferings and those of the friend he was losing, he visualized the multitudes of broken hearts, the victims of their own weakness, the oceans of tears shed by slaves fast bound by fetters of their own forging.

To make a fresh attempt, to see Dolma again, he knew, beforehand, would be useless. Something divided them which was neither the will of Tenzin, nor any other extraneous cause. The obstacle came from elsewhere; it was occult, anchored in the depths of their being. Dolma had been his fellow-wayfarer often, for ages: to-day she was loitering on the path, at the cross-roads; but she would rejoin him anew, later, on a day when they would surely remember the many, many stages which they had traversed together, and the many, many halts which had momentarily separated them.

Mipam rose and called the Tibetan woman.

'I am going,' he told her. 'It was your wish to come as far as this; I can't have you escorted back to the town; can you pass the night somewhere in the neighbourhood?'

'You are very kind, *Kushog*; do not trouble yourself about me; quite near here there's a shrine dedicated to the water deities; it is large enough for me to shelter in until daybreak. My only wish is to serve you. I could. . . .'

'That will do,' interposed Mipam. 'This is what you must do. Some day or other, when a chance occurs of approaching Semo Dolma when alone, you must say to her: "He who sent me has gone. He wishes you to be happy, and will never cease to love you. He carries your promise away with him; it will be fulfilled in another life." Repeat what I have told you.'

The woman repeated it.

'Do not forget. Now, here are the hundred silver coins which were to have rewarded your success. You have not earned them, but I don't wish you to be distressed and to think of Tenzin's daughter with bitterness.'

'I am your grateful servant, *Kushog*,' murmured the woman, with timid deference. 'I will repeat to Semo Dolma what you have told me.'

'Now go!'

Mipam followed her with his eyes as far as the darkness permitted; then he mounted his horse, and accompanied by Kalzang he rode away from Depung, and was soon swallowed up by the night.

By the side of the track the three men from Dangar in Mipam's service awaited their master. Following his instructions, they had neither unsaddled nor unloaded the animals, so as to be ready to start the moment he arrived. Neither had they made a fire, and so had to go without the tea that is such a comfort during the watches of the night. Mipam's conduct seemed to them very strange, but they did not suspect its motive, as their comrade, who had been let into the secret, observed the strictest discretion. Ah! there was Mipam, at last, emerging from the shadows! They could barely distinguish his expression, but the abrupt 'Forward' which he threw over his shoulder, without even reining in his horse, had a resonance in it quite unfamiliar to them. Kalzang was nearly as curt as the trader.

'Hurry up!' he said to his companions; but to tell the truth, he didn't know why they ought to hurry, nor why his employer was pushing on ahead so rapidly. Since his friend was not with him, there was no fear of pursuit. It would be wiser to camp by the side of the first stream they came to, make tea and go to sleep, but the honest lad knew that Mipam was sad and unhappy, and that it was useless to expect him, for the moment, to behave reasonably. He pitied him, and silenced the others when they wanted to question him.

'Don't chatter, and don't make a noise; our master has need of quiet.'

As they all loved Mipam, they blindly obeyed, and the little troop rode silently into the great silence of the night, leaving behind them Lhasa, Dolma, and, further to the south, the village of Tromo and the cemetery on the mountain-side, where, under two crossed boughs, lay a few ashes of the gentle Changpal . . . all Mipam's childhood.

They resumed the journey: it was even more mournful than that of the winter, when Mipam had been hurrying to Lhasa. The excitement that spurred him on then had subsided; he no longer urged his men onward, being in no need to hurry, and feeling no desire to arrive anywhere. Why was he returning to Dangar? He had no idea, and he did not even ask himself why. He was merely obeying the automatic impulse that drives men and animals to return to their homes. With spring the temperature had become milder, the tracks were free of snow, and the abundant grass afforded ample grazing for horses and mules. Sometimes Mipam would suddenly call a halt, and stop for a whole day, betaking himself out of sight of the camp, where he lay for hours together on the ground, inert, and thinking of nothing. On certain days, also, he would hear all about him the distant voices of an invisible choir, tirelessly repeating one single musical phrase, dulcet and slow.

Lulled by this music, Mipam lost contact with his surroundings, and with his very self, and took his flight to an alien world, where he felt himself floating on a calm sea of a luminous whiteness. . . .

Kalzang saw that no one troubled his master's spiritual isolation, but as a good pupil he could not forbear introducing an element of commerce into the journey. Mipam was carrying no merchandise from Lhasa, and a certain number of mules being available, Kalzang had asked permission to see if there were any furs to be bought from the herdsmen; and his employer, who had ceased to interest himself in anything, had given his consent. Kalzang in this way found scope for his activities and those of his companions, while their chief remained immersed in his strange contemplation.

Slow as their progress was, the travellers eventually arrived in the neighbourhood of Dangar. Then, one afternoon, as Mipam, according to his habit, had wandered by himself far from the camp, he had a dream or a vision. He could not say which of the two it was, for he did not really know whether he was awake or asleep when the incident occurred. He felt himself attracted by an irresistible force, as though sucked in by it, and borne away to the room of the seer of Dangar. The seer placed his two hands on Mipam's shoulder, as at their last meeting, and, as he did so he repeated the mysterious words which he had then pronounced: 'The last watch of the night!'

From the old man's eyes darted rays of light that penetrated Mipam, who felt as though a sheath in which he was enveloped was being consumed by fire; he shook himself, striving to get rid of the calcined remnants that still clung to him, but all in vain.

'The last watch of the night!' the old man repeated once more. 'The awakening and the dawn are at hand. Go to meet them; return not to Dangar!'

On returning to his normal state of consciousness, Mipam found that he had formed a resolution not to return home with his men, and not to continue his life as a merchant. To amass a fortune was of no avail to him now, seeing that it would not help him to obtain Dolma, and now the riddle of the seer's declaration seemed to be solved. 'The last watch of the night!': that might be a final stage in the darkness in which ignorance steeps our minds, and the 'dawn drawing near' might be interpreted in the sense of a spiritual enlightenment destined to dissipate the phantasmagoria of a life which was not *his own*. In all his pursuits, his hopes, his fears, his triumphant joy and his present grief, had he been aught else but a shadow moving among shadows? Was he about to awake, a little child, in the forest, after sleeping and dreaming at the foot of a tree on his journey toward the 'land where all are friends?' Oh! this time he would not let himself be persuaded to hurry back, to return only to share the painful turmoil of those who are immersed in a thousand cares, in all but the one longing that is needful: the longing to be good, to love.

Two days before the date on which the travellers were to reach the monastery of Dangar, Mipam called Kalzang and gave him his instructions.

'I'm going to leave you,' he said. 'You will continue your journey together: you and your three companions, who will be returning to their monastery. You will deliver the letter which I shall give you to the steward Paljor; until I have made other plans you will remain in his service. He will continue to look after my affairs, in conjunction with Tashi, who has remained in Dangar during our absence. I intend to make a pilgrimage round the sacred Blue Lake, and to visit other holy places of the district. . . . I can't tell how long I shall be away.'

Mipam wrote a letter in which he told his friend Paljor of the check he had suffered at Lhasa, and of his decision that he would not for the present resume the management of his business, which he begged that Paljor would continue to look after. He sent no message to the seer, convinced that the latter knew all that had happened to him at Lhasa, had even known of it beforehand, and had revealed it to him in the vision of Dolma, fading away and engulfed in an impalpable ocean of mist. He was obeying the order which he had received, and was not returning to Dangar; he was setting off on a pilgrimage, not toward the gods of the Great Blue Lake, as he had informed Kalzang, but toward the 'dawn' and the 'awakening.'

At Sharakuto, the first village one comes to on leaving the desert tablelands, Mipam had a commercial agent, a little Chinese merchant who was in business relations with some of the tribes of herdsmen encamped in the surrounding territories. From him he obtained fresh supplies, borrowed money on his credit account, and took the road to the lake.

'What on earth is the matter with our master?' asked the three monks of Kalzang, whom they supposed to be better informed than themselves. And Kalzang, considering that his discretion had lasted long enough, and happy to be able to discard it, replied:

'He went to Lhasa to fetch the girl he loves; her father refused to give her to him, and she couldn't summon up the courage to run away with him.'

'If it's only that, he'll console himself,' said one of the men. 'When the fine weather has gone and the snow has covered the land once more, he'll return to his pretty house, and then, see-ing his stores, his merchandise, and his clients again, he'll soon become the cunning trader we knew.'

'Unless he becomes a saint,' Kalzang answered after a pause. 'All his thoughts are turned toward religion; he is absorbed in meditation. . . . I once saw him with a halo of golden light round his head.'

'Wonderful!' exclaimed the monks, astounded beyond mea-sure. 'Then he won't come back!'

And all, overcome with respect, raised their hands, with the palms joined, to their foreheads, and then, as when worshipping

283

the gods and the holy sages, gazed in the direction which their young master had taken when he left them. Human love affairs count for little in Tibet, and the only stirring adventures on which the heroes admired by the crowd embark are those of a spiritual order.

Dolma, now a prisoner, went up to her room. She knew that on the following day the heavy gates of the courtyard would open once more, and that on each successive day material possibilities of escape would present themselves, but with an even greater certitude she knew that when she had wavered and shrunk back into the courtyard the bonds that had bound her to Mipam had been irremediably broken. More clearly than she could have seen him with her eyes, she visualized him riding away from Lhasa in the night: never would she be his wife. How had a thing so contrary to her desires come to pass? Had a demon, jealous of her happiness, paralysed her limbs? Who, then, had interposed between her and the woman sent to take her away; who had suddenly pushed her back into the courtyard? She could not understand it. She was feverish, and confused and terrifying pictures rose into her mind.

When Tseringma came home on the following morning, after passing the night in performing acts of devotion, she found her stepdaughter delirious. She seemed to be obsessed by a sound, by the loud sound of something falling, or the deep tone of the long trumpets used in religious music. The invalid imitated the sound; it seemed to torture her, and neither her father nor her stepmother could guess that what haunted her thoughts was the clang of the massive gates closing in upon her, separating her for ever from the man she loved.

Dolma's strange and sudden illness must have been caused, thought Tenzin, by a demon or spirit whom either she or he had unwittingly offended. These beings are extremely susceptible, and avenge themselves for the slightest lack of respect by overwhelming human beings with terrible ills. Certain of these invisible enemies will even take delight in acting thus out of sheer devilry, without waiting for reprehensible conduct on the part of their victims.

Tenzin called in a famous doctor, and respectfully solicited the good offices of a lama magician. It was on this latter more especially that he relied, for the attacks of evil spirits are not to be repulsed by medicines. War against them is waged by the aid of exorcisms, conjurations, threats and bargaining. To detect the enemy's identity, and the means of appeasing him or reducing him to impotence, calls for a perspicacity and a knowledge that the great magicians alone possess. Tenzin, whose means permitted him to offer very high fees, had applied to one of the most eminent among them. In a room placed at his disposal the lama installed a score of monks, his pupils, and the celebration of the rites commenced. From time to time the master entered to preside over them, seated on a sort of throne. Tenzin's house echoed with the sound of hand-bells and drums, with thunderous ritual cries and the droning of psalms. To Dolma, burning with fever, and with an aching head, that pandemonium represented, magnified a hundredfold, the loud clang of the massive gates closing in front of her. For most of the time she lay almost unconscious, perpetually living over again the drama of her lost happiness. One day, when she was a little more lucid, she had begged her father to stop the uproar that tortured her. Tenzin had referred the matter to the magician's acolytes; and they, partly in good faith, partly because they did not wish a season of substantial repasts to be curtailed, or fees for which they were hoping to be reduced, stoutly maintained that the sufferings of the young girl were an excellent sign, denoting the efficacy of their rites. The demon, having caused the illness, was growing wroth, they explained, at seeing his designs frustrated. He was striving, therefore, to put an end to the celebrations of the rites which were shattering his power, and in order to achieve this end he was inflicting pains upon the invalid which she attributed, wrongly, to the noise made by the ritual instruments and the recitations of the monks. . . . As a matter of fact, it was not she but the demon who was tormented by the noise, for the sound of the bells and the drums, the melodies of the hautboys and the voices of the officiants, formed a concert pleasing to the ear and beneficial to the patient; they must take good care not to deprive her of it.

What would the lama magician himself have thought? Tenzin, rebuffed by his pupils, dared not ask him. He counselled Dolma to be patient, as he repeated the explanations which had been given him, and assured her that the happy results of the lama's intervention would not be long in showing themselves. The uproar continued, therefore, and with it, poor Dolma's sufferings.

In spite of everything, after several weeks of fever and semiconsciousness the young girl began to mend; her weakness, however, was very pronounced, and the greatest precautions were necessary.

Dogyal returned from India during Dolma's illness. There could be no question of celebrating the projected marriage; it was indefinitely postponed. Of this the bridegroom elect had to inform his father, who was proposing to be present at the wedding.

Puntsog was much annoyed when he learnt that Dogyal's marriage was indefinitely postponed, and that Dolma, after having been seriously ill, was apparently making a very slow recovery. If she happened to die before becoming Dogyal's wife his son's situation might be compromised. Tenzin, undoubtedly, regarded him with affection, but his principal object in adopting the boy was to assure for Dolma, his only child, the enjoyment of the considerable revenues of his business. He wished her to be both the lady and mistress of his house after his death; Dogyal was for him an instrument for achieving this end; but if Dolma were to die, would Tenzin feel sufficiently interested in his assistant to make him his heir? He had nephews who could not at present advance their claims upon him, for Tibetan morals strictly forbid marriage between blood relatives, but with the disappearance of Dolma Tenzin would possibly prefer them before a stranger. It was urgent, then, that the marriage should take place as soon as possible. If Dolma were to die after that, the situation of Dogyal, having been definitively adopted, would suffer no prejudice, especially if his wife had given him a child, Tenzin's grandchild.

Puntsog wrote to his son, acquainting him with the nature of his reflections, and Dogyal did not fail to recognize their pertinence. As it happened to be the year of the great pilgrimage to Tsari, which takes place only once in twelve years, this circumstance supplied Dogyal with an excellent pretext for pressing Tenzin to hasten the celebration of his marriage. He was anxious, he said, to take Dolma to Tsari, where she would assuredly recover her health, and before he could travel with her they must needs be married. Both Tenzin and Tseringma, who were very pious, and had great faith in the efficacy of pilgrimages, were highly pleased with the idea. Dolma appeared to be gradually recovering strength. All three, then, were of one mind in fixing the date of the marriage shortly before the departure of the pilgrimage, and they agreed that they would not communicate their decision to the young girl. Tenzin had his own reasons for not doing so. Without suspecting anything of the miscarriage of Dolma's abduction, he was inclined, on due reflection, to think that the grief felt by Dolma when Mipam left Lhasa was just as likely as the malice of the demons to have been the cause of her illness. At all events, a relapse must be avoided. Dogyal, satisfied with his future father-in-law's decision, did not ask himself what motive had prompted the latter's request that it should be kept secret. Dolma's state of health justified certain precautions; the excited interest of an affianced bride in the preparations for her marriage might be harmful to her.

Mipam was fleeing with all speed across the northern solitudes. But his flight was a hopeless one. The sorrow that tore at his breast rode with him, hovered round him, encompassed him, clutched at him, went before him, to rear itself at his horse's feet, in the shape of Dolma, shrinking back into the courtyard, and the vision of the great gates closing in upon her.

He knew them, those heavy gates: every evening, during his stay with Tenzin, when a servant was closing them, he had heard the dull sound of their two halves clanging together, and, now, as Dolma did, he heard it clanging without respite, tolling the knell of his youthful love.

He fled until he felt that his horse was tiring; then he halted on the bank of a stream, ate a little barley meal, and drank some water, too heedless of himself to light a fire and make tea. Often enough he even neglected to pitch his small tent, and slept in the open while his horse grazed near him.

There were clear nights, lit by the witchery of the stars, and moonlit nights when the solitudes, bathed in a blue light, were peopled by mysterious shadows. There were stormy nights, and on the heights there were sudden snow-squalls, which brought the wolves howling around Mipam, and compelled him to keep awake until daybreak, holding his frightened horse by the bridle.

Aimless, the young man wandered hither and thither, doubling back, and skirting the green-clad mountains. He renewed his supplies from the herdsmen whom he met; a little sufficed him: he was never hungry.

He had passed several days on the banks of the Koko Nor, gazing fixedly at the island on which live certain hermits, separated from the world by the wide waters of the lake.[1] In the far distance the summit of the island rose from the azure waters. In such a retreat he might perhaps find peace, but peace was not what Mipam sought. The misery of created beings, their helplessness, their pitiable attempts to snatch at

---

[1] From the nearest point of the shore to the island, the distance is about twenty-five miles. There are no boats on the lake. The hermits' supplies of food are brought to them by the faithful during the winter, when the lake is frozen hard and can be crossed in sledges.

happiness, forced itself afresh upon his thoughts, more urgently than ever. Dolma's shipwreck and his own was but a single episode amongst millions of other tragedies just as poignant. Misery! Sorrow! He, the compassionate, did he not crush, day in, day out, under his horse's hooves, thousands of tiny flowers, blades of grass, and insects that aspired to live . . . to be happy in their humble way?

One evening he drew rein near a large herdsmen's camp, in the neighbourhood of which there happened to be a 'black tents' monastery.[1] Next morning a feeling of pity for his exhausted mount induced him to defer his departure. His arrival at nightfall had not been noticed, but in the morning, at dawn, some of the tribesmen perceived his tent, and came to see him, curious to know who he was, and what had brought him to their neighbourhood.

'I am the trader, Mipam of Dangar,' Mipam told them.

A trader of Dangar: the traveller was not then a suspect foreigner. What business transactions had he in view?

'None for the moment,' declared the young man. 'I'm making a pilgrimage to the lake and the sacred places of the district.'

'Splendid!'

Pilgrimages are held in great honour in Tibet, and pilgrims are always well received, more especially when, as in Mipam's case, they are well-to-do people who do not beg their way. The herdsmen were pleased that this merchant should get into touch with their tribe. Although his present journey had piety for its object, he might remember them, and return to see them with a view to buying wool and other products of their herds. Would it not be a good idea to detain him for several days, by way of establishing friendly relations with him? The chiefs of the camp decided to invite him to be their guest for at least a week. A little rest, they suggested, would do his horse good.

---

[1] *Banag* = black tent, in the regional dialect. The term is applied to a monastery which, instead of comprising stone buildings, consists of tents which are moved about according to the seasons.

This argument, agreeing with what Mipam had in mind,
induced him to accept the invitation, but he stipulated that he
should remain under his own tent, which he would pitch at
some distance from the camp, so that he would not be disturbed
in his devotional exercises. This request, which was quite
consonant with the Tibetan practice, appeared a perfectly
natural one. The herdsmen led Mipam's horse away, to put it
among those grazing under their eyes, and the young man was
left to his meditations. Every day women brought him tea,
boiled meat, butter and curds, and Mipam had in his bags a
provision of barley meal.

With the understanding of the spiritual life that even the
roughest Oriental possesses, the herdsmen were careful not to
intrude upon their guest's privacy. Though they themselves
were incapable of profound reflection, they were aware that
outside the commonplace cares of their manner of life there was
another field of mental activity, and that silence and tran-
quillity were needful to those who desired to enter it. The
Tibetans, from their earliest childhood, learn this from the
example of their hermits, and of those who go into retreat
from time to time for more or less protracted periods.

Although the herdsmen abstained from visiting Mipam, he
from his tent saw them coming and going, and followed the
details of their daily occupations. This scene, which he had at
first regarded mechanically, ended by rescuing him from the
sorrowful reveries in which he had been absorbed since his
departure from Lhasa. Mipam descended once more into the
drab world of realities, and once there, passed drastic judgement
on his conduct. This, now he came to consider it, appeared
inexplicable. Just as Dolma asked herself whether a demon
had not thrust her back into her father's house when she had
already crossed the threshold to go and join her friend, he now
asked himself whether a demon had not driven him to flee
Lhasa by night, leaving Dolma there, instead of renewing his
attempt, going, if need be, to snatch his well-beloved from
her father's house with his own hands, and carry her off.

Further, without imagining feats of this nature, there were many ways of enabling his beloved to escape; she was not a prisoner in her father's house. Had not the woman whom he had seen told him, at Depung, after her failure, that she knew how to prevent its recurrence? Why had he not listened to her? That was the really inexplicable thing. Inexplicable, too, were his return to the Chinese frontier, and his present aimless wanderings across the grassy solitudes. Who had been making sport of him by leading his mind and his will astray? But now he had come to himself again. Very tardily, alas! More than three months had elapsed since he had left Lhasa. What had happened during that time? Was Dolma married to Dogyal? Possibly, but that marriage would not stop him. It was robbery. Dolma had promised herself to him; no one had the right to take her from him.

He was resolved to leave on the instant for Lhasa; but a difficulty occurred to him. On leaving Sharakuto he had supplied himself, at the hands of his Chinese agent, with a sum of money sufficient to meet his very modest needs in a country of herdsmen, but entirely inadequate for undertaking a journey to Lhasa. Must he return to his own house, in Dangar, to obtain what was necessary, and to secure the attendance of the faithful Kalzang? That would mean much time lost, but Mipam saw no way of avoiding the delay.

As he was still deliberating, a flight of wild geese passed trumpeting over his head, flying northwards.

'That's an omen,' he thought. 'It must refer to my journey, since it coincided with the moment in which I had resolved to leave. Was it good or bad? It would be useful to know what it signified, but who could give me the explanation? Would there be, by chance, in that tent monastery, a diviner who would be competent to do so? I'll go and find out.'

A large black tent, of a thick fabric woven of yak's hair, served for the temple of this primitive monastery, and for a place of assembly for its monks. On an altar built of unmortared stones stood the statues of the Buddha, of Tsong

291

Khapa, the revered founder of the sect of the *gelugspas*, and of the patron deity of the sect. On the sides of the altar were ranged a certain number of volumes of the Holy Writings. Stretching from the altar to the entrance of the tent, two strips of black and white striped material, which were also woven of yak's hair, served as a carpet, on which the monks sat in two rows, facing one another, leaving between them a passage that ended at the altar. Close to the latter, at the end of the strips of carpet, were the seats of the head of the monastery and the leader of the choir, consisting of several cushions piled on the top of one another. Around this tent-temple were pitched the tents of the monks.

As Mipam approached, one of the monks, who was chatting with his fellows, noticed him and eagerly advanced to meet him.

'Welcome, *Kushog*,' he said; 'I had the pleasure of meeting you in the monastery of Dangar, where one of my uncles lives who buys wool from us. Do you remember me? We drank tea together in your friend the steward Paljor's rooms.'

Mipam did not remember him, but pretended to do so out of politeness. While the monk, very proud of his acquaintance with a wealthy merchant, continued to converse with him, the head of the monastery came up and invited Mipam to enter his tent. All those present considered themselves included in the invitation, and followed Mipam into their superior's tent, where tea was served.

After a general conversation on various topics of no importance, Mipam came to the object of his visit there. He wanted an answer, through divination, to a question of great importance which could be treated only by an expert diviner, who must be capable of interpreting augural signs. Was there one among the honourable company of the members of the monastery?

The monks glanced at one another, hesitating; then their superior spoke:

'There are several of us who often oblige the herdsmen in the neighbourhood by performing rites of divination for them; but if the matter concerning which you desire predictions and counsels is as important as you say, I advise you to consult *alak*[1] Wangchen. He is a magician and a seer beyond compare; he can discern the most hidden things, and there is not a single prediction of his that does not materialize. He will enlighten you fully as to anything you want to know.'

'I should like to see him. Where does he live?'

'A good way from here. Even without loitering on the way, a good horseman would take three days to reach his camp.'

'Oh!'

'I will accompany you with pleasure, to show you the way,' proposed the monk who had previously met Mipam at Dangar.

'That is very obliging of you,' answered Mipam, who considered the proposal in silence.

Three days to go and three days to return would make six days. If the diviner was thorough and capable he would not confine himself to the common practices of counting the beads of his rosary, throwing dice, and referring from the numbers thrown to a corresponding division in a book on divination. No; he would invoke his tutelary deities, would solicit their presence and their aid, and this would take time. Altogether, Mipam would have to devote nine or ten days to the journey.

On the other hand, he must supply himself with money before he could return to Lhasa; he had already allowed for this, but he now realized that he need not increase the delay caused by his visit to the diviner by the time it would take him to reach Dangar.

'Is there in camp a very good rider, provided with a strong and speedy horse, who would be willing to carry a letter to Dangar? He would have to ride quickly.'

'If you pay him well for his trouble, Lendup will be glad to go, I'm sure of that,' replied a monk.

'How many days would he be on the way?'

'Four days at the most. He will change horses on the way,

[1] In Northern Tibet, the title *alak* is equivalent to that of lama.

if necessary. One of his married sisters lives in a camp almost on the Dangar road; he could pick up a fresh mount at his brother-in-law's.'

'That will do. Will one of you be so good as to ask this man to come to my tent to speak with me? I am going there at once to write the letter he will have to take.'

'I'll go, I'll go,' cried several of the monks in chorus, counting on a reward for their zeal.

'I depend upon you to take me to the diviner,' said Mipam to the monk who had offered himself as a guide.

'Certainly, *Kushog*, I shall be very happy to do so. If you wish it, we will start to-morrow at daybreak.'

'Agreed.'

'While you are in that part of the country,' suggested the superior, 'push on as far as the Ngarong monastery. You've only to continue further northwards; the road is good. Have you heard of the Ngarong monastery, *Kushog*?'

'I've a vague idea that I have,' Mipam replied. 'It's a monastery of anchorites, is it not?'

'Precisely. The greater number of the Ngarong monks are hermits who assemble only from time to time. Have you not heard of the miracles of Ngarong, of the tame beasts and of the tombs of the monastery Grand Lamas?'

'I have not. Please excuse me, I must go and write the letter I'm sending to Dangar. It isn't late; perhaps the messenger might even start to-day.'

At any other time, Mipam would gladly have listened to what the amiable superior had to tell him. Although he had heard hundreds of them, stories of prodigies still interested him. He was far from blindly believing all their details, but he was also far from being wholly incredulous. However, for the present his mind was taken up with his imminent departure for Lhasa, the arrangements to be made for the journey, and his plans to enable Dolma to escape. To have his friend trotting briskly by his side, to cross the Chinese frontier in her company, and to take her to Dangar, to his house, was the only miracle of interest to him, the only one for which he hoped.

Back in his tent, Mipam at once sat down to write to his partner and friend, Paljor. In a few words he explained to him his bitter regret at having so suddenly abandoned the contest at Lhasa, and of his decision to secure, this time, what he wanted. He begged that Paljor would continue to watch over his business interests, and that he would send him, by Kalzang, as large a sum of money as he could, and ample provisions Kalzang must once more accompany him to Lhasa, and he would be glad if one of the men who had previously gone with him might again be a member of his party. Kalzang and his companion must be provided with sturdy horses, and must bring with them three strong mules to carry the baggage, a good horse for Dolma, and another for him, as his own had had no rest since his return from Lhasa. Horses and mules could be selected from his stables and Paljor's; the provisions could be found at once in the monastery itself; a day or two would suffice for the preparations. Kalzang and the manservant would start off in company with the herdsman, who would lead them to the camp where he, Mipam, would be awaiting them.

All being thus arranged, Lendup left for Dangar that very day, and Mipam set off at daybreak on the morrow.

CHAPTER XIII

*A*LAK WANGCHEN was a Khampa, who, after the vicissitudes of a stirring and wandering life, had come to settle, far from the land of his birth, among the herdsmen of the Koko Nor. For the space of ten years he had practised in their midst, in the dual role of magician and doctor, and thanks to a judicious combination of his twofold talents he had acquired some wealth. His success, it might be, was due in great measure to the prestige of his personality. Wangchen was a handsome giant with a haughty demeanour. Under the steady, steely gaze of his large dark eyes women would tremble and men feel ill at ease in his presence. The magician was a married man without children, as is fitting for adepts of the doctrines which he professed. His wife took part in the celebration of the rites which he performed; her occupations as housewife were confined to supervising the work of the two pairs of servants who had charge of the cattle. The oft-repeated gifts of Wangchen's clients, and the fertility of his herds over a period of ten years, had conferred upon the latter a certain importance. They consisted, in all, of a thousand head of sheep, yaks and horses, and the revenue which the married pair derived from them was considerable. Wangchen's tents were pitched far from all camping-grounds, in perfect solitude; they were three in number, of different dimensions, and were made of black material like those of the herdsmen. In the largest of the tents dwelt the husband and wife; their servants occupied another, and in the third, which was smaller, the magician performed his secret rites and retired for communion with his tutelary gods, or gave himself up to meditation.

In accordance with custom, when Mipam, with his guide, had arrived in the neighbourhood of the camp, the guide went

on in advance in order to announce his coming. He did not fail
to paint the visitor in the most glowing colours, nor to emphasize his predominant quality, that of being a man of substance.

Wangchen felt flattered by the fact that a townsman, and an
opulent trader, moreover, had come to seek his ministrations,
and without departing from his majestic bearing he gave the
traveller a gracious welcome.

'I do not wish, this evening, to hear the questions you desire
to ask me,' he declared to Mipam, as soon as the latter had
presented him with a scarf, in one knotted end of which he had
placed some silver ingots, and when the customary courtesies
had been exchanged. 'Reflect well during the night. Recall
to your mind any details which may modify the direction of
those questions, and may supply a motive for others; then,
to-morrow morning, you will come to see me again, and will
formulate them as explicitly as possible.'

This opening impressed the young man. 'Here is a serious,
understanding person,' he thought.

The evening meal was served; the conversation turned upon
various subjects in which Mipam was not directly interested;
and he presently retired to the tent which he had brought
with him.

He pondered afresh over the questions which he had prepared, and which did not appear to him to require modification.
It only remained to repeat them to the diviner in the form in
which he had originally conceived them.

On the morrow he once more stood before his host.

'Will you be good enough,' he said, 'to reply to the following questions:

'Are the circumstances favourable to the undertaking of the
journey which I have in view?

'Will the issue of this journey be as I desire?

'Is the person who has given me this reliquary—a girl born
in the year Earth-Bird[1]—married?

[1] A name referring to the *Lo Khor* or cycle of sixty years in the Tibetan
calendar.

'Four days ago, at the moment when I had decided to undertake my journey, a flock of wild geese flew over my head, making for the North. What does this omen mean?'

'Is that all?' asked Wangchen.

'It is all.'

'Very well. You told me yesterday, that the result of the
journey was of the utmost importance to you.'

'That is so.'

'I shall not content myself, therefore, with exercising my
powers of clairvoyance only. I shall have recourse to those of
my powerful tutelary gods. As far as the question of this girl's
marriage goes, I can also verify the accuracy of my clairvoyance
by sending one of the genii attached to my service to make sure,
on the spot, that I have made no mistake. These are simple
precautions which I shall take in order to give you the certitude
which you require, but which are, in reality, superfluous. I
am never wrong.

'You may go now; when I have obtained the information
which I desire I will send for you.'

Thus Mipam found himself immobilized for an indefinite
period. He informed his guide that he did not know when he
would return to the camp, and the guide, who had work to do
in the camp, took his leave of him.

The magician then withdrew to his little tent, and Mipam
wandered about in the neighbourhood of his camp, trying to
contain his impatience. Three days elapsed, and Wangchen did
not reappear. His wife took him his meals into his tent; he
slept there, also, or possibly kept awake, for during the night
the dull sound of rhythmic drum-beats could be heard. The
diviner-magician was undeniably engaged in a serious task,
which, though it inspired Mipam with confidence, was to his
thinking taking a very long time. Kalzang would soon reach
the herdsmen's camp with money, beasts and provisions; time
was pressing.

Mechanically complying with the customs of his country,
Mipam had preferred to consult destiny before setting out

on his journey, but he had quite made up his mind to make that journey, whatever the diviner's answer might be.

On the fourth day after his arrival, at sunset, Wangchen sent for him and told him what he had discovered.

'In the first place, there is no reason for making the journey which you are planning. This answers your first two questions.

'Secondly, the girl is not married.

'Thirdly, the geese were showing you your way.'

Mipam remained dumbfounded.

'There is no sense in what you say!' he exclaimed. 'My journey has a very definite motive. I didn't ask advice in that regard. There is all the more reason for it if the girl is not married. These two answers are quite contradictory. And what road were those geese showing me? They were flying toward the North, while the place to which my affairs are calling me is in the South. All this is perfectly absurd.'

'My answers are never absurd!' shouted Wangchen, suddenly flushing with anger. 'You are the first to dare to contradict me in this way. It is all the worse for you if you are not capable of discerning the truth which is presented to you. Some demon must be the cause of your blindness!'

Mipam, who was unaccustomed to being spoken to in this tone, took offence.

'Say what you will, I, who know the object of my questions and the facts to which they refer, am convinced that your replies have no connection with them.'

'Very well. Go, then and consult those who are wiser than I, if you can find them. . . . Now, listen: go to Ngarong monastery; it is not far from here; you could pass the night at the foot of the throne of Yeshes Nga Den, before the tombs of the Grand Lamas of his spiritual lineage. It is said that these lamas send dreams or visions to those who ask counsel of them. Yes, go there, by all means. The dead lamas will doubtless inspire you with greater confidence than I; but this I can assure you, if their answers differ from mine they will be false. I am never wrong. Come now, get you gone! It is well for you that I am inspired by charitable sentiments. If that were not so, I should already have summoned the demons whom I command, and should have ordered them to give me vengeance for your insulting incredulity.'

'I had no intention of giving offence, *Kushog*,'replied Mipam, who, though by no means a coward, had no wish to incur the enmity of a magician 'I only mean to infer that your answers do not apply to my questions, and . . . .'

'That will do!' interrupted Wangchen, whose anger was increasing. 'I don't wish to hear any more. I hope you may not have to suffer the evil effects of your stupidity!'

To insist any further was out of the question. Mipam bowed and withdrew. 'I've wasted my time and my money,' he told himself on his way to his tent; 'I have been enlightened only in this one particular: Dolma is not married. That is, after all, the point that interests me most. I'm vexed with myself for having annoyed the diviner. That's regrettable. Whatever he may have said, he might take it into his head to avenge himself on me or on Dolma. Ah! no, not that! . . .' The thought that his dear one might be exposed to danger distressed the young man. He wished at all costs to appease the irascible magician: to offer him a gift was the best means of doing so.

Mipam turned aside and went to meet one of the men who was driving the sheep back to the camp.

'You must bring my horse up to my tent this evening; I leave to-morrow before dawn,' Mipam told him. 'Go, also, and ask the lady mother if she will come and see me for a moment: I have something to say to her. I will give you your present this evening, and please tell your mate to come with you, to receive his.'

'Very good,' said the man. 'I will do your bidding as soon as I have penned the sheep.'

'Where on earth is Ngarong monastery? Do you happen to know?'

'I do, *Kushog*.'

'Is it far?'

'If you were to leave at daybreak, and did not linger over the midday meal, and if you were to do the same on the following day, you might reach Ngarong in two days.'

'How should I find the way?'

'I would willingly accompany you, but we must ask my master for his permission.'

'Don't do that,' said Mipam, quickly. 'I have no intention for the moment of going to Ngarong. I am expected at the camp from which I came.'

'Oh, very well. But if you changed your mind, you could find the way by yourself. You would only have to turn to the right behind the hill you see over there, and follow the valley till you come to a pass. From that pass you can see a river flowing beyond a very wide plain; you must cross the plain and make for the river bank: there are some herdsmen encamped there, of whom you could ask your way.'

'Good, good,' said Mipam. He had given little heed to the man's directions, for he was thinking of other matters. Ought he not to start immediately? He could cover a short stage before nightfall, which would lessen the distance to be travelled. The sooner he was back at the camp the better. His men were due to arrive in camp the day after to-morrow, or the day after that, and then he could start for Lhasa immediately.

Having thus decided he regained his tent, and there awaited the wife of the diviner. She was long in coming. Mipam expressed his regret that *alak* Wangchen had misunderstood his sentiments, which were in no sense uncomplimentary to him. He did not question the magician's great knowledge, and he gave substance to his excuses by presenting her with a scarf in which he had knotted some silver ingots. The lady was then extremely gracious; she repeatedly pressed Mipam not to leave without seeing her husband again, and invited him to supper. Mipam politely resisted her entreaties, and at last she left him, but much time had been wasted in waiting for her and conversing with her. It was too late to make a start. Mipam resigned himself to postponing his departure until the morrow.

He slept little, turning over in his mind the incoherent replies which he had received from the diviner, and endeavouring to reconcile them. Could it be that the journey which he was about to make, and the means he proposed to employ in carrying Dolma off to China, were not the best way of achieving his ends? Ought he to follow quite another course? Would he obtain light on the subject if he asked for it at Ngarong? It was the second time he had heard of this monastery. The head of the tent monastery had mentioned it, but Mipam could not remember what he had said about it. Ought he to see a sign in this repeated meeting, and would the counsel he was seeking be given him at Ngarong, if he went there to ask for it, or was an aberration like that which had seized upon him on the evening of his departure from Lhasa at work again, dragging him this way and that, and delaying his departure? While he was lingering, Dolma, who was 'not yet married', might marry Dogyal. To judge from what Tenzin had told him, the marriage might even have taken place already. No, he would brook no further delay.

The night was drawing to a close. Mipam folded up his little tent, fetched his horse, which was picketed near by, saddled it, fastened his light baggage to the saddle, mounted, and rode off in the direction from which he had come. He rode at a slow trot, for it was still dark, and he could hardly distinguish the track, which ran through grassy country, and sometimes was indistinguishable.

The thoughts which he had revolved in his mind during the night recurred to him; his indecision increased as he endeavoured to weigh the pros and cons of two alternatives: whether to obtain further enlightenment before leaving for Lhasa, or whether to start without further delay, as he had decided to do. His perplexity afflicted him with a sort of panic; he no longer doubted that some demon was endeavouring to lead him astray and mock him.

'No!' he cried abruptly. 'I shall listen to nothing; I have

no need of divination. Whatever obstacles the demon may
set in my path, my love will overcome them. I shall start
for Lhasa immediately.'

And arousing himself from his reverie, he dug his heels into
his horse's belly and broke into a gallop. The sudden change
of pace restored him to the full awareness of his surroundings.

It was broad daylight, and the sun was rising. He found
himself in a narrow valley which he did not recall having
traversed on his journey to the magician. The way to the
diviner's camp, he remembered, lay across a wide plain. He
ought, moreover, to have had the rising sun on his left, whereas
the rays which announced its presence came from the summits
on his right. In his inattention he had allowed his horse to
take the wrong way. Ought he to turn back? Behind him
were three valleys which converged upon that which he was
following. By which of these had he come? He had not the
remotest idea. What was he to do? A horseman cannot lose
himself irremediably in the pasture lands, especially in the
summer, when the herdsmen camp in the open. Sooner or
later he would come upon their tents and would be able to
ask his way. *Sooner or later;* but Mipam did not like the notion
of this 'later'. He had come by one of the three valleys which
opened out below the spot in which he now found himself;
that was certain. He might retrace one of them, at random,
and if it did not bring him to Wangchen's camp, he had only
to turn back and tempt fortune by taking another of the three;
and if he was wrong again, he had only to return once more
and take the third valley, which must infallibly bring him to
the point where he had lost his bearings. However, the
prospect of these comings and goings was by no means agreeable; they might well take up a whole day.

What evil fate was pursuing him?

The faintly-marked path on which he had entered climbed
at a gentle gradient toward a mountain crest. From the summit
he would perhaps be able to distinguish the direction followed

by the divergent valleys and the plain from which he had come. The summit did not appear to be very far away; it might be as well to negotiate it, rather than attempt the valleys. Though he disliked the notion of diverging still farther from his course, he decided to push forward.

He had greatly underestimated the distance to the summit. Seen from the spot from which he had observed the path, it had seemed to run gently up a single slope. A fold in the mountain was responsible for this illusion. In reality, having reached the top of a preliminary slope, the path dropped into a valley, whence it climbed again, zig-zag fashion, up a second slope, which Mipam had taken for the uninterrupted continuation of that which he saw before him. It took him two hours to reach the summit. From that point he saw, far below him, a wide tableland. Beyond this to the north, a river flowed along the foot of another range of mountains. He suddenly recalled the description given him by the diviner's servant: 'a wide plain and beyond it a river. . . .' He was on the road to Ngarong.

In such circumstances no Tibetan would have doubted that an occult power had been responsible for the behaviour of his horse in changing its direction, and for his own want of attention in noticing the fact. Mipam, petrified by surprise, saw in the incident the hand of the same power which appeared to rule his life and thwart all his plans. His flight from Lhasa, and the obstacles of his own making which were delaying his return, were the work of an extraneous will whose plaything he was. Was it his good or his ill that this mysterious force desired? A being, whether god or demon, invisible to him, was undeniably spying on him, marking his surprise at finding himself where he was, grinning maliciously, perhaps, because he had still further delayed his return to Dolma.

What was he to do? Should he go to Ngarong as he was being driven to do, or should he continue to resist, retracing his course, and attempting to return to Wangchen's camp by one of the three valleys? Mipam, encompassed by a disturbing sense of mystery, felt thoroughly unnerved.

'Dolma!' he murmured; 'my dear little Dolma! . . .'

His eyes filled with tears.

'I'll go to Ngarong!' he decided, wearily. 'There, perhaps, I shall find an explanation of the diviner's obscure replies. The plans which I have made may not be those which will assure me of success.'

A thousand times he had already scrutinized, or thought to scrutinize, these same ideas: in reality, he was subject to their influence. They automatically unfolded themselves, passing and repassing in his mind, harassing and crushing him.

On the river bank he found the camps of which Wangchen's man had told him, and inquired his way to the Ngarong monastery.

'I can reach it by to-morrow, can I not?' he asked the herdsmen.

'To-morrow!' they exclaimed. 'Indeed, you cannot, *Kushog*. By the evening of the day after to-morrow, perhaps, or the day after that.'

Mipam made no rejoinder. It certainly seemed to him that the diviner's shepherd had told him that the journey would take only two days, but he might have misunderstood him, or the man might have been mistaken. He was prepared for the worst.

On the farther bank of the river the path, continually dipping and rising, plunged into the heart of the mountains. Mipam passed the night close to a tiny lake set in a miniature amphitheatre. The following day passed with no sign of the proximity of the monastery, and at nightfall Mipam drew rein in front of a large cave, at some little distance from which there flowed a brook. There was grass in plenty; his horse would enjoy good grazing, and he could find shelter under the coping of the rock.

Mipam unsaddled and left his horse at liberty while he supped, and then, having carried his baggage into the cave, he picketed his mount, giving it a long tether. After attending to these matters Mipam lay down immediately, and fell asleep at once.

The sound of soft steps padding round him, and a hot breath

305

upon his face, awakened him. The night was not dark, and he saw beside him a bear, which was examining him with outstretched neck. It was a bear with a yellowish coat, of the kind known as *demo*. Bears are numerous in the northern solitudes. At a similar encounter in the previous winter, Mipam had believed that the beast had realized the sympathy which he felt for it, and had responded to it by returning to the den from which fear had driven it. Still, on that occasion he had not found himself in the actual den of the animal; an appreciable distance had divided them, and he was accompanied by four armed men. Mipam was no longer the little boy who was ingenuously ready to play with a leopard. He had more than once heard it related that solitary travellers who had taken shelter in a bear's den when the animal was away had been mauled by it on its return to its lair. He knew that these stories were true, but he was not of those who attack out of fear that they may be attacked. The bear did not appear to be adopting a threatening attitude; the immobility of the intruder whom he had found in his lair might reassure him, and result in his moving off. After sniffing for some time at Mipam the animal lay down against the rock, on the other side of the cave. Mipam remained motionless, unable to go to sleep again so close to this disquieting companion. And as he could not sleep, the similarity of the situation recalled to his memory the *tête-à-tête* in the forest with the leopard, and his instinctive motion to save its life when it was menaced by his brother's poisoned arrow. He recalled, in its smallest details, that strange adventure of his childhood; he remembered, moreover, the feeling which had actuated him at the time, and his dream of universal friendship. He had loved the friend with the spotted coat who had come to lie at his side. Did he also love this great bear, sleeping, or perhaps ruminating, only a few paces from him? Would he be ready to repeat the gesture of his childhood, if the same danger were to threaten the cumbrous animal which had examined him so attentively? He questioned himself, probing the most secret depths of his being, and in response to this investigation the old mystic fire that was smouldering within him was suddenly rekindled, invading him and burning him divinely. Yes, he loved this hirsute, lumbering bear as he had loved the graceful leopard, to the peril of his life, and as he had loved his yaks, braving poverty for their sake, saving them from death at the price of all that he possessed. He loved all sentient beings: both the feeble, and those which, seemingly strong, are the feeblest of all! Why was he not a powerful god, capable of flooding the world with a wave of happiness!

Beside him the bear slept; Mipam's reveries were lulled by its even breathing, and the ceaseless purling of the neighbouring brook.

'They have taken Dolma from me,' he murmured, talking to himself, 'and I love her, my Dolma; but may she be happy without me, if her happiness would be greater than that which I could give her. I don't wish you to be a captive, Dolma; I open the arms that longed to clasp you, to seize you, to carry you off, to keep you. Dolma, it is not myself that I love in loving you, it is you, yourself alone, little fairy of my childhood!'

Dimly the young man distinguished a procession of luminous faces that entered the cavern; a choir of remote voices chanted words that he could not catch . . . he sank into a state of ecstasy.

When he regained consciousness of his surroundings the day was beginning to dawn. The bear still slept. Mipam threw him a friendly glance and quietly stepped out of the cave. Beside the brook he ate a ball of moistened barley-meal and drank some water, saddled his horse, and resumed his journey.

Toward noon, as he was descending a very steep slope on foot, some gazelles bounded in front of him, and instead of fleeing they followed him as far as the valley. Seeing a little stream 'meandering at the farther end of this valley, Mipam decided to make his midday meal there. He sat himself down near the stream and unpacked his food, while the little group of gazelles continued to gaze at him.

307

'This region must be very little frequented, and hunters certainly do not come here,' thought Mipam, 'Nowhere have I seen wild animals so tame.' Having eaten, he moistened some meal with water, making it into a number of little balls, which he laid on the stones.

'I invite you to this humble repast,' he exclaimed with a smile, addressing the graceful creatures. He then moved off, climbing the sloping side of the valley. He had gone only a few yards when the gazelles ran forward and ate the offering which he had left them; then they began to graze and frolic in the meadows.

The path which Mipam had taken grew fainter and fainter, and he was beginning to be afraid of losing his way, when, shortly before sunset, a defile which he was following widened out and made a sudden turn, and the Ngarong monastery suddenly rose before him.

The site was a singular one. The monastery itself stood up on a ridge consisting of white rocks, which looked as though they had been shaped by human hands. From where he stood Mipam could distinguish colonnades, porticos, pyramids and crenellated walls. The architects of the monastery had utilized these natural structures, contenting themselves with completing them. In front of the monastery, at the foot of the cliff, on which it was perched, stretched a wide plain on which five valleys detracted. Here and there, hidden in the depths of these valleys, or towering aloft, on the slopes that enclosed them, numerous hermitages could be seen, many of them having been hewn, like the monastery itself, out of caverns or rocks that formed natural chambers. Streams coursed down the mountain-sides, falling into a river that flowed peacefully amidst the alpine pastures. The whole scene exhaled a happy peace, and conveyed a sense of absolute solitude.

So this was Ngarong! Only the climb to the monastery lay before him. There was no means of approaching it from the cliff, but apparently a path leading out of the valley which it overlooked led up to it by making a circuit. ' Mipam crossed the plain, which was of no great width where he had entered it, forded the shallow stream, and scaled the path which he had seen from a distance. As he drew near a gong sounded in the monastery. Then silence fell once more.

On his upward way Mipam passed beneath a hermitage. The door was closed, and no sound betrayed the presence of an inmate. The path ended in a plateau, on the pointed extremity of which stood the monastery. No one was visible. Mipam went up to a roughly fashioned door, which was very massive, and recessed in a wall of rock; finding it closed, he knocked upon it. Some time elapsed, and then the wooden bolts were drawn and a monk appeared. He did not speak, but questioned the traveller with his eyes, without admitting him.

'I am a merchant of Dangar, and am known by the name of Mipam. I wish to ask a question before the tombs of your lamas, the successive incarnations of Yeshes Nga Den, with a view to obtaining a reply by sign or dream. The counsel of which I have need has to do with a matter which is dearer to me than my life. Could I be granted an audience of your present lama?'

The monk looked curiously at the petitioner. Without a word, he stepped back and opened the door until the horse could pass through. Mipam concluded that he was permitted to enter.

He was conducted along winding lanes, fantastically flanked by rocks transformed into dwellings. Their grotesque forms, left unaltered by the builders of the monastery, gave the latter a strange appearance. Mipam was ushered into a room with an irregular vaulted roof, lit by an opening in the rock. Through this aperture the plain was visible, stretching far into the distance, and just opposite the monastery was the entrance to the valley by which he had come.

'Put your baggage down,' said the monk, laconically. 'I will show you the way to the stables.'

Mipam obeyed, and once more followed his taciturn guide.

There were three horses in the stable, but this could not have been the only one, for at some little distance the stamping of other horses could be heard, and from the same direction came the characteristic odour of manure. The three horses were loose, and when Mipam was going to tie his own, the monk signed to him not to do so. He then showed Mipam, in an adjoining chamber, some sacks of corn, peas, and beans, and beyond this a long vaulted recess in which hay and straw were piled.

'Give your beast a feed,' said the monk. 'If you follow the lane outside, you will come to a stream where he can drink. I expect you can easily find your way back to your room.'

Without giving Mipam time to reply, or to ask for any further explanations, in case he should be doubtful of the direction to be followed in that labyrinth, the monk went off and disappeared round a corner.

Mipam had never seen a monastery of this kind.

When he re-entered his room he saw that a brazier had been brought, filled with red embers, on which rested a large teapot full of buttered tea. A bag of barley-meal, a lump of butter, and a wooden pot containing curd were laid on a projecting rock, shaped to serve as a table.

At nightfall the gong which he had already heard as he was making his way up to the monastery sounded three times. Then once more silence fell, a silence deeper than any he had known in the course of his travels through the solitudes; a silence which made itself felt with an irresistible force, and extinguished even the sound of thought, imperceptible to ordinary human beings.

Next morning Mipam went to water and feed his horse. When he returned to his room, the cold brazier had been replaced by another, on which was steaming a teapot full of fresh tea. No one, however, was visible. Had not the door-keeper understood him? Ought he to go in search of another monk and explain the object of his visit? Mipam hesitated to make any exploration of this strange monastery; its lama might possibly be annoyed by his curiosity.

310

In the course of the morning a monk wrapped in the yellow mantle of the hermits entered his room.

'Welcome to Ngarong,' he said with friendly courtesy. 'I have been told of what brings you here. Few pilgrims are admitted for the purpose of asking advice, or of putting questions before the tombs of our lamas. Before they can be authorized to do so, it is necessary that the end which they are pursuing should be of really major importance. One of our brethren has made some astrological calculations about you. They have given some surprising results. I cannot communicate them to you. I can tell you only this, that you are permitted to undergo the desired ordeal; but first you must calm your mind, examine your intentions, and purify them during a ten days' retreat. Such is the rule. You are ready, are you not, to submit yourself to it? If not, we would furnish you with provisions, and beg you to leave our monastery to-morrow morning.'

A fresh delay! Ten days! The time to have rejoined his men and be already well on the way to Lhasa! Why had he come to Ngarong? Into what fresh trap was he about to fall? . . . To leave next day seemed to Mipam the wisest course; but he was incapable of taking it. The fantastic monastery had taken possession of him. From every rock-hewn turret and ornament of its bristling roofs, from every recess of its tortuous streets, from all the irregular windows of its fantastic buildings, cords like tentacles seemed to ensnare him and bind him fast. Escape was impossible; a mysterious process of fusion was at work. Mipam felt that Ngarong was entering into his bones, was becoming an integral part of his being, while he himself, expanding, was being incorporated into every stone of the monastery.

'I shall make the retreat,' he answered in a low voice.

'Good. You will remain in your room. Don't trouble to look after your horse; it will be cared for.'

And without another word, the monk left him.

•　　•　　•　　•　　•

That very day, Kalzang, supplied with money and provisions
for a long journey, reached the herdsmen's camp. The man
from Dangar, Tharchin, who had accompanied Mipam to
Lhasa, was with him. In addition to their own two horses,
they brought two others, and three mules.

From what the messenger sent by Mipam had told him,
Kalzang expected to find the trader in the camp, but the days
went by without sight of their master. Kalzang and Tharchin
began to grow uneasy, and talked of going to look for him.
The herdsmen, who had taken a fancy to the young trader,
and who anticipated doing some profitable business with him
in the future, would gladly have joined in the search, but the
fact that he had gone to see Wangchen made them hesitate.
The magician might have some special reason for detaining his
visitor. He might perhaps be performing secret rites for his
benefit, and in that case an inopportune intervention might
anger him. And the herdsmen were not at all anxious to incur
the dreadful animosity of a magician. It would be better, they
thought, to seek advice through divination before taking action.
Several divinations, undertaken separately by different monks
of the tent monastery, tallied in dissuading them from search-
ing for Mipam, and in the face of this unanimity no one dared
go further in the matter. The chiefs of the tribe had made a
conquest of Kalzang. While they regaled him on beer and
boiled meat, they praised the special excellence of the wool and
meat of their sheep, the remarkable quality of the butter made
from the milk of their yaks, and the incomparable quality of
their fabrics, woven by their own women from the hair of the
yak. They hoped that the favourable reports of his employee
would induce Mipam to come to them for supplies.

As for Tharchin, who belonged to the lower clergy, he
passed his time in the company of his brother monks of
the tent monastery. The talk often turned upon Mipam's
strange absence, and each monk hazarded a conjecture of his
own.

'The trader must have gone to Ngarong,' the head monk

suggested one day. '*Alak* Wangchen would not have detained him so long.'

'And why should he linger so long at Ngarong?' asked Tharchin.

'Why? That I can't tell you, but Ngarong is an odd place, and its monks are not monks like the rest of us.'

'What is there special about Ngarong?'

'It is a monastery of hermits who wear yellow mantles. That's not the curious thing about it; there are other monasteries of anchorites; but Ngarong is a mystery, a miracle.'

'In what way?'

'To begin with, the monastery wasn't built by man; it is self-created.'

'Oh!'

'And then, again, all kind of prodigies happen round about Ngarong, and its lama *tulkus* are always extraordinary people.

'It is said that the last but one of these, Yeshes Nga Den, the seventeenth lama of the line, was a veritable Buddha. His learning and his goodness were beyond compare. It was enough for sick men or beasts to look at him to be healed; the wickedest beings became kind and charitable if they passed only a few days in his company. Scores of demons, who formerly delighted to do evil, now dwell in the mountains close to the monastery, and there live the life of anchorites, meditating on the Infinite Compassion, and protecting the inhabitants of the neighbouring regions. For a wide area round the monastery the wild animals have become tame. They don't fear men, they don't fight one another, and hunters cannot kill them. Out of bravado, some have made the attempt, but without success. Their dogs have begun to play amicably with the gazelles, wild asses and wolves: their rifles have refused to fire, or have dropped from their hands; and however they tried to cleave to their hardness of heart, they ended by sitting down beside the animals they had come to kill, and caressing them!'

'That's marvellous!' cried Tharchin, and continuing to question his host, he asked:

'Have you ever seen these wild animals coming right up to you?'

'I've never been to Ngarong.'

'How is that? Have you never felt that you wanted to see the monastery that had reared itself up so miraculously, or to have a look at all those tame beasts?'

'Yes, but I thought it more prudent not to go near places that are haunted by gods and demons. Unless one is a holy man, a sage very deeply versed in religious matters, it is better to keep away from prodigies and those who work them.'

'Does our master know of Ngarong?'

'I told him a little about it, but I saw that he wasn't listening, and was thinking of something else.'

'What was that?'

'He wanted to find a very learned diviner, to consult him about something that was, he told us, of the very greatest importance to him.'

'The trader, Tenzin's daughter!' thought Tharchin.

'We advised him to go and consult *Alak* Wangchen, a great diviner and magician. I was going also to tell him that those who put their questions before the tombs of the Lamas of Ngarong receive the answers to them through the medium of a vision or a dream; but he was intent on his own ideas, and paid no heed to my words.'

'Perhaps this diviner advised him to go to Ngarong.'

'I doubt it. He doesn't love the hermits of Ngarong. But your master may have thought of the monastery. He had heard it spoken of, he told me.'

'But why should he remain there so long?'

The head monk made a gesture, implying that he hadn't the least idea.

Tharchin reported this conversation to Kalzang as soon as he was alone with him in their tent. Kalzang did not even know the monastery of Ngarong by name, but after he had heard what people said about wild beasts becoming tame, and demons being reclaimed, he declared:

'There's no doubt whatever that *Kushog* Mipam is there: prodigies of that kind are precisely what he longs to see. I told you and your friend that when he left us at Sharakuto, on the way back from Lhasa. He's quite capable of becoming a saint. At Lhasa, when we were staying with the trader Tenzin, his clerks said that our master was a magician.'

'That's just foolish gossip.'

'Perhaps not. He was more or less the disciple of a lama of Kham who was the guest of a petty chieftain in the Tromo district. Our master comes from Tromo. This lama quarrelled with the chieftain, who wanted to have him slain by a sorcerer, but they found the sorcerer strangled in the walled-up hut where he was performing the murderous rites. Then there's another thing. It's not very clear: this chief's son and *Kushog* Mipam had had a quarrel, and the young prince was found dead at the same time as the sorcerer was, a few paces from his hut.'

'And *Kushog* Mipam was there?'

'No, he was said to be at Shigatze at the time, with the trader Tsöndup, *Kushog* Tenzin's friend.'

'Well, if he wasn't there. . . .'

'That proves that he killed the prince by magic. A waistcoat of his was found in the undergrowth, near the spot where the prince was lying with an arrow through his heart.'

'A waistcoat cannot shoot an arrow.'

'Ah! That's what you think. . . . You are not very well informed for a member of the clergy. Most certainly it could if its master possessed the power of quickening it by infusing his will into it.'

'That I can't quite believe,' said Tharchin shaking his head.

'You've not got a very open mind.'

'But didn't you say that *Kushog* Mipam had certain leanings toward becoming a saint? . . .'

'Precisely, a very great saint, not just a poor humdrum good man. That young prince was vicious—it's easy to guess that he was about to do wrong; *Kushog* Mipam foresaw this, and killed him out of charity. He spared him the grievous consequences which his bad actions would have provoked, and saved those who would have suffered from the effects of those bad actions. Can't you understand that?'

'Hm!' said Tharchin unconvinced. 'What do you say to our going as far as Ngarong, to see if *Kushog* Mipam is there, and if he doesn't need us?'

'No,' replied Kalzang. 'From what you've told me about Ngarong, I'm certain we oughtn't to go there to look for our master. *Kushog* Mipam is very good, but he doesn't like people to interfere in his affairs. I have served him now for several years and I do know that. He'll return when he pleases, and if he needs us, he'll send for us. It's not good to interfere in matters of religion.'

'There's nothing to prove that it has anything to do with religion. . . . I should dearly like to see the monastery built without hands. . . .'

'It's more prudent to keep at a safe distance. To make our reverence to it from here will suffice to gain us merit.'

'We could try one more divination.'

'In a few days' time, if *Kushog* Mipam has not yet returned.'

Night had fallen. The two men spread each a blanket on the ground, closed the curtains of their tent, and went to bed. Kalzang soon dropped off to sleep. Tharchin thereupon sat up, and crossing his legs, took his rosary, which he had placed near the bag he used for a pillow.

'In the name of the Threefold Jewel . . . ' he murmured.

Then, telling off the beads of the rosary, and counting them in a certain fashion, according to a divinatory rite, he endeavoured to gain enlightenment as to the puzzling personality of his master, the mystery of the adventure which he was pursuing, and the risks which he, Tharchin, was incurring by following him.

CHAPTER XIV

EIGHTEEN *chortens* (reliquaries) in solid silver, overlaid with gold and precious stones, were ranged in a line, on an altar, at the far end of the rock-temple. The last on the right was provided with a niche in which stood a statuette representing a lama. These *chortens*, whose height was about that of a man, were the tombs containing the ashes of the lamas who had succeeded one another, in order of their 'reincarnations,' as spiritual lords of the monastery of Ngarong, since the day when, in the eleventh century, a son of a noble race, Mipam Rinchen, the disciple of Jowo Atisha,[1] taking up his abode in one of the natural chambers of the rock city, had founded the existing monastery.

The story of Mipam Rinchen, who, after embracing the religious life, became the Lama of the Five Wisdoms, Yeshes Nga Den,[2] is a strange one.

One day, as the result of circumstances whose causes he could not discern, Mipam Rinchen was ushered into the room where Jowo Atisha was teaching several of his disciples the doctrine relating to the Five Wisdoms.

He spoke of the Wisdom that like a mirror reflects perceptions—the Wisdom, acquired by Contemplation, which apprehends the fundamental identity in all things—the

---

[1] Jowo dje palden Atisha (the noble and illustrious Lord Atisha) was a learned Hindu philosopher, born in Bengal about the year 980. He belonged to the royal family of Gaur, became a monk, and having nearly reached his sixtieth year, repaired to Tibet as a Buddhist missionary. He died there about fifteen years later (seventeen years according to certain chronicles). His tomb is in a small monastery at Nyethang, a village situated to the south of Lhasa. Atisha is the author of a great number of philosophical works.

[2] An abbreviation of *Yeshes nga dang denpa.*

317

Wisdom that discerns, differentiates and classifies things according to their particular properties—the Wisdom applied to works, assuring their success—the universal Wisdom which penetrates everything, detects the elements of which things are formed, and then the elements which constitute each of these first detected elements, and so *ad infinitum*, and by the virtue of this process destroys the illusion of the permanent reality of form and personality.

Mipam Rinchen, inasmuch as he was a layman, had never heard the dissertations of the lama philosophers. He was enchanted to acquire the knowledge of so exalted a doctrine, but the vainglorious and egotistical satisfaction he felt in acquiring it was like a veil that hid for him the meaning of the lessons which he had received, and prevented him from perceiving that they have no practical value unless they are combined with goodness. On his return home he declared to his wife, whom he had but recently married, that he was going to leave her, to become an anchorite, as he wished to pass his life in meditation on the Five Wisdoms.

His bride was a girl of good family, of little learning, but endowed with intelligence. She besought her husband not to abandon her; she assured him that she too was disposed to retire from the world, and implored him to let her live, as a nun, in the neighbourhood of his hermitage, that she might see him from time to time, and be instructed by him in the precious doctrines which he had received from Jowo Atisha.

Mipam Rinchen disdainfully refused her request. A woman, he said, was incapable of understanding so lofty a teaching. For his part, he made the vow to be reborn an unlimited number of times, becoming a hermit monk in each of his lives, until he had absolutely mastered the meaning of the Doctrine of the Five Wisdoms, and was competent to spread it throughout the world, for the good of all sentient beings.

'You are very farsighted, *Kushog*,' his wife made answer. 'Thinking of the good of beings that are yet to come, you are neglecting that of your loyal and loving wife. I also make a

ཿ རྗེ་བོ་རྗེ་དཔལ་ལྡན་ཨ་ཏི་ཤ །

Jo-Wo Atisha

vow: the vow to be reborn as often as you, and to rejoin you in each of your lives, that I may prevent you from attaining your end.'.

They separated. Mipam Rinchen left his house and property, and, travelling northwards, reached the place where the five valleys meet. Their number, tallying with that of the Five Wisdoms, seemed to him a sign which pointed to that spot as the place where he ought to remain. According to certain traditions, the fantastic city of rocks was not in existence in those days. The plateau ended in sheer rock, and the genii of the mountains must have scooped them out in a thousand fantastic ways, to provide lodgings for the future disciples of Mipam Rinchen.

Amongst the successors of Mipam, two lamas abandoned their abbatial seats to marry, and died almost immediately after the wedding. Despite their defection, they remained 'incarnations' (*tulkus*) of Mipam Rinchen. The monks of Ngarong claimed their bodies, and having cremated them, placed their ashes in the *chorten*-reliquaries in the monastery temple.

The last, in point of time, of the *tulkus* of the Five Wisdoms met with a singular end.

It was his practice, every year, to camp for a space of two months on the shores of the Koko Nor—the great Blue Lake, in the north-east of Tibet—with all his monks. He devoted the time to expounding to them the Doctrine of the Five Wisdoms, on which they were afterwards to meditate, each separately, in their respective hermitages.

Yeshes Nga Den, the eighteenth reincarnation of the founder of Ngarong, was on the shore preaching to his disciples, when he interrupted his discourse to say to them:

'I have often spoken to you about the Fifth, the loftiest Wisdom of all; its possession is indispensable, if compassion, generosity, and all the actions which we accomplish for the happiness of others are to be efficacious. For years now I have striven to avert the sufferings of men, beasts, and other beings.

I am aware that in the course of my previous incarnations I have pursued the same end, but I still have not completely attained it. I attribute this fact to my not having absolutely mastered the meaning of the Fifth Wisdom.

'Now, I have decided, in a week's time, when we strike camp to return to the monastery, to shut myself up in a hermitage, there to live the strict existence of a recluse, without speaking to anyone, without seeing a single person, for three years, three months, three weeks, and three days.[1] If, at the expiration of this period of meditation I have won the knowledge I am seeking I will teach you all that I have learnt as to the means of being truly and efficaciously charitable. If I have not attained it I shall not quit my hermitage, but shall continue my seclusion.'

The monks, surprised and sorrowful to think that they would no longer see their lama in their midst, were silent, hesitating, out of respect, to beg him to renounce his project.

Suddenly Yeshes Nga Den rose and gazed in the direction of the lake.

'Oh! the poor goat!' he said. 'What is she doing there, in the meadow? She seems to be hurt. . . . I will go and see what ails her. . . .'

He set off running. The astonished monks shouted after him:

'Reverend sir! reverend sir! stop. . . . That isn't a meadow, there is no goat. . . . You are going into the lake! . . .'

But run as fast as they might to catch him, he outpaced them all. For some moments he walked upon the water; then he suddenly sank into the depths, crying: 'I shall return!'

Among the eyewitnesses of this drama some related that at the moment when the lama disappeared under the waters they had distinguished the figure of a woman standing on the spot. This gave rise to much talk. Some said the woman was a *nagi* (female goddess of the waters), who had led the lama to the palace of the lake-gods, where they besought him to accomplish

[1] A regular period of retreat in Tibet.

an act of charity; but others, referring to the story of Mipam Rinchen, the disciple of Atisha, believed that the woman of whom they had caught a glimpse was Mipam's wife, who was pursuing him from life to life. She had created the false vision of a wounded goat in a meadow, to lure the lama on and make him lose his life, in order to prevent him from acquiring the complete possession of the Fifth Wisdom during the retreat which he had in mind. It was she also, the report ran, who had previously caused two of the lamas in whom Mipam Rinchen was reincarnated to fall in love with her, and had induced them to forsake the monastery in order to marry her.

The body of the lama was never found, but several months after his disappearance in the lake the waves washed his mantle ashore on the anchorites' island. The anchorites showed it to some of the monks of Ngarong, who, in the course of the following winter, crossing the lake on the ice for the purpose of taking them their supplies, recognized the mantle as their Master's.

After performing various divinatory calculations, the oracle of Ngarong declared that it was the will of the departed lama and of the gods that the mantle should remain on the island of the hermits. These latter enclosed it, therefore, as a relic, in a *chorten* which they built in the shelter of a cave. Meanwhile a silver reliquary was prepared at Ngarong in memory of the deceased, and the monks, in the absence of the lama's ashes, placed in it a statuette fashioned in his image.

Mipam was not acquainted with the story of the incarnated abbots of Ngarong, and even had it been known to him, it would probably have been of little interest to him during the period of agonizing preoccupation through which he was passing.

The ten days assigned by the chiefs of Ngarong to their guest's retreat had expired. At nightfall Mipam was led into the rock temple, which until then he had not been permitted to approach. His guide silently opened one of the leaves of the

heavy door, prostrated himself on the threshold, and signed to
Mipam to enter; then closing the door, he went to rejoin
another monk who was to keep watch with him under the
peristyle, according to the established usage of Ngarong, where
the pilgrims are not left entirely alone while they consult the
invisible oracle.

Mipam sat down on a cushion which had been placed for
him opposite the *chortens*, at the foot of the lofty abbatial throne
on which lay the mantle of the *tulkus* of Ngarong, upon which
was sewn a piece of the mantle of Atisha, their spiritual father.
He felt both wearied and overwrought. A week passed under
the stone vaulting of his cell had calmed his agitated spirit. A
strange detachment, an odd indifference invaded him; he
seemed to 'go out' of himself, to be inspecting, from the outside, the figure of Mipam seated in supplication before the
sepulchres.

He must needs formulate the questions which he hoped
would be answered. It was for this he had come. But his desire
was weakened, almost extinguished. His thoughts wandered
to other objects. The *chorten*-mausoleums, studded as with
many-coloured eyes by the precious stones incrusted in their
silver, fascinated him. Reflecting the flickering flames of the
altar lamps which quickened their manifold glances, they
seemed to rest upon Mipam, to turn away, and to fix themselves
on him anew; they searched him, questioned him, and confided
to him a secret which he could not grasp. The little gilt figure
of the lama adorning the eighteenth reliquary detached its small
rock-crystal eyes from the book laid upon its knees, which it
had been conning for twenty years, and it was Mipam, his
namesake, whom the last enthroned abbot of Ngarong, Mipam
Yeshes Nga Den *rimpoche*, was now contemplating from the
height of his empty tomb.

The young man felt troubled. How long had he been there?
He had only that one night before him. On the morrow he
must leave the monastery; its heads do not allow a lengthy
sojourn. Moreover, ought he not to leave for Lhasa? Kalzang

was awaiting him, yonder, in the herdsmen's camp. Would he be able, before he went, to obtain the blessing of the present Lama of Ngarong? He had asked this of the monk who had led him to the temple. The monk had looked at him strangely and had not answered.

He must, so they told him, first ask his questions aloud, then concentrate his thoughts on them, and wait.

In the presence of Wangchen, the diviner, he had formulated these questions in such a way as to conceal his precise object; 'the journey I had in view,' he had said, nor had he mentioned Dolma's name. But in this solitary temple these precautions were superfluous, and the effect of direct questions might be more potent.

Mipam rose, prostrated himself thrice, and said aloud:

'Are the circumstances favourable to my journey to Lhasa?

'Is Dolma already married to Dogyal?

'Will she follow me to Dangar?

'What was the meaning of the flight of those wild geese over my head, making for the North, when I was thinking of leaving for Lhasa?'

With a renewed threefold prostration, he reseated himself and waited. . . . The hours went by; still Mipam sat there, motionless. He strove to centre his thoughts on the questions which he had asked. Answer there came none, but lo! there arose from the core of his inner being a personality with shadowy features and a smile of loving-kindness that was mingled with pity and gentle raillery. It swept aside his questions, as one sweeps aside with the hand a material object, and these questions, taking shape, floated away and were dispersed, as the mists that wander in the hollows of the mountains are driven away by the wind and drawn up by the sun. Mipam wanted to hold them back, to constrain them, by the concentration of his mind on the occult Presence dwelling in the sanctuary, but his efforts were fruitless. He felt that his thoughts and the idea of the world in which they moved were together escaping him. Was it death that was drawing near? . . . Was he about to die and abandon Dolma? . . .

'Dolma! . . .'

Did he cry aloud, or was his cry of distress and appeal uttered only within himself? He had no clear understanding of this, but the force of that appeal was effectual. Standing upright on the extreme left of the row of glittering *chortens* Dolma had appeared. No longer the little fairy, clad in iridescent attire, who haunted Mipam's memory, but a Dolma with a sober countenance, wearing the dress of a nun.

Was she speaking in a manner perceptible to the ear, or was it with his heart that Mipam heard her? . . . She said:

'Mipam, I am thy wife of days gone by. Each of us made a vow, and we have accomplished it from life to life. In this vow I swore to thee, before the Jowo, that I would become a nun if I did not marry thee: I am going to be faithful to my oath. I have long been an obstacle in thy path; now I free thee for this life and for ever. To-morrow I shall die at Lhasa. As for thee, accomplish the rites which will bring about my speedy rebirth in this world, so that we may come together again during thy present life, and so that, possessed of a male body, I may become thy disciple.

'Mipam, thou art the reincarnation of Mipam Rinchen, the disciple of Jowo Atisha; take once more thy place on the throne which is thine.'

Dolma advanced toward her friend, and guiding him by the hand she made him mount the steps of the abbatial throne. There Mipam raised his arms and placed his two hands on the head of the young girl, which was bowed before him.

'May my blessing light upon thee,' he said aloud. 'Me thou hast liberated, and I, in the name of the Triple Jewel and of my Master Jowo Atisha, do now liberate thee.

'Because I refused thee the gift of what I possessed of the Doctrine, I remained for centuries unable to understand it wholly. Be thou delivered from the desire for vengeance that has brought thee back into this world for numberless sorrowful incarnations, and may I be delivered from egotism and pride, the primal springs of that desire.

'Take thy rest for a brief space in the Paradise of the Great Beatitude; then, having chosen honourable parents in a neighbouring region, and having been born with a male body, come to me in ten years' time and rejoin me here at Ngarong to be my pupil and my well-beloved son.'

The two monks who were keeping watch outside, hearing the sound of a voice, had noiselessly entered, and were standing on the threshold, too dismayed at what they saw to dare to advance. Mipam was seated on their dead lama's throne, girt in the mantle of the abbots of Ngarong, which, for the space of more than twenty years had lain on the empty throne, waiting for the nineteenth *tulku* of the line of Yeshes Nga Den, whom they had never been able to find.

Mipam did not appear to see them; he was beginning a discourse, and one of the monks, who was ripe in years, recognized in what he said, even to the very terms which he was wont to employ, the doctrines which their last lama was accustomed to teach them.

'Sound the *yeskhyil* conch,'[1] he ordered the young monk who was standing by his side. 'Our lama has returned!'

The precious *yeskhyil* conch was sounded only on the most solemn and urgent occasions, to convoke the hermits living in the neighbourhood. The regulations of Ngarong sanctioned the presence in the monastery itself of only a few monks, who dwelt there in turn, to devote themselves to its material administration. The lama *tulku*, the lord of the monastery, lived the life of a hermit in an isolated part of the building, completely separated from the other dwellings. He possessed also, on the mountain-side, his own private hermitage, where

[1] A conch whose spirals instead of turning from left to right like the great majority of conches, turn from right to left. These conches are very highly prized by the Tibetans. It is no rare thing for the equivalent of forty or fifty pounds, or even more, to be paid for them.

he resided for periods of retreat of a still more rigid character. If some special event demanded the immediate presence of the anchorites in the monastery, over and above the habitual occasions of assembly, the great *yeskhyil* conch, whose tones could be heard from afar, was sounded. Then, at whatever hour of the day or night they heard it, whatever the state of the roads, or the weather—in hailstorms, or when the deep snow levelled the paths and hollows, no less than in fine weather—all the hermits, whatever vow they had made concerning the length of their seclusion, were bound to respond to the appeal, to quit their hermitages forthwith and hasten to the monastery.

It was the deep sound of this conch that now echoed in the night. The heavens were clear and full of stars, the roads were dry. Before long the anchorites who lived nearest the monastery had arrived and entered the temple. Mipam continued his discourse, unconscious of what was going on around him, addressing hearers who were visible to him alone.

Like the aged monk who had had them convened, the oldest hermits recognized the doctrines habitually taught by the last of their lamas, the terms which he had employed, his gestures, and the very tones of his voice. One by one they fell on their knees, and as other monks entered who had known the eighteenth Yeshes Nga Den they too, recognizing their old Master in his new incarnation, prostrated themselves in front of him.

'. . . To possess the penetrating wisdom that discerns in all things the elements of which they are composed, and then perceives the elements of which these elements themselves are composed, and so to infinity; to possess the wisdom that dispels the illusion of the permanent reality of form and personality is indispensable if compassion, generosity, and every act that we accomplish for the good of others are to be efficacious. For years now I have striven to avert the sufferings of men and beasts and all other sentient beings. I know that in the course of my previous incarnations I have pursued the same end and have not attained it. The reign of universal friendship can come only with the possession of that Wisdom which breaks down the illusory limits of the "I," by making us see the "others" existing in us, and the "we" existing in others.

'This wisdom, of which I have had but a glimpse, I can neither teach it to you, nor can I render you capable of propagating it in the world. This, then, is what I have resolved. I am going to shut myself up in my hermitage for a rigorous retreat of three years, three months, three weeks and three days. If on the expiration of that period I have won the knowledge which I am seeking to acquire, I shall impart it to you. If I have not attained it, I shall not leave my hermitage, and shall continue my seclusion. It is to obtain this knowledge *that I have come back.*'

This discourse was a textual reproduction of that which the dead Lama of Ngarong had given to his disciples on the lake shore, before he fell a victim to the singular illusion which led to his death. The agitation of those present was intense, but not a single one of those monks who had known Yeshes Nga Den entertained the remotest doubt as to the authenticity of his reincarnation in Mipam, and the others, informed by them of the miracle of this discourse, which was identical with that given twenty years before, shared their faith.

'*I shall come again*' had been the last words spoken by Yeshes Nga Den as he sank beneath the waters. '*I have come back*' were those that Mipam, seated on the abbatial throne, had just uttered.

All wished to acclaim their Lord, returned to his domains, their Master, who had come back to instruct them. But Mipam, falling back in his throne, had fainted. Some of the monks hurried to him, lifted him from his seat, and laid him on some cushions.

It was long before the young man regained consciousness. When he came to himself he looked with astonishment at the monks who filled the temple. He remembered that he had

come there to formulate some questions relating to his journey
. . . and that he had had a dream, a strange and terrible dream.
He had seen Dolma, who had related to him some story of
which he no longer had any clear recollection, but he vividly
recalled the fact that she wore the monastic dress, and she had
said: 'I shall die to-morrow.' Then she had taken him by the
hand, and he had distinctly felt the affectionate pressure of that
beloved hand upon his own. . . . After that, all was darkness;
he remembered nothing more.

What did this crowd of monks around him mean? Was it
the usage at Ngarong to foregather round the pilgrim who had
come to solicit answers from the invisible oracle dwelling in
the abbots' tombs? . . . But why were they murmuring: 'Our
precious Lord'—'Our spiritual Master.' Where was the
lama? . . . Would he be able to see him? He wished to crave
his blessing.

'Do you feel better, my lord?'

'I don't know what was the matter with me: I seem to have
come out of a dark night, where I had been living a very long
time. . . . But why do you call me lord? . . . .'

'You must recover first, you must recover completely,' said
a dignitary of the monastery. 'Can you walk? If it tires you
to do so, they will carry you. Let us go elsewhere; you shall
have some tea to drink.'

'Some tea; thank you; I should like some very much. I am
quite capable of walking. It is only that I feel a little weak;
why, I do not know.'

Mipam stood up. Before leaving the temple, his eyes strayed
involuntarily toward the reliquary which contained the ashes
of the first Yeshes Nga Den, beside which he had seen the figure
of Dolma dressed as a nun.

Out of doors the dawn was whitening the sky: under its wan
light the monastery amidst the rocks assumed a fantastic
appearance. The vision of Dolma in her monastic dress
haunted the young man's mind. In his 'dream' she had said
to him: 'To-morrow I shall die.' That 'to-morrow' had just

begun with this white dawn, and Mipam felt something freeze within his heart.

Mipam was escorted by the monastery officials and its older members into the apartment of the Lama of Ngarong, and there tea was served. The physical effects of the comforting hot drink, freely buttered, quickly made themselves felt. Mipam emerged from his condition of semi-somnolence. Once more completely aware of himself and his surroundings, he realized that he had fainted in the temple, after experiencing a dream or a vision of Dolma. The kindly monks of Ngarong had looked after him, and had been very good to him, but he felt that his trouble had passed. It was time for him to rejoin Kalzang, although, if his appalling dream were true, the journey to Lhasa was now useless; as Wangchen, the diviner, had told him.

'I thank you for your goodness,' he said, to the monks who stood around him. 'I am now fit to start, and I don't wish to be a burden to you any longer. I do not know whether the answer which I received in your temple refers to a real fact, if it is a product of my imagination, or if some evil spirit has wished to make sport of me, to prevent me from making the journey I have planned, and to cause the greatest misfortune of my life. I shall have the proof of this at Lhasa.'

'*Kushog*, we beseech you to stay with us,' replied the head of the monastery. 'You have found your own abode again, and we have the joy of having found our lama, whose reincarnation we have sought for twenty years and more. Remember, *Kushog*, the discourse which you gave us from your throne in the temple. All those of us who knew you in your preceding incarnation have testified to the perfect resemblance of the teachings and expressions in that discourse to those employed by our revered spiritual father when he was about to leave us. How could you, who until now have been a merchant, have been familiar with his teachings if you had not been acquainted with them in your former life?'

'I delivered no discourse.'

'Your memory is for the moment clouded in that respect, but it will clear, and you will remember it. You sat in the throne of Yeshes Nga Den, you put on his mantle, the one which is handed down from lama to lama, and on which has been sewn a fragment of the sacred mantle of Jowo Atisha, our founder's Master.'

'I did that!' cried Mipam, terrified. 'It was an abominable sacrilege! I assure you I don't remember it. An attack of madness must have seized me in the temple! Never would I have done such a thing in my sober senses!'

'In your case, *Kushog*, it was lawful. Any other than the authentic reincarnation of our lama would have fallen dead on the spot had he permitted himself to put on that mantle and to sit upon that throne. By doing so, you revealed yourself to us.'

'I was alone in the temple; I remember that very well; after that I don't know what happened, until I saw you all standing around me.'

'It is a rule to allow two monks to keep watch behind the closed doors when a pilgrim is admitted to consult the Oracle. They heard you talking.'

'And I delivered a sermon. . . .'

'Not immediately. You were talking to someone.'

The monk who had had the conch sounded to assemble his brother monks came up, prostrated himself thrice, and respectfully addressed Mipam.

'Precious lord, you were blessing someone. You said to her: "Be thou delivered and may I be also delivered." You said: "I refused thee the gift of what I possessed of the Doctrine." And by that I recognized that you were the same Yeshes Nga Den, our founder, whose history is related in our chronicles, and who, before becoming a hermit, was called Mipam, like you, *Kushog*. . . . Mipam Rinchen.'

The old monk prostrated himself anew, and continued:

'Precious lord' . . . and his voice trembled a little. 'Precious lord, it was your wife of the days gone by whom you were blessing; she who, by virtue of a magical illusion, caused your death in the lake, in your previous incarnation. You told her to go to the Paradise of the Great Beatitude, and then to be born again, not far from here, in a male body, that she can come and rejoin you. She must be living, for the time being, somewhere in this world, without your knowledge. It was I who had the conch sounded to summon the members of the monastery.'

Mipam was once more beset by the fantastic shadows of his dream. 'To go to the Paradise of the Great Beatitude' meant death. . . .

'Dolma!' he cried, seeking refuge once more in his love, which was making desperate efforts to cling to life.

'Dolma!' said the head of the monastery. 'That was the name of the wife of Mipam Rinchen who settled at Ngarong more than eight hundred years ago. He had refused to transmit to her the teaching which he had received from his Master Atisha.

'*Kushog*, do us the favour to peruse our chronicles. I will have them brought to you' .

He made a sign, and all withdrew after him. A few moments later some young monks laid five thick volumes on a table beside Mipam's seat, and prostrating themselves before him they went out in silence.

Mipam remained alone in the private apartment of the lamas abbots of Ngarong, in the company of the books in which was written the story of his past lives.

At Lhasa, in Tenzin's house, consternation reigned. For three days women had been keeping watch in turn in the room where Dolma was lying inanimate on her bed; out of her body, but not dead.

Thinking that she was healed of the illness which had all but carried her off after Mipam's departure, and yielding to the repeated entreaties of Dogyal and his father, Tenzin had consented to Dolma's marriage.

The wedding was a splendid affair; half the inhabitants of
Lhasa suddenly discovered that ties of kinship or friendship
bound them to the great merchant, and gave them the right to
keep festival with him. Tenzin turned no one away. The
thousands of monks, members of the three State monasteries
—Sera, Gahlden and Depung—were lavishly furnished, thanks
to his generosity, with butter, tea, meat, and other ingredients
needful for the preparation of a copious repast. He offered
valuable presents to the Grand Lamas and had lamps by the
thousand lit on the altars of the Buddhas and the gods; the
beggars even, and the very scavengers[1] were not forgotten.

Wan and wasted, remote and wraith-like, Dolma remained
indifferent to everything. She had raised no objection to the
celebration of her marriage, nor had she shown either displeasure or satisfaction when her father, who clove to his
original idea, had pointed out that in the marriage-contract
Mipam's name followed Dogyal's, and that Mipam thereby
became, like his elder brother, her rightful husband. It really
seemed as though this marriage was that of another person,
which in no way concerned her. However, as the young girl's
passive attitude might have been due to shyness, no one worried
about it, neither her future husband nor Tenzin.

On the wedding-night, Dolma, as lifeless as ever, suffered
herself to be led into the nuptial chamber. The guests were
still drinking in the banqueting-room and the courtyard, when
cries were heard calling for help. Dogyal, who had just
rejoined his wife, had found her lying lifeless on the cushions
of her bed.

'Dolma is dead!' he cried in terror.

Tenzin and Tseringma, followed by all their guests, burst
into the bridal chamber. Dolma appeared to be dead, as her
husband had declared.

A doctor, summoned in haste, stated that she still lived,
and, having examined her carefully, he declared: 'This case does

[1] The *rogyapas*: those who remove the corpses of men and animals. They
constitute a despised caste.

332

Cittipatti Yab Yum

not call for medical science. What we want here is a lama. The subtle body and the consciousness of the young girl have been sundered from the material body. Who can tell whither they have taken their flight? Only an expert magician can discern the bond which, invisible to us, joins them to this material body, and can prevent it from breaking, which would cause her death.'

As soon as the monastery gates were opened at daybreak, Tenzin had informed the Grand Lama of the college of the Gyudpas (those learned in magic rites) of what had occurred, and the Grand Lama, interested by what he had been told, had repaired in person to the merchant's house, attended by some college graduates. The lama had confirmed the diagnosis of the doctor, indicating, in addition to the treatment prescribed, the appropriate rites to be performed in order to protect the young girl against accidents of an occult order. Tenzin's house was filled afresh with the clamour of the bells and the drums, the wailing of the hautboys, and the drone of the liturgical recitations. Dolma remained in the same condition.

At last, on the fourth day, at dawn, she made a movement, and presently she raised herself up and remained seated on her bed.

'Call my father,' she ordered the woman in attendance.

Tenzin hastened to her bedside.

'I am daslog,'[1] she told him. 'I have come back from the northern pasture-lands. Mipam is in the monastery of Ngarong, near the Blue Lake. He is its abbot, the nineteenth reincarnation of the Mipam who formerly settled there as a hermit, and whose wife I was, when my name was Dolma, as it is now. Mipam called me, and I went to him. I spoke to him, but he doubts what I said. To convince him you must

[1] Literally 'who comes back from beyond'. It happens, in Tibet, that people remain for several days in a cataleptic condition, and when they come to themselves they relate stories of their journey to the hells or paradises, or various countries of our earth.

333

send him as a "sign,"[1] the turquoise which he gave me when he came here to claim me in wedlock.

'Bring me now, without delay, some nun's clothing, cut off my hair, and call a lama to ordain me. I shall die this evening, and I must needs do so in the Holy Order. The body I am about to forsake is my last female body; I shall be re-born, before long, in a male body, and I shall become a monk of Ngarong, and a disciple of Mipam, so that I may learn from him the Doctrine which he refused to teach me in days gone by.'

Poor Tenzin, his wife, Dogyal, and the other inmates of the house, who had hurried to Dolma's bedside on hearing that she had recovered consciousness, all wept bitterly.

'Do not die, my dear daughter,' Tenzin implored her. 'If your marriage with Dogyal causes you so much sorrow, I will allow you to go and live at Dangar with Mipam, who is also your husband. Dogyal will not stand in your way.'

'No,' agreed Dogyal, 'I will let you go, Dolma. For a long time you have been like a little sister to me; I love you dearly, Dolma, and don't want you to die.'

The good fellow spoke in all sincerity. He had never suspected that his marriage with Dolma could lead to a tragedy.

'You are very good,' replied the young girl, 'but the time has come for me to leave you. Don't delay, therefore, to do what I've asked you.'

Tenzin was loth to resign himself to his daughter's leaving him. The lamas, he thought, will easily find some means of preventing her from dying; and he placed his hope in the magic art of the chief of the College of Secret Rites. But when the latter had heard what the young girl had to say he peremptorily ordered Tenzin not to thwart her wishes. Tseringma, assisted by the house-servants, tearfully helped Dolma to remove her silken clothes and her jewels. Then they cut off

[1] 'Signs', which may consist of a number of different things: incidents, dreams, visions, material objects, etc. are regarded either in the light of warnings, putting one on one's guard against events very likely to happen, or as evidence confirming declarations.

her long hair, and dressed her in the monastic gown and mantle. Next, when a number of lamps had been lit on the altar in the oratory of the house, Dolma prostrated herself before the statues of the Buddha, Tsong Khapa, and the symbolic deities, and then before the Grand Lama of the Secret Rites, and he, having made the gesture of cutting her hair, received her into the Holy Order.

Dolma with her own hands wrapped the turquoise which Mipam had given her in a long white silken scarf. She added just a few words: 'Soon I shall be at thy feet,' and ordered that a messenger should start for the Blue Lake country as soon as she was dead.

Then she lay once more upon her bed, wrapped in her monastic mantle, and remained silent, without moving. At sunset she raised her hands, with the palms together, in the attitude of respectful salutation.

'Mipam!' she whispered.

Her hands fell gently back on to her nun's robe. Dolma was dead. In accordance with her orders, two of Tenzin's servants, taking the turquoise and some gifts from the merchant, left at once for the road to the North.

At Ngarong, Mipam was engrossed in the reading of the monastery chronicles, but more than the biographies of the lamas, their writings interested him. He found in them a strange crescendo of sensibility. While Mipam Rinchen and his immediate successors had left only purely scholastic dissertations, the more recent abbots envisaged, in their works, the diffusion of an efficacious teaching, fitted to show men the falsity of their religious and social conceptions, and the fatal effects of these erroneous views. The last of the Yeshes Nga Den advocated the wisdom which makes men perceive that no durable happiness nor security for any sentient being can exist while other beings are a prey to suffering.

'When the cold winter's wind freezes the lakes,' he wrote,

'and shrivels up the grass whereon the cattle feed; when it liberates squalls that bring the blizzards, men and beasts feel its results. In like manner, when the baleful wind of injustice and hate blows, none may claim immunity from its effects.'

In the course of his reading Mipam came across pages that touched his heart, depicting the vast misery of the beings subject to sickness, the inevitable victims of old age and death, who add to these ills a hundred thousand others which are due to their blind egotism.

'Insects imprisoned in a pan,' said the last lama, 'who instead of striving to escape from their prison, fight one another, biting, stinging and slaughtering one another, and causing one another intolerable suffering.'

These thoughts tallied with those which he had cherished from his infancy. Like himself, these lamas had dreamt of the 'land where all are friends;' but it did not follow, Mipam told himself, that he was their reincarnation. Despite his vision, despite Dolma's words, despite the trance during which—so he was assured—he had repeated the identical words of the last abbot, Mipam still doubted the new identity which the hermits of Ngarong were endeavouring to thrust upon him. He withstood their entreaties, out of honesty, refusing to benefit by what might be an illusion on their part. But Dolma did not stand as an obstacle between him and the abbatial seat of the Yeshes Nga Den; the sad conviction that he would never see his beloved again had taken hold upon him. Before his vision in the temple had he not had another vision, in the room of the seer of Dangar, before his departure for Lhasa? Seated at the feet of the old monk, had he not seen the figure of Dolma fading, dissolving, to be engulfed in an ocean of white mist? Dolma was lost to him.

Yet at the very moment when he was accepting this painful certitude, a flame of hope blazed up anew in his heart. What if all this phantasmagoria were nought but the work of a demon foe? Over and over again this possibility entered his mind. Dangar was not so far away that he could not go there to consult the seer. Yes, the very next day he would tear himself away from this Ngarong, whither magic spells had led him, where magic spells were detaining him. . . .

The next day Mipam, pale and depressed, was leaning on the balustrade of the natural terrace to which his room gave access. Below him, on the further side of the valley, he could distinguish the path by which he had entered the enchanted citadel where he now dwelt in captivity. It rested with him to saddle up and to take the same path back. He would first repair to the camp of the diviner, and then to that of the herdsmen, where Kalzang was awaiting him; he would free himself from the hold of Ngarong, from the attraction of that abbatial throne, on which, so his hosts assured him, he had taken his seat, and which seemed to be waiting, with the calm of certitude, the day when he would seat himself there once more.

He would go . . . and yet Mipam knew that he would not go. The spell was becoming stronger and stronger, was hemming him in more and more closely. During the night that had just ended Mipam had had a dream.

He had seen himself at the monastery of Dangar, in the seer's dilapidated lodging.

'You are still inexpert, my son, in seeing through the walls which you have built in front of you, with ideas for stones,' the seer had said to him. 'The last watch in the night, I predicted to you. The moment of awakening is at hand. Have patience: you are where you ought to be.'

'I will wait,' said Mipam aloud; he was mastered and conquered. 'I shall wait for a sign.'

The interest with which Mipam read the works written by the abbots of Ngarong brought him hours of calm, restful periods of truce, of escape from his painful hesitations. Besides the five volumes of the chronicles he had had brought to his room some manuscripts which had attracted his attention when he had visited the library. One of these, in resuming the theme common to all the Ngarong Lamas—the propagation of the knowledge of the Five Wisdoms—added a sort of laconic programme:

'To arrive by meditation at a just comprehension of the real nature of the sentient beings and the close bonds that unite them with one another.

'To fit oneself to be able to demonstrate this with all the consequences which it involves.

'After the example of the Buddha, of Jowo Atisha, and of all the Sages who have preached the Doctrine of Salvation through Right Views, to preach that same Doctrine in every region, as far as our feet can carry us, with the object of lessening suffering and finally of destroying it.'

Mipam, fired with enthusiasm by this programme, never wearied of meditating upon it. How regrettable it is, he thought, that he who conceived it had no successor, able to realize such a project. The successor, the hermits assured him, was himself, but against this idea the young man continued to rebel.

Two days after his dream of the seer of Dangar, Mipam summoned the head of the monastery.

'Did you not tell me,' he asked him, 'that there exists here a private hermitage reserved for the lamas of Ngarong?'

'That is so.'

'Will you allow me to retire there?'

'You are at home, my lord; the hermitage belongs to you.'

Mipam made a movement of impatience. He was not Yeshes Nga Den. Why did they want to constrain him to play that part? But if confirmation came of Dolma's death he hoped to be admitted as a monk among the hermits of Ngarong.

.   .   .   .   .

Mipam had now lived as a recluse in the hermitage for about six weeks, when one afternoon two horsemen, guided by some herdsmen, and accompanied by Kalzang and Tharchin, knocked at the gate of Ngarong.

'We come from Lhasa,' said one of them to the doorkeeper. 'The daughter of our master, the great merchant Tenzin, was daslog,[1] and then she died. She ordered a turquoise to be brought to the trader Mipam of Dangar, who, she said, has become your lama. Is he here?'

'He is here,' replied the porter, opening wide the gates.

'A message from Lhasa, on the part of Tenzin the trader,' announced the head of the monastery, speaking to Mipam through the closed door.

The reply was a long while coming: Mipam at length drew the bolt. Tenzin's servants prostrated themselves.

'From Semo Dolma,' said the elder of the two, holding out a packet to Mipam.

'She is dead, is she not?' asked the young man, with a calm more poignant than the most passionate expression of grief.

The two men bowed their heads.

'Was she a nun at the time of her death? . . .'

'You knew it!' exclaimed the chief of the monks and Tenzin's envoys.

'Our precious lord, you are a Buddha!'

Thereupon the two messengers related all that had happened in Lhasa.

While they were speaking, Mipam had opened the packet, had recognized the turquoise, and had read the few words written by Dolma.

'See that the great conch is sounded,' he ordered the monk.

And while the monks hastened to obey, Mipam, leaving the hermitage, regained the lama's apartments. In a coffer were lying, carefully folded, the monastic robes of the last lama *tulku*, Yeshes Nga Den, which the monks had more than once shown to Mipam, begging him to put them on.

[1] One who has returned from the 'beyond'; see footnote, p. 333.

Resolutely Mipam donned the vest of cloth of gold, and wrapped the wide dark garnet-coloured lower garment round him, drawing it tight with a sash of yellow silk, put on the tall boots, draped himself in the yellow mantle of the hermits, and waited.

The conch was still sounding: the footsteps of the monks hurrying to the temple could be heard outside. Finally, all was quiet: all must have arrived. Mipam went out. Alone he entered the temple, and prostrated himself before the altar on which the statues of the Buddha and of Chenrezigs looked down upon the *chortens* of the Lamas of Ngarong. As he rose, he glanced for a moment at the tomb of Mipam Rinchen near which Dolma had appeared to him.

'I obey thee, Dolma,' he murmured.

Then, with a firm step, he advanced to the throne of the abbot. Completely master of his thoughts, Mipam no longer sought to elucidate the mystery of a reincarnation in accordance with the popular beliefs. The seer of Dangar had spoken truly; the wall which had limited his vision had fallen. From the turquoise sent by Dolma as she lay dying a light had leapt to illumine his mind. A reincarnation of the Lamas of Ngarong he was indeed, since the same spirit of goodness, the same desire to battle with suffering which had been theirs lived in him, since he was there to continue their work.

On the assembly of motionless monks, who dared hardly to breathe, he gazed with eyes that were filled with a solemn benevolence.

'My sons,' said he, 'your lama has returned!'

And silently in his heart he added:

'Changpal, my sweet mother, thy child has realized thy dreams!'

THE END

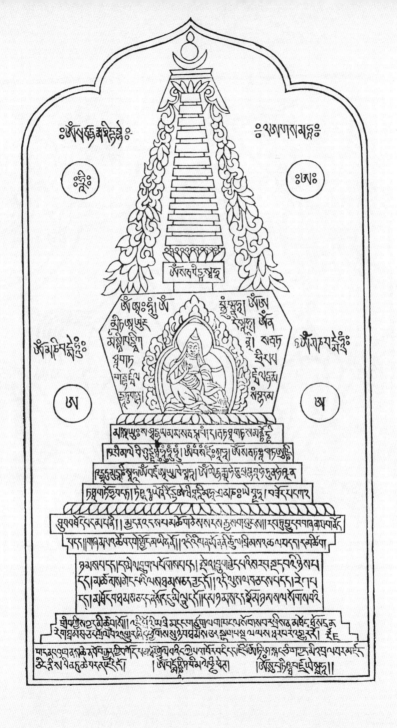

Lung Ta – Wind Horse
Prayer Flag

LO KHOR

Lo Khor (year wheel)
Tibetan Astrological Calendar

In the center is a magic square. The numbers add up to 15 in any direction.

```
4 9 2      The numbers in the square are
3 5 7      uses for devination purposes, i.e.,
8 1 6      to determine the most appropriate
           day to undertake a project.
```

The next circle is composed of the eight famous trigrams of Fu-hsi, called the "eight Kwi". They are the basis of the 64 hexagrams, which compose the 3,000-year-old Chinese oracle book called the I-Ching or book of Changes

Earth	Water
Tree	Heaven
Iron	Air
Mountain	Gem

In the next circle are the Tibetan names of the 12 animals that with the five elements form the basis for the 60-year Tibetan Calendar, which is based on the 60-year cycle of Jupiter. From the top the animals are:

Horse	Dog	Tiger
Sheep	Pig	Rabbit
Monkey	Mouse	Dragon
Bird	Ox	Snake

The New Year usually begins in February with the rise of the new moon. The first time an element appears it is male. The second time it is female. 1999 is Female Earth Rabbit. 2000 is Male Iron Dragon. Persons supposedly display the characteristics of the animal and element for the year in which they were born. The unlucky combinations of animals are Mouse and Horse, Ox and Sheep, Tiger and Monkey, Rabbit and Bird, Dragon, and Dog and Snake and Pig. The whole astrological calendar(see woodblock print on previous page) is embraced by Maya which represents illusion. Following is the current cycle.

1936 Fire Mouse	1975 Wood Rabbit
1937 Fire Ox	1976 Fire Dragon
1938 Earth Tiger	1977 Fire Snake
1939 Earth Rabbit	1978 Earth Horse
1940 Iron Dragon	1979 Earth Sheep
1941 Iron Snake	1980 Iron Monkey
1942 Water Horse	1981 Iron Bird
1943 Water Sheep	1982 Water Dog
1944 Wood Monkey	1983 Water Pig
1945 Wood Bird	1984 Wood Mouse
1946 Fire Dog	1985 Wood Ox
1947 Fire Pig	1986 Fire Tiger
1948 Earth Mouse	1987 Fire Rabbit
1949 Earth Ox	1988 Earth Dragon
1950 Iron Tiger	1989 Earth Snake
1951 Iron Rabbit	1990 Iron Horse
1952 Water Dragon	1991 Iron Sheep
1953 Water Snake	1992 Water Monkey
1954 Wood Horse	1993 Water Bird
1955 Wood Sheep	1994 Wood Dog
1956 Fire Monkey	1995 Wood Pig
1957 Fire Bird	1996 Fire Mouse
1958 Earth Dog	1997 Fire Ox
1959 Earth Pig	1998 Earth Tiger
1960 Iron Mouse	1999 Earth Rabbit
1961 Iron Ox	2000 Iron Dragon
1962 Water Tiger	2001 Iron Snake
1963 Water Rabbit	2002 Water Horse
1964 Wood Dragon	2003 Water Sheep
1965 Wood Snake	2004 Wood Monkey
1966 Fire Horse	2005 Wood Bird
1967 Fire Sheep	2006 Fire Dog
1968 Earth Monkey	2007 Fire Pig
1969 Earth Bird	2008 Earth Mouse
1970 Iron Dog	2009 Earth Ox
1971 Iron Pig	2010 Iron Tiger
1972 Water Mouse	2011 Iron Rabbit
1973 Water Ox	2012 Water Dragon
1974 Wood Tiger	2013 Water Snake

ༀ༈ རྒྱལ་བ་བྱམས་པ་ལ་ན་མོ།

Maitreya
The Coming Buddha.